THE TRIALS OF
ELDRED POTTINGER

SOLDIER, SPY, HERO...COWARD?

*Happy wedding anniversary
Best wishes*

NIGEL HASTILOW

Nigel.

RUSSIAN TERRITORY
MERV
SARAKHS
PUL-I-KHATUN
NEW BOUNDARY CLAIMED BY RUSSIA
MAIMANA
KHOJA SALEH
SHIBARGHAN
MOUNTAINS
HERAT
SAFED KOH
OBEH
KAL
HERI RUD RIVER
KHUSRU KHAN
TARSI
ASIABAD
SUBZAWUR
GHUR SIAH KOH
SAKHIR
HEZARE
MYDAN
HELMUND RIVER
SEAH KHANA
FARAH RUD RIVER
FARAH
AFGHANISTAN
HARUD RIVER
DUSTABAD
GIRISHK
KALA BUST
KHASH
SHAMALAN

When you're wounded and left on Afghanistan's plains,
And the women come out to cut up what remains,
Jest roll to your rifle and blow out your brains
And go to your gawd like a soldier.

The Young British Soldier
Rudyard Kipling

THE TRIALS OF
ELDRED POTTINGER
Spy, soldier, hero... Coward?
Nigel Hastilow

©2019
Nigel Hastilow
All rights reserved

Published by
Halesowen Press
WR11 7SA

www.eldredpottinger.co.uk
www.halesowenpress.co.uk

Printed by
Book Printing UK
Remus House
Woodston
Peterborough
PE2 9BF

Never morning wore
To evening, but some heart did break.

Tennyson

THE MAJOR CHARACTERS

Lieutenant Eldred Pottinger, East India Company
Hoosein, Eldred's servant
Captain George Broadhurst, Eldred's attorney
George Russel Clerk, a senior civil servant
Captain Trevor Whistler, Judge-Advocate-General
Eleanor Eden, youngest of the eight sisters of
Lord George Eden, Governor General of India
Sir William Macnaghten, adviser to the Governor General
Lady Frances Macnaghten, his wife
Maharaja Ranjeet Singh, King of the Sikhs
Dost Mohammed Khan, King of Kabul
Akbar Khan, his son
Sir Alexander Burnes, agent to the court of Kabul
Shah Soojah-ool-Moolk Durrani, deposed King of Kabul
Yakoob Beg, Khan of Wardak
Shah Kamran, King of Herat
Yar Mahomed, Vizier to Shah Kamran
Brigadier-General John Shelton of the 44th foot
General William Elphinstone, commander of the British forces in Afghanistan
Lady Fiorentina Sale, wife of General Sir Robert Sale

OTHER IMPORTANT CHARACTERS:

Colonel Sir Henry Pottinger, East India Company resident in Hyderabad
Mahparah, Eldred's mistress
Wasim, her son
Abdul Khaliq, a courtier to Yakoob Beg
Mohammed Shah, King of Persia
Sir John McNeill, the British envoy to the Shah of Persia
Colonel Charles Stoddart, a British envoy to the Shah of Persia
Count Ivan Simonich, the Russian envoy to the Shah of Persia
General Semineau, a French mercenary
Captain Jan Vitkevitch, Russian agent to the King of Kabul
Fatteh Jang, one of Shah Soojah's sons
Usman Khan, Shah Soojah's Prime Minister
Mohun Lal, Burnes's agent

Brigadier Thomas Anquetil

Dr William Brydon, a medical man

Dr John Logan, a missionary and cricket fanatic

Captain Christopher Codrington, commander of the 4th (Gurkha) Infantry at Charikar

Dr James Grant, a missionary, antiquarian and medical doctor

Lieutenant John Houghton, 31st Bengal Native Infantry

Mrs Alexandrina Sturt, daughter of Lady Sale, married to

Captain John Sturt, Bengal Engineers

Sergeant George Wade, 54th Native Infantry, married to Grace Wade

Lieutenant Vincent Eyre, Bengal Artillery

Emily, his wife

Captain George Lawrence, Macnaghten's Military Secretary

Captain Bulstrode Bygrave, Field Paymaster

Captain Robert Waller, Bengal Horse Artillery

Captain Colin Mackenzie, 48th Madras native infantry

Mir Masjidi Khan, an Afghan leader

Abdoollah Khan, a relative of Shah Soojah but leader of the revolt

Amenoollah Khan, another relative of Shah Soojah and leader of the revolt

Mir Masjidi Khan, an Afghan leader

Mahommed Shah Khan, Akbar's father-in-law

Saleh Mahommed Khan, a jailer

Fatteh Jang, a son of Shah Soojah

Usman Khan, Shah Soozah's Prime Minister

Lord Ellenborough, Governor-General of India

JUDGES:

Major General Sir James Rutherford Lumley, Adjutant General of the East India Company

Major General Sir Harry Smith

Brigadier Thomas Monteath

Brigadier George Petre Wymer

Major General George Pollock and **General William Knott**, commanders of the Army of Retribution

Captain Sir Richmond Shakespeare, a handsome devil

CHAPTER 1

Fort William, Calcutta, January 1843

'But you are alive though thousands are dead?'

'Yes, sir, by the grace of God I am, sir.'

'And what quality does Eldred Pottinger possess that preserves his life while those about him are dying?'

'Good fortune, sir. Nothing more than great good fortune.'

'Not cowardice then, sir?'

'Cowardice? Sir, I recognise this is not the first time I have heard that word in reference to my name but every time it has the same effect. The rage of a soldier whose every action has been in furtherance of the interests of Her Majesty, the British East India Company, his comrades and his fellow men. I am no coward, sir. I am no coward...'

I am accused of being a coward, court-martialled for surrendering to the enemy. They even accuse me misusing public funds as if I were a common embezzler as well as a man unfit to wear the Queen's uniform. Two shifty-eyed subalterns, scarcely eighteen, marched me to the commanding officer's quarters where he formally made the accusations and gave me scarcely two weeks to prepare my defence. I am so angry I cannot think straight. My mind goes over and over the catastrophe and I can find no disgrace in my actions.

I have done nothing wrong. Only my duty. Yet they want to disgrace me.

Once, they crowned me with laurels and called me a hero. Now I sit in the court in this abominable heat awaiting the Day of Judgment, denied the comfort of my bride and my friends, humiliated in the eyes of the world and refused any opportunity to defend myself in the court of public opinion.

My accusers? Dishonourable men looking for excuses. They need someone to blame for their own incompetence and cowardice – but everyone else is dead except for the chief architect of this disaster, Lord Eden, who sailed for home weeks ago. He should be returning from India in disgrace. Instead they've made him an Earl, the Earl of Auckland, while I sweat it out here, charged on my honour not to escape or have any communication with the outside world.

On my honour? Isn't that what I am fighting to preserve? My good name?

If only I had died with all the others. I wish I had never heard of that dithering incompetent William Elphinstone or met Dost Mohammed Khan, shared women with Alexander Burnes or tried to befriend our great tormentor Akbar Khan. Even my own uncle has deserted me for the South China Seas. Perhaps he, too, thinks I have brought disgrace to the family name.

All that stands between me and degradation is Brigadier John Shelton, who has to be the most hated man in the British army. Shelton is a pompous, arrogant, overweening martinet. How he survived I cannot tell. He should have died along with the rest of them. The world would be a better place for it. Instead, he is the only witness to my actions, the only man I can call to attest to my character.

The defender of my honour, my only hope, is my enemy John Shelton.

How did it come to this?

Ambition, boredom… money, of course. Why else volunteer to explore a wild country full of savages? Adventure? Adventure is an excuse. It is a way of varnishing the truth and making it acceptable to the ladies in the drawing rooms and salons of London. Call yourself an adventurer and you are a dashing hero; admit to boredom and you lack imagination; confess to ambition and you are a social-climber; tell the world you are short of money and the world turns its back on you.

So I became an adventurer. An explorer of uncharted wastes, for Queen and country. A dashing hero. I would have been feted in the salons of London if I had managed to make my way back there – even my Irish accent would have been called quaint rather than disgusting.

In the army, there are few opportunities to excel in peace-time. Few opportunities to advance one's career. Few chances to accumulate the immense fortunes one hears about.

The Company has its directors and they acquire wealth, power, privilege and titles. Generally, though, they start off with wealth, power, privilege and titles so they are already half way there. It's different for a Paddy, a bog-trotter, a tory. Especially a Paddy whose father has squandered the family fortune; a bog-trotter who has responsibility for his step-mother and her two daughters; a tory whose comrades-in-arms are disinclined to admit him into their privileged society.

The Company's army is staffed by old men. Majors in their fifties, generals in their sixties who, as young men, fought at Waterloo and enjoy regaling us with their long and involved stories of heroism. Waterloo! Imagine. These gentlemen are going nowhere; certainly not home to England. Why retire when the Company is so generous and the demands on their time and abilities are so slight? Perhaps things will change now so many of them are dead.

CHAPTER 2

Hyderabad, April 1837

We all make the most of whatever connections we have. There's no shame in it.

After six years languishing in the mosquito-ridden climate of stinking Calcutta, carrying out exercises and trying to instil discipline into Hindu recruits, with no more excitement or opportunity for advancement or entertainment than a day at the races and an evening in the whorehouses, I apply to my uncle, the Colonel.

The Colonel is my father's younger brother. Like me, he was obliged to seek his fortune in the East. Unlike me, he succeeded. The Colonel, Sir Henry Pottinger, is the Company's resident in Hyderabad, a diplomat in the court of the local king, Asaf Jah IV.

I have never understood why the Company allows people like King Asaf Jah to enjoy so much freedom but my uncle explains we only want peaceful trading relations with the Hindus; it would be absurd to try to master these unruly peoples. India is a market for us to exploit for profit and pleasure, he says. It is not a land we wish to subjugate. Why would we want to go to so much trouble, especially in such a stifling climate, when locals like Asaf Jah are so accommodating?

Unlike my father, Sir Henry is a serious man of affairs and well-connected. In his youth – he is forty-seven and still vigorous compared with most of the Company's commanders – he made his celebrated expedition all the way from the deserts of Baloochistan to Isfahan in the heart of Persia. That was 25 years ago. After the brutish Frenchman Napoleon Bonaparte threatened to extend his empire as far as in India itself, the Company wanted to know more about the unknown lands in between India and Persia. After we finally cut down the Corsican colonel, Sir Henry was dispatched from Calcutta to start mapping out the features of this landscape where no European had yet ventured. Nobody really knew if Sir Henry and Captain Charles Christie would ever come back. They were pioneers.

'You must undertake a similar expedition, Eldred,' he advises me. 'Look at Burnes.'

Captain Alexander Burnes, cousin of the late Scotch poet Robert, is only six years older than me but already rich, famous and comfortably installed as our man at the court of Dost Mohammed Khan, the King of Kabul. All because of his adventures across the Hindu Kush and the book he wrote about it. He was lionised in London and entertained in all the smartest places. He was even knighted by the King himself.

Where have I ever been? Lucknow. A wretched place where it does nothing but pour with rain.

My uncle rises from behind his huge desk, in his office draped with thick curtains to keep out the heat, and takes down his own volume from the library. 'Baloochistan. So we have some information on its geography and its peoples. But between Kabul and Persia? They call it Afghanistan. But who knows the place?'

'Isn't it all rocks and mountains?'

'Is it?' My uncle strokes his neatly-trimmed moustache. 'And the people who live there?'

'Hindus?' I ask.

'I think not. But who knows? We have Burnes's dispatches, for what they're worth. But they come from Kabul. I fear Captain Burnes prefers to enjoy his explorations closer to home these days.'

Burnes is notorious. It is common gossip among Company fellows that he keeps a harem in Kabul and debauches the wives of the local gentry. It is said Alexander Burnes is turning into an Epicurean.

My uncle takes down his book and opens it. 'Maps, my boy. The Company has need of explorers, map-makers, surveyors and gatherers of intelligence. We have enemies everywhere. Who are they talking to? Where are they? Are we vulnerable? Could an army reach the North-West frontier by crossing from Persia by way of Afghanistan? Are we safe and secure? How can we tell? We need information, Eldred, information and maps.'

'But sir, I cannot surely take leave of absence for a lengthy expedition?'

'I shall write a letter,' says my uncle.

*****

Before we part, Sir Henry takes me to one side after dinner at the palace and we walk together down to the lakeside. It is still hot, like walking through a steam bath. I ache to strip off my clothes and launch myself into the water, though I know how dangerous that can be.

Instead, we stroll along in the dark evening, illuminated only by the lamps from the Residence, smoking our cheroots – 'So good for the health, y'know?' as Sir Henry says.

'And how is Thomas, Eldred?'

Sir Henry strokes his moustache thoughtfully. I wonder what emotions arise in his breast at the sight of his elder brother's son. He treats me with nothing but kindness and consideration, as does Susanna, my aunt by marriage, but even so, thoughts of his elder brother could easily drive him to despair.

'I have to tell you, sir, my father is anxious to come out to India to repair his fortune.'

'We shall prevent him,' says Sir Henry decisively. 'My brother would not like it out here.'

'The climate?'

'Bugger the climate. Thomas has never been capable of disciplining himself. Assuming he expects to find some sort of employment with the Company, for otherwise I cannot see why he should even consider making the voyage, he would find life most uncomfortable.'

'Uncomfortable, sir?'

'Eldred, you have grown used to discipline. You have a military man's understanding of orders and hierarchy and responsibility. Your father, my brother, does not. He has never known discipline. That is how he got himself – and your poor step-mother – into this mess in the first place. How would he like subservience to younger men?'

'He has sold Mountpottinger, sir.'

'Sold Mountpottinger?' Sir Henry throws his cheroot away in disgust, turns back towards the house and marches off in a fury leaving me to trail slowly after him, ashamed of my father, ashamed of myself for my shame, angered by the humiliation of the shame.

It is true. My father has negotiated the sale of Mountpottinger, our big, stone home in Ballymacarrett, high on a hill overlooking Belfast Lough. Sitting at the open window in my room listening to the racket of the crickets, I write to my step-mother Eliza sending all the money I can spare and begging her not to allow my father to come out to India where he could expect nothing but humiliation and discomfort.

CHAPTER 3

Calcutta, June 1837

Sir Henry is as good as his word. I am breaking in a new mare when Hoosein comes rushing as best he can on his little legs across the field brandishing a missive from none other than Lord Eden himself. Or at least from one of his underlings. Or from one of his underlings' servants. Anyway, I have no opportunity to digest the news for myself because, as he toddles towards me and I dismount from my horse, Hoosein is waving the document above his head and shouting excitedly, 'Simla, sahib, Simla. We are going to Simla.'

I take the paper from my over-boisterous servant and study its three short lines. I am invited, nay commanded, to present myself at the Governor General's summer residence at my earliest convenience.

'At last,' I say to Hoosein and, as he bounces up and down on his bare feet in excitement, it looks for one appalling moment as if he is about to hug me.

'When do we leave, sahib?' he asks.

'We? Hoosein. Who said anything about "we"?'

Crestfallen is the only word I can use to describe the look on the little man's face. He hangs his head in disappointment and looks up at me with pleading eyes.

I slap him on the back. 'Of course you're coming with me, Hoosein.

I wouldn't get very far without you, now would I?' He brightens up immediately and starts chattering away about how we should make our route to Simla and what we need for the journey.

It is still unbearably hot though the summer heat is due to be exchanged any day now for the deluge of the monsoon. Strangely, the rains are late and everywhere is filthy with dust and flies. We are anxious for the rains to wash this away though, with such a long journey in prospect, it strikes me as advantageous to leave Calcutta as soon as arrangements can be made. We do not wish to keep His Lordship waiting and the sooner we depart, the further we are likely to get before becoming permanently soaked if not bogged down.

A one thousand mile march across India is not a journey to be undertaken lightly whatever the weather yet I tell Hoosein we will leave at dawn the following day. His little face falls again. 'But sahib,' he starts to protest.

'No time like the present, Hoosein, no time like the present. Tomorrow is as good as the next day.'

*****

There are few enough people I wish to take my leave of in any case. I see my commanding officer, Clements Brown. The brigadier says, 'So you're leaving us, Pottinger. Becoming an intelligencer, eh?' He chuckles.

'I am not certain what will be required of me, sir,' I reply. I am sensitive to the insult in his use of the word 'intelligencer'.

'Well good luck, man,' he says, without looking up and returning to the papers on his desk.

I write a grateful letter to my uncle.

Later I venture to the officers' club for dinner and to see who is among the company. As bad luck would have it, I find Black and Mordaunt of the Bengal Lancers, or Skinner's Horse as they like to call themselves.

With them is John Shelton. Why even the likes of Black and Mordaunt would wish to pass the time with Brigadier-General Shelton is not a question I can fathom. I know better than to exchange words with Shelton.

This is the same John Shelton who now holds my fate, my future, my honour, even perhaps my life, in his hateful hands. Perhaps it is only now, in retrospect, that I can see the disdain on his emaciated-looking face. Was he sneering at me even then? I cannot tell for sure now. I do know Shelton stands looking on, his left hand cradling the stump of his right arm, as Black laughs, 'Off on special duties, eh, Paddy?'

'Intelligencer,' Mordaunt adds and both men, fuelled by wine, laugh loudly in my face.

'Bog-trotter Potter an intelligence man?' says Black.

'Remarkable,' agrees Mordaunt.

'Gentlemen, we shall meet again,' I say as coolly as I can, turn on my heel and prepare to march out to cries and jeers from the pair and their cronies.

Then Shelton steps forward. 'Lieutenant Pottinger,' he says in his fluting little voice.

'Sir?'

'Do you not salute your superiors, sir?'

'My apologies, sir,' I say, saluting promptly. 'I was under the impression these formalities were not required in the officers' mess.'

'Then you were mistaken, sir. And if I see you here again in that apology for a uniform – no jacket, sir, no jacket – then I shall have no option but to see you blackballed. You Irishmen, I despair,' says Shelton. 'Now get out of there. Go.' He waves his good left arm dismissively and turns back to Mordant. 'Fucking Paddies,' he says and they all laugh.

*****

I venture down the back streets. Had I known then what I know

now, I should have waded into them, caused a melee and, if chance should have it, take the opportunity to call out John Shelton there and then. At least we might have settled our differences like men.

But I am excited to be leaving the city at last, I have no wish to engage in a brawl on my last night in Calcutta. I long to see the back of the place.

Gunnery and horsemanship are all very well but when there is no need for either, the constant repetition begins to pall. As I send as much money as I can spare back to my step-mother, partly in the hope of keeping my father from making the voyage out to India, I have little enough left to enjoy the delights of Calcutta's horse-racing, cricketing, partying set.

In any case, it is not the city it used to be. It is only a year since the disgrace and death of John Palmer, once the richest man in India. They say Palmer was a good man. But his bankruptcy brought the Company's whole house of cards crashing down. It inflicted poverty on dozens of good Englishmen and women. India is no place to be poor, especially if you do not even have the wherewithal for a passage back home to your friends and relatives.

As I stumble through the dimly-lit backstreets, teeming with people, considering vaguely whether to find a courtesan for one last time before I leave, I am surprised how apprehensive I suddenly feel at the prospect of the long march to Simla. In part this is excitement, in part the stimulation caused by a long hoped-for ambition finally achieving some sort of reality. But I confess I find myself regretting the loss of my quiet life. Whatever the future holds, it will not be peaceful and comfortable. I will not be able to drink claret, smoke and disappear into the depths of the city at night. Even the long journey to Simla will be a challenge. And then it is into the unknown. Who wouldn't have some reservations about embarking on such an adventure?

*****

Our great fear on the caravanserai to Simla is being waylaid by thugs, the dreadful highwaymen and bandits who rob their victims, garrotte them and bury their bodies. The campaign to rid India of this scourge is bearing fruit but the stories of their cruelty and cunning are well-known to everybody, though they tend to leave the English alone. This is why our progress is accompanied by a wide and varying collection of native fellow-travellers, who hang onto our coat-tails, as it were, for dear life.

We cannot rid ourselves of them but they make themselves useful finding food and shelter on the way.

It is already late in the season and we are anxious to make quick progress as we fear being overtaken by the monsoons. Alas, progress is slow, hampered as we are by our escort of six native dragoons, our cook and his boys as well as the dozen or so hangers-on. Scarcely a night passes without somebody waking to complain he has been robbed of some, if not all, his possessions. We post a sentry every evening to protect our little camp but, somehow, the thieves still manage to slip through our defences.

Hoosein is very unhappy. Initially my little Hindu seems to relish our escape from Calcutta but as we put more distance between ourselves and the stinking metropolis he calls home, there grows in him what I can only describe as home-sickness. It dawns on him we are were not merely on a journey to Simla but destined for a further trek, into the unknown, with no certain date for our return.

Hoosein has a young wife and a baby daughter to think about. How will he remit money to them? They cannot survive for long on the few rupees he has left behind. He knows I have arranged for a weekly payment to be made to them but he remains sceptical, his head bobbing from side to side as we discuss it.

It is one of the many perplexities in dealing with the natives. You may speak their language, as I now do pretty well, and you may be able to communicate adequately, but it is difficult, almost impossible, to read them properly. Hoosein, like many of the natives, has a capacity to shake his head vigorously from side to side but, long though I have known him, it is difficult to tell if this indicates agreement, disagreement, deep thought or something else entirely. I have learned in my time here that when we communicate with the natives, knowing the language is only part of the battle. Just as a fellow Englishman may say 'yes' when every look and sign he gives off means 'no' – and you can tell he means 'no' even if he is saying 'yes' – so it is with the Indian. Except their expressions and mannerisms are harder to interpret, certainly for someone not brought up to it and not practised in the art of understanding.

Anyhow, the upshot is Hoosein is content to stay. With me he has work and I am, I flatter myself, a considerate and not especially demanding employer. Had he chosen to abandon me half way to Simla, not only would he have been obliged to make his own way home without the protection of our small squadron and the shelter of our tents, he would have faced an uncertain future on his arrival.

So he chooses an uncertain future with me over a similar fate with his wife and child. I live to be grateful for that decision.

CHAPTER 4

Simla, June 1837

As we head North-West, the air grows cooler and we manage to keep one step ahead of the rains. The roads are pitted, rough and disappear in places. Bridges are unreliable, sometimes precarious. Two of our number become unwell and we are forced to leave them behind to recover. Neither is in fear for his life, however. I think the food sometimes leaves a little to be desired – vomiting and worse are not uncommon features of life on this continent. Most of us learn to live with it, or we die.

The natives are surprisingly welcoming, hospitable even. A few rupees generally help.

Eventually we reach the foothills of the Himalayas and trek up towards Simla, the temporary seat of Government. The hill station is quiet, beautiful and mountainous. It is how I imagine the Highlands of Scotland to be – tall pines, very green, a brisk wind, sharp sunrises. The buildings they are constructing in this small town all speak of home.

I put up in the garrison village where Hoosein and I are allocated a tent and a servant. We are otherwise ignored until an adjutant arrives as I am finishing breakfast on our second day to say I am to present myself at the Governor General's residence at noon.

I shave for the first time in weeks. I even get rid of my moustache.

I put on in my Lieutenant's scarlet dress uniform which was packed for the occasion. Hoosein fusses about polishing my boots. His nervousness on my behalf soon starts to infect me as well and I am full of butterflies when I make my way towards the Governor's residence half an hour before the appointed time.

I march briskly up the long drive towards Elysium House. It looks like a Scottish baron's home, not excessively large but accommodating. Work is being carried out to create formal gardens outside but at the moment it is largely earthworks with groups of sepoys digging and carrying. Doubtless one day it will look splendid.

At the large reception porch, guarded by two black-uniformed sepoys and a pair of tiger statues, I am told to go into the hall and await further orders, His Lordship will summon me when he is ready. I wait in a large baronial room with romantic paintings of glens and a couple of tiger heads on the wall. I stand, staring emptily at a huge painting of a tiger hunt while various servants, coolies, political officers and military men come and go.

Gradually I notice a sweet scent in the air which I can't immediately place. The day is warm, though not oppressive, and there is still plenty of sunlight amongst the gathering clouds. Outside the air is still. While I try to identify the aroma, it takes me immediately back to my step-mother's garden at Mountpottinger. I see her clearly, my ageing father's young bride, always so beautiful and kind.

'There will be a storm,' a young woman's voice says. I turn to find its owner carrying a basket with dark red roses, almost blood-red, in full bloom. 'Aren't they lovely? I pick them every day and every day there are more. The scent is heavenly. Here.'

She holds her basket towards me and I obediently inhale the fresh, watery, heady scent of the roses. 'Very red,' I say.

'Like your hair, sir,' she laughs. She has a captivating laugh, full of pleasure and amusement. She has sparkling brown eyes and her hair is bunched tightly at the back of her head. She wears a long, straight dress of striped white and blue cotton. She notices me looking her over.

'Working clothes,' she says.

'A young lady of your station, working?'

'And what station would that be, sir?' Again she smiles at me, it seems a little flirtatiously. It is clear, by her voice, her accent, her clothes, her manner, that she is no servant, just as these are no working clothes. She is young, perhaps nineteen or twenty. Not excessively tall but not short; not excessively well-fed but not skinny. Her lips are almost as red as her roses. Her cheeks are pale. Her hair is a light brown. But it is the playful smile in her eyes that captivates me.

'Well, if I may be blunt, madam, you do not seem to me to be a servant girl.'

'Oh I do not seem to be a servant girl? Is that right, sir? And what would you know about these things, Mr Pottinger?'

I am lost, shocked. She knows my name. How? Who is she? The daughter of an adjutant, an officer? 'You have the advantage of me, madam. Eldred Pottinger indeed. At your service.' I incline my head slightly and bring my heels together in a kind of half-mocking salute.

I am wearing my smartest uniform. New. Made by one of those fellows in Calcutta, all scarlet, leather and brocade. I think I cut a fine figure in my new boots with a sword at my side. My hand instinctively rises to stroke my moustache only to find it is no longer there.

I was not altogether happy with my moustache, which was red and would not grow with the kind of rakish, sharp-curling dash many fellows affect. It was a scrubby thing and I was pleased it came off though I am now disconcerted to reach for it only to betray its absence at such a delicate moment. I am suddenly conscious of the effect my gesture towards the absent moustache might have. I am momentarily embarrassed. I fear this habit may look somewhat disconcerting. This strange, instinctive twitch might remove any possibility of admiration which could otherwise come to me by virtue of my immaculate uniform and what I think of as my general air of good health and vigour.

'I think you are at the service of my brother, Mr Pottinger.'

'Your brother, madam? I fear I am a loss.'

'Clearly, Mr Pottinger,' she says and, nimbly selecting one of her red roses, she places it in my tunic. Her fingers are long and thin. She wears no ring. She carries the scent of the roses. 'We have been waiting for you to drag yourself here, sir.'

'Madam…' I want to explain the rigours of the march but she must have experienced something similar herself, otherwise how would she have ever got here?

An orderly interrupts us. 'The Governor General will see you now, Lieutenant.'

'Madam.' I bow to this vivacious young woman and our eyes meet for a moment. I would prefer to stay where I am. 'Forgive me, duty calls,' I say, with a smile and a slight bow.

She smiles and dips in a polite curtsey.

*****

It is, as I discover a long time afterwards, the day the old King died. Sailor Billy, King William IV. It takes months for the news to reach India and by then I am long gone.

For me, though, it is the day my destiny is determined. The day I set forth on that long, dreadful trek through the valley of death into the land of rocks and stones and sand.

I am conscious I have made no mark with my life and I am anxious because, by now, I should have some achievement to point to beyond an understanding of ballistics and an ability to drill a native squadron in the baking Indian sun.

I am led by the orderly, a small Englishman who wears a smart grey servant's uniform, into a wood-panelled drawing room with a low ceiling and a couple more of the large, misty, romantic Scottish scenes they seem to specialise in here. These are of highlands, rather than glens, but the difference is not very significant. They are all brown with glowering skies and surprisingly clean, though hairy, cattle gaze mournfully into the middle-distance.

It is a long room with large windows giving a view of the looming mountains, where it is still possible to see a snow-capped peak or two despite the gathering clouds.

A man in uniform sits behind a large mahogany desk, a second stands at one of the windows looking up towards the mountains. The orderly introduces me as 'Lieutenant Pottinger, sir,' and leaves.

The man at the window does not turn round, the man at the desk does not look up. I stand where I have been left, to attention, and wait for someone to say something.

Two ageing men. One of them is, I know, Lord George Eden, the Governor General of India. I have no idea who the other one is nor can I tell which is which, though I assume the man in the spectacles scribbling something at the desk is probably the Governor General. It may be his occasional grunts, the emphasis he appears to give to certain letters or phrases as he writes, or perhaps the mere fact that he is in possession of what would appear to be the place of greatest power. Whatever it is, the man at the desk certainly gives off an air of authority.

The man at the desk is small, slight and I notice the lenses of his wire spectacles have a kind of blue tinge to them. Does this mean his eyesight is exceptionally poor, I wonder. He has greying sideburns, a bald pate and a grey moustache, a thin face but, despite the strange hue of his glass lenses, he has sharp little eyes. The man at the window is taller, straight-backed, somewhat formal, it seems to me, though it is difficult to assess a man's character on the basis only of his bearing and the cut of his frock coat. He peers towards the mountains as if attempting to single out a bird of prey or perhaps track a tiger to its lair. He seems to stand on tip-toe, leaning forwards, eager to act.

The room faces north. It is gloomy and surprisingly chilly.

I wait.

The man at the desk finally completes his task and signs the document with some relish, looking up after he has done so. 'Pottinger,' he says in a surprisingly booming voice from a man so small.

'My lord.' I turn towards him and bow slightly.

At last the taller man turns, glances towards his colleague as if seeking permission to speak, and finally directs his attention towards me.

'Those mountains,' he says in a slow, high-pitched drawl. 'Are they not fabulously beautiful, Pottinger?'

I agree that they are.

'You have been here before, perhaps?' he asks.

'This is my first visit, my lord.'

'Mine also, Pottinger. Only been in this country a few months, you know. Dashed difficult to traverse, India, don't you agree?'

'It is, my lord.'

'Ruffians, thugs, terrible roads, floods, mud, dreadful food. And the Princes. All those damned durbars.'

'Now, now, George,' says the man at the desk. 'You know how much you enjoy them. All those maharajas to entertain, not to mention their wives.' The two men laugh, sharing some sort of joke to which I am not privy.

The man at the window, who I now see more clearly, is gaunt. His cheeks are thin, he has a long nose and high cheekbones. His thinning hair is drawn forward in the manner of Julius Caesar and he wears an elaborate, formal uniform, despite the heat. He looks tired and dejected.

'Tea, Pottinger?' he asks, ringing a small bell on a side table.

It is impolite to refuse hospitality so I accept the offer and wait as a servant is summoned and the order placed. 'Now, Pottinger,' the thin man at the window continues, 'Tell me about yourself.'

'There's not much to tell, my lord. I have been in the Company's service eight years.'

'Your uncle speaks highly of you.'

'He would,' says the man at the desk.

'Of course he would,' acknowledges the other. 'But Henry Pottinger, whom I have had the pleasure of meeting since my arrival in India, is not a man to promote his family interest at the expense of the Company's nor the country's is he?'

I have no answer, nor does the man at the desk. Luckily the tea arrives. The tray is placed at the far end of the room from the desk and poured into three china cups. The man at the desk rises, sighing, 'Ah, tea, thank God' as he makes his way across the dark, maroon, patterned rugs which carpet the floor. 'Come along, Pottinger, at ease man,' he says as he passes me by.

I follow the two men towards the large, uncomfortable chairs surrounding an unlit fireplace surmounted by a dark wood mantelpiece topped off with a huge, gilt mirror. I marvel that such items have made the long journey from Rotherhithe or Tilbury intact.

'You are admiring my mirror,' says the thin man. 'My sisters insisted on bringing it with us. A memento of home.'

'Home, my lord?'

'Yes, sir. Kent. Do you know it?'

'I do not, my lord.'

The thin man, who I am coming to believe is in fact Lord Eden, despite my original view, turns to his companion and says, 'Hear that? A man who has never been in Kent. Can you believe such a thing? The man sails half way across the world but has never seen dear Kent. Extraordinary.'

'I was a cadet in Croyden, my lord, which is not so very far away.'

'Croyden!' They both laugh.

'Addiscombe, my lord.'

'Of course Addiscombe, Pottinger,' says the other man. 'Half the men in India have been to Croyden, Pottinger, as if you did not know.'

He has put me in my place. I am just another Company man. We are two a penny. There is nothing to be said for Addiscombe men, this I already know.

'My lord,' I acknowledge, somewhat abashed.

'And do stop calling me my lord, Pottinger. This here,' he says, indicating the gaunt man, 'Is His Lordship. I, sir, am a mere baronet.

William Hay Macnaghten. Sir William will do for me.'

The Governor General takes pity on me. 'It's an easy mistake to make, Pottinger. Sir William rather thinks that it is he, not I, who is Governor General of India and, to be candid, I am not entirely unhappy that it should be so. I need all the advice I can get if we are to protect this unruly colony from those less fortunate nations which would seize our jewels and make off with them. Our India, Pottinger, is only ours if we remain constantly vigilant.'

'The point is, Pottinger,' interjects Sir William, all brisk efficiency. 'We are vulnerable. India is hard enough to control as it is. Then there's Ranjeet Singh.'

'Our friend, Ranjeet Singh,' Lord Eden says, emphasising the word friend.

'Indeed, for now. But Ranjeet is fighting the Afghans. Dost Mohammed's army is a formidable force. While the Sikhs and Afghans are at one another's throats then we are safe. What would happen if they were to join together and turn on us? Never forget India was once the plaything of the Afghans.'

'Mughals,' Lord Eden corrects him.

'All much the same, my lord. Uncivilised monsters from the other side of the mountains. Mohammedens, heathens, godless, bloodthirsty, cruel enemies of all that we hold dear.' Sir William is in full flight now. 'The other side of the mountains, Pottinger, lies the great unknown. The great unknown. Yes, we have Burnes in Kabul though what the man gets up to there is hard to fathom from his dispatches.'

'Other than keeping Dost Mohammed Khan friendly,' says Lord Eden.

'If that is what he is really doing, my lord. We know the Russians are never far away. Not to mention the Persians. Neither the tsar nor the shah is our friend. They cast envious eyes over the mountains. We cannot trust either of them. And what if they should combine their forces, come to an arrangement with the King of Kabul and even enlist the support of Ranjeet Singh? What then? What then?'

Sir William sits back and folds his arms across his chest, gazing fiercely out of the window. I am not accustomed to this high politics. I cannot see there is any real threat but then I am a lowly lieutenant with no knowledge or understanding of these things.

Lord Eden continues, but in markedly less fearsome tones, 'The point is, Pottinger, we need to know the lie of the land. Literally and metaphorically. We need to know more about the geography of that land beyond the Khyber Pass. We need to know more about the tribes who inhabit it. How much is it a united country loyal to its king? What is life like there? Are there trading opportunities? Can we bring Afghanistan into the Company's fold? Yes, we have Alexander Burnes keeping an eye on the King of Kabul, Dost Mohammed Khan. But beyond that, we know little or nothing. We need a pair of eyes to scout out the country and report back on everything he sees and everyone he meets.'

'That is where you come in, Pottinger,' says Sir William, having now recovered his equilibrium. 'Your mission is to become the eyes and ears of the Governor General himself. Make yourself known to Burnes in Kabul and then scour the country. Report on its topography, its defences, its military capability, indeed anything you believe might be of value to the Governor General and the Company.'

Lord Eden smiles and stands. 'In short, Pottinger, you are to be our spy in Afghanistan.'

Sir William stands as well and so do I. Macnaghten says, 'You are representing the Governor General and, indeed, the King himself. But you are not there in an official capacity. You must adopt the guise of a native and make your way across the country incognito. We do not wish to provoke an incident by allowing it to be known that we are investigating that benighted country. Do you understand?'

There are many questions I want to ask but I find myself diplomatically responding, 'It is all perfectly clear, my lord, and may I thank you for this commission? It is a great honour and I am sensible of the trust you are placing in me.' I straighten up and salute first Lord Eden and then

Sir William Macnaghten, turn sharply on my heels and march to the door.

As I am leaving the room, Lord Eden calls after me, 'Remember, Pottinger, the primary purpose of your mission – to keep India safe from invasion. We need to know the extent of the threats we face. We must guard against the Russians and the Persians, the Afghans and the Sikhs.'

*****

In the hall where I waited for this interview, I find I am perspiring heavily. The strain of meeting the two men who, it appears, are responsible for the East India Company's government of India, has shaken me more than I had expected.

Is it simply that I am unaccustomed to such a meeting or, perhaps, is it that I was straining to absorb all the information they had thrown at me? Is India truly vulnerable to invasion across the north-west frontier with Afghanistan? Were the Russians truly planning an alliance with the Persians to invade this country? Could we really not trust Maharaja Ranjeet Singh, ruler of the Sikh empire? Surely Ranjeet was even now at war with the King of Kabul and had stolen their precious diamond, the Mountain of Light, which he keeps in his fortress of treasures no-one is allowed to visit. Why should our friend and ally switch sides and tie himself to his enemy, the King of Kabul? It makes no sense to me but what do I know, an ignorant Company lieutenant from Belfast?

As I stand puzzling over this and trying to recover from my interview, I hear a familiar laughing voice. 'Where to now, Lieutenant Pottinger?'

'I do not believe we have been introduced, madam,' I say.

'But I know who you are, Lieutenant Eldred Pottinger. And I am shocked you do not know the names of the Governor General's eight sisters.'

'Madam, forgive the ignorance of a poor soldier.'

'Well then,' she says with a smile and a bob approximating to a curtsey, 'May I present Miss Eleanor Eden, at your service sir.'

'The pleasure is all mine, madam.' I am smiling and thinking how to extend this conversation when an orderly bustles into the hall and, addressing Miss Eden, says, 'Madam, your sisters Emily and Fanny are awaiting your arrival for luncheon.'

Eleanor Eden smiles at me briefly and I am struck again by the glitter and shine of her beautiful brown eyes. 'Madam,' I say, 'I must not detain you.'

'Bon voyage, Lieutenant Eldred Pottinger, I feel sure we shall meet again,' she says and turns away, swaying down the corridor with a flamboyant confidence which is irresistible.

'I shall look forward to it,' I say as she retreats and I turn for the door. The day is glowering, overcast, rain is in the air and over the mountains. The afternoon will darken further as if it were November at home, though warmer.

Hoosein, who has been loitering outside the brick walls of Elysium House, wants to hear all about my interview. I tell him of our mission as we make our way to the quartermaster's to discuss what we shall need for the trek.

CHAPTER 5

The Khyber Pass, August 1837

The tedious trek across the top of the world is worsened by the weather. The waters pour off the mountains, blocking routes, forcing us into detours and delays. The monsoon rains soak us from morning to night and it sometimes proves impossible to find watertight buildings to sleep in. Hoosein and I are accompanied by a small escort of half a dozen cavalrymen as far as Amritsar, in the heart of Ranjeet Singh's territory, where I must present myself at court. As we near the Sikh kingdom, the weather improves. That is to say, the rains give way to blinding heat, stifling and oppressive. The landscape stretches half-wild to the horizon in one direction while the mountains loom over us to our right as we travel towards the setting sun.

I am obliged to pay my respects to Ranjeet. In his palace, the old man is settled on cushions surrounded by handmaidens – it is said he enjoys three things in life: horses, beautiful women and rich jewels – when I present him with a large sapphire stone as a token of the esteem in which he is held by the new Governor General of India. I declare, as I have been instructed, that the great Lord Eden looks forward to the dawn of the day when these two great leaders meet in amity and felicity and so on. I congratulate him on his recent success in the war with the King of Kabul and on the even more recent marriage of his grandson, by all accounts a lavish business which exposed the kingdom to Afghan attack. Naturally I glossed over this and wished the happy couple long and fruitful lives under the never-setting sun of their grandfather's beneficence. Or some such rot.

I am not good with these words. Happily they are supplied for me by Sir William Macnaghten along with the gifts I have presented to the Maharaja. Ranjeet, the great warrior chief, does not look in good health – his one eye is closed off, blinded in battle many years ago; his body seems to creak as he moves; his voice is thin and reedy; his belly is well-fed. He is a squat, round man but he has an amused look in his one good eye. It may be he has a sense of humour, even a sense of life's absurdities. I glimpse him only briefly and I am then ushered out of the presence. The Maharaja has done with me in moments. He is not the kind to waste his precious time on insignificant underlings.

The next day, however, is August 12, my birthday. I am 26 and award myself a day off to investigate the delights Amritsar has to offer a weary traveller. I visit the Sikhs' temple which is covered entirely in gold, the Harmandir Sahib. Pristine and resplendent even in the rains, it is a symbol of Ranjeet's power and influence since he turned the old temple into gold. It is revered by the Sikh nation who nevertheless allow visitors into its precincts much as we might permit travellers to inspect Westminster Abbey.

The city's young women are more worthy of admiration even than their golden temple. Their light brown skin is almost golden, their figures are lithe and slim, their heavily decorated faces – bejewelled and painted – most alluring. No wonder the Maharaja enjoys their company.

That afternoon, I catch a glimpse of the old rogue as he surveys a march-past by some of his army. He is in his ceremonial robes, flaunting on his tunic the mountain of light Koh-i-Noor diamond he stole from the deposed King of Kabul, Shah Soojah, who was thrown out 30 years ago and keeps trying to re-gain his throne.

The diamond and the parade are both impressive sights. I have to confess the discipline of the Sikh army is a match for our own and quite possibly superior to that of our sepoys. But neither of them, neither diamond nor cavalry, is as dazzling as what comes next.

I have heard tell of Ranjeet's women warriors but suddenly they are riding past us in formation, perhaps sixty of them. I am dazzled, Hoosein is outraged.

The women parade past the Maharaja and his entourage at a gentle trot, riding like men with one leg on each side of the saddle. Worse still, these young women, all lithe and beautiful, are naked from the waist upwards. Though their hair is long, it rarely prevents the spectator from enjoying a sight of naked breasts which many have never before beheld and will long remember.

After this magnificent display I am naturally reluctant to depart from Amritsar but we cannot linger here. We have to move on. From Amritsar we travel through the Maharaja's kingdom, towards the great pass into Afghanistan, the Khyber, via the doomed city of Peshawar. As we travel, the weather clears. The mountains come into view, huge but not forbidding in the sunlight, capped by light clouds and surrounded by blue skies.

We are escorted by a dozen Sikh cavalrymen who remain distant and deferential but always have a threatening air of menace about them. They are big men, tall and burly. One would not wish to have them as an enemy.

They lead us into Peshawar but since the Sikhs seized the city from the King of Kabul, Dost Mohammed Khan, it has been allowed to go to rack and ruin. Only a few weeks ago there was a big battle at Jamrud, during Ranjeet's son's wedding, as the Dost tried to regain his winter palace in Peshawar. The Sikhs saw off Dost Mohammed Khan but as they pressed home their victory, they foolishly pursed the Afghans down into the Khyber Pass where a large part of the army was destroyed. Today Peshawar is a vast military camp in a state of permanent readiness for another invasion across the Pass.

How likely that invasion might be, I cannot tell. The walls of the city are strong, though the gates seem vulnerable to me. The central citadel, called Sumergarh by the Sikhs and Bala Hissar by the Muslim natives, has a series of ramparts and towers which might withstand siege. But between the city walls and the Bala Hissar, the mud-rendered houses and the filthy streets are filled with beggars, starvelings, the maimed and injured and at regular intervals the governor has strung up the bodies of Afghan invaders. There are dead bodies everywhere and the stink, in the heat, is not relieved by any passing breeze.

This was once known as 'the city of flowers'. No more. The place is filled with noise and foul smells, people yelling and cursing, selling what little they have to sell, and by troops, on horseback or on foot, parading here and there with open contempt for the people they now rule. The central mosque has four dead bodies hanging from its minaret.

Our Sikh escort ends here. I must find my own way through the Khyber Pass into Afghanistan and onto Kabul. The local Sikhs are reluctant to assist. Indeed, they come close to refusing me passage on to the Khyber Pass. Their army has been turned back at its mouth and it now stands as the border between their country and the King of Kabul's. It is, Hoosein and I are warned, a no-man's land of wild tribes who will only grant safe passage to men who come in peace and do so armed with lakhs, that is to say, thousands, of rupees.

This, at least, I have been provided with. My masters in Simla are aware of the financial realities. But I can no longer travel as a British officer. If I am to pass through Afghanistan unmolested, I must do so in secret. That's why, on the trek here, I have been growing my beard. It's pretty full now, thick and red, not entirely out of keeping with the darker ones to be found in this part of the world. Even so, I cannot exactly pass for the native horse-dealer I am supposed to become.

Hoosein and I purchase a couple of Baluchi mares at the weekly market, which seems mainly to deal in mounts stolen from the defeated Afghans. The Baluchi are fine, sturdy specimens, only about 14 hands and with turned-up ears which make them look particularly quizzical. They are supposed to be good for long journeys and you often see them trudging along with heavy loads on their backs.

We employ two boys, Ali and Waheed, willing to accept a couple of rupees a day to tend to the horses all the way to Kabul. We take our leave of the troopers and prepare to join a caravan setting out for the pass.

Before dawn on the day of our departure Hoosein bustles into my room in the filthy building where I have taken lodgings, carrying a small bowl of water. 'Spanish black, sahib,' he says, pleased with himself. 'Spanish black.'

I sit on the side of my cot and watch as he takes some powder from his pocket which he makes into a small mound in the bowl he is carrying before adding a few drops of water. He stirs in the water until it forms a thick paste. I wonder where this performance is getting us but decide to wait until Hoosein has finished.

'Here, sahib,' he says after a few minutes, taking my hand and smearing some of the stuff onto the back of it. 'Powdered cork. Spanish black. You must become brown like me.'

*****

The weather is clear, the breeze brisk but not too strong, the Hindu Kush is at its most attractive, open and smiling on our caravan as we near the entrance to the Khyber Pass. I confess I am excited and a little nervous. I know this great passageway over the mountains has been in use since time began. I know it has been a great trading route for as long as our species has exchanged goods with one another. But this is not only the first time I have ventured outside the civilised world, I know I am one of the few of my countrymen ever to have risked going this far. Like marriage, it is not something to undertake lightly.

I also know it has given marauding hordes, from Alexander the Great and Ghengis Khan to Dost Mohammed Khan himself, access to the North-West Frontier of India. Tartars, Mongols, Persians – they have all crossed this great divide to swarm down into India destroying everything in their path with their greed and blood-lust. As we approach the far fringe of Ranjeet Singh's kingdom and approach the lawless frontier, I realise Lord Eden's concerns over the possibility of another invasion are not as far-fetched as they might seem from afar. It has, after all, been done many times before so why not today when we know the slippery Tsar Nicholas is even now trying to expand the Russian empire to the south and the east?

I see a forlorn Sikh fort with its half-destroyed bastions and its scrum of beggars, traders, vagabonds and thieves. The Sikhs are carrying out repairs and re-fortifying it. There are soldiers everywhere, kicking the impoverished peasants out of the way, but there is still something forlorn and ragged about this building which stands at the border between Ranjeet Singh's Sikh kingdom and the lawless lands beyond.

The crowds milling around the fort seem to be permanent inhabitants of the entrance to the pass, feeding off the scraps thrown to them by travellers setting warily forth. Ahead of us lies the pass itself. It is policed by the local Afridi or Khyberee tribes who know no loyalty either to Kabul or to Ranjeet Singh, let alone to the British East India Company.

Hoosein is in charge now. He knows these people and, while I can speak their language, he has a greater understanding of them. We must blend in with the company we keep as we embark on this arduous journey to Kabul. Ali and Waheed on their Baluchis, Hoosein and I on our Arabs, join a caravanserai which seems to be led by a fierce man riding one of the inevitable camels which trail along towards the pass. We are perhaps 40 travellers in all and my little group endeavours to remain close-knit while the troupe stretches out along the stony road as it progresses further on up into the mountains.

We start high above sea level and move slowly but steadily upwards across a bleak landscape of rock and scrub with vultures wheeling above us, birds crying out for carrion. The mountains seem to stretch endlessly in every direction, featureless but for the rise and fall of their peaks. At first, the route through the pass is broad and wide with no obvious threat. We have our knives on prominent display just in case, while Waheed laughs and jokes with Hoosein about some of our companions on this trip.

This is a place of emptiness. After the rush and noise of India's cities, even a place as forsaken as Peshawar, we are entering a barren land, a land of rocks and stones and bleakness. Kites, vultures and eagles wheel and cry overhead, their calls as desolate as this landscape. Our caravan trudges on quietly. I think we are all over-awed by this vast open space, struck dumb by its chilly inhospitableness.

The road soon narrows into the first of the defiles in the rock through which we must pass, more or less single file, strung out for about half a mile, men, women, children, donkeys, horses and camels, constantly looking out for danger over our shoulders, up towards the rocky heights and down where our feet must tread. There are no jokes now, just grunts and shouts as the men urge on the coughing, unhappy animals.

The sky is still blue high above but in these deep passes, watered even now in midsummer by a running stream which we are forced constantly to cross and re-cross, we are shadowed in deep gloom. I look up and see the overwhelming rock cliffs, rugged with hidden clefts and ledges, and sometimes see an Afghan, one of the Khyberees, a Pathan tribe of Afridis who claim to have owned this pass for two thousand years, surveying our progress and I wonder how safe this really is. Will the Company truly be able to come and go along these passes and open up a trading route with Kabul?

My doubts grow as we reach the narrowest passages of the pass because now, placed on spears in convenient fissures, we encounter the first severed heads of Ranjeet Singh's soldiers who ventured too far in pursuit of their Afghan foes.

I have seen dead bodies before – who can pass through India without encountering them beside the road at every turn? – but not these decomposing skulls, many still wearing their turbans, each with its own crown of flies. Some of the turbans are still in good condition but the faces and skin beneath are quickly decomposing. Many have been stripped of all flesh by the marauding birds of prey. I can hear these vultures' throaty, gurgling wail as they circle overhead waiting for us to go so they can return to their food.

I cannot but look at the skulls, with their empty-eyed stares, as we pass them by. Only a few weeks ago, these were living creatures, men sent by Ranjeet to repel the Afghans and defend his territory. Now they are more haunted and empty than these passes themselves, for hidden in the hills lie the men who carried out these killings, who severed these heads from their bodies, who impaled them on spears and who placed them like lanterns to light our way towards the city of Kabul.

*****

We make it through the Khyber safely, my little group of Hindus and I, despite the stares of the local Muslims and the tributes our caravanserai is required to pay. The local Afghans are a filthy lot, their long beards unkempt and straggling, their clothes wrapped like rags around them, their heads burdened by huge turbans wrapped around their skulls, their gaze surly or threatening as we pass. I am glad to be almost as brown as my companions.

From the pass, the journey to Kabul is not without its difficulties. We spend two nights sleeping around camp fires, constantly aware of the danger of robbery. Ali, Waheed, Hoosein and I take it in turns to guard the horses and each other. The nights are cold, the sky filled with stars. I find myself thanking our Good Lord for the blessings of this life and half-praying for His protection as we venture further into this strange land.

The Khyber is the most notorious but by no means the most difficult of the passes we have to negotiate on our way to Kabul. After passing through the fortified city of Jalalabad – really not much more than a fort with a market outside its walls, though the yellowish-coloured oranges on sale there are wonderfully refreshing – our horses and camels plod on into the ten miles of the Jugdulluk Pass, where the smell of thyme hangs in the air and the apricot orchards bear more fruit than the locals can eat. This is the longest pass but not the worst. That prize goes, I think, to the Huft Kotul Pass which is so narrow you can touch both sides of the rock at the same time. It is so steep and twisted you almost feel dizzy as you descend its precarious heights.

Finally, only a day from the city, we descend yet another narrow pass, the Khoord Kabul, as the air turns thick and humid, the sky turns grey and the birds seem to take flight. Thunder rumbles far away in the mountains as we start pitching tents and preparing the evening meal.

Tomorrow we will be in Kabul. But tonight the camels, the horses and the travellers must rest.

The clouds gather in heavy clusters. The air is quiet and sounds are somehow slower, more ponderous. Hoosein, the boys and I have our tent up in no time. We feed the horses. Our supper is boiling away as the thunder grows louder. It seems to be rushing towards us. The air grows suddenly dark, the first fat raindrops splatter over us.

We are on a dry riverbed. One of the tribesmen is waving at us. 'Move up, move up,' he says and strides on to warn our neighbouring encampment. Hoosein smiles and laughs. 'These people,' he says, waving a dismissive hand after the tribesman.

The boys, though, are busily packing up our modest belongings. 'Hurry, hurry,' says Ali. 'We must make for higher ground.' Waheed is shifting the horses, which are reluctant to move, until he hits them sharply with a stick and they stumble up the steep cliffs.

Suddenly, with a roar of thunder and forks of lightning which startle the horses and have them kicking and bucking, the rain is upon us. The riverbed is first a deepening pool and, it seems only moments later, a brook, then a torrent, as the waters roll and tumble down from the mountains.

We scramble up the slopes of the valley in the gloom of day-turned-night, stumbling over rocks, tripping over ourselves and the rest of our rushing caravanserai, the horses frightened and tugging at their bridles, the camels honking like geese. Pots and possessions are left on the valley floor to be washed downstream towards Kabul as the torrent grows deeper and we stand, entirely without shelter and soaked to the skin, watching the waters rise.

We are high enough for safety but the tempest gives us no comfort. At first, the sudden drop of temperature and the cold rain comes as a refreshing relief from the humid air which has been building up all day. Now, though, I can feel the water drawing rivulets of pale skin down my face. My cotton shirt clings to my skin, my turban feels as if it is filling with water. I tear it off and pointlessly wring it out. My hair clings to my skull.

All around me are people and animals taking what cover they can find, under tiny rock ledges, under makeshift awnings which will not stay up in the wind, beneath the stomachs of their camels. Hoosein looks even more unhappy than I feel though the boys are laughing at him and, if they were not required to calm the horses, I swear they would be running in and out of the water like the little savages they are.

I watch the water rushing downhill. I keep my eyes on a bush or a log as it rushes by only to lose it again as the river boils and churns. I gaze into the waters almost dazed by the sudden onrush.

The downpour lasts almost three hours. The valley floor is awash with water and debris thrown downhill by the power of the torrent.

Eventually the clouds start to lift and night falls. The sides of the valley are too steep to build fires or comfortably sleep. Everything we possess is too sodden to be of any use anyway. The evening stars come out and the night grows cold. I make the boys do exercises, as if we are in military academy, to keep us warm. All around us are cries of indignation and discomfort, though, as far as I can tell, nobody has died.

Eventually we fall into cramped, uncomfortable and hungry sleep. I awake to a bright, warm morning with everything from the horses to our clothes starting to steam. The boys are scavenging for breakfast. The horses are docile. Hoosein is tapping my shoulder. He wants to re-paint my face.

CHAPTER 6

Kabul, September 1837

Alexander Burnes comes strolling through Kabul market as if he owns the place. Several apparently-wealthy hangers-on follow him as if he were on some royal progress. Burnes himself dispenses rupees, smiles and jests to left and right, hears a few supplicants begging him to intercede on their behalf with the King. Occasionally a young maiden catches his eye and, with the distinct encouragement of one toothless relative or another, curtseys deeply to the Great White Khan while looking boldly into his eyes.

I have only been in the city a couple of days but already I have, thanks to Hoosein, become well aware of Burnes's reputation as a ladies' man.

I sent Hoosein out from our seedy quarters to find out more about this city and engineer a contact with Burnes which would not compromise my disguise. The little man returned full of gossip.

'They say in the markets that Sikundur Burnes...'

'Sikundur?'

'Yes, sahib, Sikundur,' Hoosein insisted.

'Sir Alexander?'

'Yes, Sikundur.'

'Go on.'

'They say he is closer to Dost Mohammed than even the King's own sons, closer even than Mohammed Akbar himself. Closer than his grand vizier. And they say Sikundur Burnes has made himself popular with all the ladies of good breeding. They say he entertains, sahib.'

'Entertains?'

'Banquets. Only the best food and the best company for Sikundur Burnes. All the Khans keep coming back for more. They bring their wives with them and their daughters. But they do not always leave with their daughters. Or their wives.'

'Or their wives?'

'They say Sikundur Burnes's influence with the Dost is so strong a good word from the Great White Khan can open all doors. Favours for favours, sahib. That's what they say in the markets.'

For the maintenance of His Majesty's honour, I tell Hoosein it is nothing but idle gossip about a stranger in their midst and could not possibly be farther from the truth. Privately, I have my doubts. Burnes's reputation is well-known.

Watching Burnes's progress through this ancient marketplace I am now assured at least that he is widely-known and well-regarded among the Afghans of Kabul.

It is impossible to pinpoint exactly what smells come wafting through the market. It is so crowded with people and so full of noise I cannot concentrate. There are colours, sights and sounds which remind me of the dense streets of Calcutta, filled with thin, aggressive-looking warriors and fat merchants, dozens of small children fighting and running around, quite possibly filching things as they go. Women gossiping or haggling. There are beggars and peddlers and musicians and I see several stalls filled with spices and guns, sabres and even some of the long-muzzle rifles they seem to favour, though they look as likely to explode in your face as they are to kill a wolf let alone a man. Slaughtered sheep and cattle hang from iron hooks, their offal laid out on filthy-looking trestles and piled, leaking red, as customers handle them and put them down again. There is milk and cheese, fat eggplants, huge melons, newly-plucked apples. There is orange blossom and rose oils, a little saffron as well as parrots and other songbirds in large cages and cocks ready to do battle.

I shoulder my way through the small crowd and, as he nears me, I cry out in Pashto – as previously arranged by a private letter – 'A horse, Sir Alexander Burnes?'

'My kingdom for it, sir,' he replies in the same language, his reference to Shakespeare lost on the surrounding throng as, no doubt, he would have known. 'Come by my house this evening and we will talk of it further.' Briefly I feel scrutinised by this maharaja. In that glimpse I see a short man, no more than five feet and a half, a fat, round face and drooping moustache. The eyes are round and humorous, maybe slightly untrustworthy, perhaps a little arrogant, not necessarily sensitive. But it is only a glimpse. Burnes waves a regal hand vaguely in my direction and his little caravan plunges on, deeper into the din of the market.

*****

I next meet Burnes in his living quarters. Dost Mohammed, the King, has allocated a suite of rooms within the bounds of Kabul's massive fortress, the Balar Hissar. It is a pretty palace. He is living like Kahn, a petty prince basking in the sunlight of his King. Burnes is an intrepid, knighted hero, celebrated in a hundred London drawing rooms for his exotic mysticism, his ability to open up new worlds and spread them at the feet of society, his confidence.

Alexander Burnes may be short but he is handsome, with a confidence that comes not just from success but the belief, indeed the conviction, that everybody likes him. Cousin to the Scottish postmaster poet, now dead and none the less celebrated for that; Burnes, confidante of the King of Kabul, friend of viziers and potentates; Burnes, beloved of the people.

Yet on first acquaintance there is something not quite right about Alexander Burnes, dressed as an Afghan prince with his jewelled robes and brightly-coloured turbans. Perhaps it is his easy way with the natives. He thinks they are his friends. But if you look carefully into their smiles, there is no warmth in their eyes. He embraces them, throws his arms around them, whispers most intimately into their ears, laughs with unstudied ease. They do not laugh as uproariously, they merely smile. They do not embrace, they seem, if anything, to shrink a little from his touch. They listen to his intimacies but they do not offer their own in return.

They enjoy his hospitality but they do not reciprocate.

Perhaps it is his licentiousness. I see it immediately and it never ceases to surprise me. We all enjoy the freedoms we are given in the Company's service so far from home. The rules of civilised Christian behaviour are not always observed at this distance and we all embrace this in our different ways. We are, after all, members of a superior race. These countries are ours to enjoy. We are not shy of this nor should we be reluctant to make the most of the opportunities God has laid out for us. These are not the temptations of Satan, they are the first fruits of the Promised Land.

Yet Burnes seems to take this to excess. He has his own harem. This would surely be a scandal if it were widely known and yet he makes no secret of it. He has in his household half a dozen young women, unveiled and brown-eyed. He has the best wines the country can produce – and despite its proliferation of rock and dust some quarters of this country are positively beautiful, lush, green and fruitful – as well as Champagne, brandy and other importations from Europe.

Burnes even has opium.

'So Pottinger. You are here to get the lie of the land, are you? Well let me tell you, the Afghan is a very loyal and friendly fellow. And his womenfolk are even more friendly. My experience is that they are fascinated by the appearance of a white face, even if it is covered by a beard. But I suppose that won't really work in your case, will it? No, I suppose not. Here have some of this brandy. Now, as I was saying, you need to prepare yourself for a long and difficult journey. Otherwise how can you write a book about it?'

'I don't have that facility,' I say.

'Pity,' says Burnes, 'You should cultivate it immediately. I wrote a book about my travels and it turned out rather well, though I say it myself, made me something of a swell at home, you know.'

Burnes is pacing the room, his long velvet gown billowing out behind him, with a brandy bottle in one hand from which he fills his glass at regular intervals. I sit on his cushions on the floor of his saloon while three servants keep discreet guard at the far end of the room. I suspect if Burnes thinks of himself as a romantic hero, which I believe he does, it is not his cousin Robbie he has in mind. Lord Byron is more his style.

Burnes continues, 'You need to write it all down, Pottinger. But you can't possibly go as a horse-dealer. What on earth put that idea into your head? I suppose it was those fools in Simla, wasn't it? You can just hear them now, "Those Afghans will swallow anything, Pottinger, don't you worry. Horse dealer worked in Tibet, why not in Afghanistan?" Let me tell you, Pottinger, it will not work here.'

I look quizzical and try to ask why but Burnes is in full flow. 'The Afghan, as you know, is an expert at the equestrian arts. I have seen two men on horseback charging an enemy in full flow, one directing the animal, the other on the blind side, waiting to cut down the unsuspecting fellow who thinks he has only one rider to deal with. They breed their horses for battle, these animals are swift and sure, they don't need much food and they are among the best in the whole of Asia. The Afghan will sniff you out as a fraud at a hundred yards. Do you know much about horse-breeding?'

'I have been involved…'

'It doesn't really make any difference, they will sniff you out in no time. And they are not friendly towards spies, let me tell you. I have heard tell of foreigners being buried alive, staked out in the blistering heat of the desert and left to rot. The women are worse. Your Afghan is a friendly fellow, as I say, but vengeful, Pottinger, vengeful. They are constantly at each other's throats. Literally. Nobody trusts anybody else, for good reason. Feuds last generations. What else could you pass yourself off as? I know, a holy man.'

'A holy man? What sort of holy man?'

'The sort who says nothing and observes everything. The sort who issues blessings and peace-be-unto-yous and Allah Akbars and doesn't actually get into any sort of a conversation. Nothing more convincing of religious depths than a silent imam. You have a man?'

'Yes, Hoosein.'

'Knows the ropes, does he, this Hoosein?'

'You mean is he a Muslim?'

'If necessary, yes.'

'I suppose so, I've never asked him.'

'Never asked him?' Burnes swallows an indignant drop of brandy and continues, 'Damn it, man, ask him. Get him to teach you the rudiments. You've read the Koran I suppose?'

'A little.'

'A little is a lot more than most people in this country. The natives can't read, of course, and by and large nor can their priests. The mullahs pretty much make it up as they go along. They invoke Allah for any cause they like – from blessing a wedding feast to waging war,' Burnes pauses before adding with a rueful smile, 'Rather like we do, I suppose.'

'Except of course ours is the true religion,' I feel compelled to interrupt. Burnes put his glass and bottle down and stands looking at me.

'The true religion,' he says slowly, with voice which, in his Scottish accent, accentuates the scepticism of his look. 'The true religion, is it?'

'These people are heathens, like the Hindus and the Sikhs.'

'Are they indeed?' says Burnes. 'Well, I shall not dispute it with you old fellow. But I think there ought to be room in your universe for more than one point of view, don't you? Certainly you will need to remain open-minded about the people you are living among. Their ways are not our ways and they are, indeed, somewhat lacking in civilised sensibilities. Even so, we may have something to learn from them.'

'I am sure we shall,' I agree enthusiastically. 'And it will be simpler to pass oneself off as a Muslim if one has no sense that one is committing a sacrilege of some sort.'

'Yes, I see that. Only do not assume we know everything, is my advice to you. We can learn from these people though they can learn a great deal more from us. Or they could if only they were prepared to give it a try.'

*****

The evening is warm but the light is dying. Burnes orders in candles and wine. Three manservants in some sort of purple uniform carry in candelabra, three more carry in wine. Half a dozen women, their light saris wrapped loosely around their shoulders and hips, follow carrying plates of lamb kebabs, roasted chicken, beef and several rice dishes as well as the inevitable naan bread.

The women place these plates on the thick carpets where Burnes and I sit. The women are followed by a couple of men Burnes introduces to me as Captain Will Eastwick and Kohun Dil Khan, a relative of the King.

The servants bring in a hookah. This one is in the Persian fashion with wooden coals heating the water, the opium fumes rising to the tube through which one inhales. Burnes is the first to address this, having already tossed off a goblet of the thick red wine we have been served. Eastwick and Kohun Dil Khan follow suit before Burnes hands the tube to me and urges my participation.

I see no reason to decline and, having taken another deep draught of my wine, I decide to see what effect this opium might have on me. I have never tried it before though it is well known across the North West of India. It is disappointingly tasteless and for a few moments I remain unmoved then gradually a sense of well-being spreads through my body, I feel myself relaxing and my mind somehow seems to unwind, as if the spring of a great clock has broken and the mechanism is whirring at great speed to a sudden standstill. I watch as the others take further inhalations, start hungrily devouring the food and talking softly, slowly and languidly. I try to concentrate on what they are saying but cannot fathom the words or their meanings. Occasionally Eastwick chuckles.

'So you are the King's cousin, are you?' I ask Dil Khan but the words come out as a mumble and he just smiles at me, somewhat inanely, as I gaze at the jewels on his tunic and watch the maidservant's hair glitter and shine in the candlelight.

I call for more wine and my goblet is immediately re-filled. I take a deep draught and register this has been poured not by one of the manservants but by one of the young women. The male servants seem to have retreated to their quarters. I vaguely notice how beautiful this maiden is, with her long black hair and her deep brown eyes, her soft brown skin and her fine-boned figure. She settles down next to me on the carpet and passes me the tube. She helps me sit up and pours me more wine. She feeds me with her delicate fingers. I vaguely apprehend that Burnes and the others are being similarly attended-to. It seems the saris are not covering these women very efficiently. Indeed, I think I am seeing things I have never seen before and acts which would normally take place in private.

At some point, it occurs to me that this is an outrage against God and the King. However this thought is only fleeting. I find myself increasingly unable to think clearly, especially as the young woman at my side is caressing my body. The warmth of the room, the influence of the wine and the opium taken all together heighten my senses as they deprive my conscious mind of a will of my own.

I am given over to candlelight and the scents of my perfumed companion, who carries on her skin the scent of lemons or oranges and whose tongue, small and pink, is starting to caress my neck and shoulders.

I surrender to her attentions and feel a glorious peace descend upon me as the night draws on and the murmuring in Alexander Burnes's room seems like the sound of babbling streams on a midsummer's day in Ireland where I lie basking in a rare sun with some unknowable companion.

I try asking my girl what her name is but I am not sure I manage to get the words out. I certainly do not recall any answer other than her lips pressing on mine and her hands exploring beneath my tunic as she settles herself above me.

CHAPTER 7

Fort William, Calcutta, December 1842

The subaltern is a spotty youth straight off the boat from England. He cannot decide if I am a superior officer or a prisoner so he addresses me with an apologetic deference which, in other circumstance, I might have found amusing. As it is, awaiting my Court Martial and being neither on active service not imprisoned, I sympathise with his plight for I, too, cannot decide if I am a prisoner or an officer in Her Majesty's service.

It seems, according to this youth whose pale complexion and anxious eyes suggest he will not survive in this appalling climate for very long, that the committee of inquiry – they refuse to call it a Court Martial because I am now so well-known it would not look good for the administration to be seen persecuting the 'Hero of Herat' no matter what subsequent betrayals and derelictions of duty I am accused of – it seems, I say, that Eleanor has already left the country. She is on her way home. Lost to me and out of my life.

This boy, this Henry Lloyd, hands me a note:

Bombay, January 2, 1842

My Dear Eldred – Husband I should say – beloved Eldred

Words cannot express my fury and indignation at my removal from this benighted country and the appalling treatment you are receiving at the hands of men with no courage, backbone nor understanding. You have long been a hero, not only to me, and a guardian, friend and guide. You have saved many lives, your courage, fortitude, loyalty and honour have been an example to all and you have been recognised by your companions in incarceration as the guiding light, the wise head on young shoulders, the greatest leader of them all. Your country owes you nothing but its undying gratitude as your companions in suffering owe you their lives, their futures, their happiness, their – our, I should say – our everything.

My dear Eldred, my horror at what is happening to you is compounded by the regret that I am not with you to comfort you and support you through this latest and most outrageous ordeal.

We, your friends, know at first hand you are no coward. How the new Governor can put up with this sham I cannot tell. They are clearly seeking a scapegoat for all that humiliation and all those lost lives. They would choose my brother himself if they could though he is banished back to England already. They shall not find it in the honourable Major Eldred Pottinger.

I am being packed aboard some clipper heading for home without a by-your-leave. My brother, my sisters, all our relatives are sent home and I am in the hands – I should say the custody – of the Rev Theodore Morris, a grim-faced young man without a sense of humour and an overwhelmingly unnecessary sense of duty. "Your brother, Lord Eden, has entrusted you to my care,

Madam, and I cannot be content until I see you well under way," he says with a certain grim self-satisfaction. I am accompanied by my old amah, Rachina, who has never been out of the country. I can't see her relishing a stay in Kent but, dear woman, she is determined I shall not be abandoned. "I cannot leave you, madam, in your hour of need."

My hour of need? My hour of need? What about your hour of need? I am abandoning you, my dear beloved saviour, in your hour of need. Yet what choice do I have? The new Governor is anxious for all the Edens to be gone from India. There is nowhere for me to live here, nowhere for me to exist, as I await your vindication and your release and your recognition as the brave, true, honest soldier I and my fellow captives all know you to be. My dear, darling Eldred. That captivity, I see now, was the happiest time of my life. To be beside you day after day is to know your character in all its glory. To live alongside you, enduring such hardships, is to know you and to know how perfectly incapable you are of any dishonourable act and therefore of how absurd these charges are which have been brought against you.

Though my ship is carrying me half a world away from you, I know we shall be re-united very soon.

I was, I am, and I shall always remain,
your own

Eleanor.

CHAPTER 8

Kabul, September 1837

There are many reasons I should not have lingered with Sir Alexander Burnes that night. The next day I am not just unwell and disorientated, I am ashamed and afraid. Afraid I have betrayed my presence in the city to the Afghans. Where is my disguise? Am I exposed? What has Burnes said to his companions and they to theirs? Was this Kohun Dil Khan I passed an evening with really a cousin of the King?

I try, discreetly, to discover via Hoosein. The little man spends his day in the Kabul market where, he says, you find all the news you need to know. He says the King, Dost Mohammed Khan, is entertaining a Russian in secret. The Afghans are full of the news that Burnes's confidence in his special relationship with the Dost is about to be overthrown following the arrival of a Count Viktovitch from Moscow.

Of course Hoosein does know of Kohun Dil Khan. This is not London, this is Kabul, where everyone knows everything. Kohun Dil Khan is a younger brother of the Dost though, indeed, half-brother would be a more accurate description as they share the same father but not the same mother. It seems the Dost has several important half-brothers, perhaps fifteen, Hoosein is not entirely clear, together with a dozen or so important sisters. He has other half-brothers and half-sisters as well but these are not by important wives so they do not count, apparently.

'This is very good, sahib,' Hoosein says. 'It means, by marrying, the family can spread its influence and secure their position on the throne.'

'Secure their position, Hoosein? Surely the Dost has been in power long enough to be safe?'

It is early evening. We are sitting cross-legged on the ground outside our modest lodgings, eating walnuts which Hoosein has gathered in the market, drinking tea and watching the city dwellers come and go. The muezzin's call to prayer is widely ignored.

'In this country no King is secure, sahib,' the little man says gravely. 'The last King of Kabul is still alive, is he not? Has not Shah Soojah just tried to regain his throne? It is the tribes.' Here Hoosein raises his index finger as if proving his point, 'The tribes of Afghanistan, worse than the tribes of India, sahib, always on and on and on. Mark my words, mark my words.'

'We must get word to Burnes before we depart,' I tell Hoosein. 'Send Ali.'

*****

The next morning I am again in Burnes's residence beside the palace, in the King's great Kabul fortress. Burnes is sitting on a carpet with Will Eastwick drinking tea. Burnes neither invites me to sit with them nor to join them for tea. He makes no reference to the other night. I tell him what I know of Count Viktovitch, which is not much save that he exists and that he is being entertained by Dost Mohammed Khan. Burnes says he is already aware of the man's presence and has discussed the situation with the Dost himself but I am not entirely sure I believe him. I wonder if he is put out that I have news from his own domain which he believes he should already know, certainly well in advance of some interloper like Eldred Pottinger, disguised horse-dealer.

Eastwick, who is an amiable enough fellow with a curious accent I find difficult to place, is not in the first rank when it comes to mental agility. But he is, at least, less aggressive than Burnes. 'So the Tsar has sent some Count to chat up the Dost at last has he? Well, Alex old chap, you seem to have a rival on your turf, what? Ha! Ha! That should keep you on your toes, what? And how will His Lordship take it?'

'Very evil, sir, very evil indeed,' says Burnes, clambering to his feet and pacing the long room in the bright, sharp-shadowed morning light, deep in thought.

He turns and looks at me. 'As for you, Pottinger, you had better be on your way. If news of your presence gets out that will only complicate matters further. I have enough to worry about.'

Burnes is about to dismiss me, somewhat imperiously to my mind, when he turns back and says, 'I trust you have got rid of your horses? Good. We can't have you pretending to be a horse-dealer.'

Here Eastwick interrupts. 'Drop the disguise, why don't you old man? Don't you know, with an accent like that even the meanest Afghan would have trouble believing you were an English officer? Paddy Pottinger, that's what they call you isn't it? Paddy Pottinger. Ha! Ha!'

I do not rise to this, merely observe to Burnes, 'I think my English accent at least betrays a gentle upbringing.'

Eastwick takes a step towards me, clenching a fist, but Burnes steps between us. Our eyes meet and there is a smile in his, of recognition and fellowship. 'Don't worry about Eastwick, Pottinger. Come along now, Will, shake Pottinger's hand. No harm done.'

The man offers his hand and, reluctantly, I take it with a grim smile and agree, 'No harm done.'

'Oh Paddy,' smiles Eastwick, 'If only we had time to get to know one another we should become firm friends of that I am sure.'

Why does Burnes entertain this fool, I wonder as I make my way back out of the castle on the hill, past its huge, fortified gates and its thick bastions, and descend towards the smells and noise of the Kabul market.

piss

*****

The next day, a note arrives from Burnes. It is delivered into Hoosein's hands as he is taking chai in the marketplace and gathering any intelligence which might be of use. He comes rushing back to our lodgings, where I am writing a report for Sir William Macnaghten, the Governor General's bespectacled political adviser. I am bringing him up to date with the situation in the Khyber and between the Afghans and the Sikhs but I am not at all sure whether to mention the presence of Count Viktovich. Burnes summons me back to his apartments inside the fortress.

It is a brief walk. I am admitted by the main entrance as one of the many traders who make their way to and fro. The guards on the gates of the Bala Hissar are more or less indifferent about who goes in and out. The King's own Palace, within the fortifications of the great castle, has its own defences. Even so, I see it looks vulnerable to gunfire if one breaches the outer walls. The main Palace buildings are slightly overlooked from a parade ground which, once gained, would be an excellent location for an enemy to prosecute a further attack.

I mention this to Burnes when I am once more granted admission to his own palatial set of rooms. This time he is sitting in what might be called a Throne Room. At any rate, Sir Alexander Burnes is ensconced in a heavy wooden chair with a high back and thick cushions, so high off the ground he obviously ascended with the aid of a footstool. He is once again wearing the garb of a wealthy native, with a huge head-dress almost exploding up above, and a sapphire brooch pinned to his plain linen robes. He wears multi-coloured slippers and is studying a journal of some sort. There are three servants on one side of the room and a serving maid sitting demurely at the Great Man's feet.

'Ah Pottinger,' says Burnes, looking up from his journal. 'I sometimes like to refresh my memory,' he adds, holding up the volume which, I see, is one of his own 'Travels' books. I wonder if he is trying to make a point. You, Pottinger, he seems to be saying, intend to explore unchartered territory but never forget who got there first. Burnes smiles and it is a genuine enough greeting, as he steps down from his throne and crosses the carpet to embrace me like a long-lost brother, a strange reaction compared with our last, stand-offish encounter.

'Pottinger, thank you for sparing me the time before your departure. I am most grateful. I have something to explain to you. Come and sit down.' Once we are cross-legged on the rugs and Burnes has ordered us both some wine, he carries on. 'You see my dear Eldred, that fellow you met the other day.'

'Kohun Dil Khan?'

'No, no. Eastwick. Will Eastwick. Well, Eastwick isn't Eastwick. As far as I know, the real captain Eastwick is safe and well and tucked away in Lucknow with the 5th Lancers. No, Pottinger, I'm afraid my Eastwick is in fact Count Nikolai Viktovich.'

I do not speak but my face betrays my confusion.

'In this country, Pottinger, nothing is as it seems. Viktovich is Eastwick, you are a horse-dealer. Or are you a holy man? The King is the King unless it is his rival King who is safe and well and champing at the bit somewhere in Hindustan.

'You see, Pottinger, contrary to the gossip your man Hoosein may pick up in the market...' Burnes laughs at the expression of astonishment on my face and flings an arm round my shoulders. 'I have my own spies, you know, Eldred. It is always important for a man in my position to know the local gossip. Anyway, Viktovich and I have become well acquainted. I am trying to persuade him to withdraw from Kabul before he does any harm. Your presence assisted in my entertainment of him the other night. I have high hopes of success. Should you be sending a dispatch to Hindustan, I heartily suggest you omit any mention of Viktovich's presence for the while, lest we alarm the Governor General unnecessarily. I hope to persuade the good Count to return to Moscow at the earliest opportunity.'

'What does he want here?'

'A good question, Eldred. A good question.' Burnes absent-mindedly polishes the jewel on his tunic and, gazing into the middle distance, he says, 'If I were to fear the worst, the answer might be that Russia is seeking to establish an alliance with Dost Mohammed Khan and ally this country to the Tsar's Russian empire. As you know, the Russians are constantly trying to enlarge their dominions. The logical step would be for the Tsar to ally himself with the Persians and use this country as the route into Hindustan itself.'

'India?'

'India, Hindustan, call it what you will.'

'No, I mean, are you suggesting the Russians are interested in our Indian empire?'

'Why not? It is infinitely richer, more fruitful and civilised than contemptible little principalities like Turkmenistan and Uzbekistan. If I were the Tsar, my sights would be set on India. And never forget, Pottinger – Napoleon himself planned to invade India through Persia and Afghanistan. Tsar Nicholas obviously thinks he is the new Napoleon. That is why Count Viktovich has been sent here. To enter into negotiations with Dost Mohammed Khan.'

'But I thought the Dost was our sworn ally.'

'And so he is. But we do not spare him any money or troops to win back Peshawar from that rascal Ranjeet Singh.'

'Ranjeet is our ally.'

'Precisely. We cannot support the Dost against Ranjeet yet the two are mortal enemies. The Tsar, on the other hand, has no love for Ranjeet so he is free to offer the Dost whatever he pleases. My task is to persuade the Dost that his long-term best interests lie in friendly relations with Great Britain and not in turning his back on us and opening up a high road for the Russians into the heart of our Empire. This is high politics, Pottinger, which is why I suggest you leave it to me to deal with Sir William Macnaghten and Lord George Eden.

'It would spread unnecessary alarm if our masters were to learn there was even the remotest possibility of an alliance with the Tsar. I expect to send the Count back to Moscow without an audience with the King.

I shall certainly seek to persuade the Dost it is not in his interests to take any approach from the Tsar seriously. Though with Winter almost upon us, Viktovich's departure, if it is to be achieved soon, cannot be delayed very long.'

'You do not seem particularly anxious, Sir Alexander,' I say.

'I most certainly am not, Pottinger. One stray Russian Count cannot possibly represent more than a pin-prick on the body politic of the East India Company and Her Majesty's British Empire.'

It is as if he has slapped me across the face. 'Her Majesty?' I blurt out.

'Good Lord, Pottinger,' says Burnes with a grin. 'Are you really the very last to know what every horse-dealer in Kabul has known for at least ten days? Are you telling me your little spy Hoosein has not seen fit to pass on this news? That the King is dead?'

'King Billy? When?'

'Some time back in the summer. His heart, I believe. Never a very strong heart. Struggled on for some months, so they say. Just to spite the Duchess of Kent. Died at the end of June, just after Alexandrina Victoria reached the age of 18. We got word a fortnight ago in dispatches from Bombay. We had a day of mourning, even here in old Kabul. The Dost was very good about it.'

'So we now serve Queen Alexandrina.'

'Victoria.'

'Oh?'

'Alexandrina is her first name. But it's too Russian.'

*****

'But Sahib I thought you knew, I thought you must know. The new Queen, Victoria? I heard in Amritsar. In the market, of course.' The little man is nodding and shaking his head at the same time, in that manner he has, both asserting his point and apologising for it at the same time.

63

'You are no help as an intelligencer,' I complain to Hoosein. 'I should send you back to India with Ali and Waheed.'

Hoosein gives a look of mock-disappointment, hangs his head and then grins up at me. 'But sahib how would you carry on as a holy man if you have no-one to instruct you and guide you?'

'You are a Hindu, Hoosein, let me remind you.'

'I know as much about their religion as the average Mohammeden, sahib, you can be sure of that. They are always at war with each other and though they may profess the same faith, these people, that is all they have in common.'

'They also have one King, Hoosein,' I point out.

'Not a Queen like the Queen of England, sahib.'

'No, not like our Queen, I suppose, but then why not? Is not Dost Mohammed Khan as secure on his Throne as Victoria is on hers?'

'Sahib, in this country nobody is secure anywhere for long. The tribes, sahib, the tribes.' With that Hoosein bustles off, his little legs scurrying along, towards the market yet again. This time he is seeking out provisions to supply us for our journey. We have sold our spare horses and tomorrow the boys return to India with a caravanserai and pockets full of rupees. They seem happy enough to be going though I confess I shall miss them a little when it's just Hoosein, me, the desolate spaces of Afghanistan and its feuding tribes.

CHAPTER 9

Wardak, October 1837

The road out of Kabul crosses the river which is not deep though it is wide. There is a long, narrow wooden bridge of uncertain permanence to negotiate. It is less than a mile from the city, with some rocky, uncultivated land separating the water from the walls of the nearest houses. Before us, the foothills of the Hindu Kush, behind us the looming citadel of the Bala Hissar with Alexander Burnes and his Russian friend dancing their diplomatic gavottes.

Hoosein and I are an unprepossessing sight, dressed in the local rags, with what few supplies we manage to pack into our saddlebags, with no escorts, no protection and scarcely any weapons to our name. Our horses hesitantly stumble across the Kabul River and we gradually aim towards the south and west, with no fixed destination nor any purpose other than to understand more of this rugged country and its people. I am reminded of a Spanish book we were acquainted with back at school in Belfast. I am Don Quixote, Hoosein is my Sancho Panza. But where, I wonder, are the windmills?

*****

'Stay calm, Hoosein, they could just be merchants.' As soon as we spy five horsemen cantering towards us down the valley, Hoosein is anxious to spur our horses and see if we can outrun them. It is the most dangerous thing we could do. If they are ordinary merchants, we have nothing to fear. If they are tribesmen, bandits or worse, then galloping away will only draw attention to us. We are ordinary people, a mullah and his servant, and we are not to be intimidated by the sight of a few warlike men on horseback brandishing what, even from a distance, look worryingly like sabres.

We have been descending this pass since long before dawn. It is still chilly but, as we lose height, the pale sun is starting to warm our bones and I am looking forward to making decent progress. We have decided to stick to the main routes through this rough country. Anything unusual and we are sure to be stopped, questioned and, perhaps, exposed. I prefer to avoid trouble if possible though I can't help but fear it is always just round the next rock.

Hoosein is tugging at my sleeve. I shake him off. 'Stay calm, man,' I hiss. 'And remember, no English. We speak in Pashto. Only in Pashto, Hoosein. We are servants of Allah, peace be unto him. We are doing no harm. We have nothing to fear.'

By now we can hear the beat of their hooves as the horsemen close in on us. I wonder if my mission will be over before it has even begun. We only left Kabul a few days ago and we have been sleeping in villages, talking to the local people and I have been noting our experiences as we go. So far our journey has been relatively trouble-free but the brigands quickly gain on us. I try to ride on unperturbed but one glance at Hoosein is enough to warn me we were unlikely to escape from this encounter without some difficulty.

Hoosein is not the man for a crisis. He is looking around like a madman, staring at the new arrivals and shouting that they should leave us alone, we are only poor pilgrims. At least he is speaking in Pashto. For that, at any rate, I am grateful. 'What do you want? We are holy pilgrims. Leave us alone. Go away,' Hoosein is crying out as they come nearer. I stay silent, looking ahead down the rough track.

I see out of the corner of my eye the horsemen are the same weather-beaten, wrapped-up, bearded savages we usually encounter on the passes. They could be traders separated from a caravan, horse-dealers searching for customers, simple thieves or, as I guess, militia belonging to the local Khan. They ignore Hoosein's imprecations and gradually his yelling subsides. The horsemen take up their positions: One of them rides ahead of us, one rides to my left, another at Hoosein's right hand side. The other two troop along behind us. We are surrounded without their saying a word. They listen to Hoosein's gibbering but do not react.

I do not react either. I am a holy, meditative man. I will not be swayed into betraying my apprehension by the appearance of these characters. I look a little more closely at the one beside me, with his greying beard and unkempt clothing, in the brownish cloth they all wear. Tucked behind his saddle he carries a rifle, one of the Afghans' home-made weapons. It has a carefully carved peacock on its stock. Maybe this man is wealthy, I think, to have such an ornate weapon.

I try to look both respectful and a little anxious, smiling at this man and saying in Pashto, 'I see Allah has blessed you', indicating the weapon.

He grins, exposing what is left of his discoloured teeth. I guess he is not much older me though, I flatter myself, he already seems like an old man in comparison. 'You must come with us,' he says, loudly enough to indicate to the whole company this is an order and he is the one in a position to give it.

Hoosein begins to protest. 'We are pilgrims, we are pilgrims,' he insists. I take hold of his horse's bridle and pull animal and rider closer to my side.

'Indeed we are pilgrims, Hoosein,' I say. 'But if you must make this infernal racket they will take us for something else. Do not arouse their anger, man. Stay calm. If you refuse to stay calm, I cannot be held responsible for the consequences. For either of us.'

We trot on, all seven of us, in silence. Hoosein is clearly unhappy.

I can tell by the way he chews his fingernails as he rides. The day is warming up fast. Though it is almost November now, away from the mountains the land remains very warm. I should say it must be in the 60s, which is still hot for me, if not for Hoosein. For now, though, the temperature is bearable though sweat is starting to prick at my smock and irritate my beard. At least, I console myself, it is not hot enough yet for my brown make-up to start melting.

My sweat is not entirely the result of the growing heat of the day. It does not become an Englishman – even an Irish Englishman – to betray his nerves. He must show his steel at all times. These natives do not frighten me. I have Sir Henry Pottinger's example always before me though it is fair to say since Sir Henry's adventure, affairs in these territories have deteriorated. Hoosein and I are passing through a land at war, with the Sikhs, with each other, potentially with Great Britain. And I know what these tribes are capable of. Sir Henry has written more than enough about the dangers and I have noted more than once the brutality he was exposed to.

As we ride on, I have more leisure to inspect our escort – I would say captors though so far we are not in captivity and we have not been threatened or misused. They are all young men, their horses thin but powerful. Only the man on my left has a rifle but the others all have swords of one kind or another. It looks as if these have been put to use, possibly recently. One of them is bloodstained, though this could just be the blood of an animal.

It is unlikely our captors are loyal to Dost Mohammed Khan. He may be King of Kabul but his sway does not really reach much of the country he claims as his own. The real power, the power over life and death, rests with the local Khans who rule their own clans or tribes rather like the old Scotch chieftains of the last century. Our escort consists of members of an independent tribe or, should I say, an independent nation. Worse still, they appear to be Hazaras. They have that slightly Mongolian look about them which indicates they are direct descendants of that marauding monster Genghis Khan. It is not clear whether they owe any loyalty to the King of Kabul but, even if Dost Mohammed Khan is their enemy, it does not make Hoosein or me their friend. The people here may well hate each other but they hate foreigners more.

The rocky outcrops we are riding through gradually give way to a slightly greener valley where a small stream meanders. The winds are getting up and blowing clouds of sand around like great flights of starlings rising from a field. There are some trees though little in the way of leaf or fruit adorns them. There is some growth in the fields but nothing that seems worthy of cultivation, just enough scrub for thin cattle to graze on. About two miles from where our track is leading us, we see a village on fire. Farther on, I can see only sand and distant hills.

To our left, about five miles distant, there rises a citadel of stone and mud with turrets at each corner and a great gate. It is towards this city or prison we now inclined.

Our companions offer us a leather beaker of water. I am reluctant to taste it without first ensuring it is safe to drink and decline. Hoosein, on the other hand, has no compunction and swallows a long draught before I can advise him against it. He grins at me, looking happier than at any time since we had first encountered our escort. 'It is good,' he tells me, holding it out for me to reconsider. 'And cold.'

I am tempted but think better of it. 'I shall wait a little, Hoosein, and see if you drop down dead.' That wipes the smile from his face and he frowns. I do not think the possibility of poison crossed his mind and now he begins pressing a hand to his stomach as if testing it for pain or indigestion.

We are able to appraise the fortifications as we approach them. They stand on rising ground which gives a view back across the surrounding wastes towards the distant mountains. The fort is well-placed for defence. The walls must be at least twenty feet thick at their base, stretching perhaps a mile in one direction, three-quarters of a mile in the other. Within, I see the minarets of two mosques. The whole edifice is surrounded on the outside by an empty ditch into which the inhabitants throw their waste. The ditch may serve as a moat in the wetter seasons but its unpleasant stench can be encountered from a considerable distance as the unhealthy vapours are blown in our direction on the wind. On the approaches to the fort are huddled a few huts and tents peopled by scraps of humankind, men, women and children, sitting in the shade, gazing listlessly at us as we pass.

This place, I know from what I gleaned in advance of our expedition, is almost certainly called Wardak, an unremarkable settlement slightly off the trading routes which cross Central Asia, backward even in a backward country.

We pass over a wooden drawbridge and through the gates of this fortification to be greeted by a new gust of wind and dust. Inside are more tents and tenements either side of a main road leading directly to the Khan's Palace, which is on one side of a square with a mosque opposite and a market in the middle, with stalls under brown cloth draped loosely above them, a rudimentary affair compared with the great trading centre of Kabul.

We are required to give up our horses near the market and we are offered tea in the shade of one of the buildings behind the square. I watch our captors carefully but they neither look at us nor speak. Two women, in long smocks with scarves wrapped around their faces to hide them from the wind and the gaze of strangers, silently pour tea into small earthenware cups and hand them to us, eyes bowed, refusing to look at us or to be looked at. As everyone seems to be drinking tea and it all comes from the same pot, I am willing to risk a taste. I am thirsty after our ride and glad to be out of the wind.

The men stand in one corner muttering. Hoosein worries about our horses and possessions. I try to calm his fears. 'We are not prisoners here,' I remind him. 'We were not compelled to accompany our friends.' I say this loudly enough that, if our captors hear it, they might gather we are unafraid. Maybe I am being naïve but this seems to me the wisest approach – show fear to these people and they will take advantage of you; show steel and you earn their respect.

Soon enough, their leader, the man with the jezzail and few teeth, indicates we are to accompany him. We are led back across the square to the ornate entrance to the Palace, with its carved marble pillars. The archway is guarded by men with jezzails who look at us with curiosity but not, I am pleased to note, with much hostility. We walk in what, at home, I would call the cloisters, around a beautiful garden sheltered from the wind, with a small fountain tinkling in the silence. It is as if we have been transported to another world, of peace and tranquillity. The garden is filled with carefully-tended rose trees, still blooming crimson and white, despite the fading year. Behind them stand trees plump with fruit, mulberry, plum, pear, peach and cherry. Here is God's plenty. We pass through this demi-paradise into an inner courtyard where, it appears, some kind of ceremony is taking place.

In the centre, on a patch of ground, stand four men. They are bound hand and foot and tied to strong posts. In the shade on three sides of the small square stand maybe thirty personages who look as if they are the most senior officials of the Khan's court for their robes are clean and expensive, their beards are well cared-for and their turbans sport jewels. Everyone's attention is directed to the stone wall of the palace where, on the first floor, the Khan himself sits at a casement window.

Our captor indicates that we should stand beside the entrance, behind the great men of the court, which affords us a clear view of the proceedings. I look at Hoosein to indicate he should make not a sound. The Khan is giving a speech. He smiles as he does so and looks on his courtiers with a beneficence belied by his words.

'These curs, these cowards, these mongrels. They will know what it is to defy the word of Yakoob Beg. They shall not die, they do not deserve such mercy. They shall live to wish they were dead. He on the left, let him lose his fingers and toes. The next shall lose his manhood. The third, his ears and nose. Then throw them out of here. Let them live or die beyond our sight. This one, this one,' he indicates a boy whose beard is not even grown yet. 'Let him stay here. Do nothing to him. Do not feed him. Let him linger a day or two. He shall know what it is to defy Yakoob Beg, and his people will know what fate lies in wait for those who choose to defile their brothers and sisters.'

Immediately a small, wiry man with a devilish grin on his face leaps from behind the councillors and springs into the middle of the courtyard bearing with him what appear to be a pair of the sharpest scissors I had ever seen. With surprising deftness, which I can only conclude must come from regular practice, he falls on the first poor criminal and begins cutting off his fingers and thumbs. The blood and screams, the terror of it all, has Hoosein gagging and, I must confess, I myself am also a little disturbed in the stomach. I cannot watch but I cannot fail to hear. At one point I look up at the Khan who, I notice, has at his side a young woman who is busily eating a peach as this bloody spectacle is played out. Our captors also seem to be enjoying the sight though it does appear as if one or two of the Khan's courtiers are a little unhappy. A couple of them turn away, sip lemonade from a fountain and begin a conversation which appears to be about business.

During this time, I distract myself by telling my beads. I have on a string of glass beads which are supposed to indicate my holiness and I pass them through my hands muttering words which might be mumbled prayers as I do so.

It does not take long before the three men are cut down from their stakes and dragged by some of the Khan's men out of the courtyard. They do not pass us by, I am thankful to say, but leave through the opposite side whence, I suppose, they will be hurled from the citadel walls to live or die in the foul cess-pit that performs the role of a moat.

The fourth man – I should say boy – is limp at his post. It seems as if the shock of what has taken place is enough to make him lose consciousness. The Khan orders that he should be woken with water, which is duly thrown over him. He is forced to look at the blood-red ground and the pieces of gristle and bone lying close by. He screams hysterically until the dervish with the scissors dances up to him, slaps him several times and holds his forefinger to his lips to indicate silence.

The Khan throws the dervish a few coins, belches, spits out the stone of a peach and stands up, stroking the back of the young woman at his side. As he turns to go, our captor strides out into the sunlight, sinks to his knees, bows three times towards his chieftain and calls out: 'My Lord, we have apprehended two strangers and brought them here.'

CHAPTER 10

Wardak, October 1837

Irritated, the Khan sits down again, waves away his woman and declares, 'Show me.'

We are shoved in the back and required to emerge from the shadows into the brightly-lit killing ground. I walk with what I fancy is the solemn dignity befitting a holy man, in the way I have seen clergymen walk in my own country. Hoosein shuffles and lurches, as if he will fall at any moment. The poor man is horrified by what we have witnessed. He is gibbering again.

'Behold,' declares our captor with as much drama as he can muster, 'The prisoners.'

I can stand it no longer. I look up at the Khan, see a powerfully-built warrior whose cruelty is belied by his apparently kind eyes and his slow smile, and announce, 'We are not prisoners, my lord, we are here of our own free will to bring peace and joy unto your house and your city by affording you this opportunity to shelter two humble pilgrims who have ventured into your lands on our journey to the holy places. This gentleman,' here I indicate our captor, 'Has been our guide to your great city and, if we may, we will rest here a while before we continue on our journey.'

The Khan looks us up and down, inspecting our poor clothes, and considers our respectful manner. 'You have not burned down any homes today like those criminals I have been forced to punish?' he inquires from his perch. 'Is it not just, holy man, to punish criminals who raid their neighbours' villages, set fire to their houses and steal their cattle? Is it not the act of a wise ruler to dispense justice to such foul rats? Do you believe we have done well today?'

By all that we hold dear, I know very well the answer to this. But it is not a response this pagan warlord would wish to hear. By his lights, summary justice without trial, and cruel sentences without mercy, are the natural consequence for anyone who might fall into his clutches. It can easily be doled out to Hoosein and me at any moment. Even so, I am not prepared to let this man cow me though I have no desire to provoke him to wrath.

'It would seem by the Holy Koran that the force of justice is a necessary and Godly response to man's transgressions. And it is for our wise rulers to dispense justice in the name of Allah the Almighty, peace be unto him. Justice, though, must be fair and proportionate and must not oppress His people,' I reply, with a slowness that I feel suggests deep thought and great wisdom.

The Khan looks as if he would engage in further debate on the subject but the woman at his side – a thin but beautiful girl scarcely older than sixteen wearing a bright red Salwar Kameez – is tugging at his sleeve. He turns to her and smiles. As he stands, he tells our captors, 'These men are our guests. Treat them well. We shall see them again later.' To me, he adds, 'I have much to discuss with you, holy man.'

I look at the poor wretch strapped to his post and expiring from terror. 'What about this man?' I ask, as forcefully as I dare. 'Shall he be left here?'

'What would you have me do with him?'

'My Lord, he is a child. He cannot have been the mover in this affair. He would, if he could, beg for your mercy.'

The Khan is irritated now. He wants to depart and I am aware one word from him and I am a dead man. Yet somehow I have convinced him of my holiness and he is disinclined to ignore me entirely. 'Does the Holy Koran not demand an eye for an eye, holy man?' asks Yakoob Beg. 'This man has taken lives; I must take his.'

'My Lord, the Prophet, peace be unto him, says we cannot always exact an equal price. A good Muslim may sometimes temper vengeance with mercy and require a smaller sum in compensation. Give this youth his life; keep him in your service.'

'I shall consider,' the Khan replies and disappears. Hoosein looks at me in astonishment, clearly appalled at my attempts to intervene on the young man's behalf. His accusing eyes demand to know how I could risk our lives so needlessly.

'Be calm, my friend,' I say to him and turn smiling to our captors who, in turn, are now smiling back. They have done their duty and the Khan's pleasure is theirs. He has let us live; indeed, he seems to want to treat us as honoured guests. So that is how they, too, will treat us.

We leave the poor wretch and the blood-stained sand, retrieve our modest baggage from our horses and we are led, with much courtliness, by a young woman who does not introduce herself, to our quarters. She leads us through a heavy wooden door into a single, dark room with a low ceiling. It has whitewashed walls and a stone floor. There are gaps in the walls for the air to pass through and, opposite the entrance, an opening protected by sacking which gives out onto a terrace. On the floor of the room are a couple of horse-hair mattresses and a single wooden chair. This room is somewhere at the back of the palace but the terrace affords a view over the ramparts of the citadel to the plain beyond. The terrace is a small courtyard, overlooked on three sides, with a bench and a single walnut tree for shade. There is no way off the terrace, which is bounded on three sides by sheer walls and on the fourth by a huge drop over the bastions of the city itself.

The woman indicates we are to wait on the terrace and departs, returning ten minutes later with some food – naan bread acting as a plate for what appears to be a stew of spiced lamb, onions and other vegetables – and clean, cold water to drink.

We fall on this like starving men and Hoosein calms as he eats. We converse distractedly, exclusively in Pashto, for a while before the warm autumnal afternoon and the luxury of a good, hot meal get the better of us and we gradually drift into slumber.

We awake in the early evening but nobody comes for us. We discover we cannot escape our quarters. I try the wooden door and it is no surprise to find it is locked. We are confined to the room and the terrace. We can smell cooking, we can hear voices and horses. At a distance I hear cattle lowing. Across the plain, we see the sun set in an orange haze. We have our liberty – we are not bound in chains – yet we are not free.

The woman returns and I try to engage her in conversation but, like most of her sex in these parts, she keeps her eyes lowered and will not meet mine. She indicates the food she had brought us and departs without a word.

We remain thus for three days. While I am anxious to be on my way, I am aware that nothing happens but at the Khan's pleasure. He may well have forgotten all about us or he may simply be distracted, perhaps by the woman in the red Salwar Kameez.

*****

Hoosein will not sit still. I am trying to concentrate my attention on a cockroach or a lizard as if I am in deep meditation but the little man is so filled with nervous energy he is like a lion in a cage, pacing to and fro. He would growl in anger and frustration if he could, if he dared. Instead, he starts questioning me.

'Sir Henry Pottinger, sahib? A great man.'

'Yes, Hoosein.'

'Travels in Baloochistan.'

'Yes indeed.'

'He sent you here, sahib?'

'After a fashion, Hoosein, after a fashion.'

'The great Pottingers.' He grins at me, forgetting for a moment our plight and his fear. 'The great Pottingers.'

'Well, there's Sir Henry.'

'There will be Sir Eldred, sahib.'

I laugh. 'If you must know, our family has been around for centuries, Wars of the Roses, all that. Some great-great grandfather was Sovereign of Belfast.'

'A King! I knew it.'

'Not a real King, Hoosein, just an underling to Charles II. Who really was a King.'

'The great British royal family, sahib.'

'Indeed, Hoosein.'

On the fourth day of our captivity, our serving woman is replaced by an individual who announces himself to be Abdul Khaliq. 'The Khan will see you now,' he says.

Hoosein scrambles to his feet and looks at me anxiously. 'Not you, Hoosein,' I tell him, thinking to keep him from the coming confrontation and perhaps protect him if things go badly. Khaliq does not demur.

This is a well-fed courtier whose hands betray a man unused to the tough struggles of daily life. He is clearly wealthy – his robes are cut of good quality cloth, his beard is well-kept, unlike mine, I should say – and his head-dress is decorated with what appears to my untutored eye to be a sizeable ruby.

He is courteous but distant, leading me through cool passages into the Khan's audience chamber. It is a tall-ceilinged room, open to the elements, on the same level as the courtyard where we witnessed Yakoob Beg's form of justice. I wonder about the poor boy who was left languishing at his post. There is no sign of him now. The red blood and stains have been washed away and all outside is peace and tranquillity.

Within, the Khan sits on a thick, beautifully-crafted woollen carpet with half a dozen of his chieftains. Abdul Khaliq announces, 'Our visitor, your majesty', bows and takes his place on the carpet.

I kneel and bow to the Khan. Having not been invited to sit and being disinclined to remain kneeling, I stand up again and start telling my beads. He looks me over and smiles. It is a disconcerting sight – I know the man, I have seen what he does to his enemies, yet I cannot help being charmed by his apparent welcome. 'So, you are a pilgrim,' he declares, 'And do you have a name?'

'Liaquat Ali.'

'And you are a holy man.'

'All are holy who follow the teachings of Mohammed, peace be unto him.'

'There is no God but Allah,' says Beg.

I know this is a catch. The Hazari are Shia Moslems and, while their suspicion of foreigners is as great as that of everyone else in these lands, their fear of Sunni Moslems is perhaps even greater. A Sunni would not respond. A Shia would add, as I do now, 'I am witness that Ali is the agent of Allah.'

The Khan rocks back and laughs in satisfaction. 'Come and join us, holy man. Tell us about your pilgrimage.' He indicates a place on the rug where I am to sit. I do so, cross legged as the others are, and I am offered fruit from a large bowl. I take a peach. It is hard, a little unripe and sour. I say so and we discuss the best time to harvest various fruits before Yakoob Beg suddenly brings the chatter to an end. He claps his hands, leans forward staring at me and says, 'That youth, I spared him. He is yet living. Why should I not have him disembowelled?' To the guards stationed at the four corners of the room, he says, 'Have him brought here.'

Within minutes the poor boy is dragged in. He can scarcely stand. His clothes are filthy, he is lice-ridden and he has plainly been neither fed nor watered since he was cut down from the post. He is at the gates of the valley of death. The guards let go of him and he falls. He is too frail and exhausted to prevent his body injuring itself further as it drops to the marble floor. There he lies as Yakoob Beg contemplates the unmoving almost-corpse for some moments.

'This criminal,' he begins, 'This rogue joined with other vagabonds to steal cattle belonging to the villagers whose homes you saw aflame. Several were cut down by my cavalry who had been lying in wait for their attack, and left for the crows to peck at. A few were brought before me, as you saw. Including this wretch. Why should I not have him parted from his innards here and now?'

'There is no reason why you should not dispatch him now, my lord, none at all. You have the might and you have justice on your side. But he is young, look at him, I doubt if he is above twelve years old.'

'Not too young to be an evil pestilence on my house.'

'No, but you have imposed your punishments with justice. Now is the time for mercy. Is it not the case that the Prophet says the shedding of blood will be the first matter about which judgment will be given on the Day of Resurrection? Does he not say that "those who are merciful have mercy shown them by the Compassionate One, if you show mercy to those who are in the earth, He Who is in heaven will show mercy to you"? You have shown your terror and your rage, show now your mercy and save this one.'

Why am I doing this? The boy is as good as dead whatever I say. I am just giving the Khan an opportunity to turn on me. Yet I feel, as I quote these heathen scriptures, that I have a Christian duty towards him. This, after all, is one of the reasons why we wish to expand England's sphere of influence – to bring civilisation to barbarians. Am I to fail at the first hurdle?

The Khan laughs. 'You speak well, holy man. Very well, let him go. Cast him out,' he orders the guards, 'And be sure you give him some food and drink before he goes.' The Khan smiles around him and everyone applauds his merciful disposition. There are several speeches in praise of him. I continue telling my beads and staring at the intricate patterns on the rug.

Then one of the company turns to me and asks, 'Mullah, you speak of the Prophet, peace be unto him. But why is it that the Prophet has led some of our Moslem brethren, those who call themselves Sunnis, such as the King of Kabul, Dost Mohammed, and his Durrani tribe, into a different course? Why is it that the Shia such as ourselves are persecuted by the Sunni? When shall we have peace between us?'

The long-standing animosity between the two Mohammeden faiths is as bitter and violent as that between the Protestant Church and the Church of Rome was two hundred years ago, though with less justification and without the certainty of a true faith. I venture a few answers. But the conversation grows deeper and deeper. My inquisitors talk of rafida, which is something about rejection of the true spirit of Islam, and whether Sunnis are, in the eyes of Allah, heretical murtaddun.

As the conversation becomes more and more complicated, I can keep my end up no longer. The Khan is lying back enjoying my discomfort while several others are now rounding on me asking how it is that a Mullah should know so little.

At length I confess, 'Gentlemen, you have found me out. I am indeed a pilgrim and endeavour to be a holy man. But until recently I was a soldier in the service of the keepers of the Khyber Pass. We helped keep the Sikhs at bay in the war lately fought.'

I grin back but by now their scepticism is pricking at my skin. I am sweating. My misfortune is to wipe my sleeve across my forehead. Though my robe is of thin grey cotton, I see immediately some of Hoosein's Spanish black has come off onto it. The fool has not mixed it thickly enough. How pale is my forehead now? Is the dye coming off the rest of my face?

Then, suddenly, one of the party demands, 'Why are you so pale? Your skin is not the same shade as ours. Are you not a feringhee?'

That word. That word at last. Feringhee – the word they use to describe all foreigners, not just white men but Persians, Indians, Arabs, the entire world beyond the Hindu Kush. If I am unmasked as a feringhee, I may be a dead man.

The Khan lies on his back, looks up at the ceiling which, I notice, is painted a bright blue and decorated with stars, and declares, 'He is a feringhee. Seize him.'

I am indignant. I have to be. I stand, slowly to avoid alarming the guards, and look down at these uncivilised creatures. 'Gentlemen, I am shocked. Here I am, a humble pilgrim, throwing myself on your hospitality and all you can do is question me and doubt me. You question the colour of my skin? Why, of course you do. I am from the mountains. I was born and brought up among the snows of winter on the Hindu Kush. I have not enjoyed the sun and plenty of your beautiful valleys. I have not known the fruits of Allah's bounty as you have done. I have not looked up and seen the sun day after day. Like all my tribe, I am of a paler skin than you. Of course my skin is paler. We do not enjoy the privilege of plenty as you do. We live among the clouds and never see the great sun which warms your people and colours them a healthful colour. We are pale, you are dark. It is a sign of the blessings Allah bestows upon you. Do not take me for a feringhee just because my skin is not as brown as yours.'

They nod and smile. Of course, they say, we never doubted it. Here, have another peach. Slowly, and with a great show of reluctance, I sit back down and the conversation turns to the harvest and the coming winter.

The following day, however, three soldiers of the household are sent to confiscate our saddlebags and display their contents before the Khan. Hoosein and I are required to accompany them for the formal opening. This time, the interview takes place in the Khan's own bedchamber, an enormous room where three of his women sit draped on cushions piled high in one corner while their lord and master reclines on a divan. Standing along one wall are three of his advisers, one of whom is Abdul Khaliq.

'Liaquat Ali,' he says, 'You are a pilgrim. You will not mind if we see what possessions a pilgrim carries with him through this land.'

'Of course not, Abdul Khaliq,' I declare, beginning to unpack the first bundle.

Besides clothing and some coins – a small sample of the silver I carry strapped secretly to my body – there are one or two possessions which may take some explaining. The first is my notebook containing Pashto and Persian words. I speak both languages but feel I need a few reminders which is why I carry it with me. More worrying is my copy of Mountstuart Elphinstone's book "An Account of the Kingdom of Kabul" which was published a year before my uncle's book.

Abdul Khaliq throws this book open at a page showing one of the coloured illustrations – a Durrani villager dressed in a cloak and robes with a jezzail and a woollen hat on his head. Abdul Khaliq and the other advisers crowd round this picture in some awe declaring it must be a religious idol. At this point, the excitable Hoosein pipes up to declare it is nothing, just the sort of picture the Kizilbash merchants all have on their walls in the great houses of Kabul.

The Khan himself comes over to view the phenomenon and declares himself satisfied it was not some sign of perverse religion. I suspect the man has never seen a printed book before and is reluctant to admit his curiosity among his closest courtiers.

He is, however, struck by a couple of other items I am obliged to disclose. One is a small percussion cap gun, the new sort which are rapidly replacing the old flintlock small arms. Then there are my compass and pencils which I declare are for my study of the stars.

This, alas, shocks my companions because, though I had not known it, the Hazari regard astronomy as a forbidden science. It is only with difficulty that I blame this lapse on my former career as a soldier, thank them for their timely advice and forswear any further gazing at the heavens.

We are allowed to pack up our goods and return to our quarters, the Khan having apparently lost interest in us. And there we stay for four more days, visited only by the young servant girl with food from time to time.

Hoosein tries to cheer me with stories of his family back in Calcutta but I am not in the mood for his chatter. I get lost with all his sisters and cousins and brothers-in-law. As he prattles on I think to myself it looks as if our journey is over before it has really begun. We could be held here for months. Years even. I have heard stories of fellow officers incarcerated by these petty princes and left to die, forgotten and denied by their own countrymen. I, too, would be deniable – a freelance traveller with no connections to the Company or the British Government, wandering alone in the wastes of this lawless land.

Hoosein and I debate our predicament. Can we escape? It might be possible to scale walls and descend the ramparts of the city under cover of night. But we will not have our horses and escape, on foot, will be hard going while detection means instant death. But can we be sure we were not being kept for a purpose – the Khan is notorious, as are so many of the rulers of these territories – for enriching himself through the slave trade? He may be waiting to sell us to a passing caravan of merchants. We could be dragged off in chains to some pagan place like Bokhara. We try not to dwell on this but I confess it does lead to a lowering of our spirits.

We are coming close to determining on a plan for flight when, one morning, we are summoned with our bags and baggage and told to present ourselves to the Khan in the courtyard where we first saw him sitting at his window dispensing what he calls justice.

Perhaps this is it. Perhaps the Khan is bored of us and will set his fiend onto us. We fear the worst. I embrace Hoosein and tell him he has been a good companion. The poor man can scarcely hold back his tears and his legs are so weak I have one arm round his waist to support him as I help him into the open square. It is still early, the air is chilly. I am refreshed and ready to defend myself. I have my pistol in my belt, hidden but ready to use, and a knife I have kept concealed all this time. I will not give up without a fight.

The Khan could not be more charming. 'Pilgrim,' he says, speaking from his window, 'Thank you for allowing us to offer you hospitality, we trust you have been comfortable.' I assure him we have been. 'Then you may now take your leave of us.'

'Your majesty, we leave with regret but we have far to go and we are grateful to you for your hospitality.' I still fear a trick so I think I should ingratiate myself with him. 'Allow me to present your highness with this small token of our thanks and our esteem.' I step towards the window and stretch up with the pistol, handle towards the Khan. He cannot reach and a soldier is obliged to take it from me and run up to him with it. In the intervening moments, I explain to the Khan how to make the gun fire and he says he understands.

The man and the gun arrive and he inspects the weapon again. 'How did you come by this, again?' he asks.

'It was taken from the body of a Sikh who may have had it from the English,' I reply.

He dismisses us with an imperious wave of his hand and turns to study the pistol.

We leave, as hurriedly as it is possible to do whilst retaining an appearance of calm. Our horses have been well fed and are, of course, rested. Hoosein and I are led by a party of six of the Khan's horsemen through the citadel's gate, across the festering and empty moat and past the tented villages. We are heading west and after a mile or so, our escort turns for home.

We ride slowly on, scarcely believing we have escaped the place unharmed. I tell Hoosein yet again to stay calm – we are still visible from the citadel. Eventually, we crest a rise and descend into another valley, out of sight of Wardak for the first time. It is hot and we are tired despite our days of idleness. I think it is because of the strain of captivity more than any physical exhaustion, so we seek out the shade of an orchard to sit out the mild mid-day sun.

It is a fatal error. We have only been resting there for a matter of an hour or so when, over the brow of the hill, we see our original escort, all six of them, one more than we encountered on our original visit to Wardak. They see our horses and make straight for us. They are heavily armed, each with his own jezzail, as well as a sword. When they insist we must return with them immediately, we are in no position to argue.

CHAPTER 11

Wardak, October 1837

We cannot escape. We return with Yakoob Beg's henchmen. We trot back across the plain into the tumbledown town of Wardak and the Khan's palace. I see out of the corner of my eye that Hoosein is muttering away to himself as we go. The poor man is clearly terrified. No doubt he is thinking, as I am, of Yakoob Beg's tame devil, that prancing little dervish responsible for hacking people to death for his master's entertainment.

Why should we assume the worst now? We survived our residency in Wardak unscathed and left on congenial terms with Yakoob Beg. The hour-long ride back to the city takes place in silence but for Hoosein's mutterings. The men sent to track us down either do not know the purpose of this summons or they are under instructions not to respond to our questions.

They are polite and respectful, though. It does not seem as if we are being treated as prisoners. They are, it seems to me, a little more friendly than the men who first forced us to enjoy Yakoob Beg's dubious hospitality. I find this encouraging and point it out to Hoosein who hisses in reply, 'This is the respect they afford the dying.'

I cannot resist replying, 'I didn't know they offer the dying any respect.'

I am more curious than nervous but I cannot deny some apprehension as the walls of the citadel loom over us and we pass the ditch filled with its rubbish, animal carcasses, burned-out bonfires and who knows what other disgusting contents, concealed in among the dust, rocks and stagnant pools of stinking water?

Our escorts lead us to the palace where servants take the horses from us. They are smiling and promise the animals food and water. 'Look Hoosein,' I say, 'They are expecting to see us again. That should cheer you up.'

'Nothing will cheer me, sahib, except the walls of this terrible city receding in the distance,' he says.

'Very poetic, Hoosein,' I say, trying to sound as light-hearted and jolly as a holy man can reasonably expect to be when he is being summoned to pay his respects to an important – not to say cruel – local chieftain.

As we are ushered towards the inner courtyard of the palace, there is a loud explosion. The Khan is standing in the courtyard itself, rather than looking down from above, and he is holding the gun I gave him. He is grinning at his courtiers though in one corner a goat is breathing its last. The Khan hears the tramp of feet and turns to see us arrive with an appropriately holy shuffle. Waving the gun towards us he says, 'Ah yes. We don't need you now after all. As you see, I have made it fire. You may go.'

There is a pause as Hoosein and I take in this news. I am turning to go when Hoosein, his face taut with anger and, it may be supposed, tension, demands, 'Do you mean you have dragged my holy master all the way back here just because you could not fire his gun? Is this the sort of ignorant behaviour we must expect from you Hazari? Have you Mongols learned nothing since Genghis Khan came to shit on these lands? Fuck your mothers, you filthy sons of bitches.'

It is the tension, I don't doubt. Hoosein has been so afraid of what might happen he lets himself be carried away in his indignation and relief. But he is in danger – in very grave danger – of turning the Khan against us again. No petty chief likes to be berated by a little Indian in scarcely-fluent Persian, especially one who is holding a gun which he knows how to fire, and has his own court demon, much as English monarchs might once have enjoyed the entertainment of a Court Jester.

To maintain my disguise I am forced to listen to this outburst without betraying any emotion. How should I appear? Shocked? As angry as my servant at the Khan's unreasonable imposition? Simply relieved we are free to go again? As it is, I fix my gaze on a purple plant growing out the stone walls of the courtyard, keep my head bowed and hope Hoosein shuts up quickly.

Happily for Hoosein – and me – his tirade is interrupted by Yakoob Beg, who seems to see the funny side of the situation. No doubt pleased with his recent gift and anxious to try it out again, all he wants is for us to be on our way.

'Little man,' he says to Hoosein, 'Holy man,' he says to me, 'Be on your way with the blessings of Allah and Khan Yakoob Beg to keep you safe on your journey.'

He turns away. Hoosein takes a step towards him as if to renew his attack. I seize his arm and, squeezing so tightly the little man winces in pain, I march him away from the Khan and back towards our horses, the town gates and relative safety.

*****

Finally we are outside the town walls once again, this time without our escort, and turn our horses Westwards towards what is now a setting sun. A ragged woman appears, it seems, from the dry, filthy moat which surrounds Wardak, dragging a filthy child with her. She throws herself on the ground in front of our horses. Hoosein, who has not yet calmed down, yells, 'Out of the way woman, move and take your brat with you.'

The woman is crying, begging us; almost, it seems, worshipping us. It is difficult to catch what she is saying but the gist is that we should take her with us, and her son, because they owe us their lives and they are our slaves. Hoosein, still angry, is yelling back and telling them to get out of his way. He spurs on his horse, it rears and plunges, and he eases his way past them, more gently than his aggressive shouts might suggest, though he does raise his whip and threaten to bring it down on the woman if necessary.

The boy, on the other hand, takes hold of my horse's bridle and begins to stroke the animal's nose while shyly looking up at me with a smile of pleasure which, I suppose, is the result of his close proximity to the horse. I think I recognise him. He looks like he may be the boy who I persuaded Yakoob Beg to release a few days ago. I therefore conclude the woman might well be his mother. 'Take us with you, take us, sahib,' she pleads holding two hands above her head, palms together, as if in prayer.

'Do you have horses?' I ask.

The mother stops her noise, as if she has been slapped in the face, and looks at me squarely. Despite the rags and filth, she is a striking young woman with lustrous hair and dark brown eyes. She cannot be more than, what, twenty-four? Can this be her son or is he her brother? She stands and Hoosein backs up his horse a little to listen to this conversation. The boy carries on smiling and stroking my horse.

'No, sahib, we do not have horses. But we can walk. Take us with you, we are your slaves.'

'We have a long journey ahead of us and we cannot be delayed by a mad woman and her brother.'

'Son, son. Wasim is my son.' She strokes his shoulder as he strokes the horse. She looks afraid and proud at the same time. 'You saved him. He owes you his life. You saved him. I owe you my life.'

'I did no such thing. I just asked the Khan to spare him.'

'You saved him, you saved him. Take us with you. We cannot stay here. We will assist you on your journey.'

Hoosein intervenes, 'No, woman. Go away. You will slow us down. Go away. Come sahib, we must leave this filthy place.' He spurs his horse and trots ahead.

I fish out a few rupees and give them to the boy. 'Here. Now we must be gone.'

He will not take the money. He looks at his mother. 'You must take her, sahib. She can help you. She is a good cook.'

'How can I take her? We have horses, you do not. As my man says, we have a long way to go, we cannot afford to wait for you to catch us up every day or travel as slowly as a boy and a woman on foot can go. No, I am sorry, we have to go now and we cannot take you with us.'

I spur my horse on and hurry to join Hoosein. He is waiting some distance away. I catch him up and he wrinkles his nose at me in a sort-of smile. 'She cooks?' he says.

'She cooks,' I confirm.

'And the boy. A groom? Since we lost Ali and Waheed we have had to care for the horses ourselves.'

'We have only had two horses to worry about, Hoosein.'

He nods agreement and pauses for thought. 'But good cooked food, sahib.'

'How can we take them with us?'

'A great English general must have his entourage, sahib.'

'But I am not a great English general, Hoosein, remember? I am a simple Muslim holy man.'

'With followers,' he says with a grin, looking back towards mother and son who are trotting after us and closing the distance as we converse side by side under the shade of this fig tree.

'How are we to transport them?'

'The boy with me, the woman with you, until we find them horses of their own.'

'Your responsibility, Hoosein,' I say with a sigh. 'You find them horses within the next 24 hours or we leave them wherever we happen to be.'

'Forty-eight hours, sahib,' he bargains with a grin and one of his all-purpose shakes of the head.

'Agreed. Forty-eight hours and no more. And she'd better be able to cook.'

'She had better,' Hoosein agrees, turning to explain this agreement to the woman and child.

*****

That evening Hoosein presents the woman with the few ingredients we have to hand and leaves her to manage as best she can.

I watch from my makeshift tent spread over the branches of a tree as I write up my journal and take some measurements. I am trying to compile a map as we progress on our journey and it must be as accurate as possible. Hoosein disappears to a nearby village, on what errands I cannot say. The woman and her boy busy themselves building a fire, which they light easily, and she sends him off to collect water.

She is competent, calm and methodical in her approach to the task. She is clearly experienced in the art or science of cookery and occasionally hints at exasperation or frustration at the lack of facilities and ingredients available to her. She sighs and tuts and curses quietly while her son, back from fetching water, is boiling it up on a separate fire he has built under her instructions.

It is amusing to watch them work together. The boy is tall and thin, like his mother. He dotes upon her, watching her every move, awaiting her slightest command, rather like a dog stares devotedly at its master, waiting for the slightest indication of recognition or encouragement, his large brown eyes never leaving her face, which glows in the twilight and the light of the fires.

She, by contrast, scarcely notices the boy. Occasionally she utters a single word or two and he immediately responds, fetching water, passing her a knife or stirring the pot while she does something else.

The work lasts about an hour, which is fifty minutes longer than I am accustomed to wait for Hoosein's dubious concoctions. My servant returns just in time to be handed a plate of naan covered with rice in an aromatic, spicy sauce with choice pieces of lamb presented hot, not luke-warm, and tasting more wildly exotic yet appetising than anything I have had since leaving Burnes's palace apartments in Kabul.

What has she done? Where did she find the spices? I ask Hoosein to explain but the little Indian eats eagerly, demands more, grunts his satisfaction but otherwise makes no comment.

The woman and her son, I notice, are not eating. She shrugs when I ask why. Plainly there is not enough to go round. I tell Hoosein to hand back his second helping. He looks up. 'But sahib we took them so they could cook for us.'

'Yes, but not starve for us.'

Hoosein, I realise, is a little the worse for drink. That is where he has been, seeking out the local potcheen, some kind of brandy I believe. Unless he has been eating the opium again. 'Let them starve,' he says, and giggles.

I kick him, not hard but with enough force to alert him to the fact that I am displeased. To the woman I say, 'You must eat as well. And your son.'

She does not speak but hands the boy the lion's share of what is left.

*****

We sleep in the open, in the cold, on the rocks and stones. It is difficult to find any comfort. The woman and her child lie beyond us, with no blanket, no rug, just the rags they have on. I look up at the stars, that great unfathomable firmament, for some time before rising from my makeshift bed and, unwrapping the rug I had earlier pulled tight around me, step over Hoosein, past the two tethered horses and make my way down the slight slope to the spot where I last saw the woman and the boy.

They lie bathed in the silver light of the full moon, huddled together for warmth, both – as far as I can tell – fast asleep. The woman is curled around her son, her arm across his chest, both of them lying on their right sides, his back against her stomach. Spooning? Isn't that what it is called?

I gaze on them for a moment, transfixed by their beauty. This is no Eden and they are not innocent children and yet in that white light, in this vast, cold wilderness, in this moment of silence, this young woman and her urchin son strike me as if they have been made new by the Good Lord and placed among us for the edification of mankind. I know this is nonsense yet there is something sacred about this mother and child, their vulnerability and – I suppose – their trust. Their trust in me and Hoosein. They sleep because they are sure we will not rob them or worse. They are safe with us, or at least reasonably safe, in this land where nobody is ever safe for long, this land of constant danger, of eternal vigilance.

I make my way back and lie down once again. But I cannot sleep.

CHAPTER 12

Herat, November 1837

Heading West, as we are, it is inevitable we should reach Herat eventually. It is, after all, a famously beautiful place set amid orchards and pastures, on the old Asian trading routes, filled, according to Hoosein, with palaces and poets. My little entourage, Hoosein, Mahparah and Wasim and I, look down from the surrounding hills towards the city as it basks in its fertile valley in the late autumn light. It is becoming chillier but at about 60 degrees it is still much warmer than Novembers at home. This evening we are content to sit overlooking the town some five or six miles distant across the plain. We will stay here tonight and make our way into Herat tomorrow.

We have developed a routine. I write up my journal of the day's encounters, such as they are, and attempt to map out the route we have taken. Hoosein scouts around the local area to establish how safe, or otherwise, we might be, whether the local landowners or chiefs should be avoided or encountered, to see what gossip and provisions might be obtained. He usually comes back with one or two people, plenty of food, wine, fruit and, on rare occasions, a little opium which we all smoke until we fall into a pleasant haze. Wasim constructs our shelter for the night. This is not easy. He has to improvise using whatever the local vegetation affords, together with the cloths we fling over our horses, our coats and other possessions until he has created three separate sleeping quarters: my own; his mother's; and one he shares with Hoosein. Every night Hoosein complains about these arrangements, on the grounds that he deserves a shelter of his own, and every night I point out he is welcome to one if he would care to construct it for himself.

True to her promise, Mahparah builds a fire and starts to cook a meal for us all. This is usually based on whatever Hoosein manages to forage the day before though she does have plans and carries certain herbs and spices with her, collecting others when the chance arises, as well as fruit and vegetables which she packs into saddlebags. This is all limited, of course, because we move on every day and there isn't much we can easily carry with us. Sometimes Mahparah and Hoosein go off together in search of provisions, though usually when we are near a larger village or a prosperous-looking farm.

I watch her from where I am sitting pretending to write. She is so young to be a mother. She can't have been more than twelve when Wasim was born. Yet you can see the lines of care on her forehead, even perhaps a stray grey hair tangled up with the black. She moves with a natural elegance, as if she is dancing, and her expression is calm. She looks contented and happy, I am pleased to note, for she really is an excellent cook. Even Hoosein is generally prepared to overlook his natural aversion towards travelling with a woman in order to accommodate Mahparah. He went so far as to acquire a horse for her and another for her son, at a knock-down price after a long evening of hard bargaining and hard drinking.

Tonight Mahparah has plenty of lamb and rice for us as we settle down in this orchard amid the unpicked apples – there are simply too many for the local people to harvest. We have apple juice and tea. I consider whether we should introduce cider-making and remember I am a Muslim holy man not an English peasant-farmer.

The following day we strike camp and make our way slowly through the orchards and vineyards towards Herat.

*****

The city stands on a low hill overlooking the fertile plains of Western Afghanistan. In the outskirts are some ramshackle homes and farms but all the life of the city takes place within its walls. There are two sets of these, an outer wall which would slow down but not stop an invader, and the inner wall, taller and surmounted by ramparts, turrets and towers. As we arrive, I notice work being carried out to shore-up some of these defences and commission Hoosein to find out more when he sallies forth later in the day to discover the gossip.

Our first task is to find accommodation. It seems we are about as far west as we can decently go in Afghanistan before encroaching into neighbouring Persia, a country well-known to us and therefore not worth further exploration.

I decide to stay here for a week or two before making a return journey to Kabul. We will remain long enough to test the city's loyalty to Dost Mohammed Khan. It is questionable how far, if at all, the writ of the King of Kabul runs in this Western edge of his supposed domain.

We secure lodgings in a house close to the palace. The houses here, like many in this country, seem to turn their backs on the public world and concentrate instead on their internal affairs. The exterior walls of people's homes are all tall, blank stone with just a small doorway for an entrance. Yet once through this door, the visitor is confronted by flower gardens, fruit trees, tinkling fountains, cool verandas, balconied rooms looking down to a central courtyard, furniture with intricate designs and a sense of calm. All this disappears the moment you return again to the noise, smells and commotion of the streets. We have two rooms in the roof-space of a house which has been divided into a number of lodgings. It is busy with people day and night but the facilities are adequate for a Muslim holy man and his followers and one advantage is the rooms have small windows from which I enjoy a view across the square towards the palace and the minarets of the city.

After stabling our horses, settling in and taking some food, Hoosein and I venture out into the city while we leave Mahparah to make whatever domestic arrangements she can – I have already decreed she and her son will have to sleep on the stairs or the roof as I have no intention of sharing a room with Hoosein or anyone else.

We take a walk around the city walls. We are not allowed up onto them but, as we noted on the way in, building work is taking place to improve the city's defences. Why this should be, we cannot tell. What we do see, as we reach a gate in the north west of the city, is dust being raised on the road from Persia by a long troop of soldiers.

Hoosein immediately engages in conversation with a passing builder, who looks towards the parade, shrugs, spits and declares, 'Yar Mahomed.'

'The Khan?' asks Hoosein.

'The Vizier. The Khan is Shah Kamran. He's there too. Look, two troops, both the same. One for the Khan, one for Yar Mahomed.' He spits again after naming the Vizier.

As the procession draws near, it becomes clear it is actually two separate parades. The first apparently includes Shah Kamran, the official ruler of Herat. We can see him, outstretched on his raised litter being carried by a dozen bearers. His parade starts with a troop of mounted soldiers carrying short spears and scimitars. They lead a procession of men – and some women – in chains. I count 150 of these wretches, stumbling, dejected, starving, half-naked.

'Slaves,' Hoosein points out, rather unnecessarily it seems to me.

Alongside the slaves come more troops, this time on foot. They occasionally encourage the stumbling slaves to keep up through the liberal use of sticks and whips. They are followed by several men in bizarre red hats which rise perhaps two feet above their heads and end in a point. After some discussion with our friend the builder, Hoosein establishes these are the King's executioners.

'Why does he want so many?' asks Hoosein.

'Many enemies,' says the builder, whose name is Baseem.

The executioners are accompanied by criers, who seem to be yelling the praises of the Shah, alerting the populace to his glorious return to their city and to the triumphant nature of that arrival, crowned as it is by the achievement of capturing so many fit and healthy Persian slaves to be sold in the market. After the heralds crying the glory of their Shah we see the man himself. As he comes closer to the gate and, therefore, nearer to where we are standing, I study Kamran carefully but he is an unimpressive creature – slight of build and spoilt-looking, lying back and looking around him with arrogant disdain. It is notable that the procession is greeted with little enthusiasm by the locals.

The first entourage is completed by a baggage train of mules and the Royal horses, a dozen fine-looking specimens which, I assume, the King occasionally rides when he goes in search of slaves to bring to market.

We are only half way through this display of power. After a short pause while his entourage makes its way through the gate and on towards the palace of Herat, a second procession arrives, almost an exact replica of the first. There are differences. There are more mounted troops in the second parade, more slaves, more baggage, more noise from the criers, more bearers for the litter, more executioners in their ridiculous red hats – and the same lack of enthusiasm among the dwindling band of spectators.

In pride of place is not the Shah but his Vizier, Yar Mahomed. If Shah Kamran looks weak and ineffectual Yar Mahomed is well-built, though running to fat. He appears strong, purposeful and corrupt. I cannot say what it is about his appearance which seems to betray an essentially evil nature but I certainly feel this is a man who cannot be trusted, who is likely to be cruel and full of deception. There is something sinister about Yar Mahomed, I think to myself. It may be his short, clipped beard; it may be his narrow-set eyes; it may be the sneer on his lips. Whatever it is, I know I should be wary of this man.

'I shiver just looking at him,' says Hoosein. Baseem, the builder, spits on the ground as the Vizier's litter is carried past.

*****

Herat has a thriving slave trade. This should be a matter for Her Majesty's Government, slaving being an abomination to man and God, but I have no remit to protest on her behalf against this ungodly commerce in human life.

The prisoners are slung into a packed prison where they will be lucky to receive any food or water at all before they are paraded in the city's main market and sold to merchants and traders who will then transport them elsewhere throughout Asia – slaves are much sought-after in Samarkand and Tashkent. The sale takes place in two days' time and I resolve to attend. How much is a human life worth in this terrible place? A few rupees, I suppose. I am disgusted, though Hoosein points out that, as a consequence of the slave trade, the people of Herat are not required to pay any taxes or fees to their King. Shah Kamran's administration is self-financing for as long as there are Persians he can kidnap and sell to passing merchants.

'Good business, sahib,' says Hoosein, rubbing his hands as if he is wondering whether to make an investment himself.

The day after Shah Kamran and Yar Mahomed return to Herat, and before a sale can take place, word reaches the city of a great army heading in this direction. It seems the Shah of Persia has already captured Ghurian, an outlying town belonging to Kamran, and is preparing to advance on Herat itself. This appears to confirm what the city already knows, for the army commanders redouble the efforts of their men to reinforce the defences. The city gates are closed and no-one is allowed in or out without being interrogated and inspected by the guards who are now posted at all entry points.

The arrival of the Persian army is everywhere anticipated. A lull, a kind of silence, falls over the city as the news spreads through the market and from house to house. The streets are empty. The marketplace is quiet. Even the mosques are deserted. Winter has arrived. The air is cold, suddenly, and it feels like the silence before a storm.

*****

The following day a small Persian force mounts a feeble attack on the city. Hoosein and I join a crowd of interested onlookers as the Persians fire rifle-shot towards the outer walls and fall back under fire from the city's defenders. They are easily repulsed and as the Persians flee, several Heratis set off in pursuit, run them down, butcher them and sever the heads of their attackers. These heads, nine in all, are set on stakes and paraded on the ramparts of the city. The heads, still fresh and dripping with blood, are inspected by many of the townspeople and, in due course, by Yar Mahomed himself. The King's Vizier dispenses fifty rupees to each of the men responsible for these decapitations – it seems there is a bounty payable on every Persian head his men are able to separate from its body.

From the ramparts, we can see, away in the distance, the Persians' encampment. It grows day by day as the Heratis continue to reinforce their defences and despatch soldiers into the surrounding countryside to gather as much food as they can find. At the same time, the local people are streaming into the city as they flee the countryside ahead of the invading Persian army. There is talk of skirmishes between Heratis and Persians as both armies forage for supplies.

Despite all this, the slave sale goes ahead. Hoosein and I watch as each captive is auctioned off. The bidding is brisk but it seems to us the prices are modest. Certainly the Vizier's representatives at the sale look disappointed more often than not when another lot – that is to say, another human being – goes under the hammer. It seems traders from Turkmenistan are among the biggest bidders. Late in the day, the slaves, still in chains, leave in caravanserai by the eastern gates of the city unmolested by the Shah of Persia's army – even though it is the enslavement of his people which, according to rumour in the city reported to me by Hoosein, has supposedly provoked the Shah to mount his attack on Shah Kamran and Yar Mahomed.

It looks as if the Persians are settling in for a long siege rather than attempting a knock-out blow. Perhaps they think they can starve us out – perhaps they are right. There are, I should guess, forty thousand souls within these walls, including women and children. All the men, more or less, have been drafted into military service and it certainly looks as if most of them are able to lay their hands on their own weapons – rifles and swords. War is never far away from their thoughts even if they are usually farming the land.

A second attack on the city is a little more serious. A detachment of mounted troops comes close to the outer walls and fires off its muskets in the general direction of Herat but this turns out to be a decoy. A smaller, more determined group establishes a bridgehead towards the south-western corner of the city close to the outer wall and, despite constant firing from above, it cannot be dislodged. The suspicion is that this will be the place where the Persians begin mining operations in order to undermine the walls. This will take them a long time and it is reasonable to assume that constantly harrying them would probably limit their progress.

A raiding party sallies out of the south gate, rushes the Persians, engages in some hand-to-hand fighting and returns with a few severed heads. From my vantage point it is clear the time spent chopping off people's heads would have been better spent pressing home the advantage the Heratis achieved in their first attack. But of course there is a bounty to be paid for each head brought into the city and stuck up on a spike.

I find myself frustrated. There does not appear to be a great deal of discipline among the defending army. Indeed, the only tactic seems to be the severing of heads and the claiming of rewards. That will not save the city. It is also clear the Persians are awaiting reinforcements. They are digging in for a long siege. Do the Heratis really have the resources, determination and discipline to hold out for any length of time?

As a solider, I have an urge to become directly involved in the conflict. But on which side? It is hardly in Britain's interests to see Herat remain a centre of the slave trade. It is contrary to the Christian Government we have been striving to create throughout our great empire. The more our values are encountered, the greater the understanding of our civilisation, the happier and more content are the people who benefit from it. If Herat came more closely under the influence of Her Majesty's empire – I still have difficulty thinking of 'Her' Majesty, young Victoria, when I have only ever served King Billy – then perhaps it would understand the evil of the slave trade and acknowledge the greater wisdom and power of we British.

The Persians, on the other hand, are scarcely to be relied upon. They are not above trying to build an empire of their own. They may see Herat and, indeed, Afghanistan as a stepping stone towards their ultimate prize – India itself. This they may well seek to achieve with the help of, or indeed on behalf of, their ally and our enemy Russia. Reports here in Herat already suggest the Tsar's officers and men make up some of the force that is forming up within view of the city walls.

If the Russians are genuinely involved then it is firmly in our best interests to stop this siege from succeeding. If Herat falls to the Persians and Russians, the whole of Afghanistan is open to their armies as far as Kabul itself. And if Dost Mohammed Khan, the King of Kabul, is entertaining the possibility of an alliance with Russia, despite Sir Alexander Burnes's best efforts, then all that lies between India and the Russians is the Khyber Pass. And the Afghans have already invaded the Sikhs' kingdom by that route once this year.

I send Hoosein to the Palace to demand an audience with Shah Kamran in the name of Her Majesty, Queen Victoria. I am summoned to attend in the early evening.

'What am I to wear, Hoosein?' I ask. Suddenly the garb of an inconsequential holy man doesn't seem in the least bit appropriate for conveying the might and majesty of Her Britannic Majesty's Government of which I am, I must conclude, not merely the sole representative in this place today but the sole representative ever to have ventured this far from India or, indeed, from Tehran.

My servant looks crestfallen. He mumbles about uniforms left behind in Simla and asks how we could possibly have carried anything imperial or noble across all these miles of rock and sand. Mahparah joins the debate. She takes my filthy, travel-stained robe from around me, more or less forcibly, and flings me a carpet off the floor to cover myself with. She takes it to the nearest town well along with my turban to wash them, leaving me to sit and wait. Hoosein, meanwhile, points out I might like to wash and even suggests a shave. This is not a welcome idea given my beard is now very full but he may have a point as to our general state of cleanliness. It is surprising how little attention you pay to these things after a few weeks traipsing across the countryside. Still, Hoosein is right to suggest that if I am to present myself and my country to best advantage it would not do to arrive looking like a maniac tramp.

Herat's public baths are some distance from our lodgings. I am forced to borrow some clothes from Hoosein to get myself there and back but the effort is worthwhile. I return cleaner and fresher though I have made no attempt to remove my beard. I consider it too much trouble and, besides, it gives me an air of authority which may come in useful if I am to make a positive impression on these slave-traders.

How Maparah manages to dry my robes in time for the appointed hour of my interview is not something I think about at the time. Instead I fling them on and, accompanied by a newly spruced-up Hoosein, who relishes the idea that he may once again play himself rather than some holy man's guide, I make my way to the palace.

The guards usher us into the King's presence. He sits at the far end of a long, gloomy reception room lined in dark, intricately-carved wood with illustrations, tapestries, carpets and candles attempting to lift the pervasive air of unhappiness. Around the room are gathered perhaps forty chieftains, all sitting cross-legged, a few drinking, one or two smoking, all looking agitated as if I have just interrupted an argument.

I walk towards the Throne where Shah Kamran, the King, sits. Next to him stands his Vizier Yar Mahomed. I realise that, apart from me and Hoosein, Yar Mahomed is the only one standing. His hair seems to have been slicked back over his head, his thin beard seems to have been trimmed carefully since we last saw him, his clothes are the finest cotton, his shoes have the brightest gemstones, his headdress boasts what must be a diamond. His eyes are narrow, his nose is pointed, his lips are thick and generous. The King, by contrast, is less well-dressed, seems less intelligent and appears to be half asleep. There is a goblet at his side which makes me wonder if he likes a drop of the hard stuff.

'Your Highness,' I say, bowing low to Shah Kamran, 'I bring you greetings from the Queen of England, ruler of India, sovereign of the greatest empire the world has ever known. I am a humble soldier in her vast armies but have the pleasure of being the first to venture to your famous city.'

There is a pause. The King looks quizzically at me. I see in his eyes a sense of relief, perhaps, or hope. But it is Yar Mahomed who speaks.

'That's all very well, but what can your Queen do to help our city? We are besieged. We shall surrender.'

There is a murmur among the chieftains which makes it clear this is the argument I have just interrupted. The Vizier, it seems, is for capitulation, the King is not so sure.

'Surrender by all means,' I tell them. 'If you want to die like dogs or be sold into slavery, let us surrender the city now. If you want your women and children to be slaughtered, let us surrender the city now. Nothing is easier. Open the gates. Let the Persian horde into Herat. Let us waste no time but have done with it. I shall take my chances with the Shah. He will not want to antagonise the English Queen, I shall be safe. But you, your majesty, and your court...' I ignore Yar Mahomed and make this speech to the others.

'We cannot defend this city,' says Yar Mahomed, stroking his clipped beard.

I wonder if he has already come to an arrangement with the Persians.

'No?' I say. 'You surprise me.'

Now several other voices speak up arguing the city's defences are sound, its men resolute, its supplies plentiful. 'We can withstand a siege,' the King says, finally. 'If we are not afraid.' He looks at the Vizier.

'I am not afraid.' Yar Mahomed is indignant, he looks as if he would like to slice off the King's head. 'I am not afraid, Kamran. I know these people' – he waves an arm to encompass all the men in the room – 'They are brave only to save their own necks. They will fight only to protect their own. They will defend only what is theirs to defend. They will not save the city, Kamran, they are cowards.'

At this, two or three reach for their scimitars and make towards Yar Mahomed. The King stands unsteadily and slumps back down again as his Vizier goes on, 'Well, let us see. Let us defend ourselves. It is better than surrendering. This Englishman is right. It is better to die a noble death than be sold into slavery by these heathen Shia scum.'

The meeting breaks up into small groups of people discussing different aspects of the defence of the city. Some talk about supplies, others about weapons, a third group is debating where the walls are most vulnerable and where the strongest defences need to be established. The King sits in some kind of wonderment, listening but not able to stamp his authority on proceedings. The Vizier, meanwhile, has taken three or four men aside and is whispering fervently to them. I stand in the middle of the room with just a silent, slightly over-awed Hoosein for company wondering if it was my intervention which swayed the chieftains from surrender to defence and, more importantly, trying to identify the city's military leaders.

The King descends from his throne and meanders slowly through the groups of men towards me. He is a short man, no taller than Hoosein, and of similar build; thin and anxious-looking. He is clearly nervous – I suppose this is the first time in his life Shah Kamran has felt his authority challenged or his rule in danger. The man is in his thirties, I would guess, but he has apparently been King of this city and the surrounding area for twenty years.

Hoosein tells me the gossip in the market is that the Vizier is the real power hereabouts. Yar Mahomed has been with King Kamran for most of his reign and between them they have been able to do as they pleased. It seems to me they can't afford to surrender and I wonder what game the Vizier is playing that he would even contemplate it.

'Lieutenant Pottinger,' says the King, 'You see we are not well prepared for this outrageous assault on our city. We have already lost some of our lands and towns to this Shia devil. We are Sunnis, we can expect no mercy from this wicked army. We have no choice but to resist them. You must help us. Your Queen must send us an army. We need money, we need troops, we need guns, we need men. You must secure them for us. You must help us.'

'I shall write immediately, your highness, but I have no great hopes of success. Herat is a long way from Hindustan. Our Sovereign and her Governor General have greater concerns than the protection of a far-away slave-trading city state.' I think of adding a few more choice epithets about the insignificance and unimportance of this place in the middle of nowhere but decide it would be unwise to antagonise the King too soon. There may come a time for that but why push my luck so early in our acquaintance? 'In the meantime,' I continue, 'Perhaps I could consult with your military commanders. My own military experience may be of help in preparing and manning our defences against the siege.'

It will take at least three weeks, if not longer, for a letter to reach Kabul and even if Burnes were to act on it without delay, the best he could do is write to the Governor General or Sir William Macnaghten in India seeking their advice, guidance, money and men. It will take another month at least for Burnes's letter to reach its destination. Longer, I suppose. After all, it is now the end of November. Given the snows shut the Khyber Pass in December and January, any message from Burnes will have to travel south, on the much a longer route through Baloochistan, if it is to reach the Governor General. And where will Lord Eden be anyway? If we are lucky he will be in Bombay but he could be anywhere in the great continent of Hindustan. Burnes's letter may take six months or more simply to find him.

All these calculations make me conclude first, that I am on my own and cannot expect any orders or assistance from elsewhere for a considerable time; second, that I should endeavour to communicate directly with Sir William as well as via Burnes, in the hope that one of us succeeds in tracking him down; third, that as Her Majesty's representative here it is my duty to remain, resist the Persian siege, and support the Afghans unless and until I receive orders to the contrary.

'Do you understand this, Hoosein?' I ask him, having set out my considerations at some length.

The little man nods and shakes his head as he says, 'Of course you have no choice, sahib.' He does not look entirely convinced.

'And you shall take my letter to Sir William Macnaghten.'

Hoosein says nothing. His expression is that of a sulking child.

'I thought you would be pleased, Hoosein. You can deliver the letter and then go home to your wife and child.'

'I am being dismissed.'

'No, Hoosein, not dismissed. No, not at all. I need you to carry a letter for me to the Governor General's headquarters, wherever that may be, and convey the urgency of the situation and the importance of a response. You are not being dismissed, this is the most important service you could perform for me.'

Hoosein looks a little happier. 'And then I am dismissed.' There is an edge of misery in his voice still.

'No, Hoosein, not dismissed. You have been, you still are, the best servant a man could hope to have. I shall miss you desperately when you are on your travels. But you will be performing a great service for me and if it is money that worries you...' He vigorously waves away the very idea but I continue, 'You will be well provided-for, I assure you.'

There is a pause while Hoosein considers the proposition. We are sitting on the battlements of the city watching the sun going down over the orchards to the west of Herat and glinting off the encampment of the Persian army. 'It is dishonourable.'

'Dishonourable?'

'To leave this city and my master when he and the city are in danger.'

'Not when the express purpose is to get help to relieve the danger, Hoosein. That is wise and bold and sensible.' I wonder why I have the patience for this debate. I should just order him to go and leave it at that. But I think, if Hoosein can be persuaded of the wisdom of what I propose then somehow there is more likelihood he will accomplish his mission successfully and – perhaps this is more to the point – live to tell the tale. Many messengers set out, few return.

Will Hoosein survive? Who can tell? Would he be any safer here in Herat? Almost certainly not. As I consider what to write in my letters to Burnes and Macnaghten, it is clear to me the city has only a modest chance of holding out against a determined Persian attack. It certainly could not survive indefinitely if the Persians surround us and determine simply to starve us out. It is surprising, though, that so far only the two western gates to the city are under attack. It is still possible to pass freely through the other three, leading to the North East, East and South East, away from the enemy. Indeed, for the past few days soldiers have been scouring the surrounding area gathering in all the provisions they can lay their hands on. They are even chopping down the orchards, which seems a short-sighted approach to take. But if we are in for a long siege, we don't want to leave supplies for the Persians or crops that will grow again next year and supply them with food. So a scorched-earth policy is adopted and I have to say I told Yar Mohamad I thought it made good sense.

Hoosein sets off a couple of days later. I embrace him and he sheds tears because he is an emotional little man. We have bought him clothes and food for the trek, and he joins a caravanserai bound for Sindh. From there it's a simple enough journey on to Bombay though it still takes time. Maybe, I suggest to Hoosein, you should go by sea but the idea appals him so I tell him to do what he thinks best. There are a few slaves in Hoosein's caravanserai, I notice, and tell him to note if any of them is taken as far as Hindustan and, if so, he is to discover their destination and report all to the authorities. He promises faithfully to do so though I am more concerned about whether he will survive the journey himself than I am about the fate of some Persian slaves.

Refugees join the train heading for Sindh. Some will only disappear into the countryside, others may go as far as Kandahar. There is a not unnatural desire among the wealthier people of Herat to protect what they have, make the most of the Persians' lack of initiative and leave while it is still possible to do so.

Shah Kamran is indifferent to this exodus but Yar Mahomed sees in it an opportunity for enrichment. Everyone who leaves the city is forced to pay a tax. One hundred rupees. Many cannot afford to leave. I refuse to pay for Hoosein's departure. We argue. Yar Mahomed concedes but with ill grace. He will not forget.

I am, though, pleased to see Hoosein depart. It is one thing less for me to worry about. I would rid myself of Mahparah and Wasim as well only Hoosein insisted he would travel more swiftly alone and I think he is right. I do not want to be a protector for this young woman and her child. They are nothing to me. We have become accidentally attached. I must deliberately detach myself.

CHAPTER 13

Herat, December 1837

The Persian army grows by the day but even after six weeks it is still not numerous enough to surround Herat in safety. So we are able to send the cattle out to graze every morning on the eastern side of the city and return the animals in safety at the close of the day.

There are skirmishes. The number of heads impaled on stakes along the city walls continues to grow. From time to time, enemy soldiers are captured, interrogated and tortured by Yar Mahomed's henchmen. I am invited to attend these sessions but decline. Few prisoners escape alive. Nevertheless, some information is worth knowing. It is confirmed that several of the Persian regiments are under the command of Russian officers and that Mohammed Shah, the King of Persia, is being closely advised by a Russian count called Ivan Simonich.

Lord Eden is right to worry. The Persians are being used by the Russians to promote the Tsar's empire-building and the Tsar cannot be trusted to satisfy himself with a share of the influence over Western Afghanistan. Today Herat, tomorrow where? Kabul, Lahore, Bombay? I write further letters to Burnes though I receive no reply and have no great hopes my communications will reach their intended destination. By day, I take command of a division or two of the Herat defences. There are few commanders other than Shah Kamran, who has no understanding at all of military matters, and Yar Mahomed, who knows as little as his King but thinks he has great command of the subject, thus making him the far more dangerous of the two.

The local chiefs, at any rate those who have not already fled the city with their followers, take responsibility only for their own little clans. One group may occupy the tower over the south gate, another the inner or outer walls in the south west quadrant but these two groups will not co-ordinate their activities. All they seem to have in common is their desire to claim bounties on the heads of any Persians unfortunate enough to get his head chopped off. They are certainly not prepared to submit themselves to a central authority and would rather die than work together under a commander other than the tribe's chief.

It's the beheadings I worry about most, though. I argue several times with Yar Mahomed that beheading your enemies is not merely a barbaric activity, it is doing the defence of the city no good at all. In fact, it is positively harmful.

On one occasion it looks as if we are finally about to remove the Persian advance column from its dug-in position close to the south-west bastion. It is clear they are using this as the base for their tunnelling activities which may, if they are not checked, undermine the city walls and create a breach the enemy can pour through. We send a detachment of men on a raid early one morning and catch the Persians by surprise. Our men leap into the trenches but, instead of striking an opponent dead and moving on, they spend time and energy trying to remove their victim's head from his body.

This is gruesome work and not as easy as it may seem. A great deal of hacking and sawing is sometimes necessary. From a military point of view, this wastes valuable time. The momentum of our assault is fatally slowed by the eagerness of our men to sever the heads of their enemies. As a result, the Persians regroup, fight back and ultimately prevail. Many of those who lost time hacking away at the necks of dead men, just to claim Yar Mohamed's fifty rupee reward, eventually lose their own lives as a result. The rest are forced to abandon their heads as they flee back to safety.

That evening I protest once again to the Vizier and the King. 'You waste time as well as money,' I say. 'It is unnecessary. A dead Persian is a dead Persian. You do not have to remove his head from his body to make him dead. And as our men struggle to secure their bounties they lose our advantage over the enemy and many of them lose their lives as well.'

'I don't care if they lose their lives,' the Vizier laughs.

'You will if they give the enemy an advantage he can exploit. If enough of our men die, we may be left exposed to a counter-attack. And all because you want to parade your enemy's heads along the ramparts.'

'It deters them. They are frightened by the sight. That is why they have not pressed home any advantage. No, we carry on with the bounty, Mr Pottinger. You do not command our army yet.

*****

A couple of days later, yet another head is presented to the Vizier, Yar Mohamed, this time by a toothless, filthy man with tatty robes and an ingratiating grin. The Vizier, a look of amusement creeping across his fat face, inspects the head which has been laid at his feet. 'But this man has no ears,' he complains.

'No, they must have been removed as a punishment before,' says the man.

'But these wounds are fresh,' complains the Vizier. 'Come here.'

The man, who has been shrinking away from the Vizier, turns to escape from the courtyard where Yar Mahomed is holding court but finds his way blocked. He turns back, a grin baring his toothless gums. The Vizier has a knife in his hands. 'Seize him,' he tells two guards, who take hold of the wretch. The Vizier seizes one of the man's ears and cuts it off with his knife as the man screams in pain. 'Did I not pay a bounty only yesterday when someone – was it you? – presented me with a pair of ears, claiming they were all he could recover?' This question is addressed to his officers. A captain confirms that fifty rupees were indeed paid out on a pair of ears.

The wretch wails, 'Not to me, sire, not to me.'

'To whom, then?' demands the Vizier seizing the man's remaining ear.

A name is screamed out but it is not enough to save the ear, which is hacked off just the same. The second man is sent for. The first one is slumped in the arms of his captors and seemingly lacks any energy. As we wait – who can tell how long it will take for the second man to be tracked down? – the Vizier looks again at the head. 'This is a Persian's head, I suppose?' he asks.

How can one tell? Is the skin the colour you would expect of a Persian or a Tajik? Is there a difference and how obvious is it a couple of days after death when the head has been wrapped in a filthy cloth and kept who knows where in the meantime? The company of chiefs inspects the head and examines the man who presented it with suspicion while the man himself looks increasingly fearful.

'It was not my idea, it wasn't my idea, not my idea, no, no, no,' he starts yelping.

The Vizier holds the knife to the man's throat. 'What is that?' he asks, smiling.

'It was not my idea.'

'What was not your idea?' The Vizier hisses and draws blood at the man's neck.

'He said take any head, any head, who can tell the difference, who's to know?'

'So this is not a Persian? This is not one of our enemies? Is that what you are telling me?'

The man collapses, the knife scraping across his cheek as he slumps to the ground despite the efforts of his captors to hold him up. The Vizier kicks him as he lies squirming on the stone floor. A second man is marched in. He takes one look at the scene before him, turns and struggles to escape. But he is held fast by his captors and made to stand to attention before Yar Mahomed. The Vizier comes close to him and hisses, 'Ah, so this was your idea, was it?'

The man clearly cannot decide if honesty or denial is the better policy. He chooses denial which encourages Yar Mahomed to take the knife to him. One ear follows the other. Blood and screams and pain inevitably follow until eventually the two men are taken to a tower overlooking this courtyard and thrown off. Nobody bothers to look to see if they die from their falls or whether they are condemned to slow and painful deaths in the dry moat beyond the city wall.

The Vizier wipes his blade on the skirts of one of his servant's tunics and turns to me with a wry smile. I think how vile this man is. 'Perhaps you are right, Lieutenant Pottinger, perhaps this bounty has served its purpose. Let it be known,' he tells us, 'We shall no longer be paying bounties on the heads of our enemies. The practice must stop. It is wasteful and it encourages criminals. I shall have no more of it.'

This does not help the troops' morale but it does improve their effectiveness.

*****

The nights are not safe. Every morning, bodies lie dead in the streets. Some may have died of starvation but most are victims of the Vizier, Yar Mahomed. Traitors, spies, suspects of any kind are dragged to his personal palace, which is the administrative heart of the city, and tortured either by the man himself or by his henchmen. It is difficult to know whether the Vizier's vigilance is justified or whether he is taking advantage of the siege to indulge in one of his favourite recreations.

The red-capped public executioners are also kept busy though most Persian prisoners have so far been kept alive. Food is becoming scarce and Shah Kamran is encouraging women, children and anyone unfit for combat to leave Herat while they still can.

The night after Hoosein sets off in search of the Governor General of India, Mahparah creeps into my room after we have gone to bed and slips under the blankets beside me. It is a chilly night and she is wearing her usual cotton sari but it slips open and in the moonlight I see the beautiful shape of her breasts and the lusciousness of her lips.

'I was lonely,' she whispers and kisses my ear. 'And I thought even the Queen's Ambassador might sometimes feel lonely too.'

She smells warm, a little of the rice she has been cooking, a little of the spices she has seasoned the curry with, a little of something like lemons, a little musky. Her body lies close to mine as her hands caress my skin and I realise she is right, I have been lonely. Soldiers rarely enjoy simple human affection. It has been weeks since I enjoyed the body of a woman and what a body Maparah's is – still young and firm but soft and yielding at the same time. Strong and energetic yet meek and submissive. Naïve and experienced, shy and brazen. We sleep little and awake only when the sounds of the morning skirmishes reach our room.

'You know you have to go, don't you Mahparah?'

'Go? I did not please you?'

'Go from Herat, leave this city, depart for somewhere safer, taking Wasim with you.'

'Without you?' She looks at me from under her long black hair with a smile and a pout on her lips. She doesn't know if I am serious or teasing.

'I am serious, Mahparah. You have to leave. This siege will get a lot worse before it gets better. There will be more blood, starvation, death and disease. You need to leave while you still can, the Persians will soon surround us and lock us into this place for who knows how long? You must escape while you can.'

'Without Lieutenant Eldred Pottinger, our saviour and guide?' She runs a hand across my chest and down under the blankets, a smile in her eyes.

'I mean it. You are not safe here. Neither of you.'

'There is nowhere else I would rather be,' she says as her fingers caress me, 'And besides who would take care of Major General Eldred Pottinger esquire?'

'Mahparah.' It's all I can say before she stops my mouth with kisses. We resume the conversation at intervals over the next couple of days, however. I offer her money. I tell her to head for Kabul and throw herself on the mercy of Sir Alexander Burnes. I promise to give her letters of introduction from me. I promise to find her when the siege is over. She laughs and smiles and kisses me and pretends she doesn't understand.

'If not for yourself then for Wasim,' I say.

'Wasim is not a boy any more, he is a man. He must play a man's part.'

'Is that his view as well?'

'Ask him?'

I do. He says the same as his mother and swears his loyalty to Her Majesty Queen Victoria and her envoy Lieutenant Eldred Pottinger.

'I am yours to command, sahib,' Wasim tells me.

I send him to Kabul with more news for Burnes. At least this way I can get the boy out of Herat even if I cannot shift his mother. Though, of course, the truth is I do not wish to shift his mother. She is happy to see her son leave while the roads east are still reasonably safe but she does not want to go with him. She says her job is to help me. And I would certainly miss her by day and by night.

The days of the siege begin to fall into a routine. There is a skirmish most mornings, some ineffectual artillery fire from the Persians, a lull at lunch time when both sides seem to have reached a mutual agreement not to take up arms for the three hours of siesta, a resumption of hostilities in the afternoon, a lull towards sunset and very little activity during the night. It is almost as if each side is waiting for the other to take some drastic step which will make or break their fortunes. An English army would have reduced this pox-ridden city to rubble in a matter of days.

In the meantime, I retire early to spend evenings in Mahparah's arms.

She tells me of her family. How she comes from a small village near Kandahar, how her mother was one of the wives of a local chieftain, how she was farmed out to a relative at a young age, how she was forced into a relationship with the son of the household, how she was cast out when she fell pregnant and how she wandered across the country looking for food and shelter for herself and her child. She says she was taken in by the villagers near Wardak and fed and housed in return for working in the fields. It was hard work but she felt safe and befriended by these people. They were occupying the land illegally, according to Yakoob Beg, the King of Wardak. He sent out his thugs to burn down their hovels, destroy their crops and imprison or murder their menfolk. That is why the villages were burning when Hoosein and I were forced to become Yakoob's 'guests' and how Wasim came to be his captive.

I tell Mahparah about Ireland. I tell her about my father and his spendthrift ways and about my beautiful young step-mother. I tell her I am a poor man in my own country. She refuses to believe me. She asks why I am in Herat. I tell her I am in India to make my fortune or at least earn enough money to keep my family provided-for now my father has squandered what might otherwise have been my inheritance.

'I grew up in a great house called The Mount – though my father insisted on calling it Mountpottinger – overlooking Belfast lough. It had wonderful views,' I tell her. 'The land there is green and lush and full of rain. Not like this dry-as-dust country with its baking heat.'

'Is it a beautiful house?'

'Not as beautiful as you. It's was big house but as we grew poorer we couldn't afford so many servants and we rattled around in it a bit. My father is not a rich man. And what money he has, he spends. Eventually we had to sell Mountpottinger to a banker.'

The muezzin issues the last call to prayer of the day though I suspect most of the men and women within the walls of Herat will disregard it. We certainly do. 'You should understand that my father, Thomas, is not an adventurer nor is he an industrious merchant nor even a military man,' I tell Mahparah as she lies with her head on my chest.

I look up at into the darkness and pull her close to me. I do not know if she is interested or even listening, but it does me good to tell her these things. 'My father,' I say, 'He is, not to put too fine a point on it, a gambler and a wastrel. I say this with a heavy heart for it is not becoming in a man to speak ill of his parents. He has dissipated not one but two fortunes. The first he inherited from his frugal and industrious father. That money he had more or less exhausted by the time he met my mother Charlotte Moore. Happily for him, she brought with her a considerable dowry from her father.

'By the time my mother died, most of her money was gone. My father quickly re-married, this time to Eliza. She is half Indian, you know. Her father is English but her mother is called Beebee Poll. Eliza has been my mother since I was three years old and she has been everything a young man could hope for in a loving and affectionate parent. She has borne my father two brothers, John and Tom, and my sister Harriet, all of whom I have the utmost affection for.

'Yet my father has treated us with shocking indifference. He sails his pleasure boat around the shores of Ireland and England for months at a time or spends weeks at racecourses, returning only when his resources have dwindled away to nothing while my mother Eliza is obliged to shift for herself with only three loyal servants and bailiffs constantly at the door. After they sold Mountpottinger the family has moved to Kilmore in County Down. That place, alas, is mortgaged to the hilt and before I left India I wrote to my mother advising her to have my father pass the property over to her entirely with the assurance that, as long as I continue to receive my £250-a-year Company pay, I shall assume responsibility for the discharge of this debt. I have to prevent my father from squandering what remains of our family's resources. He has a wife and children to think of. He must be persuaded of the need to exercise some prudence in his financial affairs.'

I sit up and force Mahparah to come out of whatever doze she may have slipped into. Thoughts of my father make me indignant. 'The man has been suggesting he come out to India, where John, Tom and I are already trying to make our way, to restore his fortunes,' I tell her.

'That would be a fine thing, to bring father and sons together again,' she says somewhat sleepily.

'It is the last thing I could contemplate. I have enlisted my uncle's support in begging him to stay at home and not bring us disgrace over here as well as ruin at home. I believe he acquiesced, though not before tapping Sir Henry for a loan which will never be repaid.

'If I sound angry at my father's improvidence,' I say to Mahparah, distractedly stroking her hair in the dark, 'It is not on my own account. For myself, things have worked out as well as I could have hoped. The early prospect of becoming a Lord of the Manor in little Belfast was never one which held much attraction and, happily for me, though unhappily for my mother, his extravagance and thoughtlessness forced me to join the Company which riches and position would certainly have denied me.'

'Were you a brave little boy at school? I am sure you were,' she asks, biting me gently on the shoulder.

'I went to the Belfast Academy where we have a fine tradition of revolution.'

'Revolution?'

'Revolution. It is in our blood. About 25 years ago there was a boys' rebellion. Eight boarders and two day-boys barricaded themselves into the mathematics classroom and withstood a siege just as we are doing here in Herat. It lasted two whole days. They started shooting at the enemy. They shot at the Sovereign of Belfast and the headmaster's wife.'

'But why?'

'Because the headmaster, a clergyman called Billy Bristow, abolished the Easter holiday. The boys took it very badly and insisted the holiday should be restored.'

'What happened?'

'The headmaster begged them to surrender but they refused until he met their demands. They wanted the holiday restored and a promise of no reprisals, no punishments. Eventually Bristow gave in.'

'They won? The boys?' Mahparah is excited at the thought.

'No, alas, for Billy Bristow may have been a man of the cloth but he was not a man of his word. He promised to meet all their demands but as soon as they handed over their gun, the boys were surrounded by soldiers, marched into the great hall of the school and beaten until they bled, in front of their own school-friends.'

'That is terrible.'

'And then they were expelled from the school, which is one good reason why we cannot come to terms with the Persians and offer to surrender Herat. What happened at Belfast Academy many years ago will happen here as well. Only this time it will be even more bloody.'

I brood on this for a while and then add, 'It's a very religious school. It belongs to St Anne's Cathedral.'

'Cathedral?'

'Like a huge mosque where Christians pray. It was there I learned to love my God and the Protestant religion and there I came to understand how divine providence had smiled on our English nation.'

'Every nation is chosen by God,' Mahparah says cynically.

'Is that so? And how many nations do you know of, madam?' I ask, biting her shoulder in return.

'The Hindus, the Mohammedens, you Christians, the Sikhs as well. All chosen by God.'

'God is not on the side of the big battalions, as that monster Napoleon claimed,' I say. 'God has blessed my nation and made us the greatest nation on earth.'

Mahparah is bored of this conversation. I can tell because she is licking my back and nuzzling against my neck. Her naked flesh is warm against mine and I, too, discover that conversation is not uppermost in my mind any longer.

CHAPTER 14

Herat, March 1838

The Shah of Persia is not in the mood for a discussion. 'This city belongs to me. To us. To my country. This city has always belonged to me. To my country. This city – that I shall reduce to a pile of rubble in a desert if it will not surrender to me what is rightfully mine – this city you say you are speaking for, this city is mine and that filthy dog seizes my people and sells them as slaves. What am I to do? Tell me, what am I to do? Am I to sit and watch as these stinking Afghan sons of bitches raid my country, enslave my people and laugh at me from the turrets of my own city? No, Mr Pottinger, it is not to be endured.'

We are in his imperial tent surrounded by courtiers and generals. I have invited him, in the name of Her Britannic Majesty Queen Victoria, to lift his siege and make his way home. I have told him Shah Kamran is a friend of Her Majesty and of the Governor General of India and is, therefore, under the protection of no less a power than England itself.

This is the message I have already agreed with Sir John McNeill to convey to the Shah of Persia during my audience because it supports what McNeill has already been telling him. It doesn't make much difference. McNeill has been trying to talk the Shah out of this siege for months now.

It was only three days ago both sides granted McNeill a safe passage into the city to negotiate with Shah Kamran and, I have to say, it was a great pleasure to meet a fellow countryman, even in these circumstances.

I'd never met McNeill before but when we were told an envoy from the Shah of Persia was to visit Herat, Shah Kamran insisted I be there as a negotiator.

The sense of delight which coursed through me at the sight and sound of a fellow countryman is difficult to describe. The sound of a voice speaking English was like being washed in clean, fresh water after months crossing a burning desert, though McNeill's heavy Scottish accent makes his language almost as difficult to decipher as his Persian, which he employs in conversation with Shah Kamran. Herat's king nods wisely and frowns seriously but it seems to me he is as baffled by McNeill's Scottish-Persian as I am.

Even so, my countryman is an imposing figure, handsome and tall, unlike so many Scots. He is clean-shaven with dark, black hair and some kind of uniform of a blue woollen tailcoat with silver braid which looks impressive but must be unpleasant to wear now the weather is heating up again.

McNeill's message is not one Kamran wishes to hear. The Shah of Persia demands the surrender of the city. He says it would spare further slaughter. The Shah of Persia demands an end to Herat's trade in Persian slaves. He also demands Kamran pay homage to him and accept the sovereignty of Persia. 'The Shah asserts his country's historic rights over Herat and calls on Shah Kamran to acknowledge the true state of things, bow his knee to the inevitable and live in peace and amity with the Great King of the Persians,' McNeill concludes, reading from the speech he was given to convey. 'And by way of a token of your Highness's good intentions, the Great King asks you to send back with me your Grand Vizier himself, Yar Mahomed.'

I admit he does this with a straight face and in the apparent expectation Kamran would, there and then, surrender his city to the Persian. There is a silence. I look not at Kamran but at Yar Mahomed, on whose face there is a sly grin rather than the shock or outrage I had been expecting. I wonder, not for the first time, whether the Vizier is plotting his own future without Shah Kamran and if this ruse will secure his safe passage out of Herat.

Kamran's other advisers discuss this among themselves though few seem to welcome the prospect of surrendering to the Persians.

'Mr Pottinger?' Kamran asks.

What can I say? McNeill and I have not discussed this in advance. I am unprepared. What is it my country wants? War with Persia or surrender to the Shah?

'Surrender is quite out of the question,' I say, addressing both McNeill and Kamran. 'But it may be Your Majesty and the Persians could come to terms. Perhaps we should consider further and respond with some suggestions of our own. And, in the meantime, perhaps we should invite Sir John to counsel us as the Queen's representative with the Shah. Sir John?'

We back out of the King's audience chamber into a cool corridor. McNeill whispers to me, 'You, Pottinger, should come back with me to the Shah of Persia and explain the position to him, as I have done repeatedly but to no avail. Make it clear the King of Herat will desist from enslaving the Shah's people.'

'I'm not sure Kamran would even agree to that, let alone Yar Mahomed,' I reply.

'Never mind that, nobody expects a King to keep his word. This is all about face, the saving thereof.'

'Kamran might agree to that but we can't possibly take the Vizier Yar Mahomed with us. I wouldn't trust that man further than I could spit,' I say. 'He is the very embodiment of nastiness. There's something about his sneer.'

McNeill chuckles. 'Pottinger, you need to adopt a more flexible approach if you are to make a career in diplomacy. Opinions are all very well but they are best kept to oneself. Even in official dispatches, I might say. Never say something your superiors don't want to hear, never criticise today's enemy because tomorrow he may be your friend.

Always remember, optimism breeds confidence, pessimism generates suspicion. It will do you no harm and it never matters if your optimism is misplaced. You will be forgiven excessive optimism, nobody forgives a pessimist; they just blame him for the disasters he warned about all along. Now, Pottinger, let us go back to the King of Herat and tell him what he wants to hear – that we will act as intermediaries with the Shah of Persia, that we will seek to persuade the Shah of the King's honour and good intentions and that we do not think it would be wise or diplomatic to place the King's Vizier in the jaws of his enemy, so to speak.'

'Yar Mahomed won't like that.'

'So much the better.'

*****

Now, though, having been rebuffed by the Shah, I make my way back inside the crumbling fortifications of Herat with nothing to show for my efforts but a couple of days of relative peace, a gift of fruits for Mahparah and a growing concern this isn't just about the re-establishment of the Persian empire or Kamran's slave-trade raids over the border.

During my brief stay in the Shah of Iran's camp, McNeill takes me into his confidence and reveals the reason his attempts to bring a conclusion to the siege are so unsuccessful – the Russians. A few days ago, McNeill had talked the Shah out of mounting an all-out assault on the city. The Persians bombarded us for days. The roof of the apartment I share with Mahparah took a terrible blow, bringing down half a wall and covering all our things in a layer of filth, dust, plaster and laths. Mahparah spent three days trying to make the place habitable again and, sweet thing that she is, she found drapes and thick cloths and carpets which she hangs from the gaping wounds in the building and decorates it more sumptuously than before. Yet the bombardment was meant to be a prelude to an all-out attack. The Persians massed just out of gunshot and we were braced for a fight when, all of a sudden, the cannon-fire stopped and the army stood down.

It seems McNeill somehow talked the Shah out of the attack by suggesting negotiations instead. But Count Simonich is expecting the arrival of a troop of Cossacks. 'Bloody man isn't even a Russian, you know,' McNeill complains. 'He's a Frenchie, or as good as. Comes from Dalmatia, served Bonaparte. Never forgiven us for Waterloo.'

It seems McNeill knows Count Ivan Simonich from the court back in Tehran where they vie for the ear of the Shah. Simonich declares he will help the Shah command the army and has with him several Russian officers who are apparently ready to oversee operations.

The sight of Russians at the gates of Herat alarms McNeill as it alarms King Kamran and his Vizier. It doesn't exactly encourage the people of the city either. I tell the King we have sent word to the Governor General asking for reinforcements and money but, as McNeill has already told me, we won't get either. I am close to despair. How can I keep this city out of Persian and, more to the point, Russian hands, protect the honour of Her Majesty, and the lives of the people who remain here?

Mahparah greets my return with a show of affection which I find difficult to reciprocate. Her fate is in my hands and as I grow increasingly fond of her, my concern for her safety rises together with my sense that I cannot protect her as I should. We have little food, though we have more than many. There is little to drink. Our living conditions are deteriorating by the day. The whole city smells of sewage, rotting flesh, dust and dirt. We are no more savoury though Mahparah still somehow retains a scent of fresh oranges.

Can we bribe the Persians, I wonder. It seems McNeill has laid out some of Her Majesty's treasure already but, as I have nothing to offer in the way of hard cash, there is not much I can do. Promises of future payment might work, I suppose, but there are two difficulties with that – the first is the Persians may not trust our good faith; the second is they would be right to mistrust us because I have been assured most positively by McNeill that his masters would not contemplate the outlay of even a few sovereigns in defence of Herat.

On the other hand they do not know the city is under siege not just from Persians, who may be of little account, but from Russians. As everyone knows, Tsar Nicholas is pushing his empire further and further towards the East. If he can take Herat then the whole of Afghanistan could fall under his influence. And if he can take Afghanistan, who knows, he could take India itself. I feel certain the Company, and indeed Her Majesty's Government, would not begrudge the expenditure of some small sums of money to prevent such a catastrophe from befalling the British Empire. Yet I have no authority to do more than fire a cannon or wield a sword and no credibility to promise more than my own blood.

CHAPTER 15

Fort William, Calcutta, December 1842

I am beginning to lose my temper. I can't be polite even to the servant who brings me my meals. He is a perfectly decent fellow aged about fourteen in a starched white outfit which would grace an officer's mess. He serves the food silently, efficiently and conscientiously. He is respectful and solicitous. I want to reprimand him, shout at him, even kick the little man.

It's not his fault. This incarceration is beyond a joke. I deserve better. It is unconscionable I should be kept under close confinement – not quite in prison but not free either – and branded before the whole world as a coward.

No accusation is more terrible for a soldier. Even when this court martial is over, I shall have to live with the ignominy. A coward? The man they once called 'the hero of Herat'. They want a scapegoat and most of their possible victims are already dead. We few survivors must carry the burden of defeat. They want us – they want me – to accept responsibility for the fiasco.

And they are using Shelton to fire the ammunition.

Shelton. It is almost unimaginable they should rely on that man for anything. My enemy. The man who made the misery of captivity more miserable still by his arrogance and stupidity. The man who could have averted the whole Kabul disaster is now the main – actually the only – witness for the prosecution.

How did he engineer it so I should be blamed and he should be cast as the victim? Is it his sightless eyes? They glaze over and stare blankly into the middle distance whenever something uncomfortable comes up. He says nothing, seems to shrink into the background and waits for others to fill the silence. It gives him a spurious power. No doubt he has allowed his questioners to answer their own questions for him.

Those eyes speak of violence. They tell the onlooker this man is capable of anything. They look down on everyone. Shelton's eyes betray his cold, hard soul. There is no passion in him. No blood. But he is brave, I'll give him that. He doesn't lack courage. I have seen him risk his life many times. As I have heard him moan, not from pain but with contempt for his superior officers Elphinstone and Macnaghten. When they sawed off his right arm in Spain, they say he stood throughout the ordeal and never made a sound.

Why didn't he advise? Why didn't he take charge? Why didn't he lead? Why did he simply roll around on the floor wrapped in an Afghan rug groaning like a man on his deathbed? Why was Shelton so arrogant he was happier to watch an entire army being condemned to death than use his courage and experience to come to its aid? Why did he never offer advice, support or help? Just because he wasn't a full general like Elphinstone even though he was a superior officer in almost every way? Because he was a Company officer and Elphinstone was a Queen's officer? Perhaps it was because he, Shelton, had missed Waterloo? Who can tell what turns a man vile but Shelton is the vilest man I have ever met. Vile to his superiors, vile to his fellow officers and even more vile to the troops who have to serve him. Stubborn, ill-natured, uncommunicative – how anyone thought he could lead a pack of hounds let alone an entire army is beyond me to comprehend.

We got back from Afghanistan, we survivors of that terrible expedition. You and I, my dearest Emily, were free at last. Free of our fellow prisoners, free of the fear, free of the disease and deprivation, free to tell the world of our love.

You report to the Governor General's house only to find it's true, what we had been told and not told, that your brother and sisters have gone, disappeared, returned home in a hurry, in disgrace, and left you, abandoned you, forgotten all about you. Almost, anyway.

They left word you were to follow them home to England without delay.

You could have stayed. You should have stayed. We were going to visit the Taj Mahal, remember? The temple to love, you and I, to celebrate our love and declare the truth to the world. But I was arrested and escorted here, to Calcutta.

Why didn't you follow me there?

That orderly. He said: 'Major Pottinger? I am obliged to hand you this, sir, and you must come along with me.' I open the letter, read it quickly, hand it to you.   You are so shocked you cannot speak. Your delicate face grows pale. Tears well in your eyes. 'Oh Eldred,' is all you can say before you turn and run from me towards the Governor's house. I have not seen you since.

Why have you abandoned me?

You write to say you have not. You say you are working for my release. You tell me to keep alive the dream of our visit to the Taj Mahal. But you do not talk to me, I do not see you, I do not even know where you are – back in England with the Earl?

Where are you? Can you not understand why I am angry, bereft, full of grief? After all we endured together. After all that time in captivity. After all that love.

Soon it will be Christmas. I am promised the court martial will take place as soon as the year turns. Meantime I write letters, stare across the empty parade ground from my quarters, discuss the case with my attorney, Captain George Broadhurst, who has every confidence in the outcome. 'You will be thoroughly vindicated my dear boy,' he says. 'There is no need for any concern on your part.'

He is an amusing fellow, I confess. We play at cards together, drink port wine and smoke cheroots. Broadhurst is an old hand at this. 'Done dozens of Court Martials, old fellow, but none as straightforward and clear cut as this. All we need is for Shelton to tell the truth and we're home and dry. Home and dry,' and he chuckles as he lays down another winning hand. 'All we need is for Shelton to tell the truth....'

I receive letters from my uncle, my brother, my step-mother. Lady Sale is very solicitous. Even Lady Macnaghten has the grace to be outraged on my behalf. Lieutenant Eyre and his wife are determined to resign the service and go back to England to raise a hue and cry on my behalf if I am convicted of any crime. A poet wishes to tell my story in verse. A newspaperman from 'The Times' has been assigned to the case. He is a thin, weak-looking fellow who finds the heat out here overbearing. I very much doubt if he will live to see the court in session. I would be happy if he were to survive that long; I am anxious for the truth to come out. The question is whether that will happen, especially if I must rely in Shelton to be the truth-teller.

CHAPTER 16

Herat, April 1838

King Kamran takes the news of the Shah's rejection with equanimity if not despair. He is tired. Even the Royal apartments look frayed at the edges. Many servants have fled, slipping away in the night. The guards look under-nourished and exhausted. They, too, would flee if they could but Yar Mahomed's spies are everywhere, ready and willing to slit a throat at the least opportunity.

Yar Mahomed is less calm. 'I shall visit the Shah myself,' he declares. Kamran merely looks at him, as if trying to calculate the level of his Vizier's treachery, and drinks from the goblet he keeps on a small table beside the throne.

The king's council is debating the severe food shortage. In the few days since the Cossacks arrived, the siege has grown more serious. The exits from the city are all now barred – the Eastern gates no longer accessible. The cattle left in the fields are in enemy hands. The scorched-earth policy ordered by Yar Mahomed has put paid to this summer's crops but already it seems the Persian army is setting about planting the fields again. They are settling in for the long run – long enough to grow their own food, at any rate. At the moment, they are probably as hungry as we are. Their supplies must come across the mountains between here and Tehran. We in our citadel probably endured the winter in greater comfort than they did in their tents.

Yar Mahomed says, 'Yesterday we executed seventeen cowards and traitors who were hoarding food from our own soldiers. We took their food and their money. There is more where that came from. I shall collect all the gold in Herat and offer it to the Shah to withdraw. We shall soon see the back of him. Money, that's all these filthy Persians understand. I shall visit the Shah.'

Other chieftains argue Yar Mohamed's summary executions are depriving the city of defenders, sapping morale and leaving the citizens as prisoners under a reign of terror. The Vizier says all the more reason, then, that Herat must come to a deal with the Shah.

I sit cross-legged on the carpet along with the other advisers, watching the King. One moment he is lying across his throne, eyes closed, right hand stroking his beard, half-listening to the discussions around him. A moment later, his legs twitch involuntarily, his jaws grind his teeth. He sits upright in the large, carved-mahogany throne, folds his arms across his chest. Now he is scratching his head, now he is reaching for a drink, now he is looking distractedly from one man to the next. Our eyes meet.

'Lieutenant Pottinger,' he says. 'What do you say?'

I stand. I prefer to stand when I am addressed by the King. It makes me feel a little more in control of the situation and of these strange people with their furiously warlike features and contempt for human life.

'Your Highness, you have no choice. You must fight on. Your Vizier may wish to seek an accommodation with the Shah but any arrangement will be nothing but a surrender. If this city were going to fall, it would have fallen by now. The Persians do not have their heart in this fight. If you, Your Highness, were to treat your own people equitably, distribute what food we have left among them all equally. If you were to forgive them their understandable desire to feed their own families. If you were to urge them to redouble their efforts to protect their city from the invaders…'

Yar Mahomed interrupts, sweeping across the carpet towards me and laughing. 'The British Pottinger wants to see us all starve. Every day another part of this city crumbles beneath the Persian guns. Would the British Pottinger have us buried in our own city?'

'Some people have already been buried, Your Highness,' I say, addressing the King rather than his fierce-faced Vizier. 'We would do better to preserve the lives of those we have left. Instead, we drag them from their crumbling homes and hang them, slit their throats, behead them and worse, in front of their wives and children. And for what crime?'

'For hoarding,' says the Vizier with a sly grin. He turns to the King. 'Your Majesty,' he is at his most obsequious, 'We cannot protect this city for much longer. It has been months since the Persians came to Herat and now he has handed control of the siege to the Russians. The Russians, Your Majesty.'

This is Yar Mahomed's trump card. He throws it down with the satisfaction of a big winner at the gaming tables. The King is suitably taken aback.

'The Russians?' he asks me.

'Indeed, Your Highness. But we have known of their presence in the Shah's camp since the beginning. You can see the Cossacks as they gallop across the fields before the city walls.'

'But now the Russians are in charge,' says Yar Mahomed. 'With the Russians in charge, for the first time, the Persians have commanders who know how to conduct a war.'

This is undeniable, but the alternative to resistance is surrender. Yar Mahomed is trying to ingratiate himself with the Shah of Persia by engineering the surrender. If he were allowed to leave the city, he would not return except at the rear of a conquering army. I dislike him enough to do my damnedest to prevent that at least.

'We will not surrender,' says the King with some determination, 'With British Pottinger's help we shall fight on. But we need more food – or we need fewer mouths to feed. How many slaves do we have?'

'Forty-three men, seventeen women and nine children,' says an aide quickly.

'They are in the cellars?'

'Most of them.'

'The others.'

'Working on repairs, Your Highness.'

'Sell them. Sell them all.'

'But they are Persians,' warns the Vizier. 'If the Shah discovers this, he will seek revenge. And who will buy them? How shall we get them out of the city?'

'With a raiding party. There are merchants here, I suppose?'

'There are.'

'And they do not wish to stay?'

'They do not.'

'What could be better?' says the King, rubbing his hands with glee. 'We sell the slaves to the highest bidder and help the buyer leave with his merchandise. Meanwhile, the merchants who remain, we shall kill.'

This appals me. 'Kill, your highness?'

'Of course. Fewer mouths to feed. And we can confiscate their money.'

'Let it be known,' he declares, rising unsteadily from his wooden throne and trying to sweep out of the room in a magisterial and decisive manner but failing to do so because his maroon shoes slip on the carpet and he is almost felled. Luckily a servant rescues the collapsing King and rights him again but the drama of the exit is somewhat lessened by what would have been a comical incident if it were not for the decisions the King has now made.

*****

The sale takes place two days later. The slaves are bought by a merchant from Turkestan who says he will take them to Balkh where the Emir pays high prices if the men and women are healthy. The children, he says, he will discard en route.

A raiding party rushes out from one of the Eastern gates accompanied by the merchant and his train. They find little resistance as they escort the merchant some miles from the city. His entourage is then deemed safe enough from the Persians and our troops head back to Herat. They are cut down in the saddle on their return and just half a dozen reach the great gates only to find the Vizier has ordered them to remain closed.

'Even fewer mouths to feed,' says Yar Mahomed with a smile of satisfaction.

The sale of the slaves does not go unpunished by the Persians. The following day, about one hundred of Herat's soldiers, taken prisoner over the preceding months, are paraded in front of the city walls. Chained and manacled, they are dressed in filthy rags and look starved. Nobody fires on their guards for fear of hitting one of our own. This little army is marched from the northernmost citadel to the southernmost so everyone in Herat can see them and, in many cases, recognise their friends, brothers, husbands or fathers.

Then the guard marches them to the summit of a small hill, still well within sight of the city but beyond the reach of our most powerful jezzails, which have almost twice the range of own Brown Besses. The Persians line up their prisoners and methodically work their way down the ranks disembowelling each man in turn. A knife is stabbed into the victim's stomach, his killer plunges his fist into the entrails, drags them out and holds them aloft amid the piercing yells of the dying and the screams of triumph of their Persian captors.

This appalling sight is greeted by a fruitless rain of musket and cannon fire while a raiding party is hastily assembled at the South East gate. I urge them to stay put because it is obvious to me the Persians will have a reception party laid on in expectation of just such a sally but I am ignored as 35 men on horseback charge out of the city towards the site of the massacre and we are forced to watch from the battlements as they are gunned down by the Persians who have been hiding in the trenches awaiting just this opportunity.

I am not squeamish. I am a soldier. I have seen dead bodies. I have seen men meet their doom. I have seen men cut off the heads of their enemies and relish the bloody task. Yet the joy which possesses the Persians as they disembowel their prisoners is more than I can take. Later, when I am with Mahparah, I find I am physically sick as I recall the hideous deaths.

*****

A few days after this massacre, Yar Mahomed announces there is so little food we must further reduce the number of people kept alive in the city. There are only two choices, he tells King Kamran. We must either kill anyone who is not making a useful contribution to the defence of Herat or we must throw them out of the city and onto the mercy of the Persians.

I see the logic of this. There isn't enough food to go round, there hasn't been for some time, and people are already dying of starvation on the streets. Their bodies are unburied, or sometimes thrown over the city walls. The constant stench is abominable. Only the rats prosper.

If we could reduce the numbers inside the city, we might be able to hold out for perhaps an extra month, though by September, if the siege is not lifted or we cannot drive the Persians from here, there will be no option but to submit ourselves to the Shah's mercies. I have written to Sir Alexander Burnes in Kabul telling him this but I do not expect any response.

Shah Kamran is, as usual, not sure what to do. He listens as Yar Mahomed demands that all the elderly, all the children, most women and the infirm are rounded up and then forced out of Herat. 'Not my wives,' Kamran pleads.

'Of course not your wives,' the Vizier answers with a cold contempt. 'Nor your servants. Of course not. But all those mouths we can no longer feed and which serve no purpose but to deprive our fighting men of sustenance. They must go.'

King Kamran looks at me, as if expecting me to raise an objection. I feel I should do but I can see the logic of the Vizier's case. If we keep all these people inside the city, and there must be perhaps five thousand of them, we shall all die. Without them, we who remain might live a little longer. 'But what is to happen to them?' I ask. 'If we force them from the city, what fate will befall them on the other side of Herat's great walls?'

'They will die,' says the Vizier simply. 'If they stay, they will die. If they go, they will die. But if they stay, we shall all die; if they go, we may live.'

'Can we not secure their safe passage somehow?' I ask. 'We could make a request of the Shah via Sir John McNeill.

'You have twenty-four hours, British Pottinger,' says the King, as Yar Mahomed frowns in frustration.

*****

It is impossible to escape the city under a white flag and believe yourself safe but as I ride out from the Western gate in something the scarlet of a British uniform, provided by McNeill at our last meeting, the Persians refrain from murdering me and allow me passage towards their camp. Once I am there, McNeill is waiting for me and I explain my mission.

'I cannot help, Pottinger,' he says. 'I am bound for Tehran tomorrow. I cannot stay here and see Her Majesty undermined and disparaged at every turn by this wretched Russian. Count Simonich has taken control of the army. He has captains from Russia under his command and I must warn you they are preparing a more formidable assault than anything your city has dealt with so far.'

McNeill is hot in his thick uniform but his agitation is not merely from the scorching weather we were now enduring. 'I must tell you, Pottinger, my servants have been attacked. The Queen's messengers have been turned back. I am denied access to the Shah. I am forced to remove my small encampment from one position to another, every time further from the Shah and his counsellors and, every time, another party of Russians takes my place.'

We stroll through what remains of an orchard. Most of the trees were chopped down in the early days of the siege but a few remain and, though the blossom is coming off, their leaves give us some welcome shade. McNeill's face is red, but with fury not heat. He cannot stand still but paces between the trees clutching the hilt of his sword as if he would draw it and run his enemies through.

A pair of Persian guards stands a short distance from us, no doubt listening to our conversation. McNeill's servant arrives carrying a jar of cold lemonade, some chicken, bread and fruit. It is the most sumptuous repast I have feasted on in days, for all Maparah's skills as both a cook and a scrounger, and I fall on it like one who has trudged through a desert and at last stumbles on a water-hole.

I sit, cross-legged on the ground to concentrate on the food, while McNeill continues to pace before me.

'These Russians, Pottinger, they have ingratiated themselves with the Shah. They have paid the Shah's troops out of the Tsar's own pocket. Soldiers are obedient to gold if to nothing else and the Tsar's money has served its purpose. The Persians – even their officers – are happy to submit themselves to this Russian's rule. The Shah's own commanders take a backward step and defer to Simonich in all things. I can scarcely win an audience with Mohammed Shah any longer and, when I do, I try to explain he is playing with fire but he will not listen. I think he is bored out here in Herat and wants to go home. He thinks the Russians can bring this siege to a swift end and he would be immensely relieved to return to his Palace in Tehran.'

'Why can't he leave now?' I ask, somewhat naively, as I gnaw on a chicken bone.

'He can't lose face. If he leaves now, the siege will collapse within days, even with the Russians still here. The army would melt away. If the Shah leaves, he can only do so if he is prepared to admit defeat. And he won't do that in a hurry.'

'What have you said about the Russians?'

'I have told him he is making friends with a nation which is Her Majesty's enemy. I have explained the Russians are not helping the Persians out of the kindness of their hearts. They are doing so because they believe it undermines Her Majesty and her armies. They have designs on more than just Herat. They would conquer the whole of Afghanistan. And why do they wish to do that?'

McNeill pauses and I am not sure if this is a rhetorical question or he is expecting an answer from me. I venture, 'India?'

'India, precisely. India. India with her riches and her trade and her treasures and her English armies. India. And with India, the Far East – all the trade from India to China. The Tsar has designs on Her Majesty's territories far and wide. If it isn't the filthy French, it's the untrustworthy Russians. We are never safe from the designs of these filthy foreigners. And I have explained this in no uncertain terms to the Shah.'

'Does he not realise he cannot ride both horses at once?'

'I don't think he does, no. My withdrawal from here will make it clear to him, I trust, that Her Majesty is not to be trifled with in this way. I have, of course, made our Prime Minister and the Governor General aware of the situation and the Russian adventurers. You know there's another envoy in Kabul, I suppose?'

'In Kabul? What about Burnes?'

'What indeed. Dost Mohammed Khan, the King of Kabul, is playing the same dangerous game as the Shah, negotiating with Burnes and, at the same time, behind his back talking with some mountebank captain of the Russian guard.'

'And in the meantime, you can do nothing for the Heratis who are about to be expelled from the city?' I ask, getting to the point of my mission.

'I can ask the Shah for mercy tonight when I take my leave of him but it is a formal occasion and the Russians will be hovering to persuade him against any show of clemency. They think the more ruthless the Shah is, the more they will destroy morale among the Heratis and the sooner the city will fall.'

'They may be right,' I say ruefully, thinking of what I must return to within the hour.

McNeill seems to be reading my thoughts. 'You must impress on them your importance as Her Majesty's envoy to Herat. I shall do the same here,' he says. 'It would not do for the Shah to allow any harm to come to you nor, I think, would the Russians want to run the risk of sparking a diplomatic incident. At least not yet, though these fellows are not to be trusted. What happens to you in the heat of battle, now Pottinger, that I cannot vouch for. You must take care of yourself whether Herat falls or no.'

*****

I take my leave of Sir John McNeill and return slowly to Herat, protected by my white flag, despondent at our chances of survival and in despair over the prospects facing the citizens who are to be thrown out and onto the mercy of the Shah in the morning.

I present my compliments and regrets to King Kamran and one of his servants presents me with two letters from Sir Alexander Burnes in Kabul. The first, dated three months ago, is in reply to my appeal for help:

'Pottinger, I have no reassurances for you. The situation in Kabul is not promising. Your Count Simonich has spies here, as well, and I learn he is putting the Tsar's money out in support of the Shah of Persia's assault. At the same time my old friend Dost Mohammed Khan, the King of Kabul, is also subject the blandishments of Captain Viktevitch. He insinuates himself into the favour of the Dost to the point where the poor man cannot see what is perfectly obvious to you and me, which is that his best interests are served by remaining loyal to Her

Majesty. We cannot have this, Pottinger. I have nothing practical to offer you, I regret to say, but my best wishes and warm encouragement in your resistance to the Russians and the Persians. I shall, of course, pass on your comments and my own assessment of the situation to the Governor-General. I am aware Lord Eden is taking a personal interest in affairs on our side of the Hindu Kush and this may be to our benefit in the long run though, as you know, the Company is anxious to minimise its expenses at present and is unlikely to sanction any liberality on your part.'

A second letter is also handed to me. This, too, is from Burnes, dated a couple of weeks after the first. It says:

Pottinger, I am returning to Hindustan. The Dost's behaviour is insupportable, accepting money from Viktevitch and promising some kind of treaty with the Russians. He needs to understand it has taken Her Majesty some pains to restrain Ranjeet Singh and that, in the event of an alliance with the Tsar, we cannot be answerable for the Sikh king's actions. The King of Kabul's brother in Kandahar has already signed some kind of alliance with the Tsar. You must hold out in Herat on your own, to demonstrate the power of Her Majesty in these treacherous lands.'

The King of Herat expects some comment from me to explain the content of these letters. I am at a loss to know what to say but eventually declare, 'Her Majesty sends Your Majesty her greetings and assurances of her continued devotion to Your Majesty and your city of Herat. Her Majesty, moreover, urges Your Majesty to be strong in your resolve to turn back the Persian horde at the gates of your city and Her Majesty dedicates your humble servant Eldred Pottinger to your cause. Her Majesty says Your Majesty can be assured of Great Britain's continuing good will and support, trusts you will not be in want of supplies or men to further your endeavours and feels certain you will prevail in the fullness of time.'

'But no money? No men?' smirks Vizier Yar Mahomed.

CHAPTER 17

Herat, June 1838

It is another day of merciless heat and raw, burning wind when the elderly, the infirm, most of the women and almost all the children are shooed, beaten and thrown bodily out of the West, South and North-West gates. There is screaming and wailing, stumbling and begging. Limping old men try to head eastwards or simply sit on rocks looking perplexed and wait for whatever will happen next. The women cry out to their menfolk on the battlements; the men left behind to defend Herat, meanwhile, scowl, weep and look mutinous. Children scamper and throw rocks at the city walls. Babies wail. One or two elderly horses carry a few old women. The Palace guards use knives and swords to prod and shove the crowd out of the gates.

To start with, the Persians simply watch from a safe distance as the commotion continues.

Mahparah is exempt from banishment because she is regarded as my slave, though I make a point of telling the Vizier she is here entirely of her own free will and may leave whenever she wishes. I try, half-heartedly, to encourage Mahparah to join this exodus but I cannot say if she would be safer in Herat or among the city's refugees and she is insistent she will go nowhere without me. 'You will keep me safe, Eldred,' she says with her lovely smile, which has not disappeared despite the privations which are taking their toll on everyone around us.

'I am not sure I can,' I say but she replies, 'I would rather be in danger with my Eldred by my side than safe without him.'

Later on this dreadful morning I am pleased I did not press the point further because the crowd of refugees, which has been trudging towards the Persian lines, is forced to turn back and flee when it is fired on by the enemy. The Persians do not mount an all-out attack on the refugees but one or two are killed by the gunfire, which immediately creates a great panic, and we are forced to stand on the battlements watching as some old folk and a few small children are trampled underfoot as Herat's outcasts run back to the city which has just vomited them out and is barred against them.

We stand aghast as the dust rises and crowds dash pell-mell towards the dry, stinking moat and beg at the feet of the walls to be allowed into Herat. The Vizier, Yar Mahomed, stands at the turret above the Eastern gate with his arms folded firmly across his chest and a defiant expression on his unpleasant face as he orders his retainers to shoot into the crowds, which they dutifully do. Now the refugees are trapped, unarmed and defenceless, between two hostile armies with nowhere to go and nothing to hope for but death.

I try to reason with the Vizier but he is in no mood for pleas to his better nature. There is no such thing. Besides, his logic is inescapable. 'If we let them back into the city,' he says, 'We will all starve to death within days. We might as well surrender the keys right now and throw ourselves on the Shah's mercy. And we know Mohammed Shah is not merciful, do we not British Pottinger?'

I confess the disembowelling of the Herati prisoners a few days ago does not bode well for the fate of those left in the city if and when it falls to the Persians.

'If we let them in we starve and die; if we refuse to allow them to return, our little food will go a little further and we will last another week or two. And who knows, Sahib Pottinger,' and here he grins wickedly at me, 'Perhaps your English Queen, perhaps she shall step in and save us all.'

The Vizier's voice is thick with irony. He has no love for me or my Queen. He has no hope of relief from this quarter. He has only the expectation that he can somehow negotiate his own safe passage out of Herat and behind the Persian lines. He feels, I am sure, I have somehow thwarted him so far and is biding his time.

Meanwhile, from his castle keep he watches the tragedy unfolding in the destroyed orchards and burnt-out fields outside the city.

The refugees' ordeal lasts for hours. There is a respite during the heat of the day when both armies are in the habit of seeking shade to rest. But after the bloodshed of the morning, the refugees are forced to camp out in the blazing heat with no water, food or shelter other than whatever they managed to carry with them out of the city. As the heat begins to die down late in the afternoon, the clusters of old men, women and children are once again assailed by intermittent gunfire from both sides. They have nowhere to turn, no-one to ask for help.

Eventually three elderly men with long, grey beards and dignified bearing hobble slowly towards the Persian lines under a flag of truce to be met by a Russian officer on horseback who, from what I can see, addresses them with civility and prevents the soldiery from firing on them.

We watch as negotiations take place. Eventually, it is clear, the Persians grant the refugees some sort of safe passage through their lines so that, as the sun finally sets on the blood-stained gardens and abandoned orchards which once graced the outskirts of Herat, the hundreds of survivors are permitted at last to trudge away from their city towards a future which holds neither hope nor promise.

*****

The sight of their wives and parents, their children, relatives and friends being ejected from Herat and thrown on the dubious mercy of the Persians does not help secure the resolve and determination of the soldiers left behind, marooned in the city. There is no escape for them, not from the Persians, the enemy on the other side of the city walls, nor from the Vizier Yar Mahomed, the enemy within.

He, in turn, finds no escape from subservience to King Kamran. Each man has his followers, his personal guard, his chieftains and his alliances. Neither trusts the other but if they were able to choose, I believe a majority of the clan chiefs now in Herat prefer the King to the Vizier. Yar Mahomed is a dangerous man, not to be trusted, never a friend even to his nearest and dearest. I have seen him have cousins killed. He treats his wives with contempt – he forced most of them from the city in the great evacuation. He bends his knee to the King because he knows his power is still too weak to do otherwise. But I do not trust him so when I receive news that another British envoy has reached the Shah of Persia's encampment, I keep it to myself.

Mahparah has gleaned this piece of intelligence from one of the wives of one of the King of Herat's more senior military leaders who maintains a ring of spies in and around the Persian camp in order, among other things, to negotiate his own safe passage to freedom when – I should say if – the city falls. This unreliable source of information says the British envoy Sir John McNeill will not come back from Tehran, having withdrawn in frustration at the Shah's dealings with the Russian, Count Simonich. In his place, Sir John has sent Colonel Charles Stoddart.

Colonel Stoddart was on the Governor General of India's staff when I was in Simla so I'm surprised he has made his way to Persia and even more surprised to learn he has trekked all the way out here.

While I am wondering how to contact Stoddart, he contacts me, riding under the flag of England to the very walls of the city and demanding entry in the name of Her Majesty Queen Victoria. He is florid in his fury when he is initially denied access to the city and sent back to the Persian lines with a few volleys of buckshot following his hasty retreat.

I am summoned to the King who is, as usual, undecided. Should I be allowed, encouraged even, to make contact with Stoddart or should the King of Herat remain defiant? I persuade him we should at least hear what the British envoy has to say though, of course, the Vizier thinks this is a trap and argues against any contact with the enemy.

I am growing tired of this nonsense. The city is a crumbling, stinking, foetid, starving, half-derelict settlement with scarcely a quarter of the inhabitants it started with a year ago. King Kamran maintains the fiction of his rule and the Vizier finds it convenient to assist him in this pretence. The chieftains allied to this pair are uneasy and their allegiances seem to be perpetually fluid. One or two have sneaked out of the city with a few followers and thrown themselves on the mercy of the Shah. They seem to have been welcomed, or at least they have not been put to death, though they are soon to be seen deployed on the forward lines thus endangering their lives almost as much as they were imperilled before.

'We must negotiate,' I tell the King of Herat. Eventually he agrees and under the banner of surrender I am allowed to ride towards the Persian lines as the baking June heat of the afternoon sun is slowly dying down and the brilliant light of its setting blinds my eyes.

Squinting into the fierce glare, my emaciated pony and I plod slowly towards the enemy braced at every moment for a final bullet to put one or both of us out of our discomfort. None arrives and in time I am met by a Cossack on horseback and a dozen foot-soldiers.

The Cossack, one of Count Simonich's officers I assume, speaks to me in Persian. 'Lieutenant Pottinger. You wish to see your countryman.'

I feign ignorance of the language and reply in English, 'I am here on the Queen's business. Take me to Colonel Charles Stoddart.'

My enemy recognises the name but is puzzled by the rest. My horse walks slowly on toward the Persian camp and I more or less ignore my escort. I am alone but have no fear of these foreigners. The blessing of our Lord God is shield enough; the strength of the mighty Great Britain is my sword. I am untroubled by these heathens all around me.

As I felt sure he would, Stoddart emerges from one of the semipermanent buildings they have erected over the last few months and calls out, 'Pottinger, good afternoon.'

'Colonel Stoddart, sir.'

He walks towards me with a boy who runs ahead to take hold of my horse and allow me to dismount. I cross to Stoddart, realising how filthy and dusty I am, how alien my native garb must seem to this Englishman and how wild my beard has become. I salute, as one should, my senior officer and he returns the greeting in kind.

Stoddart is a slight figure in his smart scarlet uniform. He is a young-looking man, though he is five or six years older than me, with thick, black curly hair, clean shaven, with a slightly shocked expression, a permanent frown on his forehead, as if whatever he sees somehow meets with his disapproval. But he greets me warmly enough, after our salutes, with a shake of the hand and an invitation to dine with him in his tent.

This is most welcome. Stoddart is well provided for, as befits an envoy of Her Majesty. We eat heartily as his servants – he seems to have seven of them – ferry in red wine and roast chicken, Port and roast beef, Madeira and pears. I fear I eat with more greed than manners but excuse myself on the grounds that food is scarce in the city of Herat.

We discuss Sir John McNeill's withdrawal from the Shah of Persia's presence, Stoddart's own mission to separate the Shah from the Russians, and the activities of Count Simonich.

'The Russians,' Stoddart explains, 'Are behind it all. They put the Shah up to this in the first place. They don't care a fig about slavery. They have their eyes on India, Pottinger. Today it's Herat, maybe, but next year, who knows? Bombay? Calcutta? The tsar is an ungodly tyrant and must be stopped this side of the Hindu Kush. That is why your defence of Herat is so important to Her Majesty.'

'My defence?' I laugh. 'I have done very little. The truth is, if the Persians were dedicated to their task they could have taken Herat weeks, if not months, ago. Instead they seem content to starve us out.' I say this as I suck on another chicken bone, my lips greasy with fat, my stomach more satisfied than it has been for weeks. I do not even think of Mahparah as I gorge myself.

By now, it seems, the wine has taken effect on both of us. Stoddart sways as he stands up and almost falls over. 'Peace, Pottinger,' he drawls, 'Peace cannot be achieved while the Russians are running this confounded show. That is why,' and here Stoddart collapses down onto the rug again and whispers into my ear, 'Spies, Pottinger, spies,' he says. He leans away and calls loudly, 'Spies! I don't care. Go on then, listen away, I don't care, I have no secrets for you to carry to your Russian masters.' He finishes his glass of Madeira and, leaning towards me again, whispers in a voice as sober as his previous expostulations sounded drunk, 'Now listen Pottinger, the Shah is in for a nasty surprise any day now. You will know all about it when it happens. Until then, we just have to play along with this ludicrous game. Spin it out, keep talking, it will soon all go away.'

I am incredulous and gasp out a few incoherent words. Immediately Stoddart is back to his former drunken self. 'I have it on good authority,' he says loudly so any spies within half a mile will be able to hear, 'I have it on good authority, Pottinger, the Shah, peace be unto him, the Shah I say, Pottinger, the glorious emperor of Persia, King of Kings, is willing to make a peace with that renegade tyrant Kamran of Herat. He stipulates only the following conditions...' Here Stoddart gropes around in the gloom of the darkening tent for a piece of paper. 'Ah here, here,' he waves the document in triumph, 'The word of the Shah himself, Pottinger, the word of the Shah himself,' he says, waving it under my nose. 'His Imperial Majesty stipulates he is willing to raise the siege and return home without pressing his advantage any further on condition, Pottinger, on condition, on these conditions, these conditions I say...'

It comes down to peace in exchange for the return of all Persian prisoners now held in Herat, the provision of a contingent of trained and equipped soldiers from Herat to join the Shah's Persian army and a promise that Shah Kamran will never again carry out slaving raids into

Persian territory.

'One other thing, Pottinger,' Stoddart says as he stands and falls forwards, almost flat on his face, and I am required to help him right himself. Suddenly he is quiet, urgent and entirely sober. 'The Russians are planning an all-out assault. The Shah's Vizier, Haji Mirza Aghasi, tells me. You may or may not know that Mirza is a friend of the Company's and Her Majesty. We are lucky enough to be able to persuade the Vizier to lay out some of Her Majesty's treasure among the wiser officers in the Persian army. The Vizier will do his best to keep the impact of this attack to a minimum. We have supplied him with fresh funds and I think we can take his word for it. He has been friendly to us in the past and richly rewarded for his loyalty to Great Britain. We can trust Mirza. He will do all he can but with the Russians running the show we cannot be sure his efforts will be enough. You must be aware, Pottinger, this peace offer is a diversion. An attack, a serious attack coordinated and led by the Russians, is coming very soon and we cannot buy off every officer in the Persian army.'

The following day I carry this offer back with me to Herat, having enjoyed a companionable breakfast with Stoddart and taken a fond leave of the man, my saddlebag crammed with fresh fruit, some meat and even fresh naan for Mahparah.

Back in my rooms later, I discuss all this with Mahparah but all she is interested in is Her Majesty. 'You have a Queen?' she asks, fascinated. 'A woman. Is she beautiful?'

'Yes, she is.' I have no idea whether that is true but what else can I say?

'Tall? Fair? Who governs her?'

'Who governs her? God, I suppose, and the Prime Minister.'

'And her husband?'

'I don't think she has a husband. At least not yet. I think she is only 18 or 19.'

'Old enough for a husband. No good comes of Queens. Perhaps she will marry my Eldred Pottinger. King Pottinger. That would be fitting would it not?'

I stop her mouth with kisses.

*****

King Kamran's court is growing ragged. Some of his chieftains have disappeared, one or two have died. His women are depleted – he threw out some of the older ones in the Great Exodus. The Vizier stands in dark corners and glares. The daylight filters through the windows but there is an air of filth and defeat. Even the King is hungry now. He is setting an example to his chiefs by only eating once a day. Unfortunately this increases the impact of the alcohol he drinks incessantly, which in turn means his decision-making is even more erratic than ever.

His followers are supposed to restrict the amount of food they eat as well but some of the stouter men do not look particularly deprived by this latest edict. I know the Vizier, Yar Mohamed, has a cool, well-stocked cellar which is still open to his closest cronies. He, unlike his King, does not look to be starved.

'Your Majesty, the Shah of Persia sends greetings and a request that You Majesty might at last agree to his terms for a lasting peace between His Majesty and Your Majesty,' I say to the King and the assembled chieftains, who spit and shuffle and cough idly.

'This is all preposterous,' says the King.

'How can it be,' intervenes Yar Mahomed, 'When Your Majesty is as yet in ignorance of the Shah's requests?'

This irritates the King, who declares, 'I will hear no more.'

'Your Majesty is right to ignore these overtures of peace,' I say. 'The Shah wishes to give us false hopes of a settlement while even now he and his traitorous Russian allies are preparing for the biggest assault on this city we have yet encountered.'

'Assault on Herat?' the Vizier laughs. 'What has he been doing all these months, then?'

'Your Majesty,' I say, 'The Shah has been given new heart by his

Russian supporters. You are aware of the activities of Count Simonich and his officers? We must reinforce our defences at once.'

Naturally my urgency does not impress the King or the Vizier, though for different reasons. I am more and more convinced Yar Mohamed has his own channels to negotiate with the Shah and would not be unhappy to see the surrender of this city. No doubt he would replace Kamran as King under Persia's tutelage.

'What is the Shah of Persia's request?' the King asks me.

'That you return to him your Persian prisoners, that you provide him with a regiment of your soldiers and that you desist raiding his territory and selling his people into slavery. It is a good offer, Your Highness, and should not be refused. But it is a meaningless one. He is trying to encourage Your Majesty to let down your guard while he plans his assault.'

'There will be no assault,' laughs the Vizier again, 'And as for the prisoners, we should carry them up to the East Gate and slit their throats in full view of the vile Persians and spit in their faces.'

'Your Majesty,' I say, 'I must see to the defences. We do not have the opportunity to debate this. The assault should be expected imminently.'

*****

Yet nothing happens for two full days. The King sends the Vizier to talk terms with the Shah of Persia. The King thinks a peace may be negotiated. The Vizier, somewhat to my surprise, returns with a grim face and tells the King the Shah of Persia wishes to have tokens of good faith. The King must free the prisoners before any further progress can be made. The King says he will sleep on it.

The next morning, the assault finally begins.

It is another still, hot day and as soon as dawn breaks, the Persians mount cannon-fire on the city, aiming at the three nearest of the city's five gates, the South, West and North-Western gates. We cannot afford to leave the other two unmanned and yet there is no sign of an attack on them.

The assault continues with rockets, deliberately used to burn the wooden buildings within the city walls. These rockets began to set fires, up and down the streets. The heat, an easterly breeze and the thatched roofs employed in many of these hovels are enough to create a conflagration which rushes and leaps towards the apartment I share with Mahparah.

I order a small contingent of soldiers to beat back the flames as best they can. This includes pulling down the intact wooden buildings surrounding them to stop the fire spreading but not before our own building is engulfed. I watch this from my post on the West gate, torn between my duty to defend Herat and my concern for the young woman who has been my constant companion and friend these past months.

I hear screaming and a tremendous crash as another building collapses into the flames. The noise from the assault is growing but I swear I can hear Maparah's agonised cry through the mayhem. I descend from the tower as quickly as I can and make my way through the thick smoke and apparently leaderless soldiers towards our apartment. I cannot reach the building, the flames are scorching everything in their path. A young woman rushes past, her hair ablaze. Water is in short supply but a couple of men are throwing what they can at the fire, to no effect. Then I hear Mahparah's voice distinctly. It is a cry which seems to carry my name on it. Looking up, I see a figure engulfed in fire on the upper balcony. It must be Mahparah. I can get no closer, I can offer her no help, I can do nothing. The body disappears in another wave of flame and, when I peer through the fire again a moment later, there is no sign of her. The rockets have killed my Mahparah, the flames have consumed her young body, her wise soul, her loving heart.

I stand like an idiot, incapable of thought or movement. The smoke stings my eyes. They weep.

*****

I cannot control my anger. I rush to the Northern gate where the Persians are trying to climb the ramparts. We rain down fire on them. I lead a contingent out of a sally port and into the thick of the enemy. I thrust my sword into every body I come close to, possessed of a fury I do not recognise. I scream and swear and stab and thrust with no thought but it seems to inspire those around me and soon the Persians are in full retreat.

We do not rush after them for it is clear the West gate and the Southern are still under siege. The assault on the West peters out as the Persians see the flight of their comrades and follow suit. It may be, though I will never know for sure, that Haji Mirza Aghasi, the Vizier to the Shah of Persia, has been liberal in the distribution of Her Majesty's treasure among these elements of the Persian army for it is not entirely clear the Heratis are in overwhelming command of the gates when our enemies flee.

The struggle at the South gate is more serious. By the time I reach the area, the Persian cannon-fire has brought down a sizable length of wall, perhaps three yards long, beside the gate itself. The rubble offers a route into the city. It is unstable and precarious but for a determined enemy assaulting in numbers it is not too daunting. The city is in danger of being overrun.

I see from the still-standing tower over the gate that operations are being directed by Count Simonich himself, on horseback overseeing activities from a position just out of the range of our guns. This does not stop the Heratis wasting precious ammunition taking pot shots at him when they should be concentrating their fire much closer to hand, where scores of Persians are clambering up the ramparts towards the breach in the city wall, led by a filthy Frenchman called Georges Semineau.

Who would have thought a Frenchman and a Russian could fight on the same side after Napoleon? I suppose this is all we can ever expect from the French and the Russians; these people are never happier than when they are plotting the downfall of England.

The difficulty for Semineau is that the breach in the walls looks wide from his side but actually narrows quickly. Only one or two men at a time can advance the last few yards. This means both sides can only be championed by one or two men at a time, the whole siege is reduced virtually to single combat. Semineau is close to the front of his line, distinguished not only by his pale skin but by the cocked hat and blue silk frock coat he wears – a prime target for a good shot, perhaps, but also a rallying point for his men.

Pitted against him is a squadron led by none other than King Kamran himself. He stands on a wooden platform close to the breach in the wall urging and threatening his soldiers, hacking away at any man who shows fear and yelling curses at his troops. Yar Mohamed is nowhere to be seen. I see the King shoot dead one of his own soldiers who steps back from the narrow breach even though it seems to me the man was simply seeking somewhere sheltered to reload his jezzail.

We can rain down shot on this concentration of men but we cannot know whether we are hitting friend or foe. The King is screaming. I leap from the tower onto the battlements and thence, over the rubble, to the King's platform. 'You can't inspire men by shooting them,' I say angrily, 'If you want to keep this city you must show an example and lead your men into battle.'

The King cannot hear me above the din. He cries, 'It is hopeless, we are lost,' and in full view of his own soldiers, who are sweating and bleeding to death to save his city, he slumps to the ground in defeat and resignation.

He is drunk. I can smell the alcohol. Some lethal fortified wine, I suppose. I do not have the time or patience for this. I grab the King by the collars of his ornamented shirt and drag him back to his feet. 'You damned well get a grip on yourself, man,' I yell at him. 'If you give up, look, your men are giving up too.'

Already a dozen or more have retreated down from the ramparts, preparing for flight. Others watch hesitantly, ready to flee but not entirely convinced their King has finally abandoned all hope. He is, I realise, well gone in drink but if it can induce defeatism, it can surely summon up courage as well.

I force the King to accompany me from his platform. I yell orders to the soldiers to mount the battlements and attack the enemy. I drag Kamran through the stumbling and sweating ranks of his men towards the thick of the fighting, yelling at our soldiers to clear a way for us.

'Now, Kamran, now,' I shout at the King and, pulling him along with my left hand, start to cut a swathe before us with my right. I find I am yelling and screaming, without thought or coherence, as I thrust the sword again and again at the bodies lurching up in front of me. The King has no choice but to follow suit. The alternative is death for him and defeat for his city. He and I are now at the narrowest part of the breach and pushing onward. I can see the Frenchman up ahead in his velvet coat, his grey moustache and fleshy lips smiling as if he can taste victory.

I carve a way towards him and, slashing indiscriminately, I am upon him. He sees me and thrusts his sword at me ineffectively while mine pierces his ribcage and I drive it deep into him, as deeply as I can. I blame Semineau for Mahparah's death. As he slips to the ground, I think of her son Wasim, who I saved at Wardak, and what I can tell him when next we meet. I stand over the body of the Frenchman and expect, any second, to receive a sword thrust or a bullet which will put me out of my pain. Instead, I see Persians clambering back down the rubble of the demolished wall and rushing back towards their own camp.

Fifty yards away I see the Russian Count Simonich on his horse, wildly yelling and swearing at his retreating soldiers. He tries to manoeuvre his horse to cut them off but when a shot, which may well have come from one of the Persian soldiers, flies close to his face, he flinches, looks briefly towards Herat, spits an order to the man at his side, reins in his horse and trots angrily away.

I try to restrain the Heratis from pursuing their retreating foe but most of them ignore me and chase after the enemy only to become involved in hand-to-hand fighting in which many of our men die or are seriously wounded. Some return with severed heads to show off on the battlements but others crawl back to die. I try to organise a party of men to begin the urgent task of rebuilding the defences in the wall; even something impermanent will be better than the gaping hole we have at the moment.

In truth, though, I am exhausted and my head thumps but I know any time on my own will be spent dwelling on Mahparah's terrible fate. I have never known someone so close to me to die before. Of course my mother died when I was a child but I have no memory of her. My step-mother is the only mother I have known or loved and, I pray to God, she is fit, well and living safely far away in Belfast. Oh, to be there now, in the cool wet of Ireland, all green and fertile, not burning to death under this foreign sun amid these strange and ungodly people. What possessed me to come out to India? What? To volunteer for this mission to the heart of nowhere?

CHAPTER 18

Herat, September 1838

It is the 280th day of the siege. I am once more in council with the King, who is, as usual, under the influence of drink, and the Vizier, Yar Mohamed, who is anything but.

The garrison is reduced to no more than a few thousand people, mainly men, together with one or two women of King Kamran's harem and a few servants. The King's council chamber carries the scars of the war. Its furnishings are makeshift and battered. Much of the wood was burned during the coldest nights of winter, even some of the intricately-carved panels are gone. The hangings, rugs, curtains and mats are either stolen, ripped or filthy. Dust is everywhere. The smell, across the whole city, is a virulent combination of filth, sewage, burnt-out buildings and dead bodies. The heat of the summer has not started to die down, we are plagued by flies and there is nobody to keep them off us any longer.

The chieftains are arranged around the chamber in the shade, their backs to the walls, while Yar Mohamed marches up and down the centre of the room yelling and declaiming and Kamran lounges, a goblet of red wine in his hand, chuckling quietly to himself.

An emaciated youth is led in by one of the guards. He demands to see 'Colonel Pottinger' but he cannot identify me. I suppose I am as brown as the rest, my blue turban is filthy and no longer identifiable by its colour, my trousers are ragged, my shirt may once have been white but it is now grey with dust and grime. Yar Mohamed seizes the note the lad holds in front of him, breaks the seal, studies it closely then hands it to me. Clearly he cannot read it and, even if he could, he does not understand English but he turns away, giving a convincing impression of a man who has already gathered whatever news the note contains.

I look at it. It is from Charles Stoddart. It reads simply, 'My dear Pottinger, The Shah has mounted his horse Ameerij and is gone.'

I read it aloud to the assembled chieftains and even the King deigns to look up from his semi-stupor and smile. The others throng around me, shaking my hand, kissing me on both cheeks, hugging me and demanding to see the note itself which none of them can read. The Vizier, of course, is aloof from all of this but even he cannot entirely feign lack of interest.

Over the next few days we watch from the city walls as the Persian army strikes camp and makes its way Westwards, over the horizon and away from Herat. After a week Stoddart arrives, with some supplies and I have a chance to find out why the siege has been lifted so suddenly.

He tells me the attack a few weeks earlier was Count Simonich's last throw of the dice. The Tsar had ordered him back to Moscow even before the final assault. 'You know, the bloody fellow seems to have done a Nelson,' says Stoddart. 'Simonich turned a blind eye to the order in the hope their last foray would see Herat overrun and he could return in triumph.'

'Having paved the way for a Russian invasion of Afghanistan and then, perhaps, of India itself,' I add.

'Quite possibly,' Stoddart agrees.

According to Stoddart, McNeill had not been idle since his departure from the Shah's camp. He wrote to Lord Palmerston in London and Lord Eden in Bombay urging them to relieve Herat and warning the interference of the Russians represented a threat to India herself.

Stoddart, with rare excitement at this great diplomatic triumph, says, 'The Company sent six hundred men from Bombay to the Persian Gulf. You see, Pottinger, your exploits have not gone unnoticed. McNeill said you were holding the line in Herat but you couldn't hold on for ever. Lieutenant-Colonel William Sherriff's force has landed on the island of Karrack. It's just a desolate bit of sand, I believe, near Bushire – you know Bushire? The place the Royal Navy has been using as a base to sweep slavery out of Arabia? Anyway, the Shah was afraid it was the start of a full invasion of Persia. It was enough to encourage him to beat his hasty retreat from Herat. He summoned Simonich, told him Persia didn't want anything more to do with the Russians, summoned me and swore his allegiance to Her Majesty.'

'Whatever value there is in that,' I say. 'These Muslims are all the same – utterly untrustworthy, always at war with someone, constant only in their inconstancy.'

'They must all be women,' jokes Stoddart.

*****

The weeks after the end of the siege of Herat are desolate times. The city has been ransacked for anything that could be used in its defence. Only about one in five of its people are still alive and in residence. The place has been almost razed to the ground – all its buildings are badly disfigured if not destroyed. The beautiful old mosque is a wreck. King's palace is the most well-preserved though Kamran himself lies in his couch for days on end as if he is dying. The man is exhausted, defeated mentally and physically, and soaked through with alcohol. The Vizier, Yar Mahomed, meanwhile, is busily shoring up the defences of the city and his own position among the surviving chieftains.

It is over. I want to go home, back to India at least, though Ireland is my dream. Soft, green Ireland. Never have I pined for Belfast so much. Even the prospect of meeting my father after all this time doesn't seem unbearable. Only Stoddart, with his unquenchable optimism, makes things bearable.

As the Persians march away, some of the city's displaced refugees come crawling home. Their homes are destroyed. There is no trade. There is nothing to eat. There is stench and rotting bodies, a drunken King and a scheming Vizier.

I search for the apartment where I lived with Mahparah but the building was consumed in flames. There is no sign of her, no sign she even existed, just charred wood and the smell of smoke, which hangs over the whole city. There is nothing of the woman herself, no body to bury, nothing to remember her by unless, perhaps, I meet her son again. Poor woman. I clamber up the blackened stones and over, under or around the beams which remain, up towards the room we shared but it has gone, there is nothing but the blue sky, cruel heat and the unflinching glare of a bitter sun.

I sit for a long time and gaze sightlessly about me as some of the locals try in a desultory fashion to start cleaning up their city. I think of Mahparah and already her image is fading from my mind. I can smell her, though, the aroma of fresh orange that seemed to stay with her even at the worst of times. This I shall always have to remember her by.

I write letters to Burnes, to my uncle Sir Henry, to my step-mother Eliza, and a report to Lord Eden, but receive no instructions from any quarter. Stoddart, whose orders came from McNeill in Tehran, says we should seek to establish a British bridgehead in Herat, help with the rebuilding and embrace an alliance with King Kamran.

But Kamran is not the man he was even a few months ago. The administration of the city is now entirely in the hands of his Vizier, Yar Mahomed, who is arresting all the returning refugees, incarcerating them as best he can, and selling them as quickly as possible to passing Turkmen slave-traders.

'How else am I to rebuild this city and provide for all its people?' he demands when I point out, yet again, that his enslavement of Persians caused the siege in the first place and that Her Majesty's Government is dedicated to wiping out the disgusting and un-Christian trade. 'We must bring back the bazaars, we must start making carpets again, we must trade with the Turkmen and the Mongols, the Uzbeks and even the Persians. Your Great Britain, your East India Company, what are they to me?'

We say Britain can re-supply and re-arm the city. We say Her Majesty's Government is willing to offer money, material and men. 'But first, Your Lordship,' says Stoddart, 'You must abandon this trade in human flesh. These slaves are but people like you and me.'

The Vizier laughs. 'Like you, perhaps, but not like me. They are slaves. I am not.'

'They were not born slaves.'

'So much the worse for them,' says Yar Mahomed with another laugh. 'It shows how worthless they are if they cannot even keep themselves out of slavery. They are nothing, nothing, scum.'

'They are your own people.'

'Not mine,' he says. 'Now, tell me what help your Queen can offer me.'

We negotiate a little. One day the Vizier is willing to entertain the possibility of help from Her Majesty, the next he is dismissive of everything we offer or stand for. Stoddart is more patient about this than I am but even he becomes exasperated after a few weeks of vacillation from the Vizier.

A messenger arrives. I am to report to Sir William Macnaghten who will be seeking an audience with Maharaja Ranjeet Singh, King of the Sikhs, in Amritsar. There is to be no delay. I receive many false promises of eternal friendship from Yar Mahomed and a brotherly hug from the lurching King Kamran, who gives an incoherent little speech to his chiefs and invites me to return at the earliest opportunity. He swears to honour Great Britain, her eternal Queen Victoria, her children and her children's children and so on and I take my leave of the pestilential place.

*****

I am not sorry to be going, though I worry about poor Stoddart's prospects dealing with Yar Mahomed. The trek back to Amritsar is as long, slow and uncomfortable as the outward journey was. This time, though, I have the benefit of an escort of half a dozen men sent by Macnaghten and a guard of 20 supplied by Yar Mahomed himself. It is my belief the Vizier wishes to see me escorted out of the country never to return and requires his men to bear witness to my banishment.

We return via Kabul, where there is some commotion and no Burnes. The commotion is over rumours that the King, Dost Mohammed Khan, is preparing for war. The gossip in the bazaars is of an attack in the spring on Ranjeet Singh to recapture Peshawar. There is also talk of an alliance with the Russians and even discussion of making war against the British.

We press on after only a couple of nights in the city. Winter is almost upon us now and the passes are already thick with snow, inhospitable and bleak.

There are so many passes to negotiate. Less than ten miles from Kabul is the Khoord Kabul Pass followed by the short, but steep and narrow, Huft Kotul Pass and the ten-mile-long Jugdulluk Pass before we even reach Jalalabad.

We march as briskly as we can in these confined and forbidding places. The men and supplies are adequate to the task while I am pleased the funds provided by Macnaghten are sufficient to pacify the local tribesmen when they come, heavily-armed, to exact their tolls. We grin and smile and exchange compliments and buy their rugs, their woollen caps and their boots. The clouds and snows close in. We trudge through narrow defiles into the teeth of howling gales and driving snow. One of the Heratis contracts frostbite. Our doctor, William Brydon, sent with the expedition by Macnaghten, cuts off the man's left foot and we pay for him to be taken in by the natives for the winter. Whether he will survive and make it back to Herat is a moot point. Frostbite and amputation may be the lesser of two evils if the alternative is to linger at the mercy of the Khyberees who are about as trustworthy as Yar Mahomed and less friendly.

*****

Macnaghten makes me wait a full two days before he deigns to grant me an audience. I dismiss my escort of Heratis and kick my heels in his camp outside Amritsar, more or less ignored by my countrymen, their servants, the Sikhs, everyone. I have spent over a year at Her Majesty's service in a most abominable place and yet nobody is willing even to give me a civil word.

Eventually I understand why. Macnaghten regards my service in Herat as a singular failure. He summons me before breakfast on the third day and as he is poured more coffee – I am not invited to join him – he says, 'You have not ended the slave trade, you have not made close allies of Yar Mohamed and Shah Kamran, you have failed to secure the city for Her Majesty.'

I explain, as calmly as I can, that Kamran is a puppet King and the Vizier is entirely untrustworthy. He will take money from us and make endless promises but they will last only as long as he sees it as worth his while. He is open to the highest bidder but this is one auction we should not participate in.

'Do you know what is going on here, Pottinger?' Macnaghten asks, gazing at me through his blue-tinted spectacles with a frown on his brow. 'I am here on the Governor's business. Today or tomorrow, His Excellency Lord Eden will issue a declaration of war.' He puts down his cup of coffee with a flourish and looks at me with triumph. I am shocked.

'War? Against Ranjeet Singh?'

'Don't be ridiculous, Pottinger, of course not against the Maharaja. He is our loyal ally and the sworn enemy of our enemy.'

'Our enemy?'

'Dost Mohammed Khan, the King of Kabul.'

'Our enemy?' I ask again. 'How has it come to this? Burnes…'

'Sir Alexander Burnes quit Kabul some time ago, Pottinger, as you know very well. He could not persuade the Dost to ally himself with Her Majesty. And as you also know, the Tsar's men are everywhere hereabouts – in Herat it was Count Simonich, in Kabul there was the pestilential Captain Viktevitch. And the Dost showed himself ready to ally himself with our enemies. We know the Tsar's ambitions. You, Pottinger, temporarily thwarted Russia's Emperor at the gates of Herat – for which,' Macnaghten grudgingly concedes, 'You deserve our congratulations and thanks – but he will return. Afghanistan is the gateway to India; we must slam those gates firmly shut now, while we still can. That is why your failure to secure the peace in Herat is such a disappointment to us.'

'Sir, I don't understand. Are you saying that because the Shah of Persia failed to invade Herat, we must invade Kabul?'

'Don't be ridiculous, Pottinger. The fact is, Dost Mohammed Khan cannot be trusted. He is prepared to betray us to the Russians and he is a man of war who will not rest while the Sikhs control Peshawar which, I do not have to remind you, is on our side of the Hindu Kush and therefore way past the gates and half way up the drive to India itself. Which, in turn, means if the Dost takes Peshawar with Russian help, the Tsar has his route into India and we are at his mercy. This is our vulnerable frontier. It must be defended and we shall defend it.'

Macnaghten calls for more coffee and a servant rushes to pour while the Governor General's ambassador lights a cheroot. In a cloud of smoke, Macnaghten says, 'I am sending Darcy Todd to Herat. He will negotiate with Yar Mohamed and King Kamran and secure the Company's influence over the Western border of Afghanistan. Todd is an accomplished diplomat, Pottinger, not some soldier adventurer.'

I take it this disparaging phrase refers to me and it is all I can do not to protest. I know it is not in my best interests to contradict a man of such power and influence so I merely lower my head slightly in a humble bow and say, 'Well at least he won't have to deal with a siege when he gets there, and he will have Stoddart for company.'

Macnaghten concentrates on his coffee as, without once looking at me, he says, 'Stoddart will also be relieved of his duty in Herat.'

'Also?'

'Also.'

'I am being relieved of my duty?'

'Pottinger, you have been away for more than a year. You have conducted yourself with outstanding bravery and the Company is suitably grateful. But the world moves on, the political situation has changed. The Queen requires us to do our duty.'

I am now indignant to the point of anger. I say firmly, 'I have been doing my duty, Sir William.'

'So you have, Pottinger, so you have. And now your duty lies in another direction. You must return to Calcutta and write a full report of your activities and adventures. But first you must present yourself to Lord Eden. The Governor General is anxious to be reacquainted with you and hear more about what he is pleased to call your great success. You will find him in Ferozepore where I shall be joining you, along with Ranjeet Singh and his army, a few days after you. From Ferozepore, you will be going to Calcutta, Pottinger. We will be invading Afghanistan.'

I speak as calmly as I can, and slowly, measuring my words. I do not wish to turn what I expected, and hoped, to be a triumphant return into a disaster. But I certainly feel I am being undervalued for all the privation and danger I have endured. 'Todd has my best wishes, Sir William, but reaching any lasting agreement with Yar Mohamed and King Kamran will be a Herculean task; the King is a broken man, a drunk who commands no loyalty or respect any more. As for the Vizier, he is quite simply an untrustworthy, sly, duplicitous, cruel and ambitious man whose word is worthless.'

'I have every confidence Todd will succeed where others have failed, Pottinger.'

'I trust he will be well furnished with rupees, then, Sir William. The only thing that might bind the Vizier to us is money and then only for as long as the funds last.'

'As you know well, Pottinger, the Company requires us to practice economy at every opportunity. Todd will not have a fortune to dip into. He will have a couple of lakhs of rupees, perhaps, but that is all.'

'Then I regret to tell you, Sir William, that his mission will not be crowned with glory.'

Macnaghten frowns and stares at me for the first time. 'Pottinger, you are the hero of the hour but do be careful. Remember, sir, you looked for this service, we did not seek you out. You have behaved with nobility and courage. But do not waste your credit. Your superiors are your superiors still.'

*****

There is a lot to absorb. I am not going back to Herat. This I welcome, though not Macnaghten's view that I have somehow failed in my mission there. Todd will have no more success than Stoddart and I, especially as Macnaghten will strictly control his expenditure. Sir William is very keen on economies. He is not a Scot for nothing. When it comes to money, one would be forgiven for thinking the British East India Company was on the brink of bankruptcy, Sir William is so parsimonious. And nothing but money will keep Yar Mohamed loyal.

Still, I console myself, this is no longer my problem. I have the bleak prospect of exile in Calcutta to look forward to when everyone else is setting forth on a great adventure into Afghanistan. First, though, I must make my way to our camp at Ferozepore, less than a hundred miles away, to watch the army set out to conquer Afghanistan.

Happily, I have Sir Alexander Burnes to accompany me. Burnes is desperate to get back to Kabul.

'This business with the Russians, it was only a flirtation,' Burnes assures me as, accompanied by a squadron of light dragoons, we make our way to meet the great army assembling from all across India to take part in the invasion. 'The Dost wants Peshawar back, he's desperate for it. The place does actually belong to him and he will ally himself with anyone who will help restore it to him.'

'I can't see what he sees in it. It was a tumbledown wreck of a place when I was there,' I say.

'And so it will remain while Ranjeet Singh holds onto it. He is using it simply as a buffer to protect his kingdom. A fortress on his border, not a city. But he won't give it up. Why should he when he has won it through the right of conquest?'

'So the Dost can't have his city back?'

'No, he can't. So he won't declare himself unequivocally and uniquely our ally. He continues to flirt with Russia though the Russians have now gone home. Foolish man. It's all too late for him now, I'm afraid.'

'Too late?'

'The Governor General has declared Dost Mohammed Khan our enemy. They have issued what they call "The Simla Manifesto". It does not read well, Pottinger, it really doesn't. It starts by arguing my mission to Kabul was purely to promote trade with Afghanistan then it goes on about Persian designs on Herat, on Afghanistan and even on India itself.'

'Persian?' I turn in the saddle to look at Burnes, very smartly got up in his dragoon captain's uniform.

'Exactly. Nowhere is there any mention of the real enemy. Nowhere does this manifesto talk about the Tsar and the Russians. It uses the siege of Herat alone as evidence of Persian ambition and somehow conflates this with a suggestion that the Dost has shown what it calls "a systematic course of disrespect" towards me. You have to bear in mind, Pottinger, that this manifesto was issued before they knew the Persians had abandoned the siege of Herat, which is a bit embarrassing all round. Your great victory in Herat should put an end to all this nonsense about the Persian threat. Instead, it seems to have spurred Macnaghten and Eden into greater determination to get rid of the Dost.'

'And then what?'

Burnes halts his horse so I follow suit, bringing the whole escort party of thirty to a standstill. The land here is fertile and full of growth after the rains of summer. Even now, in early November, the temperature is up almost to eighty degrees, but with a brisk breeze to make it bearable.

Sir Alexander gazes ahead at the fat, rolling clouds and doesn't speak for a moment. He sighs and turns in his saddle to look at me. 'Dost Mohammed Khan is a good man, Pottinger. A good man. He is confused about what is in his best interests and he will not give up hope of regaining Peshawar. I did try to reason with him. I did warn him. I did my best to persuade him...' Burnes breaks off and stares ahead again at the darkening sky.

Burnes is clearly unhappy. 'Why did I leave Kabul, Pottinger? Because the Dost gave me no choice, the stupid man. He doesn't understand. I tried to explain. Perhaps I failed.'

'Failed?'

'Failed to make him understand just how powerful our nation truly is. Just how easily our army can crush him. If I had made him understand, he would not now be facing this ruin. And I failed with the Governor General and with that idiot Macnaghten.'

I laugh nervously. I have no reason to like Macnaghten but I am shocked to hear Burnes call him an idiot. 'Why an idiot?' I say.

'Because Macnaghten thinks he can replace one King of Kabul with another and all shall be well. He thinks Dost Mohammed Khan is not trustworthy. But why would he think some other King would be more honest and straightforward? My experience in Kabul tells me these are people given to no more than temporary alliances. Whatever is convenient or profitable suits them very well. But if something better comes along, old alliances are shrugged off and forgotten. There there's the tribalism, the factions, the territorialism and the blood feuds. Nothing is forgotten. Every slight has a price, every death demands another. It is not a straightforward place.'

'Does Macnaghten have a new king in mind?'

'Of course he does. We've kept one in reserve these thirteen years for just such an occasion. The new King will be the old King. Eden and Macnaghten will get rid of the Dost and replace him with Shah Soojah-ool-Moolk Doorani. It's all arranged. Soojah is already at Ferozepore with an army we have provided for him and is looking forward to getting his throne back.'

As we walk our horses on towards Ferozepore, Burnes explains Shah Soojah had not taken much persuading to become the figurehead of this expedition.

'Macnaghten went to the palace we provided for Shah Soojah in Ludhiana armed only with the gifts of a pistol, 500 rupees and the promise of an army to re-take the throne of Kabul,' Burnes continues, 'And within an hour the Shah was furnishing Macnaghten with a diamond ring to show his gratitude.

'I'm not surprised the old man was happy,' Burnes continues. 'He'd probably given up hope of ever getting his throne back again. After all, he's been trying to regain it for 30 years or more.'

'He was deposed by the Dost?' I ask.

'No, by the Dost's brother Fateh Khan. But Fateh Khan was killed and the Dost took over. Shah Soojah was King of Kabul for only six years. He took over from his brother, who was blinded by his enemies. Soojah is the last of the Dooranis who created the Afghan empire about a century ago. But Soojah was kicked out after he lost the Battle of Nimla in 1809. Beaten by his half-brother Mahmoud, not the Dost.

'Soojah spent years travelling from one tribe to the next, all over the Hindu Kush before someone sold him to Ranjeet Singh, King of the Sikhs. Soojah was forced to buy his freedom – the price set by Ranjeet was the most precious thing any King owned, the Koh-i-Noor diamond.'

'The mountain of light? I've seen it on Ranjeet,' I say. 'He wears it on his tunic.'

'It is the biggest diamond in the world,' Burnes says, 'And it has a long history. They say it was first stolen by Babur, the Mongol emperor, from some Hindu monks when he overran India about the time of our King Henry VIII. It was owned by Shah Jahan, who built the Taj Mahal. He had the diamond placed on his Peacock Throne. Since Soojah used it to buy his freedom, he's been a guest of the Company in Ludhiana but he's made three failed attempts to get back his throne, the last one, believe it or not, in an alliance with Ranjeet Singh. The Sikhs took Peshawar while Soojah reached Kandahar before being defeated in battle by Dost Mohammed Khan and fleeing for his life once again.

'Soojah refuses to accept that he was actually defeated. He says he simply ran out of money. Soojah says it costs 100,000 rupees a month to maintain an army in Afghanistan and even though he mortgaged or sold all the property he owns, and borrowed more, he came home deeply in debt.'

'Well I suppose it was a gamble which didn't pay off,' I say. 'So he bit Macnaghten's hand off when he was told we would regain the throne for him, I fancy?'

'Well yes and no,' says Burnes, 'As I said, at first Soojah was delighted, even gave Macnaghten a diamond ring to show his gratitude. But the next day he seemed a lot less impressed. Why, he wanted to know, had the Company waited thirty years for this? Why had the Company waited until he, Soojah, was old man?'

'How old is he?'

Burnes does not like the interruption and replies brusquely 'He is 53' before going on, 'Why, he wanted to know, was it planned before anyone deigned to consult the Shah himself? Why did this plan involve that dog Ranjeet Singh who had stolen the Koh-i-Noor and why were the Sikhs promised possession in perpetuity of Peshawar? Why were we treating him as a radish?'

'A radish?'

'A puppet, I think we might say,' Burnes smiles.

'You'd think Soojah might have despaired of ever regaining his throne,' I say to Burnes.

'I think he had. After he was turned back at Kandahar I do believe he thought the game was up. He had lost his country, he had lost his diamond and only a few weeks ago he lost his chief wife, Wafa Begum. Ironically, she is – was, I suppose – Dost Mohammed Khan's sister.' Burnes laughs bitterly. 'She was the one who negotiated his exile and won him a pension from the Company.'

'A pension?'

'Yes, 50,000 rupees a year though even that isn't apparently enough for the Shah and his seven wives, his innumerable concubines, his four sons, their families and all the other hangers-on at his court in exile.'

Burnes falls silent and we ride slowly on. The clouds are rolling around and the air is thick, damp and sultry. I shiver despite the heat.

'You know what, Pottinger?' says Burnes eventually. 'I have to go along with this invasion. I don't have any choice, do I?'

'Well, we all have orders,' I agree.

'Macnaghten will become Chief Minister and Envoy to Soojah in Kabul and I shall be his deputy.'

'Congratulations,' I say with a chuckle. 'I am delighted you will be able to return to the city where you have made so many friends.'

'I know, so am I. But in these circumstances, Pottinger? How will we dispose of Dost Mohammed Khan and his followers? He is a good man. I feel wretched for him and responsible, too.'

'Burnes,' I hear myself say, 'This is not your fault. No failing of yours is responsible for this invasion. If you want to lay the blame anywhere, look no further than that damned Frenchman Napoleon Bonaparte. If he hadn't thought about invading India with the help of the Russians, the Russians would never have got the idea for themselves. We defeat Napoleon but his mad scheming lives on and now we have to defend ourselves against the Tsar.'

'It's not the Russians we will be fighting, Pottinger, it's all the tribes of Afghanistan. And if there is one thing they enjoy even more than feuding among themselves, it's fighting a common enemy.'

CHAPTER 19

Ferozepore, November 1838

It is dusk. The plains are dusty and dry and there is a faint scent of jasmine in the air. There is peace. For the first time in months I can simply stare into the sunset and enjoy the sight without anxiety.

I have arrived in Ferozepore with Burnes, who immediately reported to the Governor General. I secure a lodging and I even find Hoosein, who is delirious to see me, jumping around like a dervish and calling out to a tall, gangling, handsome youth with lanky black hair who turns out to be Wasim, Maparah's son. Wasim falls to his knees and kisses the hem of my filthy trousers. I have to tell him about his mother's fate and the poor boy changes instantly from a confident youth to a bereft child.

I leave Hoosein to look after Wasim and go in search of Lord Eden, the Governor General. I should have tidied myself up a bit first but it doesn't occur to me. I am so accustomed to living with dust and grime, in threadbare native clothing and with my thick, unkempt beard, I never even think about the need to make myself more presentable.

It is obvious where the officers and Company men are dining – a vast marquee, brightly lit in the gloaming, with servants rushing to and fro and music from the military band carrying across the parade ground to where I stand contemplating the sunset.

At last, as the orange glow fades behind the mountains, I approach the durbar marquees with some caution. No sentries challenge me so I loiter by the entrance waiting for an opportunity to introduce myself to the Governor General.

As I stand watching the proceedings, several uniformed Indian servants try to shoo me away thinking I am a native. A couple of officers approached and one says, 'You, man, get out of here immediately. Go on, now, go. We don't want your sort here.' A couple of impressive-looking Sikhs in impeccable uniforms try to intimidate me into withdrawing without further fuss.

Before I utter any of the responses on the tip of my tongue, I see a young woman in an elegant pale blue ball-gown cross towards us. Her firm step clearly indicates a firm purpose. The fearsome Sikhs step back at the sight of her.

She – that is to say you, my dear, you, my Eleanor, my dear girl, you – you kneel in the deepest of curtseys, a slight smile playing on your lips and a much brighter smile darting from your eyes as you say, 'Lieutenant Pottinger, the Hero of Herat. It is my pleasure to welcome you back to India, sir, after your noble service to your Queen, your country and your God.'

The officers step back, appraise me anew, seek Miss Eden's permission to speak and greet me with cheers and smiles. 'Pottinger! The hero of Herat!' they cry, a refrain which sweeps the marquee as you, Eleanor, take hold of my arm at the elbow and guide me through the throng towards the top table where your brother sits in state. The band strikes up a new tune. I find out later it is called 'The Conquering Hero Comes' but everybody seems to know it already. The gentlemen rise to cheer, the ladies applaud. There are cries of approbation. Even three cheers.

This is a triumph. I cannot prevent a smile from spreading across my face. I may be as black as a native but my heart is the white, true heart of an Englishman, and this rapture is such balm to my heart it almost mends the wounds it has suffered over the last few months.

Lord Eden descends from his dais, or, as it were, his throne, and walks to meet us. 'Eleanor, how is it you know this brave man?' he asks his much younger sister, but with a smile.

'I met him at Simla, sir,' she says, looking at me, also with a smile, 'I knew him to be destined for great things, George. And now, here he is, the hero of Herat.'

'Here he is indeed,' says Lord Eden, shaking my hand with the utmost warmth as he raises his voice so what looks like a private conversation is turned into a speech, which silences the rowdy welcome as everyone hushes himself and his neighbour to listen to the Governor General of India as he says, 'Pottinger, my congratulations and, on behalf of Her Majesty, my thanks. All of India owes you a debt of gratitude, sir. Single-handedly you have defended Her Majesty's precious possession of India from the perfidious Persians. By your action, you have preserved this Empire. You have done your duty, Pottinger, with courage and fortitude. You have shown all the many virtues which have given our nation its pre-eminence among the peoples of the Earth and we must all learn by your example. You left India Lieutenant Pottinger; welcome back Major Eldred Pottinger.'

At this, His Lordship shakes my hand again, to whoops of approval and applause from the assembled company, and leads me to the table closest to his own, occupied by Generals and their wives. Miss Eden orders a place to be set for me at her side and I am required to greet my neighbours. On my left is Brigadier-General John Shelton of the 44th foot, a man I should have occasion to remember.

On this night, however, I bask in my triumph and the attention of the beautiful woman on my right hand side. I am lost in the scent of her perfume and the cacophony of noise – the band, the cheering, the laughter, the chatter, the servants as they come and go. I do not notice the Brigadier's reaction to my success.

Now, looking back, I realise he is angry. Eleanor makes him jealous by chattering away to me without addressing a single word to Shelton. He spends the evening staring at his food with a scowl on his face – I can visualise it even now, that hot, bulging-eyed, furious stare of his.

He says scarcely a word though I do remember him quoting, to no-one in particular, 'Pride goeth before destruction, and an haughty spirit before a fall.'

*****

I am clean, shaved and dressed in a fine borrowed uniform. I am invited to join the Governor-General's party and find myself once again sitting beside Miss Eden to view the meeting of Lord Eden, Ranjeet Singh and Shah Soojah. Burnes calls this carnival 'the field of the cloth of gold'. Certainly the meeting between King Henry VIII and some French king in the fifteen-hundreds was extravagant, so they say. This, though, must exceed it for splendour – Henry did not have cannon and rifles, he lacked fireworks and camels. He certainly never had any elephants while the pearls, rubies and diamonds on display, even assuming there were any, cannot possibly have matched those being shown off by the thousands of Sikh cavalrymen in their yellow and red satin uniforms mounted on chargers which are themselves kitted out in gold and silver tissue with sparkling diamonds on their reins. The magnificence is unmatched.

The fearsome and elegant followers of Maharaja Ranjeet Singh meet on the plains of Ferozepore with Lord Eden who is wearing a most impressive bright blue, braided rig-out leading a parade of his most senior officers all riding elephants, led by a marching band, supported by their own cavalry. Our European and native soldiers are all outfitted for the parade ground, flashing crimson and gold, their swords rattling in their sheaths, their horses' accoutrements shining and new. The constant salutes of our cannon, are returned by those of the Sikh army, and the cheers of the thousands of observers. The clouds of dust and the smells of horse, camel and elephant all mingle together to create a giddy sense that this was at once the greatest display of military might and pageantry the world has ever seen and at the same time one of the most chaotic.

The Maharaja is drunk, as it seems he often is. His servants carry small bottles of some firewater wherever he goes. It's supposed to have herbs and rosewater and who knows what else in it. I tried something similar once. It tastes a little like raw gin and seems to be pretty much pure alcohol. The Maharaja's endless consumption of this liquor helps to explain why, as his elephants approach the parade ground, he stands up unsteadily in his howdah, pulls down the trousers of his bright red outfit – red trousers, red tunic and red turban – and takes a piss, indifferent to the fate of those in the seething crowds standing nearby.

I see Shah Soojah in his howdah. He and his retinue approach from the east as Lord Eden comes north while Maharajah Ranjeet travels south to the parade ground and the durbar tents. This is my first sight of the next King of Kabul. Soojah is dignified, I suppose; sober at least; a little world-weary as he might well be, given this latest spin of fortune's wheel. He wears a long beard down to his waist which would certainly be white if he did not apply some kind of dye to it regularly. His face looks grim and serious, unlike the maharaja, who smiles and grins all round, and unlike Lord Eden, who looks gratified at this great parade he had conjured into being.

'How old Shah Soojah looks,' Eleanor whispers to me as we wait, along with the Governor General's family and entourage, on a specially-erected viewing platform.

'Yes, he is an old man,' I agree. 'All the better for us, I suppose. A puppet king in a puppet state.' I do not add that I worry whether Soojah will be accepted by the Afghans themselves, who do not take kindly to foreign interference. They may see Soojah as a foreigner himself now, after all this time, and they will know where he gets his orders from so they will treat him with the utmost suspicion.

Even so, my fellow officers are desperate to be part of the Army of the Indus, as this force has been named. Rumour has it the commander-in-chief, Lieutenant General Sir Henry Fane, has decided to reduce the number of regiments required for the invasion now we are not facing a threat from either the Persians or the Russians. There is great concern among Company men that many will be deprived of the adventure, excitement and advancement this invasion represents. It seems the lucky regiments will be chosen by lot. It is rumoured Fane has decided not to bother leading the expedition and will leave the job to Sir Willoughby Cotton of the British army. This will infuriate William Nott, who is also here in Ferozepore. Nott is also a Major General, the same rank as Cotton, but Cotton is in the service of Her Majesty the Queen while Nott is only in the service of the British East India Company and we Company men are all of the opinion the Government in London, as well as the Governor General and his staff over here, see officers in the Queen's service as automatically superior to officers employed by the Company.

There is no reason they should be seen as our superiors. We have the same training and we in the East have greater challenges and responsibilities. We have even seen active service, which is more than can be said for most of the Queen's men, who bought their commissions and secured their promotions through marriages and connections rather than through the hard work and hard-won experience of men like William Nott. They haven't taken part in a single skirmish since Waterloo.

*****

Before the Army of the Indus marches away, there is a celebration dinner for Shah Soojah and Ranjeet Singh. It is a magnificent display of silverware and glass, regimental flummery and uniforms.

Miss Eden asks, 'Tell me, dear Major Pottinger, why are we going into Afghanistan? The Persians failed to take Herat, thanks to you, and the Russians have gone home. They have abandoned Dost Mohammed Khan in Kabul. So the threat my brother describes in his great manifesto,' Eleanor giggles as if the idea of her brother, the Governor of India, issuing a manifesto justifying a war which might seem a little absurd, 'The threat in his manifesto has gone away. Surely there is no threat.' She giggles again. 'Is that not the case dear Major Pottinger?' She looks at me with wide brown eyes as if this is the most innocent question in the world though she knows well how subversive it is.

'Your brother the Governor General has set out his justifications, madam,' I say as diplomatically as I can. I do not fear our being overheard for there is a din all round us and we sit some distance from the top table at this banquet in honour of what the Governor General calls the triple alliance.

'Well, Major Pottinger?' asks Miss Eden again, her eyes smiling though her mouth looks stern, 'It looks to me as if we are swapping one untrustworthy despot for another. How can we trust Shah Soojah any more than we can trust Dost Mohammed Khan?'

'You may have a point, madam, and my own experience in that country suggests one can have little faith in any of these Mohammedans. They betray each other regularly. Whole families will hold a grudge for generation after generation. They will fight to the death for a cause which has been lost in the mists of time. We would be unwise to trust any of these people too much, I agree. Shah Soojah may be no better a despot than Dost Mohammed but Soojah is at least our despot and therefore more likely to act in our favour than the Dost.'

'Not according to Sir Alexander Burnes or so I hear,' says Miss Eden with a smile.

'I could not say, madam.'

'You are acquainted with Sir Alexander, Major Pottinger?'

'I have had that privilege, madam.'

'Then, saving your presence, you will know he is our greatest living expert on Afghanistan. You will have read his treatise on his travels there.'

'Of course.'

'So if Sir Alexander disapproves...'

'Sir Alexander does not disapprove.'

Here Miss Eden once again giggles and hides her amusement behind her napkin. The noise of competing bands, the cheering and clatter of the diners, make it difficult to hear what she is saying. I lean closer, apologising for missing her comment. She still smells of roses and I am almost overcome by the scent and its reminders of wet, green, beautiful Belfast.

'Well, if he does not disapprove, you know why he does not disapprove, I suppose, Major Pottinger? Shall I tell you?' She stares at me with her glittering, mischievous eyes. 'Sir Alexander has been promised Sir William Macnaghten's job once we are settled in Kabul and Shah Soojah is safe on his throne.'

I draw back, sit upright, stare ahead at the people opposite – one of the Maharaja's Ministers and Miss Eden's sister Emily, an old spinster of forty – more than twice Eleanor's age – who takes the role of wife for her brother. Does this mean Burnes has been bought off? Despite all his misgivings about getting rid of Dost Mohammed, has his ambition got the better of him?

My Miss Eden has a look of smug satisfaction, having imparted this piece of gossip. She follows my gaze, wipes the smirk from her face, pats my arm gently and changes the subject tactfully. 'There are eight of us sisters,' she says, 'Emily is more of a mother to me than anything else.' Her sister catches her eye and frowns across the candlelight at her. My Miss Eden chuckles. 'There's also, as far as I can remember, Fanny, Pamela, Theresa, Agnes, Mary and Harriet. I also have six brothers – George, of course, but also William, Robert, Gilbert, Ashley and Arthur though I hardly know any of them, they are mostly so much older than me. I had to come out here with Emily and Fanny because nobody knew what to do with me otherwise.'

'And are you enjoying yourself, Miss Eden?' I ask but before I receive an answer there is a commotion and one of the Sikh bands strikes up a new tune as thirty lithe and sensuous young women begin to dance in front of us, much to the delight of the Maharaja. I can see most of the English ladies are by no means as attracted to this display of almost-naked flesh. I sneak a glance at Miss Eden, who looks agog at this display, but then I glance over at her much-older sister and see my own interest thoroughly disapproved-of as I catch her eye and note her stern frown.

I look back at the girls as they seem to sway and roll to the baleful caterwauling of an ancient old crone with few teeth, the not-very-rhythmic beating of drums and a tuneless howl created by flutes of some sort and an instrument which is played a little like a violin, though without the melodic notes which often accompany such a thing. I admit I do not have a good ear for music but this racket assaults the ears even as the dancers ravish the eyes. The Sikhs and most of the Europeans are enthralled, however, and this may have something to do with the circulation of the strong liquor so beloved of the Maharaja, much to the disapproval of ladies such as Miss Emily and Miss Fanny Eden, not to mention others like Lady Sale and Lady Cotton.

As the celebrations continue, I think back on my audience yesterday with Lord Eden in the Governor-General's private quarters. After our dinner the night before, I was ordered to present myself the following day to make a further report on my experiences. Macnaghten was there, having arrived ahead of Ranjeet Singh. The Secretary was silent throughout our meeting. It was hard to remember only the other day he described my activities in Herat as a failure.

I gave Lord Eden an account of the siege and my own role in it. I do not exaggerate and try to be plain, straightforward and honest. Mostly, I tell him, there was little I was able to do to influence the outcome one way or the other.

Lord Eden begs to differ. In the presence not just of Macnaghten but his senior commanders including Generals Fane, Nott and Cotton and even Brigadier General Shelton, Lord Eden formally announces my promotion, says it is back-dated by a year and that my pay shall increase by 1,000 rupees a month, also back-dated a year. This pleases me enormously as I am now able to remit substantial funds to my step-mother as well as pay Hoosein for the first time in over a year.

Lord Eden gives a little speech. 'Gentlemen,' he says, 'As we set out with our Army of the Indus to bring back honour and justice to an uncivilised and difficult territory, allow me to present to you Major Eldred Pottinger, late of Herat at the Western edge of that country. Major Pottinger has done this Company, her Majesty and this nation great service in single-handedly holding off a determined and pestilential attack on Herat and, therefore, on our own possessions in India, for almost a year, to the despair or our enemies and to his and our great honour. It was a most chivalrous adventure. Major Pottinger is widely admired for his noble conduct, his fortitude and bravery which achieved extraordinary results. Gentlemen, I trust our army is filled with similarly brave young men but in the meantime it is my duty and great pleasure, as the representative of Her Majesty the Queen, to bestow Major Pottinger with this medal to signify he has been admitted as a Companion of the Most Honourable Military Order of the Bath and to present him with this sword of honour.'

I say I wish to have an active role in the war, a chance to return to the Bombay Artillery and join the invasion, but Lord Eden says the information I gathered during my time in Afghanistan is too valuable to lose. I must go to Calcutta and write a full report.

I am satisfied. Never mind Macnaghten, Lord Eden has honoured me, in front of the generals of the army. I am held up as an example of honour, courage and fortitude. Now, tonight, I sit beside his beautiful youngest sister whose animated features and glorious smile suggest these whirling dancers are not offensive to her but, if anything, exotic and exciting. Never mind Macnaghten, I tell myself, and never mind that fool Shelton with his Bible quotes. Here, I am honoured; here, I am hopeful; here, I am happy.

CHAPTER 20

Fort William, Calcutta, December 1842

It is all so petty, this cavilling about money. One of the charges goes right back to Herat. So long ago. So much blood. So much treasure. Eight hundred rupees? Burnes used to spend more than that in a single night. The Company spent thousands… hundreds of thousands…

When the Shah of Persia left us in Herat to the pestilence, starvation and emptiness of a victorious and defeated city, he also left us deep in debt. For months I had to borrow from a moneylender in what was left of Herat's bazaar, at exorbitant rates of interest. Stoddart was able to repay my debts out of Government funds provided by McNeill. One of Stoddart's servants was required to complete endless paperwork which I was obliged to sign.   Little did I know this entirely necessary transaction would come back to haunt me – papers signed Lieutenant Pottinger from four years ago are now being used as evidence of how I have misused Company money. I have not repaid the money because these were expenses incurred in defence of our country and on behalf of the Company. To pretend otherwise is laughable. And yet these funds, only eight hundred Rupees, are included in the charges against me.

And there is no Stoddart alive to defend me. He escaped the Afghan massacre but only because he was prisoner of the mad King of Bokara.

That was thanks to Yar Mahomed, the vile Vizier of Herat. In Bokara they actually boasted about Yar Mahomed's request that Stoddart be tortured and put to death. The poor man was thrown into a dungeon for months, forced to become a Muslim and eventually hauled him out for a public beheading alongside his would-be rescuer, Colonel Arthur Connolly. And the Company didn't lift a finger to prevent it though the two men were incarcerated for many weeks before they were murdered.

I mourn for Stoddart, a decent and humorous fellow whose death will, alas, go unavenged.

*****

A servant presents me with a copy of 'The Times of India' which has published a letter from my brother John. He concludes: 'I suppose some example must be made "pour encourager les autres" and to satisfy the nation that a British army is not to be led into a trap and then left to be slaughtered, with impunity to their leaders. I beg your assistance to prevent such a possibility as my brother being made one of the scapegoats for errors which he had no authority to prevent, and which were perpetrated in direct opposition to his wishes and advice.'

CHAPTER 21

Ferozepore, November 1838

It's always pleasant to enjoy a little flirtation. There is something immensely encouraging when a young and attractive woman flutters her eyelashes, takes hold of your sleeve, looks up into your eyes with a spark of wit, a smile on her red lips and a laugh rising in her slender throat. After weeks of travelling through enemy territory and months of trial by siege, to meet Eleanor Eden again is one of those unexpected delights which offer more satisfaction even than a promotion or a pay rise.

It is a pity our time together is so short. Miss Eden is to depart with the Governor General's entourage for Simla. I must report to Calcutta.

'You are so much thinner, Major Pottinger,' she says with a laugh, when I present myself to make my farewells. I am in my dress uniform with my new insignia. I am also clean-shaven and Hoosein has gone to some trouble to ensure I am got-up more like an officer and gentleman than for many months past. I suspect I even smell reasonably pleasant. 'We shall have to feed you up again before you go back on active service,' says Miss Eden.

We are strolling across the parade ground a few days after the great Army of the Indus finally departed for Afghanistan. There is no news of any significance yet, of course, but the sight of all those horses, camels and elephants, camp followers and servants, not to mention the regiments themselves marching off towards the mountains could not but stir mixed emotions in my breast.

I am envious of all those destined for battle and glory. A proper fight against our own country's enemy is far to be preferred to the long, slow attrition I faced in Herat. On the other hand, I cannot help saying to Miss Eden, 'Thinner I may be, madam, but I am at least fit for a fight.'

'Why Major Pottinger, are you suggesting our army is not?' She stops and shields her eyes from the glare of the sun to look up at me.

I do not want to discuss the military capabilities of our regiments bound for Kabul or the competence of their generals. I want to discuss the way the sunlight plays on her hair, I want to stroke her cheek, I want to kiss her on those lovely lips and pull her to me in her light-blue gown. I feel sure my attentions would not be unwelcome. Yet how can we pursue any passion on a parade ground, in full view of the remnants of the Indian army, as her brother the Governor General and his staff prepare for their departure? We cannot.

'Miss Eden,' I say.

'Major Pottinger?' she says lightly.

'Miss Eden,' I say again but I cannot carry on. I find myself tongue-tied.

'What is this? The Hero of Herat, the famous Major Eldred Pottinger, lost for words? How can this be?

'The army, Miss Eden, will you follow it?' I cannot say anything more intimate.

'We are departing for Simla, Major, as you know. And you are bound for?'

'Calcutta, madam.'

'Ah yes, there to retire and write your memoirs like all good old folk,' she says and resumes our stroll across the parade ground towards the recently-constructed pavilions which hosted the great durbar involving the Governor General, the King of the Sikhs Ranjeet Singh and the once and future King of Kabul, Shah Soojah.

'Not exactly,' I say, rising to her bait. I know she is laughing at me but I feel some need to justify my retreat to India at a time when we are at war. 'I have to provide your brother and his officers with as much intelligence about Afghanistan as they require. It will take some time to make a full report to them on the condition of the country.'

'The condition of the country?'

'The lie of the land, as it were. The geography, the flora and fauna, the rivers and mountains, the temper of the people, their tribes and trades, their superstitions and so on. You forget, madam, that most of us even here in Hindustan live more or less in ignorance of life on the other side of the Hindu Kush. We need to accumulate as much information as possible…'

'In case we invade their country and are caught out by our own ignorance?' She stops and looks at me with a glint in her eye and an expression of intelligence and seriousness which belies her usually frivolous attitude.

'Well…' I hesitate.

'Well? Well. Of course well. It would indeed be in our interests to know as much we can about a country before invading it.' She smiles and skips away as she adds, 'I do so agree with you, Major Pottinger, though I have yet to hear any of his advisers make that point to my brother. And besides, it is too late now, is it not?'

She steps out ahead of me and I am obliged to stride swiftly to catch up with her. 'You are apprehensive about our little war, Miss Eden?'

'No war can be entered into lightly, Major. And most wars are contrary to God's laws.'

'As for that, madam, it is surely right that we protect these lands from invasion. One of the results of doing this will be to encourage more Hindus and Muslims to convert to our faith, Miss Eden. Surely this is doing God's work.'

'Cleverly argued, Major. You should be a lawyer.' She smiles briefly but wrings her hands at the same time, her expression changing again, a frown creates a line of perplexity across her high forehead. Her eyes seem to be watering a little. 'I am afraid, Eldred. I own it, I am a little afraid.'

I resist the temptation to take a step towards her, fling my arms protectively around her shoulders, draw her close to me and kiss the top of her head. We are in public. She is the Governor General's sister. I would be disgracing her, perhaps.

Instead I step between Miss Eden and the sun, to cast her into shadow and save her from squinting at me as she has been doing. I stand with my arms folded across my chest, realise I look like a large sentry and awkwardly wonder what to do with my hands. I am embarrassed as I say, 'There is little enough to be afraid of, Miss Eden. Our army is far superior to anything it might meet. We have an alliance with Ranjeet Singh whose Sikhs are fearsome warriors. The Afghans, you know, are not one people but several – divided into tribes and factions, set against each other, not one to be fully trusted, always falling on one another's throats. We shall have no difficulty with the Afghans as long as they carry on having difficulties with each other. There are so many different clans, worse even than the Macdougalls and Campells and...'

'The Burneses and Macnaghtens?'

'Just so. There are the Afghans, of course, who call themselves Pathans or Pashtuns but there are also Belochees, Tartars of all descriptions, Persians, including Tajiks, Indians such as Kashmerians, the Hazari, the Kyberees who guard the infamous pass, the mad Ghilzai mountain men and so on. And while we have divisions between Scots, Welsh and Irish, it is nothing to these people – their feuds are personal and go on for ever. Nothing is forgotten; nothing is forgiven. Dost Mohammed Khan may be King of Kabul for a few months more but he has never ruled the whole country from the mountains to the edge of Persia. His successor will be no more successful in creating a single, united kingdom ruled from a capital city.'

Miss Eden takes hold of my arm between the wrist and elbow as if she would march me off to her brother there and then. 'So you think our invasion is a foolish thing, Major?'

'I have no opinion on the politics, madam. I have every reason to believe the Russians constitute a threat to the security of India. They certainly have designs on Afghanistan and they cannot possibly want it for its own sake – the country is too poor and unstable to interest even an imperialist like the Tsar. If the Russians moved into Afghanistan it would only be to get closer to India and threaten our interests here. So, of course, politically, your brother Lord Eden is right to seek a method of protecting this country, and the Company's interests here, from the Tsar. Whether invading Afghanistan and replacing Dost Mohammed Khan is the best way of securing this is not a question I am qualified to answer.'

'But you can say whether it is likely to be a success, can you not, Major Pottinger?'

'It will be a success, of course, Miss Eden. We have the overwhelming force, the discipline and the resources necessary to pull it off without too much effort. Taking the country is the easy part, I am afraid. Holding it will be more difficult, I think.'

'More difficult?'

'It will cost us a great deal of money. To keep the Afghans on our side we will have to lash out thousands of rupees, I fear, Miss Eden, and the resources of the country are insufficient to generate those funds for us.'

Miss Eden laughs at me and relaxes, bouncing up and down on her toes as if she were about to start dancing. 'Oh well, if it is all just a question of money, we have nothing to be afraid of. We are the richest nation on earth and India is our gold mine, isn't that so Major? How delightful…'

*****

With an escort of half a dozen native dragoons, as well as Hoosein and Wasim, I leave Ferozepore for Calcutta. It is as cool as it gets in the Punjab today, which means it would be a pleasant spring day in England, making our 1,000-mile journey seem a congenial way of passing the time. Unhurried, well-fed, more or less safe from danger, I feel myself relaxing for the first time since I set foot in Afghanistan.

Miss Eden and the Governor General's entourage left two days ago. The Europeans in their howdahs on the back of their elephants, followed by the dragoons on horseback and the laden camels last of all.

Lord Eden's youngest sister promises to write to me and tells me we shall meet again. I do hope she is right. I find myself lapsing into daydreams of marrying Miss Eden and idly wonder whether such a match might be possible now I have made something of a name for myself and her brother, the Governor General, is full of praise for my exploits. I doubt if I could do much better for myself than to marry into the Eden family.

CHAPTER 22

Fort William, Calcutta, December 1842

That was then. Now Eleanor is on her way back to England in the wake of her disgraced brother who, despite everything, is now the Earl of Auckland. I, meanwhile, am confined to my quarters here in Calcutta overlooking a courtyard as I celebrate Christmas at Lord Ellenborough's pleasure with my jailer Henry Lloyd and George Broadhurst, my attorney.

Fort William is our great Company headquarters in this city, built of stone and almost certainly – though it has never been tested – secure from any attack. The place covers 1,200 acres, has a handsome new church of St Peter, and houses two infantry regiments and the artillery as well as the Supreme Court. Beyond its walls is the river on one side and a huge expanse of open land between the fort and the teeming, filthy city, which gives us a commanding view on all sides, makes an attack unlikely to succeed and preserves us a little from the stench of the backstreets.

The Company has even decided to create a special garden for the natives, which was originally to be called the Auckland Gardens but has already been re-named Eden Gardens. It seems Ellenborough, the new Governor General, thinks naming it Eden rather than Auckland is a way of expunging his predecessor's name from the annals of shame while still showing a modicum of respect because Eden is Auckland's family name as well as the name of Paradise on Earth before the Fall of Adam and Eve. He can pretend to himself the name is Biblical rather than commemorating a failure.

Captain Broadhurst is a large and humorous fellow who has spent his entire career with the Company as an attorney – 'the original barrack-room lawyer,' he says in his jovial way – and has failed to gain preferment largely because he constantly takes the part of the accused man rather than the Company's side. 'It's not through any desire to see justice being done, I assure you,' he tells me. 'It's just that none of the other fellows will stoop to defend the natives when they're accused of stealing from the Mess or raping one of their own.'

'So I am relegated to the ranks of the natives, am I?'

Broadhurst and I are sitting outside my little room of a prison with Lloyd hovering in the background, part servant, part spy. We are celebrating Christmas with some gin he has procured for us from the Mess. I am allowed in the Mess but my fellow officers shun me, as if frightened that charges of cowardice and misuse of public funds might somehow be infectious. I don't know any of them anyway. Since the massacre, most of the fellows I might once have counted as friends are dead – except for the hostages who survived with me, now blown to the four winds while I await my court martial and the evidence of that idiot Shelton.

I receive letters. My brother John, of course, is still busily pleading my innocence to anyone who will listen. I warn him not to make too much of a fuss for fear of destroying his own career as mine has clearly been ruined no matter what the outcome of my impending trial.

Fiorentina Sale is a regular correspondent, wishing me well and praising my devotion to her and her companions. Lady Macnaghten deigns to offer her condolences and support. My uncle Sir Henry writes to tell me he has every confidence in my acquittal and inviting me to join him in our new city of Victoria which is on an island called Hong Kong on the fringes of China. He says we are setting up a colony there to ensure the continuation of our trade in opium. Sir Henry says 'this is a superb country, my dear boy, and every single hour I have passed here has convinced me of the necessity and desirability of our possessing such a settlement as an emporium for our trade and a place from which Her Majesty's subjects in China may be alike protected and controlled.'

I suppose if I ever get out of this confinement I may as well go and join him. No doubt there is work to be done there and I do not see how I can continue to serve the Company in India whatever happens in this ridiculous court martial.

I tell Broadhurst this and he laughs. 'Victoria? Nothing to be gained there, old man, but an addiction to opium. I have to tell you, opium is not as pleasant as some people say it is. I have eaten it myself. I lived a hundred years in one night and swore never to try it again.' We have some more gin with quinine tonic. They say it's healthful though I have my doubts.

'Now as to the evidence, Pottinger,' Broadhurst continues, 'We need to consider the accusations you are facing and how we shall respond to them.'

'What evidence?' I sit up in my chair and lean across our small table to confront my lawyer. 'There is no evidence.' I slam my palm down to emphasise the point.

'Well, Eldred, that is not strictly true is it? The evidence may not be substantial but we will have to present a counter-argument which undermines whatever the prosecution witnesses may say. For instance, there's the money?'

'The money?'

'The lakhs of rupees you promised to buy the hostages' freedom. Not to mention the eight hundred rupees you received in Herat.'

'Necessary expenses. If you spend over a year in a city on the edge of nowhere promising payment to various traders, thieves, black-marketeers, Ministers, Viziers and so on, you have to spend money and when there is none forthcoming you have to borrow it from a moneylender.'

'Of course, of course,' says Broadhurst, 'But you failed to itemise these expenses. Naturally the Company is concerned to know whether the money was disbursed on Company business.'

'What other business do you suppose I had in Herat than Company business?' I am exasperated and find myself being aggressive with the man who is, it seems, my only friend at the moment but I cannot restrain myself. 'I was not there for any other reason than to defend the God-forsaken place on behalf of my Queen and my country. Are you seriously suggesting I spent any of that money unnecessarily? It's a libel.' I stare out across the fort's courtyard as a small party of native soldiers haphazardly go through the exercise of loading a cannon. 'It is all so wicked. When I came back from Herat I was hailed as a hero and praised by the Governor General himself. Now...'

'The Governor General has been replaced, Eldred, as you know,' says Broadhurst in a calm and reasonable voice intended to coax me back into humour, 'The new regime wishes to distance itself as far as possible from the chaos of the invasion and everyone involved in it.'

CHAPTER 23

Kabul, August 1841

Major General Sir William Elphinstone would once have passed for a tall man. I imagine in his youth he might have been a ramrod straight officer with a full head of hair and a patrician attitude. The sort of fellow, though Scotch by birth, who was energetic, strong and indefatigable. He'd have to be. When he was young, he was in Wellington's 33rd Regiment of Foot.

That's 25 years ago and even then Elphinstone was 33 years old. Now they have brought him out of semi-retirement to take charge here in Kabul and we must pray very hard there is no fighting to be done. The man is clearly unwell and quite probably not right in the head.

My interview with him is short and to the point. 'Ah Pottinger,' he says quite genially, pouring himself a glass of port and indicating I should take one as well. 'I have heard all about you, the Hero of Herat and all that, isn't it? Yes? Yes?'

The General sits on a threadbare sofa with his legs propped on a footstool, wearing no boots, merely thin white cotton socks. A cigar rests on a small table at his side. Elphinstone is clearly doing his best to recreate the atmosphere of his club in London.

'A while ago now, sir,' I say.

'Modesty, Pottinger, modesty, eh yes? Yes? I like that in a man.

Wellington was never modest you know. No. Never modest whatever his other virtues. Great man, though, Pottinger, Wellington, yes? Yes?'

'Indeed, sir, indeed.'

'Now sit down, Pottinger, sit down, have some port man.' The General indicates a chair. I feel obliged to do as he asks though it is still only half past ten in the morning. The port is light, almost pinkish, and very sweet. I sip it with pleasure, despite the hour. 'The Duke, Pottinger, not even in Government now. Did you know that? I know how slowly news travels in these parts. That dreadful man Melbourne, would you believe it?' As Elphinstone goes on about politics back at home, I have a chance to study him. Though he remains seated, it is clear his natural stance is now stooped, his body has run to fat and his limbs appear to hang heavily on him. His uniform is untidy, his bald pate glistens with perspiration though the day is not especially hot. He slouches in his chair, legs propped up on a stool. Rumour has it he suffers from gout. He certainly pauses, breathes heavily, resorts to his glass regularly, and speaks in a reedy voice, without any natural authority, hissing his Ss in a whistle like the old man he has become. 'Melbourne,' he is saying, 'Is the young Queen's favourite but she will soon see the merits of the Iron Duke, yes? Yes? Yes? And Sir Robert of course. Peel the reformer. Are you interested in politics, Pottinger?'

'Well I am here as a political officer, sir, so it would be a brave man who said he was not but the affairs of our Government on the other side of the world are not my first concern, sir.'

Elphinstone isn't listening. He is rubbing his right arm. 'Confound it all,' he says. 'I seem to have ricked a muscle. I am a martyr to ailments, Pottinger.' He smiles wryly, 'Can't imagine why they picked on me to command this ludicrous outpost, yes? Yes? Still, needs must, I suppose. Queen and country and all that. And why are you here again? Remind me, my boy, remind me.'

'I am paying my respects, sir, on my way through Kabul. Though I have yet to receive an audience with Sir William, sir, I believe I am to take up a position as Political Officer in Charikar. We have a small garrison there…'

'Do we indeed? Very well, then, Major Pottinger, my boy, very good. This port, first rate, considering, don't you think? Some of those idiots killed themselves on brandy on the march over here, did you know that?' Elphinstone chuckles and as a consequence dribbles of port stray onto his grey whiskers. 'Thought brandy would quench their thirst. In the desert? Can you believe it? Ha!'

I do not know what to say so I remain silent. I have heard this story. It is one of the many minor mishaps which befell our army on its long, almost disastrous march into Afghanistan. 'Anyway,' says Elphinstone conversationally, 'Soon as they name my successor I shall be gone from this place. Kabul. Seen much of it yet, Pottinger? Not much to see really. The palace and the castle, I suppose. The bazaar of course. That's it. Filthy streets, little alleyways, flies everywhere. And goats. Have you ever seen so many goats?'

'I was here a couple of years ago, sir,' I remind him.

'Of course you were, of course. On your way to where was it now? Herat? Is that it? Yes, yes, well, well. Herat, of course. The Hero of Herat. That's you, isn't it my boy.' Elphinstone raises his glass in a good-natured salute, drinks off its contents and motions to the boy for more.

A voice is raised outside on the veranda of the General's house. A native guard says, 'The general is in conference, sir.' 'Conference be damned,' declares a more forceful British voice as the door crashes open and in strides Brigadier General John Shelton of the 44th Foot. He does not bother to introduce himself but strides across the wooden floor to where Elphinstone is ensconced and declares: 'Elphie, when is that damnable house going to be ready then? When?'

The General winces slightly, looks up at his inquisitor apologetically, reaching for his re-filled glass as a form of comfort or protection, sips briefly and declares, 'They said in three days' time, brigadier.'

'They said in three days' time over a week ago. It's simply not good enough you know Elphie. Not good enough at all. I have already had to put that man Mackenzie on a charge.'

'Mackenzie? A charge? Why, brigadier?'

'Requisitioned a team of sappers to improve some damned-fool part of the cantonment when they should have been completing my residence, Elphie. Told Mackenzie it was none of his damned affair to requisition my builders.'

As Shelton talks, he struts to and fro in front of Elphinstone, his leather boots emphasising his irritability by drumming their own tattoo on the floor. I wonder why the General hasn't acquired some carpets for the room, given that they are one of the few products of this country to be generally admired. Shelton is a short, thin man with a furrowed, untrustworthy face and close-set eyes. He still has most of his hair, though it has largely turned grey, as well as a thick, grey beard. He is in his fifties, I suppose, and has an air of furious disappointment about him which may well have been exacerbated by the loss of his right arm. The empty sleeve swings unnecessarily from his military greatcoat as if it, too, were emphasising Shelton's points for him and shared his irritation.

'This won't do, Elphie, this really will not do.'

'Have you met Major Pottinger?' Elphinstone asks, waving a hand vaguely in my direction, 'He is the Hero of Herat, you know. We are most honoured to have him come among us.'

'Yes, Pottinger,' Shelton says without breaking stride, acknowledging me with the slightest nod of his head – I salute briskly in return – 'I shall tell Mackenzie to report to you directly, Elphie. You will have to deal with it. This is just too bad, too bad.'

And with that, Shelton storms out of the room again, slamming the door so hard the whole wooden structure of the General's house seems to shudder.

'Oh dear,' says Elphinstone. 'They say he is a very brave man but I do wish he could be a little more accommodating, I do indeed.'

*****

Assured and relaxed, king of all he surveys, Sir Alexander Burnes looks down from the fortified battlements of the Balar Hissar across the city of Kabul towards the army encampment, a cantonment where work is still going on to build more permanent residences for the senior officers. It is an attractive view: The town has several mosques and a huge market on our left, with its winding streets, its shouts and cries, the smells of cooking mingling with those of animals, its several mansions with their fertile, well-watered gardens hidden from the view of the passing street urchins. Further away, the mountainous Khoord Kabul, foothills of the Hindu Kush, climb inexorably towards the Khyber Pass and ultimately to India and home.

'You've seen the General, then?' Burnes asks casually as we enjoy the view. Towards the Kabul River a peasant is trying to manoeuvre three recalcitrant goats across a narrow wooden bridge. Their protests can be distinctly heard above the parade-ground shouts from the cantonment, the occasional cawing of the King's peacocks, the cries of the vendors in the market, the rumble of wheels, the protests of camels and the bleating of sheep, not to mention the unspeakable wailing of the muezzins calling the Muslims to prayer, which, collectively, seem to be the never-ending background noise of this place.

'Elphinstone? Of course. First port of call.'

'I suppose so.' Burnes strokes his neatly-trimmed moustache and gazes into the middle-distance. 'What did you make of him?'

'Doesn't seem terribly… what shall I say? … energetic.' I pause. Burnes does not react. He is clearly waiting for me to ask, 'What do you think?'

'Man's a blithering idiot. A superannuated buffoon, too old, too infirm, too indecisive, too feeble. And then there's that awful man Shelton.'

'The Brigadier-General?'

'Thinks he should be in command. Nothing but contempt for Elphie and not shy about demonstrating it at every opportunity. Troops hate Shelton, Shelton hates Elphie, Elphie loves everybody. God help us if we ever get into a fight.'

I point towards the encampment. There are low earth walls surrounded by a dry ditch, gates on each side manned by a couple of sentries, a few cannon and several wooden huts for stores, barracks, stables, officers' mess and married quarters as well as lines of tents and the Union Flag fluttering in the breeze in the centre of the parade ground. 'You wouldn't want to have to defend the camp from an attack,' I observe cautiously. It does not do to criticise, though some flaws are so obvious it would be difficult for a soldier of the meanest intelligence to miss the fact that his headquarters were indefensible.

'Army should be here, inside the Balar Hissar,' says Burnes, slapping the solid stone battlements. 'This castle's impregnable. These walls are built into the rock in places and they're ten feet thick in others. It would take days of heavy pounding to breach these walls and the Afghans don't possess the artillery to put a dent in them.'

'So why are we out there on the plain?'

Burnes ignores my question, following his own thoughts. 'You realise the stores aren't even in the same place as the men, don't you? They're over there in that fort,' he points to a building about half a mile from the camp, 'And in that one.' He points to another fortified building made mainly from wood a quarter of a mile further on still. 'And the Treasury's over there,' he says, pointing in the opposite direction to yet another building, this time closer to the town, mainly built of stone, at a distance of maybe a third of a mile from the camp. 'And where do you think the ammunition's kept?' he asks, turning to his left towards the centre of the town where a large house flies the Union Flag. 'Over there, right in the thick of it. Everything everywhere. We might just as well give them the whole lot. It's theirs for the taking, after all.'

'But we are not at war with them, are we? Macnaghten says the whole of Afghanistan is peace and tranquillity. Everything is quiet, the King is widely welcomed and much-loved. According to his despatches, Macnaghten says the country is content.'

'He says that does he?' Burnes spits on the ground. It is a gesture of contempt I find hard to reconcile with the urbane ambassador of my recollection. For me, Burnes is the ideal envoy to a foreign potentate. Charming, sophisticated, well-connected, relaxed and cheerful. To see him angry enough to spit comes as a shock. His dark hair now has flecks of grey. His sunburnt features display frown lines of intense anger suppressed with some difficulty.

'Burnes, we have not met for more than a year. What's caused this change? You're usually so calm.'

'Frustration, dear boy, sheer frustration,' he laughs. 'Frustration with Elphie, to be sure, and his idiot Brigadier-General Shelton but much more with that damned man Macnaghten.'

'I have to present myself to him tomorrow and await orders.'

'He wants you out of town,' Burnes tells me. He turns away from the vista before us to look intensely at me with his hazel eyes. There is something in his expression, an apprehension and confusion, I have not seen there before. 'He's off, you know, Macnaghten. Back to Bombay to become the governor. His great ambition realised. He's due to depart before the winter snows. He wants to leave everything calm and tranquil, he wants the Afghans to be compliant and quiescent because then he can get away and wash his hands of the place. So he has created this fictional peace.'

'Fictional? There is a peace. The King is in his castle. We are teaching the natives horse-racing, even cricket, I hear. How can it be a fiction?'

'Macnaghten is a politician. He's playing the game. He does not understand this country as I do, he does not see what I see, he certainly does not hear what I hear. And yet...'

'And yet?'

'How can I tell him the truth, Pottinger? How can I warn him and prepare him for what's to come? Insurrection, rebellion. I sense the way the wind is blowing but, if I warn him, he will not believe me because he will not want to believe me. And if he did believe me, I would be writing my own political epitaph.'

I was confused. 'Why should that be?'

'Because I am to succeed him. I am to become our ambassador to the court of Shah Soojah. The Queen's representative in Afghanistan.'

'Congratulations, I'm delighted.' I reach out to shake Burnes's hand but he holds his own firmly by his side.

'There's nothing to congratulate me for,' he says. 'It's too late. I am finally going to receive my due – the post I should have had if they hadn't sent out Macnaghten in my stead. It is my due, my right. And I am not going to lose it by delaying his departure and disabusing him of his belief that all is well. But it is a poisoned chalice, Pottinger. Macnaghten's getting out while the going's good – it's the rest of us who will have to pick up the pieces and who do you think they will blame when this fictitious peace breaks down? Only the Envoy, Sir Alexander Burnes. My name will be mud. Everything I have striven for will be washed away. They will talk of me as the man who failed to keep the peace in Afghanistan. But the damage has been done.'

'Should you be telling me all this, Burnes?' I ask. 'It's not every man who would confess his innermost thoughts to a stranger.'

He is annoyed by this. He fiddles with his moustache with his right hand and grips the parapet firmly with the left. He squints into the distance, screwing up his eyes and betraying a glint of frustration. 'You are no stranger, Pottinger. You and I are friends, are we not? You have dined in my house. I have taken you into my confidence in the past.'

I acknowledge this is true and add I have nothing but admiration for Burnes but ask again if it is wise to express his views quite so openly. And I go on, 'If you let Macnaghten leave and you are right and there is some kind of uprising, you will be responsible for handling it and for quelling it.' Burnes waves this away as if it were trivial and I add, 'But if you are right to say you will also be blamed for allowing it to happen in the first place, under your supervision, not Macnaghten's, then you must force him to recognise the true position now, before it's too late.'

'Do you think I haven't thought of that?' Burnes pounds a fist on the grey-stone wall of the castle. It must hurt. 'That is my dilemma. If I let him leave in the belief that all is peace and tranquillity then I shall be blamed for what is to come. But if I warn him, and if he believes me, and he feels the need to remain, then I shall not succeed him. He would make sure of that. The blame would be mine in any case, Macnaghten would see to that. We have had disagreements already. Many of them.'

'But your duty to the Governor-General, to the Company, to the Queen?'

'My dear Pottinger, never forget my duty has been suborned already. My arguments in favour of Dost Mohammed Khan, the old King, have been taken and used against me. My argument that the Russians are no threat to us in Afghanistan is seen as naïve or even treacherous. Some people have said I was in the pay of Count Simonich. Can you believe that?'

'Surely not.' I had heard such a thing during my time in Calcutta and I had done my best to dismiss the claims but once a lie gets abroad, especially one that may have been deliberately put there by Macnaghten's men to discredit Burnes, it cannot easily be killed off.

'That's the story – don't say you haven't heard it,' says Burnes. 'Macnaghten does not trust me. If I said the Dost's friends were planning a revolt, he would tell me it was my imagination. Or – worse – he would accuse me of encouraging it.'

'Tell him. Your conscience is clear. You are not in communication with the Dost, are you?'

'Not directly,' Burnes says, 'But, of course, I see some of my old friends now and again and hear what they say. And I have my agent, Mohan Lal, who keeps his ear very close to the ground.'

This worries me. 'You must tell Macnaghten and write to Lord Eden. Make your apprehensions known now so you cannot be blamed later. If nothing comes of it all, it will be forgotten. If you are proved right, you will gain the credit you fear to lose.'

'I wish it were that simple. I shall prove it to you tomorrow. We shall visit Macnaghten together.' Burnes shakes off his melancholy, turns brightly away towards the great interior of the castle and goes on, 'Tonight, though, you must come with me. We have an entertainment in my home tonight. Some of the local girls will be joining us. They will be leaving their husbands at home.'

Burnes rubs his hands together and chuckles, his gloom lifts as we march away from the battlements, across the wide open parade ground towards the gatehouse in the castle's inner walls and thence downhill into the town of Kabul.

*****

The streets are crammed with hawkers and goats, whores and horses, the sellers of food and the eaters of it, drinkers and drunkards, British soldiers, the Afghan King's soldiers and other militia-men belonging to some of the warlords summoned into town recently by Macnaghten for a durbar. There is a terrible din but by and large everyone seems friendly enough. There doesn't appear to be any enmity between the Europeans and the natives. Occasional fights break out, or disputes at least, but these are only over money. The people of Kabul complain our presence here has led to a rise in prices which makes some basic commodities unaffordable for the Afghans themselves; but others are making their fortunes. Yet when an Afghan asks a few rupees for a rug or a coat, our soldiers assume, without any evidence, they are being grossly over-charged and, instead of entering into one of those long bartering sessions beloved by so many traders in this corner of the world, they cry 'Cheat!' and try to provoke a fight.

'Wellington was right about our soldiers, you know,' Burnes says casually as we elbow our way through the narrow streets accompanied by three of his household guards who are supposedly clearing our path while two more are protecting our backs. 'Scum of the earth, scum of the earth.'

'Ah yes, but he did say how wonderful it was the army turned them into such fine fellows.'

'Did he indeed?' Burnes asks as he strides ahead calling 'Make way! Make way!' with growing impatience.

As we barge through the streets I find my own man Hoosein pulling at my sleeve. Burnes is some distance ahead of us now, separated by the seething mass of men and beasts. 'Sahib, sahib,' says Hoosein, 'News sahib. News.'

I do not stop but take Hoosein by the shoulder and half drag the little man along with me. 'What news, Hoosein?'

'Dost Mohammed Khan, the King, sahib.'

'What of him?'

'He is coming to Kabul to surrender himself to the Governor, sahib, and ask for asylum in India.'

Now I do stop and look down at Hoosein's eager little face, lit up with the delight of carrying important news which he believes only he knows. His white tunic is dusty and his jet black hair is glistening. He has been running to find me and I feel grateful for his devotion but I say, 'Alas, Hoosein, I fear your informant is misleading you. Dost Mohammed Khan fled into the Hindu Kush weeks ago.'

'Yes sahib and now he is coming back.'

'I don't know who you've been speaking to, Hoosein, but I think we would know already if the former King were planning to surrender himself to Sir William Macnaghten and seek refuge in India.'

'He wants to move into the same palace you British gave Shah Soojah.'

'And how do you think you know this? Come along, I have lost Burnes now. We have to find his house.'

'Down the next street on the left, sahib, the one with the large green wooden doors and the walls covered with clematis. White clematis. There is a bell. But sahib,' he goes on, taking the lead to direct me to Burnes's house, 'It is well-known in the markets. The Dost has fallen out with his hosts and thinks sanctuary with the British is a safer option than being passed from one castle to another. It is all costing him money and he is running out, they say. In exile the British will give him a pension and he can wait for Shah Soojah to die before coming back to Kabul. That's what they are saying in the markets sahib.'

We arrive at Burnes's mansion, windowless walls overgrown by clematis with a pair of large green doors facing the street where Hoosein grabs the bell-pull to summon the servants before melting away again into the crowd with the words, 'Well we shall see' and a look of disappointment on his face at my undoubted scepticism.

*****

I tell Burnes this extraordinary news and we enjoy a chuckle over Hoosein's credulity as we await the arrival of his guests. But then my friend hesitates. 'Suppose it is true,' he says, 'What then? Is it not evidence supporting Macnaghten's assertion that all is well? If the former King surrenders himself to us and applies for exile in our lands and at our expense, that would make Shah Soojah more secure on his throne. For now, anyway.'

The party is a more extravagant version of the hospitality I enjoyed at Burnes's previous residence in Kabul before the invasion, when I was on my way to Herat and he was confident he could control the Dost. The young maidens are certainly delicious, sinuous and lithe, cheerful and willing. The hashish is of the finest quality. The food, heavily spiced and fiery, is as well-prepared as one can reasonably expect in a town where goat and chicken are the staple diet. The wine is plentiful, the brandy strong, my fellow guests, both the British and the Afghan, are in good heart. The talk is all about the day's horse-racing, last winter's skating on the frozen lakes – a new sport widely embraced by the Afghans – and the difficulties of entertaining the English ladies in Kabul over the summer months.

Later, though, as I am about to retire with one of the ladies of Burnes's harem, he pulls me to one side. 'On the other hand,' he say, without preamble, 'If Dost Mohammed Khan were to give himself up, all it means is he cannot win the support he needs among the tribesmen and chieftains to try to regain his throne. And that means the people are divided.'

'Surely that's a good thing – divide and rule, isn't that what we want?'

I say as a young woman strokes my arm and the fragrance of her perfume invites me to follow her into the inner rooms of the mansion.

'Maybe, maybe.' Burnes contemplates this a moment. 'Or there are others who would seek the throne and the Dost thinks his best chances of survival are to be as far away from the coming conflict as possible.'

'Always assuming my man Hoosein hasn't been dreaming,' I say with a laugh, slapping Burnes on the back and wishing him good-night.

*****

Before we present ourselves to Sir William Macnaghten, Her Majesty's Envoy to the court of Shah Soojah-ool-Moolk Durrani, Burnes's man, Mohun Lal, arrives with a very similar story. He says the Dost is only three days from Kabul. Burnes insists the information must go no further. 'With a bit of luck we can look forward to Macnaghten accompanying the Dost back to Hindustan,' he says with a grim chuckle. 'But I still don't think this is good news.'

'My dear Alexander,' I say, 'I think you have too much of the Scottish pessimist in you.'

'It means Macnaghten will be free to leave Kabul believing his own propaganda, that all is peace and tranquillity. He won't realise it's just the Dost's latest move in a longer game.'

CHAPTER 24

Fort William, Calcutta, December 1842

Broadhurst comes over, in his smartest uniform and with a serious frown on his face. I do not fail to notice the marks of spilt coffee on his tunic nor the unshaven face, which suggest to me my attorney has not been awake very long. Yet here he is, in my room inside the castle where I am confined, as I address my tea and broiled lamb in some kind of stew with the inevitable naan bread. I am wearing a dressing gown and trying to read 'The Friend of India' when the man stumbles in, red-faced and sweating.

'Broadhurst, have a cup of tea,' I say without rising to greet him. I try to be jovial but somehow I lack the spirit.

'I have news, Pottinger,' he says, waving a piece of paper in my face.

'Clearly,' I say, 'But do sit down and tell me slowly.'

'The trial.'

'Court martial,' I correct him.

'Yes, yes, the court martial. It will be before Clerk.'

'Should that mean something to me?' I am so resigned to this farce I cannot be moved by the news that such-and-such a civil servant or so-and-so Company man shall preside over my humiliation. I sip my tea, which is bitter and not exactly hot. I shall remonstrate with Henry Lloyd. The boy should be looking after me better.

'How's the wound?' asks Broadhurst as he slumps into my worn-out leather sofa, apparently exhausted by his rush to greet me with the news that somebody has been named to deliver judgment on me.

'Really? I thought you had important news for me, Broadhurst.'

'I do, Pottinger, but of course I want to be sure you will live long enough to answer the charges against you, otherwise Clerk will sit in vain.'

This is Broadhurst's version of light-hearted banter. When he asks if I propose to live long enough to stand trial, he thinks he is not just being funny but putting his client at his ease. This may explain why Broadhurst has so few clients. 'Be assured then, Broadhurst, that Brydon tells me every day the leg is starting to heal. Starting, mind you.'

'Good, good,' says Broadhurst briskly. 'We can't have the defendant dying before he has cleared his good name and restored his reputation, can we?'

'I don't know, perhaps we should ask Clerk, whoever he may be,' I say, attempting to return my attorney to the topic of his indecent haste.

'Clerk. You know, George Russel Clerk, the Governor General's personal envoy to the Sikhs. The man who did the deal with Ranjeet Singh's successor Maharajah Sher Singh.'

'That fat oaf,' I say, referring not to Clerk but to Sher Singh, who may have been one of Ranjeet's sons but was never blessed with the Sikh king's brains.

'Yes, well,' says Broadhurst, 'The fact remains Clerk is Ellenborough's right-hand man. And we know Ellenborough is not exactly well-disposed towards us, do we not?'

'We do.' There is a pause in our conversation as I reflect on the calculated snub I suffered at Ellenborough's hands when I returned to Ferozepore with the Army of Retribution. Ellenborough had made the journey down from Simla to greet the triumphant generals, welcome home the hostages and celebrate what he liked to term a victory which restored the Company's and the Queen's honour across Hindustan and, indeed, the world.

He wouldn't meet me. Other hostages were summoned into his Lordship's presence. Several were treated as long-lost friends. Their stories were recounted to a fascinated and sympathetic Governor-General. Their wounds inspected. Their outrages sympathised with. Their tears tolerated. Their financial losses compensated for. Yet one man was conspicuous by his absence from this fetching scene of sympathy, reconciliation and victory – that man was me.

Even Shelton was granted an audience. Even Shelton.

The thought of it still incenses me, all these weeks later. It seems Ellenborough had a court martial planned for me. The indignity still wounds. It hurts far more than this festering leg of mine. 'So this Clerk character is Ellenborough's creature, is he?'

Broadhurst looks apologetic. 'He is. I thought you should know as soon as possible.' The big man stands, comes across to the table and helps himself to some of my naan, which he chews thoughtfully.

'Just the civil servant?' I ask.

'Ah now, I am glad you asked that. Here we have better news.' Broadhurst consults his piece of paper, waves it about again, fishes for his spectacles which he has mislaid, checks his tunic pockets, cannot find them, pads his trousers, discovers them perched on the top of his head, lowers them to his eyes and starts to read, quietly, to himself. I wait expectantly. He looks out of the window, towards the parade ground, deep in thought. I feel if I do not interrupt him soon, he will turn to stone.

'Broadhurst?' I prompt him.

'Oh yes, Pottinger, I do apologise old man. I was just thinking.' Again Broadhurst comes over all dreamy.

'Thinking? Yes?'

'Well, the others are more promising, that's the thing. Much more promising.'

'Others?'

'Yes, the four other judges.'

'Four more? And they are?' It feels as if I must cross-examine my own attorney if I am to secure any new intelligence on the state of my own trial.

'Ah yes, well, two major-generals and two brigadiers.'

'Their names, Broadhurst, their names.' I fear I sound a little irritable but I would be pleased to know what I am up against.

'Lumley you know. Sir James, the adjutant general. And Harry Smith.'

'Sir Harry,' I exclaim, 'Now there is a blessing.' Sir Harry Smith is well-known as the man who tried to bring civilisation to South Africa but is really famed for the exotic beauty of his Portuguese wife, Juana María de los Dolores de León Smith, known everywhere as Lady Smith. They say a town has been named after her somewhere in Africa. It is said Sir Harry is a something of an outsider, not always willing to appease his seniors in cases where his own judgment is contrary to the prevailing climate. That, they say, is why he was forced out of South Africa. I see a glimmer of hope knowing Sir Harry is one of the tribunal. 'And the others?' I ask.

'The brigadiers, Tom Monteath and George Wymer. Now Wymer I know a little,' says Broadhurst. 'He was with General Nott in Kandahar, you know. He was there, Eldred, he saw it all.'

'From a safe distance,' I say.

'Yes, from a distance but you would hardly call it safe.'

'No,' I concede. 'No, it was active service, that much is true. And?'

'And?' Broadhurst is again gazing out across the parade ground.

'Is there something you would rather be doing, George?'

'Oh I'm sorry, Eldred. I was rehearsing my opening speech.'

'You were, were you?'

'I was, Eldred. I shall say, "Gentlemen, is this any way to treat the most honourable, dedicated, single-minded, noble, purposeful and, above all, brave servant of Her Majesty who has ever had the misfortune to cross the Khyber Pass and embroil himself among the tribes of that benighted land?" I shall say, "This is building tragedy upon tragedy, traducing the reputation not merely of the Hero of Herat, a man who has done the Crown and the Company singular service in the past, but a man who can truly be called the Hero of Kabul as well. A man who at every step along the tragic way has put his own safety, security and hopes way behind those of his country, his Queen, his fellows and their dependants. That this man of such high integrity is laid so low as to humble himself before this tribunal is an added torture he cannot have expected and certainly never warranted." I shall say…'

'Never mind what you might say if you ever get the chance, Broadhurst, what about Monteath? He was with General Sale, wasn't he?'

'He was.'

'And I was with Sale's wife.'

'You were.'

'And we have Lady Sale's own words to support our case, do we not?'

'We do, Eldred, we certainly do.'

'Shall we call her as a witness?'

'Lady Sale?'

'Why not? She was in my care for almost nine months and we were closely acquainted even before that. She has written to me with her personal thanks and subscribed to the collection in my honour. Why shouldn't she testify on my behalf?'

A cloud descends over Broadhurst's brow as he contemplates this possibility. 'A General's wife as a witness in a court martial? You know how the world will see it, especially as it's Lady Fiorentina.'

'She has been my bedfellow, you know?'

Broadhurst turns to me frowning. He is not amused. 'Come now, Pottinger, come now,' he says, unwilling or unable to say anything further. I pause to contemplate the man standing before me, who is employed by the East India Company to defend one of its servants against its own prosecution. Is this portly, somewhat shambolic character in his mid-forties really the man to rely on when one is in a tight spot? He is certainly not the man I would choose to protect my back in a gunfight. On the other hand, a florid, bookish man frustrated with his life and unable, it seems, to do anything to improve it; perhaps this is the man for me.

'Broadhurst,' I say, 'It is true. Lady Fiorentina and I have lain side by side all night and been glad of the warmth of each other's bodies.'

'Pottinger, this cannot be an...'

'Alongside several other persons of both sexes, I confess. Let me tell you, captivity in the wastes of Afghanistan is no place for the niceties of polite society. Keep warm or die, that's the rule, old boy, keep warm or die. I kept her warm, she did the same to her daughter, who in turn warmed Lieutenant Crawford, who warmed Mrs Eyre and so on. Forty of us or more.' I laugh at his discomfiture. 'You really do have no idea, do you Broadhurst?'

CHAPTER 25

Kabul, August 1841

As Burnes and I ride towards the Company encampment a couple of miles beyond the huge bastion of the Balar Hissar, he is plainly not looking forward to our appointment. Sir William Macnaghten brings out the worst in my friend but his contempt for the Company and its invasion are not confined to the Envoy.

I remark on the inconvenience of having an indefensible barracks at some distance from the castle and separated from the munitions, in one fortress, the money, in a vulnerable town house, and the supplies in a third godown standing in the orchards not far from the only bridge over the Kabul river.

'This has never been a proper military expedition,' Burnes complains. 'It wasn't an army, it was a hunting expedition. We weren't going to war, Pottinger, we were on the biggest outing in anybody's life. There may have been 15,000 soldiers, including the Sikhs who, in the event, didn't bother to turn up. But there were twice as many servants – tent-pitchers, grain-carriers, wives and bazaar girls. The girls were completely superfluous – you've seen these Afghan women? Beauties.'

'They are,' I agree.

Burnes continues his lecture, 'Even the most junior officer had six servants to care for his glass, crockery and portable bath. We had our own wine chests and supplies of cheroots. General Cottin had 260 camels to transport all his accoutrements. When we set out there were 30,000 camels not to mention the horses, oxen and elephants. It was a bloody carnival. At least to start with.

'I could have told them – you, Pottinger, you could have told them – their route into Afghanistan wasn't just a pleasant ride through friendly country. Cottin side-tracked his troops. He decided he wanted to teach the Baluchis a lesson because they kept attacking our rearguard even though I'd already bribed them to leave us alone. Macnaghten had to recall him before we got involved in an entirely separate war.

'Then there was the desert. It was hot – over 100 degrees. We starved. Food rations were halved. We had to eat our own horses we were so hungry. The Bolan Pass was a nightmare, the Baluchis didn't stop their raids. It was quite a relief to lay siege to Ghunzee, blow the gates and destroy the garrison. I can tell you the men were only too happy to spend a day or two sampling the delights of the place before we marched on.'

Burnes chuckles at the recollection. I have heard stories of rape and ransack which would have shamed the Vandals and Visigoths when they descended on Rome. Still, armies are armies and soldiers will always be soldiers even if they are fighting for God and the Queen.

'The native soldiers are reliable enough, I suppose,' Burnes says grudgingly, 'But the Europeans – our own men – are a bloody nightmare. Ignore orders, aren't intimidated even by floggings and executions, all of 'em want to go home to India, to their wives and doxies. Don't like the food, can't speak the language, object there isn't any beer. Ill-disciplined and untrustworthy.'

*****

We reach the cantonment. At the main gate a rabble of local children beg, wheedle and occasionally throw stones at the three men on duty, a European sergeant and two Indians from the 54th Native Infantry. It is a hot day, the thermometer heading into the eighties, and the men are irregularly dressed but there is no officer to tell the sergeant, in breeches and a white, collarless shirt, that he is not presenting the British Empire in an impressive light and I do not feel it is my place to do so as I have been given no military command.

The men greet Sir Alexander Burnes with a curt nod and demand to see my papers as if I were some sort of threat to the establishment. I show them to the sergeant, who gazes at them for while but plainly cannot read what is inscribed therein and instead introduces himself as George Wade from Brighton, 'You know, sir, where the Pavilion comes from.'

Wade is clearly interested in a long conversation but we cannot stay. We bid him farewell, riding past the two wooden towers and over the bridge crossing the shallow, empty ditch, which has been dug around the whole camp to increase the height of its wooden defences. They are still only six feet high. Above one of the modest towers hangs a limp East India Company flag, with its red and white stripes and a Union Jack in the top left-hand corner.

The camp itself consists mainly of row upon row of tents overlooked by hills on all sides. There are a few solid buildings constructed from the local rock, of which there is a plentiful supply, including shops and offices, half a dozen bungalows and three more substantial houses. Here live General Elphinstone, Lady Fiorentina Sale, wife of General Sir Robert Sale, who is now in Jalalabad and, in the most superior, if such a word can be applied to such modest accommodation, Sir William Macnaghten and his wife, Frances. It is a stubby, ugly building of three stories with a peremptory veranda boasting a pair of rocking chairs on which, I assume, the Envoy and his wife relax as they overlook the constant comings-and-goings laid out before them across the camp.

Today there is no sign of Sir William's wife and a pair of liveried servants greets us at the steps while a couple of native boys rush to take hold of our horses and help us dismount. I am clean-shaven and broiling in my new blue-braided uniform as a Company diplomat and

Major in the Company army. My boots are new, the leather stiff, the spurs disconcerting, the sword swinging at my side, and I wipe my sweating face with a cotton handkerchief at regular intervals. Burnes, by contrast, is dressed like an Afghan in a long, flowing robe and one of those bizarre turbans they wear which seem to be three times the size of the head they surmount. He is not particularly perturbed by the heat.

We are led into what appears to be a dining room, with a large table and a dozen chairs, heavy chintz curtains, dark-wood panelling and a huge fireplace, empty now but for some logs awaiting another freezing Kabul winter. The room is shaded and dark with a light breeze wafting through it from the open windows but it is still hot. I can smell the wood as it dries and warps; obviously it is not properly weathered.

Sir William sits at the head of the table, surrounded by papers set out, in some apparent order, in different piles. Two secretaries, one of them a European, the other an Indian, sit nearby proffering the Envoy requests and orders awaiting signature while, almost hidden in the shadows, stands a young Afghan man who is evidently present to translate, explain and offer whatever insights he may be able to conjure up from his imagination, as an adviser to the Government.

Sir William carries on reading as I stand to attention, salute and remain waiting for him to acknowledge my presence while Burnes slips into a chair as far from Sir William as possible, while curtly proffering an unnoticed nod of greeting with the words, 'Morning, William.'

I am reminded of my earlier encounters with Macnaghten. His decision to relieve me of my duties in Herat was particularly galling. I am inclined to ask how my successor is getting on but first I must await the great man's pleasure.

Eventually Sir William looks up. 'Pottinger,' says this negligible clerk with his blue-glass spectacles and his thinning hair. 'I did not look to see you here.'

'You will have received notification from the Governor-General, sir?'

'Of course but I must say I thought we had got rid of you and Afghanistan is the better for it. I am sorry to see you back again so soon, Pottinger. I trust this time you will take greater care with the Company's money and not go incurring debts in future. You will find the Company is anxious to avoid greater expense here than is absolutely necessary and, indeed, we are reaching the bottom of our purse. Afghanistan will have to start paying its own way, isn't that right, Burnes?'

My friend begins a lengthy, and somewhat confusing, lecture on how he is reforming the taxation system of the city. Kabul is a crossroads for international trade and Burnes is attempting to impose some sort of regularised levy on the whole thing. He is confident of success though my man Hoosein tells me the money is rarely paid to the King or the Company and what is handed over is greatly resented.

'You see, Pottinger, prudence in all things,' Macnaghten resumes, still seated, still peering through his thick spectacles, still gazing somewhere six feet above my head and still requiring me to remain firmly to attention. I will not let myself relax unless this man invites me to do so. 'You have a reputation for profligacy.'

I try to interrupt to explain some of the financial difficulties involved in defending a city in a far-flung corner of a virtually-unknown country without any resources, financial or otherwise. But I am talked over. 'We are all well aware of your elevation to the status of a hero. But anybody can buy himself a reputation and, in my book, Major' – he hisses the word contemptuously – 'an indigent Irishman is just the fellow for such an endeavour.'

I start forward and cry a word of protest but Burnes is up from his seat and laying an arm on mine to calm me down again. 'Remember where you are, Pottinger.'

'Hot-headed, the Irish,' says Sir William with a conspiratorial grin in Burnes's direction. 'Lucky the administration is in the hands of the Scottish, eh Burnes?'

Sir William goes on to tell me the administration of Afghanistan has cost the Company £1 million in the past year and, while he will shortly be leaving Kabul to take up his new post in Bengal, he is disinclined to leave behind any unnecessary financial difficulties for his successor. 'We shall be levying more taxation,' he says, 'And while the natives won't like it at any rate we shall be more welcome than Shah Soojah's tax-gatherers, eh what Burnes?'

My friend is silent so Sir William continues, though with less alacrity, 'The King of Kabul, my friend Shah Soojah, has some disconcerting habits, I must admit. But it is our duty to support him in his rule so when some of the locals came here to protest at the way Soojah's tax-gatherers cut off the ears of people who will not pay the taxes they owe, I was forced to have them taken out onto the parade ground and whipped for their impertinence. They were some of the better sort of Kabulites. They will not be complaining about the taxes we levy any longer, I think we can be quite sure of that. Eh what, Burnes?'

'But of course, my fine Irish friend,' Macnaghten continues, finally looking me in the eyes though I cannot see his through his bluebottle lenses, 'Raising taxation is only one way of reducing the cost of this exercise to the Company – the other is to reduce our expenditure and that is what I expect of you in Charikar. You are there to uphold Her Majesty's law and maintain Her Majesty's peace. But you are not there as a soldier, Pottinger, and don't you forget it. We want no expensive heroics from you, sir. We have had more than enough of those already. We have a Ghurkha regiment in Charikar who are perfectly capable of doing that, thank you very much. In any case, Afghanistan is in a state of miraculous tranquillity – miraculous tranquillity, sir – and we can't have Irish hotheads upsetting the applecart, now can we?'

I grit my teeth. 'No, sir.'

'Good. Now I shall ask Shelton to arrange an escort for you in a couple of days' time. You are dismissed, Pottinger.'

'Sir.' I salute and turn to leave but Burnes, who has been silent all this time, interrupts my departure.

'One piece of news, Sir William. We think it may be of importance.'

'We, Burnes?'

'Pottinger and I.'

'Pottinger has only just arrived. Unless it is intelligence from India, he cannot have news I am myself not already acquainted with,' Sir William says, waving a dismissive hand in Burnes's direction.

'It concerns Dost Mohammed Khan, Sir William. He is said to be on the point of surrendering himself to us and asking for exile, in India, at Shah Soojah's former palace in Ludhiana.'

Macnaghten laughs, removing his glasses to reveal tired, blinking eyes which he wipes with a handkerchief as he deals with his tears of mirth. 'My dear Pottinger,' he says with singular contempt, 'When you have been here as long as we have, you will learn to dismiss such fairy-tales for the nonsense they are. I trust you did not pay your informant too many rupees for this piece of fiction. If the Dost were planning to give himself up, I assure you I would be the first to know. We have been taken in by these people once too often on that score – do you remember the melon-seller, Burnes? He led us on a wild goose chase and cost us a small fortune. Money, I might add, we could ill-afford. Never again, never again. Economy is the order of the day. Next time you see your informant, Pottinger, give him a whipping on your own account, for having made you an object of mirth, and give him another from me for his damned effrontery. Now go, sir, go. And mind you practice the utmost economy. The utmost.'

*****

'That went well,' laughs Burnes, clapping me on the back. We stroll through the camp towards the officers' mess where we order some water and wine to quench our thirst and sit in the shade of an awning as men come and go, greeting Burnes with varying degrees of affection. I am introduced to them all though there are so many unfamiliar faces I immediately forget their names. Burnes catechises me: Walpole Clark, a Lieutenant, aged about 19 and straight out of college; John Sturt, Captain in the Engineers, married to Alexandrina, daughter of Sir

Robert Sale; Lieutenant Vincent Eyre, a man I know a little from our days together in the Bengal Artillery; Robert Waller, a captain in the Bengal Horse Artillery; Dr John Logan, yet another Scot, who is here as a Missionary for the Church of England.

Logan sits with us for a while and I agree to his request to accompany me up to Charikar in a few days' time. He then offers to take us to the afternoon cricket match which has been got up by the men – the Bengal Light Infantry, a European regiment, is answering a challenge laid down by the 37th Native Infantry.

We collect our horses and ride a couple of miles further out of town to an area which has been commandeered for sporting pursuits. Around the periphery is a horse-racing track which, to my eye, looks about the same distance as the course at Epsom in Surrey, which I visited during my time at Addiscombe. A small stand has been built near the finish line and beside it, facing away from the course, is a large pavilion which serves as the headquarters for the cricket field laid out within the race-course.

A game is under way when we arrive. The Europeans are in the field while the Indian side contains four of its European officers. 'They do the batting, while the natives practise their spin-bowling on the enemy,' Logan explains.

For a pious churchman, he is highly knowledgeable about the game and invites us to join the queue at the betting booth where we are given the opportunity to wager a few rupees on the winning team and, should we wish to do so, wager some further coin on the man most likely to achieve the highest score. Careful of my funds, most of which I must remit to my step-mother, and mindful of Macnaghten's warnings about exercising economy, I limit myself to placing 50 rupees on the European team. Burnes, who has seen these games before, opts for the Indians, declaring they have two infantrymen capable of bamboozling even the most lively of batsmen. Native Afghans cluster round the bookmakers, a couple of shady Londoners who seem to have made their way to Kabul after the conquest, with the primary purpose of promoting and exploiting various entertainments. The Afghans show little interest in the proceedings on the field but they are eager to debate the odds of one side winning and the other losing. It seems the Europeans are favourites from the very fact that we British invented the sport, brought it with us from home and must be the superiors in this struggle. On the other hand it is noted some of the leading cricketers on the other side are also European, despite being members of a native regiment, and, besides, the natives have the two most guileful bowlers. 'It is the flexibility of their wrists,' says Logan, 'There is something in the Indian which gives his wrists a greater strength and flexibility than most of our own men possess.'

There seem to be at least 15 fieldsmen, not to mention the two umpires, a bowler and a wicket-keeper on the European side. This, Logan assures me, is normal. It is also notable that some of the bowlers are adopting the new round-arm method of throwing the ball. This, Burnes says, is tantamount to cheating because the ball travels faster and gives the batsman less chance of hitting it. That said, it looks as if one of the batsmen, who is named by Logan as Major Charles Griffith, is dealing admirably with these thunderbolts, allowing them to slip off his bat behind the wicket-keeper and into unmanned spaces which permit him and his partner to saunter for a couple more runs at their leisure while some wheezing old sergeant lumbers after the ball.

As all this exercise is conducted on the field of play, under the unbearable heat of the early afternoon sun, I see a group of ladies and gentlemen enjoying the shelter of a marquee where cold drinks and hot tea are being served by smartly-uniformed Indians. We wander over to join them and, to my surprise, I see Miss Eleanor Eden among a group of ladies sitting together in the shade fanning themselves as they sip lemonade.

Miss Eden sees me as well, I am sure of it, but she gives no indication she has done so. Instead her soft face disappears behind her white fan and she turns to the lady on her right. Logan and Burnes, who are acquainted with everybody, gradually make their way over towards this gathering of ladies dressed in light cotton dresses, high waists, long sleeves, with bonnets which seem to me to speak more of fashion than they do of comfort or convenience in this terrible heat.

We reach the ladies eventually, armed with cups of tea, and Logan makes the introductions. There are a dozen ladies, including Antoinette, the wife of the batsman Major Griffith, Lady Fiorentina Sale, wife of the General in command at Jalalabad, her daughter Mrs Alexandrina Sturt and, in their care, it seems, Miss Eden.

'All these exotic names,' I say as I am introduced, 'Fiorentina, Alexandrina, Antoinette. And Eleanor, of course.'

Finally she looks at me and smiles, somewhat shyly, I think. 'Miss Eden, it is a pleasure to be reacquainted.'

'Major,' she says, somewhat brusquely and turns to Mrs Sturt. 'This is the Hero of Herat I think I mentioned before,' she says to her companion. 'You know, the Irishman.'

Mrs Sturt nods demurely, as befits a recently-married woman, and says quietly, but not so much that I cannot hear her, 'He's very big, isn't he?' The two young women giggle to themselves while I turn away towards the cricket, where Major Griffith charges down the wicket to a slow lob from the bowler, misses the ball completely, turns to re-gain his ground, inelegantly falls over, sees the wicket-keeper seize the ball and remove the bails. There is polite applause from the tent and wilder whooping from the native troops confined to the far side of the field. The bowler is congratulated and the bookmakers alter the odds that suggest Major Griffith may record the highest individual score of the game. Burnes slips away to place some more rupees on the question while Logan tells the assembled company how he has seen the 37th native infantry in previous encounters and he would swear by their two spinning bowlers. I am beginning to become bored already by Dr Logan and I have only known him a couple of hours.

We gentlemen stand behind the ladies while the 37th continue with their innings. One of their sepoys is almost as proficient as Major Griffith. 'That man has a natural genius for the game,' declares Logan.

'I have seen him block for an hour to the frustration of his opponents and then score at the rate of a run every ball. Difficult to dismiss...' At that moment, the man lashes a ball straight back down the ground only to see the fieldsman remove his cap and catch the ball in it signifying the end of his innings. 'I'm not sure that's allowed,' says Logan. 'If you look into the laws of cricket, I think you will find that catching the ball without use of the hands is not regarded as in the spirit of the game.' Despite this, the man walks back to the players' makeshift pavilion and another sepoy steps out.

The sun blazes down, the heat rises, in the distance a haze settles at the foot of the mountains, the players trot and stumble and the spectators – especially the sepoys of the 37th – applaud loudly while those of us in the marquee politely notice the more outstanding efforts of either side.

I am bored. The play is sedate, to say the least. I say to the spectators around me, though intending it for one person in particular, 'I have a mind to take a stroll. Would anyone care to accompany me? Mrs Sturt? Miss Eden? I would be glad to carry two parasols.'

They both look at Lady Sale who nods acquiescence. I gather their parasols from one of the servants, open them and offer shelter on either side of me as we perambulate slowly around the cricket pitch, trying to avoid the native boys who come begging at our heels, the beer tents which the men of the European regiment seem to prefer to the game itself, and the sepoys who are crushed together in some sort of enclosure policed by a couple of stout sergeants from the Envoy's own guard.

Captain Sturt, who has arrived late, rushes to join us. We are introduced. He is a tall, polite officer with a harassed look. 'I am trying to persuade Elphie we should consolidate our supplies in a single place and construct more robust defences but he will have none of it,' he says before taking his young wife's parasol from me and marching her ahead of us.

'It is some time, Miss Eden,' I say.

'Two whole years, Major Pottinger. You look better fed than when we last met, I must say.' She almost slaps my stomach which, though it is by no means overweight, has, I confess, thickened out a little.

'The delights of Calcutta, madam. A sedentary existence. The absence of danger.'

'The absence of danger? Why Major I assumed you had enjoyed your fill of danger.'

'Danger comes in many forms, Miss Eden. Indeed, it can be concealed in the shape and countenance of a young woman.'

We stop and look at one another. She is, of course, even more beautiful now than she was two years ago. Reddened by the sun and heat, admittedly, her skin has turned somewhat less pale than it was; almost as dark, indeed, as some of the paler Indian girls. But her eyes still shine with a mischievous glow and her golden hair peeks from its pale blue bonnet with a becoming dishevelment. She laughs and it sounds like the ringing of champagne flutes.

'Oh I have missed you, Eldred,' she says. 'You will brighten up these tedious days I feel sure.'

'Alas not for long, Miss Eden. I am ordered to Charikar. And your own plans?'

'I return to India with Lady Sale and Mrs Sturt at the first opportunity. We expect to depart with Sir William and Lady Macnaghten. He has been appointed Governor of Bombay you know, and he is anxious to quit the field.'

'What is holding him back?'

'It is said,' and here Miss Eden whispers, 'It is said Macnaghten cannot abide the thought that Sir Alexander Burnes will take over from him and he has applied to my brother for what he calls "a more suitable replacement". Your friend Sir Alexander has something of a reputation, you know.'

'And Lady Sale is your chaperone?'

'She and Mrs Sturt, yes.'

'But Mrs Sturt, Alexandrina, cannot be any older than you are.'

'Drina is nineteen, sir. Quite old enough to be married to a captain in the engineers and therefore a woman of far greater substance than I. We also, both of us, have Lady Sale to defer to. Fiorentina is accustomed to command. She is, after all, the wife of a general with twelve children to her name. Your brother officers are besotted with her. Perhaps they look on her as their mother. Perhaps they hope her favours will benefit their careers. But she is kindly and good-humoured so it is no burden to be beholden to her.'

'Astonishing for a lady who must still be in her forties,' I say, not so much because I believe it but in the hope of being seen as gallant.

Eleanor laughs. 'In her forties? Major Pottinger, what can you be thinking? Drina is 19 but she is Lady F's youngest. The oldest must be at least, what, 35? And she can't have been younger than 15 when married. That makes her at least 50. Older, probably.'

'Perhaps it is the reflected glow of your youth and beauty which benefits her,' I say, not altogether sincerely, in the hope of both flattering and amusing Miss Eden. I succeed and she takes my arm.

'You must tell me how you have spent the past two years, Major.'

As we stroll on, I explain how I spent some time travelling to Calcutta, there to write up a lengthy report on my time in Afghanistan in general and Herat in particular though all the while wondering what the purpose of it might be when we had already invaded that country. I took some time to visit my brothers John and Tom, who are also serving with the Company in India, and I was also able to see my uncle, Sir Henry, who was setting out to become governor of one of our new colonies on the coast of China, a town called Victoria, after Her Majesty, on an island known as Hong-Kong. My conversation peters out and we conclude our walk in silence though Miss Eden does not seem entirely at ease; her small hand appears to grip my arm a little more tightly and even the way she walks is less relaxed than it was.

'I have missed you, Eldred,' she says to me quite frankly. 'I had hoped our paths would cross before now.'

A sudden fear crosses my mind. 'You are not betrothed, are you?'

She laughs. 'Not at all, but I shall be leaving Kabul soon and you are off to Charikar so who knows when our paths will cross again? My brother may be recalled to England soon and you will be out here perhaps for the rest of your life.'

'Then you shall have to visit me in Charikar before you leave,' I say and, somewhat recklessly I suppose, in such a public place, I take her hand and kiss it but it goes unnoticed because the batting team has finally lost its last man and is all out having notched up a score of 156.

*****

There is one final visit I am obliged to make before trekking the 40 miles or so to Charikar and that is to present myself to the King in the palace which lies within the walls of the Balar Hissar.

It is a huge fortification, perhaps a mile long and half a mile wide, with three separate forts, dozens of wooden and canvas structures for about five thousand inhabitants – housing everyone from the greatest Afghan nobles to their servants, harems, soldiers, artillerymen, shopkeepers and armourers. Accompanied by Macnaghten and his senior officers, including Burnes – all got up in their most courtly regalia with plenty of gold braid and plumed cocked hats – we trot through the noise and confusion of this city within a city until we reach the gardens, with their fountains even now playing merrily despite the weeks of drought.

This building is undergoing some sort of restoration. It seems the King was furious when he arrived back in Kabul to discover Dost Mohammed Khan had allowed its delicate ornamentation and its grand state rooms to fall into decline. Dozens of men are at work on wooden scaffolding repairing, repainting and re-gilding.

We are met by an honour guard and formally marched through these ante-rooms and up a wide flight of stairs into an upper chamber, which is almost the highest point in the entire citadel. The wooden arches and pillars surrounding the King are carved and painted with exotic birds and flowers while the ceiling, too, is richly decorated. Here the King holds court and enjoys a wonderful view across the city and over the valley towards the mountains. I see there is still snow on the mountain-tops. Shah Soojah also benefits, especially in these baking-hot days, from what little breeze is to be found. While my fellow officers and I struggle with the heat, the courtiers and even the King are clad in light, loose-fitting linen garments which help to keep them cool. The air is scented with the aroma of oranges.

We step deferentially toward the Monarch, our boots echoing on the marble floor, with our heads bowed. Soojah sits high up on a white marble throne too big for even his plump frame. Macnaghten presents me to the King, I step forward, bow deeply, receive a dismissive flick of His Majesty's hand and withdraw back among my fellow officers.

Macnaghten starts to discuss the refurbishments with the King while I have a chance to study Shah Soojah's fat face, his soft cheeks, his neatly-trimmed and dyed beard, his sly grin. To me they denote a man used to getting his own way, complacent about others' deference and indifferent to their fate. Here is a man for whom the life of an inferior human being is of no interest at all and, as all human beings are his inferiors, his concern for others goes no further than his assessment of what they can do for him. I can see why the stories of how he puts to death the young women in his harem are probably true.

The Shah believes in ruling through fear rather than love, it seems. When Soojah regained his throne last year, few Afghans came out to cheer even though Burnes and Mohan Lal had been out bribing the residents to do just that. His reputation had gone before him.

We are invited to dine with the King and his entourage. The British officers are required to disperse among the Afghan dignitaries and eat, cross-legged on the floor, as is the custom.

They talk about the restoration of the Monarch and the neglect of the palace but there is something boastful and arrogant about these men. They see themselves as victors and betray a sense of glee at their recently-won power and position. They can hardly stop themselves from grinning with self-satisfaction. They are in on the conspiracy to bring down the symbols of the past and they enjoy the discomfort on the faces of those they have supplanted or, more pleasurably, those they intend slowly to supplant, while savouring every moment of the discomfiture afforded to adherents of Dost Mohammed Khan's fallen regime. It seems they like to do it a little at a time while the representatives of the old guard cling onto the trappings of their power for a moment longer, smiling the gallows smiles of those who know they are about to be hanged but desperately hoping they will somehow escape the changes of the new regime even though they know there is little chance of survival. They know they are to disappear, as if they never existed. The blood they shed for the old King counts for nothing now. This is a new dawn, a new regime; change, sacrifice and blood-letting are the orders of the day.

It's an endless cycle, I suppose, and if I were on the winning side I dare say I would find it difficult to resist the thrill of power, the sense of superiority that comes with being aligned to the new regime. Yet as a disinterested observer, with nothing personally to gain or lose, I find the victors' enjoyment repulsive. Not content with booting out their enemies and – literally as well as metaphorically – stabbing former friends in the back, they cannot resist crowing and jeering.

Old scores are settled. The bodies of the losers are dragged to their graves without a word of sorrow or regret let alone any thought of recompense for the families of those who have fallen so swiftly from favour and found their lives dashed on the rocks at the foot of the victors' citadel. Or – and in some ways this is even more cruel – they blind and incarcerate their enemies and keep them chained, fed and watered just enough to maintain life, but leave them without hope.

It won't last, of course. Not even the Roman Empire lasted for ever and the life of every Emperor was constantly in danger. Hardly any of them die in their beds – even the best of them were murdered, usually by a Nero or a Caligula, who were murdered in their turn. The victors do not remember this. The victors, unlike imperial Roman generals, do not have slaves whispering 'sic transit gloria mundi' in their ears during their procession of triumph. They forget their mortality. They forget fortune's wheel turns often and quickly. Today they are immortal.

Every dog has his day and this is theirs; they will enjoy the spoils but already it is clear this great good fortune is corrupting them as it seems to corrupt every power in history. I watch them enjoy their triumph, I despise them and I know I am like them too.

Shah Soojah is no more terrible than his predecessor Dost Mohammed Khan. He rewards his friends. He doubles the size of his harem and lavishes gifts on his favourite wives. He employs musicians and eats the finest food with the courtiers who suffered with him in exile and he cuts off the heads of his enemies. His first act, as soon as he set foot back in Afghanistan with the Army of the Indus, was to line up thirty of the Dost's local ministers, in full view of the people of Quetta, and have them decapitated. The headless bodies were, by the King's order, left to rot where they lay while the heads were displayed on pikes along the town walls.

After the short siege of Ghazni, where most of the population was massacred by our own soldiers, the officers and men found cowering in the mosque were burned alive on the Shah's orders but for a couple of their leaders who were publicly disembowelled.

Burnes says it made him sick to watch and explains why, as he says he has repeatedly warned, Shah Soojah does not command much support or affection.

Macnaghten insists Shah Soojah is as popular as any King in these parts can expect to be, given the place is riven by factions, tribes and vendettas. He insists the executions were the natural reaction of a Monarch who has been denied his rightful throne for many years and says it is only the British who have a sense of decorum and a love of justice. It will take us many years, perhaps centuries, to instil our belief in civilised behaviour in the minds of such primitive people as the Muslims of Afghanistan. 'Charles the Second only executed 13 of the men who ordered the death of his father, and that after fair trials,' Macnaghten told Burnes, apparently as evidence of how much more civilised our countrymen were even all those years ago. Perhaps he is right but that is no reason for his complacency.

*****

The day our missionary cricket-lover Dr Logan and I set off with an escort of native lancers for Charikar, I am chatting with Sergeant Wade, who is again on guard duty at the cantonment and still wearing only breeches and a white shirt. The weather is hot and the mountains look grand and almost beautiful in this bright morning light.

'The boys are sick of it here, sir,' he confides. 'They want to go home. It's hot now but last winter it was cold as hell. The climate here is colder than England. When it freezes, it bloody freezes and those mountains... that wind. The sooner we quit this place, the better.'

Miss Eden comes to see us off. We take a stroll as Hoosein and Wasim finish my packing and make final preparations for our journey. It's only a day's ride away through pleasant countryside, but I do not know what I shall find on my arrival and we need to be prepared. I have acquired several books and maps, as well as guns and swords, several sets of European and Afghan clothing, tables, chairs, bookcases, some intricately-woven Afghan carpets, dining implements including silver cutlery not to mention a sustaining supply of wine, beer, spirits and six fine horses. Life in Charikar will be bearable provided I have enough to keep me occupied. I even have some scientific equipment as I plan to make a study of the stars. Packing takes some time.

I invite Miss Eden and Mrs Sturt, with Lady Sale if necessary, to visit me in Charikar when we have settled ourselves in. I say I shall write to let her know and hope it is soon enough that she may make the journey while the weather is still fair and before her party returns with Sir William Macnaghten to India.

'Anything to relieve the tedium,' says Miss Eden, with a hint of laughter in her voice. 'My friends are anxious to return to civilisation, Major. I mean, can you imagine, there is hardly a drop of eau-decologne to be had, the price of Windsor soap is frankly ridiculous and I am assured by some of your brother officers there is a worrying shortage of decent claret.'

'So I gather, madam. The price of cheroots is going through the roof. Money goes up in smoke here.' We both chuckle. 'Perhaps things will be more comfortable in Charikar. I look forward to seeing you there.' I kiss her hand and she blushes slightly before turning and walking away with what I can only describe as a lilt in her step.

The preparations continue. Wasim says I have too many carpets and must choose which to leave behind. I tell him not to be ridiculous and find another camel. He says he must have money to pay for one. I say he is to use his initiative, he is commandeering one in the Queen's name. He says three rupees are more eloquent. I give him two and tell him to look lively.

*****

Two days later, as I am meeting the Gurkhas in Charikar, we receive news from Kabul. Dost Mohammed Khan has ridden into the city, bumped into Sir William Macnaghten apparently by accident and surrendered to him. As Hoosein predicted, he is to be pensioned off and sent to live in luxury in India – in the same palace previously occupied by Shah Soojah.

A second dispatch tells us the young man I met with Burnes just the other day is now dead. Leading a troop of native cavalry on a routine patrol, poor Lieutenant Walpole Clark is involved in a skirmish with a thieving mob of Ghilzees. The poor lad was hit above the heart but told Sergeant Prendergast, 'Don't say a word. It has gone through me but I don't want to show those fellows their shot has taken effect.' Another Lieutenant, a Sam Loveday, was taken prisoner and later found half-naked, emaciated and tied to a camel pannier with his throat cut.

I wonder if Macnaghten will be accompanying Dost Mohammed Khan and return to India with the ladies before the bad weather arrives.

And, if he were to do so, whether he is getting out while the going's still good.

CHAPTER 26

Charikar, September 1841

I am told not to interfere in military matters. I am a 'political', not a soldier. That, at least, is what Macnaghten's latest missive reminds me after I point out to him the dangers involved in siting the embassy in a small fort almost two miles from Charikar castle. Not that you could really call this mound of mud and rocks a castle, especially as the rebuilding work started earlier this year is far from finished and one of the entrances is still without a gate. It is overlooked on three sides – by an Afghan castle in one direction, by a mosque in another and by our own outbuildings in the orchard beside the canal on the third. This is not Herat and will not withstand a siege but, according to Macnaghten, this is none of my business. I am a tax-gatherer and local magistrate only.

Yet we are seeing small incidents of what I might call insurrection. A musket is stolen one day, a bugle the next. Yesterday the local chieftains protested over the high taxes we are expecting them to pay. They say the old king, Dost Mohammed Khan, did not take money from them, only men to make up his army. We British expect hard cash and want them to be grateful to have parties of foreigners spreading out all across their country. Dost Mohammed Khan's family had enough money to pay for his own court through the revenues from his own lands. Now this Shah Soojah expects the chiefs to maintain him, they say, but if the British want him as their puppet king they should meet the expenses themselves.

They also accuse us of ungodly ways because our men debauch their women and they have all heard of the dreadful rapes committed by our army when we took Ghazni, which was only achieved through the treachery of one of the Dost's closest relatives. They say their mullahs are preaching against us and warn of rebellions to come. They point out that only a year ago, close to this very town of Charikar, our army was bested and our cavalry disgraced in a battle with the Dost himself.

I point out the Dost fled the scene while our General, Sir Robert Sale, returned unhurt to Kabul. I add that the Dost has now surrendered himself to Sir William Macnaghten and the country is at peace.

After this delegation has departed, Hoosein tells me how wrong we are to think these tribesmen are ready to submit to British rule and pay their taxes. 'They are scheming, sahib,' he says. 'These petty thefts, they are no coincidence. The tribes are massing. They are just waiting for their orders from Mir Masjidi Khan.' Hoosein explains Mir Masjidi Khan was furious when the Dost gave himself up and has vowed to fight on. Mir Masjidi Khan is, according to Hoosein, both rich and saintly. The people see him almost as a holy man and when he calls them to fight, they look on his battles as a holy war. 'Sahib, this town is not safe, we are not safe,' Hoosein insists.

It's certainly true we are settled in a flimsy fortress consisting mainly of thrown-together wooden sheds within the bounds of modest mud walls. The place is filled with wasps and fleas and I have only 75 Afghans and 100 Gurkhas to defend it while the main army is in the fort down the road under Captain Christopher Codrington, a florid, overweight man with no battle honours to his name.

Like so many of the officers in Afghanistan who have bought their commissions, Codrington is not the sharpest sword in the armoury. When I say to him the two camps should be combined within the fort, he agrees but still feels the need to write to Elphinstone for permission and when the General replies it's up to him to make whatever dispositions he deems wise and satisfactory, he still hesitates, asks for further advice and concludes that inaction is the right course. When Hoosein tells me the Afghan troops under Codrington's command cannot be trusted, and I pass the message on, he calls in their officers and asks if they are honourable. When they assure him they are, he is satisfied. He reminds me my only role here is to secure the King's revenue, that I am really nothing more than the local tax-collector, and when I say there are difficulties securing the payments from the chiefs of Charikar and the surrounding area of Kohistan, he tells me his men cannot help.

Still, the weather is perfect and I am sitting in a shaded arbour under the fruiting jujube trees with my bulldog Caesar, a new recruit Wasim found wandering the countryside near here and we have adopted as our own. The afternoon sun casts its rays round about and the high clouds sail serenely across the sky above me. I hear the tinkling sound of a small stream which rushes down off the mountains towards the Kabul River and birds chatter in the trees. I am reading a book about Afghanistan by Mountstuart Elphinstone, once governor of Bombay and a relative of our own dear General. I trust Elphie has read and inwardly absorbed his cousin's warning that, while the Afghans are 'fond of liberty, faithful to their friends, kind to their dependants, hospitable, brave, hardy, frugal, laborious and prudent', their vices include 'revenge, envy, avarice, rapacity and obstinacy'.

*****

The weather is still fair and Miss Eden is visiting with Mrs Sturt and various other young ladies, accompanied by a troop of young officers. Captain Codrington takes on the role of host and we are all entertained in the Charikar fortress. This takes place in sight of about 200 or more Afghan horsemen who trot to and fro on the other side of the walls all afternoon. They are not exactly threatening but the constant drumming of hoof-beats, the woops of the warriors and the clouds of dust thrown up by their exertions are not a reassuring backdrop for the ladies nor, it has to be said, for the gentlemen.

The Gurkhas look anxiously over the parapets and then back at the Europeans enjoying the fruits of an Afghan autumn in what is a calm and very English picnic on the dry and brown lawns of this half-built bastion.

I tell Miss Eden I am pleased, but surprised, to find she is still in the country. 'The Dost Mohammed Khan has already set off for exile in India, I gather, but I assumed Sir William and the ladies would depart with him.'

She smiles, pleased to be able to confide in me. 'Ah but it seems, Major, that Sir William awaits his replacement from India before he can return.'

'His replacement? Is it not to be Burnes?'

'It seems not, Major,' she says, leaning in towards me as we sit, cross-legged on the ground drinking Champagne and eating salmon brought all the way from Aberdeen in sealed containers, 'Your friend Sir Alexander is not popular with Sir William. Sir William thinks he is too much an epicurean.'

'An epicurean?'

'I think that's the word he used. You know, someone who enjoys the good things of life a little too much – food, drink and so on.'

'And so on.' We both laugh and she slaps my thigh lightly.

'Poor Burnes. Does he know? And who will the new Envoy be? Has your brother told you?'

'My brother does not communicate with me very much, Major. All my intelligence comes to me second or even third-hand, from Mrs Sturt or my sisters Mary, Emily and Fanny who are all with my brother in Simla. Fanny is engaged to a dashing captain in the hussars.'

'My congratulations,' I say, not wishing to see the subject changed from the political gossip Miss Eden seems to possess. 'Do I know him?'

'Samuel Parsons of the 22nd.'

'No. I don't think I do. And Burnes's replacement.'

'Major Pottinger, I do believe you are more interested in the comings and goings of the political establishment than you are in romance and love. I am most dismayed.' She turns her face away from me and is immediately engaged in conversation by the officer on her left.

Is she genuinely upset I have shown little interest in Miss Fanny Eden's engagement or is she being coy? I cannot tell but I feel the absence of her attention like the sting of a nettle. It is trivial but it hurts. I would have her to myself if I could. No young woman has captivated my attention so completely. I think of poor young Mahparah, killed during the siege of Herat, and try to compare my feelings for her then with my feelings for Miss Eden now. There are differences, of course: culture, complexion, circumstances. I would never have taken Mahparah for a wife and she would never have expected it. At least I suppose she would not have. We never discussed it. But then, in a city under siege, when every day could be your last, there is no point discussing the future. There didn't seem to be one. Today, sitting in the warm autumn sun amid this party of visitors from Kabul, dressed as if for the races at home, it seems we have great grounds for optimism and hopes for the future.

If it were not for these infernal horsemen cantering up and down outside the castle walls waving their swords and firing their guns into the air.

*****

As our visitors are escorted to their quarters for the night, Mir Masjidi Khan presents himself at the gates of our fort. Captain Codrington admits him and the chief, along with a dozen of his lieutenants, marches into the only large room in the castle. He is a tall, handsome man not much older than I am, with thin cheeks, a big, unkempt beard and hooded eyes which seem to suggest a certain humility. He is not the kind of arrogant native one comes to expect. Mir Masjidi Khan speaks slowly, calmly and rationally.

'If you English had only come here as our friends, we would have welcomed you and sought to become your friends as well,' he says. 'You are not here as our friends but as invaders. You are foreigners, you are our enemy. You have placed your puppet on our throne and deposed our rightful king, Dost Mohammed Khan.'

Captain Codrington, as is usual with him, launches into a long and tedious explanation of why the Dost had to be replaced, about his dealings with the ungodly Russians, why British civilisation will be such a benefit to the people of Afghanistan and why its people are now under the protection of the greatest and most Godly empire in the history of the world.

Mir Masjidi Khan listens politely. He looks as if he is truly thinking about what Codrington tells him. When, finally, the Captain runs out of words, there is a moment of silence as Mir Masjidi Khan looks around him, appears to consult his friends, bows deferentially towards the other officers in the room and sighs. 'It is a sadness to me,' he says, 'That such a great empire and such a respected nation should come among us as tyrants and thieves. You mistreat our women, you force us to pay high taxes, prices go up, food is in short supply and you call this civilisation. If this is how you treat people you call your friends then Allah help the people you call your enemies. I am here, gentlemen, to ask you now, politely, and for the only time, to withdraw from my family's lands in Kohistan and I will allow you to depart unmolested. You may return to Kabul and then we shall see. But leave these lands at once. This is my request and this is also my warning. You have one week to make your preparations and I shall hope to see this castle empty within two weeks.'

Captain Codrington is silent but clearly furious. Other officers are fondling their swords with a view to striking the man down here and now. I do not blame them and perhaps that is the right thing to do but instead I step in and say to Mir Masjidi Khan, 'Sir, we hear your words and we will consider them carefully but now you have delivered your message, you must go. I would not wish to be guilty of mistreating a guest but I do fear for your safety if you were to remain for long.'

*****

We rush our visitors back to Kabul the following morning at dawn, sending Dr Logan with them. Miss Eden and I have no chance for a prolonged farewell though I do ask her to tell Burnes how worrying the situation here is. I have been up most of the night writing a despatch to Macnaghten telling him the garrison in Charikar needs to be urgently reinforced. A couple of cavalry divisions would probably be adequate but they must be sent immediately otherwise I fear Mir Masjidi Khan will make good on his threats and our own defences, both men and dispositions, are not adequate to fight off a large force of Afghan warriors.

Two days later a message arrives from Macnaghten. 'Troops cannot be spared,' he says, 'And your apprehensions are in any case exaggerated. There is no cause for this alarm. Take a firm hand and do not let the natives get the better of you.' Instead of reinforcements, the damned man demands the return of 25 men from my escort.

This cannot be a sensible reaction to the threat posed by Mir Masjidi Khan. I consult Captain Codrington and he agrees we need more men but he says if Macnaghten won't send them there is nothing to be done but trust to God. I suggest moving my mission into the fortress but he says he is not sure there is room for another two hundred men. I urge him to rebuild the defences and move our field guns to more prominent positions overlooking the ungated entrance. At least he does this, though it takes a dozen men all day to manoeuvre our one 18-pounder into position.

'I don't see any reason for all this alarm, Pottinger,' says Codrington. 'My Gurkhas are as fine a body of men as any in the Company's army.'

'But what about our Afghan soldiers?' I ask. 'Are they to be relied upon?'

'I see no reason why not. But if you think they are untrustworthy, we could throw them out I suppose.'

'And have them reinforce the enemy?'

'No, perhaps not.'

*****

Time is running out. I return to Kabul with my 25 escorts to see Macnaghten in person. He keeps me waiting all evening and eventually grants me an audience at midnight, as he is about to retire to bed. He is in his drawing room drinking brandy. His wife Lady Frances is with him, fussing over three ginger-coloured cats which she calls Shaddie, Meeshie and Abbey.

I apologise for disturbing them at such a late hour – though the disturbance is entirely of their own making – and explain about our interview with Mir Masjidi Khan, add the local intelligence Hoosein has gathered, discuss the taxation question and say the immediate deployment of two detachments of cavalry would, in my opinion, deter any serious insurrection and, should such a thing occur anyway, allow us to put it down without much ado.

Lady Macnaghten, who maintains a commentary to her cats throughout my speech, does not give her husband time to respond before she says, in an accent which my step-mother would describe as 'common', 'Pottinger? Irish are you?' I confirm the truth of her observation as politely as I can. 'Another Irishman, William. Really.' She tuts and turns back to Shadrach, or perhaps it's Meshach, saying, 'And what do we think of the Irish my little fluffy bunny?'

Sir William, however, remains silent. I stand before him. I have not been invited to sit let alone offered any of his brandy. Eventually he sits up in his leather armchair and says, 'Pottinger, if you were not so well-known as the "Hero of Herat" I should say your alarmism smacks of – what shall I say? – a certain nervous disposition. This country is tranquil from Herat to Kandahar and no-one shall gainsay that. I am leaving here any day now, my appointment as Governor of Bombay awaits only confirmation from Lord Eden of my replacement, and I am not prepared to depart this country if there is any suggestion of turmoil or disturbance. I hold you personally responsible, sir, for maintaining cordial relations with the local chiefs. It is not beyond the wit of man to deal with these people and keep the peace. Or is it, Major? Are you not capable of the diplomacy for which you are employed? Would you prefer a transfer back to the Governor-General's staff?'

Macnaghten is mocking me. He smiles and sits back, puffing on a cheroot. 'Sir William, the position is serious and I do not believe an uprising can be prevented by diplomatic means alone. If I were to rescind all taxes and, indeed, offer payment of a couple of lakhs of rupees then perhaps we could prevent an immediate disaster...'

Behind his blue spectacles, Macnaghten's face contorts with rage though he does not rise from his chair or raise his voice. 'I beg your pardon, Major, but for a moment I thought you were suggesting we buy off our enemies by remitting their taxes and offering them a bribe of two hundred thousand rupees.'

'That is the only alternative to a show of military force, sir,' I agree.

'Have I not explained already how this country is draining our resources? Have I not told you we cannot carry on as we are? That the Afghans must be made to pay for their King and their army? And you want to reverse this policy at the first sign of a little discontent. Get back to Charikar, sir, get back there immediately. I want to hear no more about it. Go, sir, go.'

*****

I visit General Elphinstone, who does not seem to have moved since my last interview. The only difference is that a fire is burning in the grate and three of his senior officers are sitting at a table a distance away playing cards. At least Brigadier Shelton isn't present – he has taken the 44th to be garrisoned in a village about five miles off, though no-one seems able to explain why. I ask Elphie for reinforcements but I feel obliged to admit Macnaghten has already turned down my request.

Elphie is pleasantness itself. He gives a regretful smile and reaches for his morning brandy. 'My dear fellow, if it were up to me, then of course your request should be granted. Of course, of course. But alas…' He throws his free hand into the air and allows it to fall by his side in a gesture of helplessness. Elphie smiles and says over my shoulder to the three officers at the table, who are pretty much indifferent to our conversation, 'We know who's the General round here, do we not my fine fellows? Yes? Yes? Yes? Alas, Pottinger my hands are tied.'

As I leave, one of the officers follows me out and introduces himself as Captain John Sturt. 'We met when they were playing at cricket,' he reminds me.

'Of course,' I apologise, acknowledge his salute and shake his hand. We stroll away from Elphie's headquarters beside the rows of tents, which look a little more flimsy somehow now that autumn is upon us and the weather is starting to turn chilly.

I explain the situation and appraise him of my fears. 'I do believe, captain, that the very least we should be doing now, as a matter of urgency, is to evacuate the women and children before the winter sets in and the passes are cut off.'

Sturt, a tall, handsome man with a determined look in his eye, takes me by the arm. 'What I am about to tell you, Major, is known to very few but you need to know. Elphie has resigned his commission and ostensibly is already in retirement. We await a replacement but this is not official yet because we are all hoping against hope that Shelton will not be appointed as commander in chief in Afghanistan. The men hate him. And he hates this country. For weeks now his constant refrain has been that we should leave. He will not be your ally any more than Macnaghten is. For now, we maintain the pretence that Elphie commands the army for fear of someone worse. I'm not sure how long we can keep this up and we anticipate news from the Governor-General any day.'

'But in the meantime, if the situation worsens?'

'We have to shift as best we can.'

'Without reinforcement? Without even evacuating ladies and the children?'

'Impossible, I fear, until Macnaghten and Elphie depart and we know who their replacements are to be.'

'Not Burnes, I gather?'

Sturt hesitates. 'Sir, I am a recently-married man. My dear wife is expecting our first child.' I offer my congratulations but he waves them away. 'No-one is more anxious for the safety of our families and friends than I am but Burnes...' His voice trails away and he kicks the dirt with his boot, staring at the ground with a pent-up frustration. Quietly, Sturt goes on, 'Sir Alexander is... Well, Sir Alexander is not what he once was, I fear.'

'How do you mean?' I ask. 'He is still the same sophisticated and charming man he has always been.'

'Macnaghten doesn't trust him, says he behaves like a pasha. Debauches the local women, indulges his senses, all that. And he has never been reconciled to the new King either, for that matter.'

*****

Sturt takes me to his mother-in-law's house, where I find Lady Sale, Mrs Sturt and Eleanor. The ladies are embroidering kneelers for the new stone church which is being built inside the cantonment to replace the wooden edifice which was the first building to be constructed on our arrival in Kabul. It is considered a matter of the utmost importance to establish a permanent Christian presence in the city before Logan and other missionaries can proceed with the important work of trying to convert some of the heathen Afghan Muslims to the true faith.

None of the ladies is particularly interested in her work and they appear grateful for the interruption, though the news I bring is not so welcome. Lady Sale says she is still in communication with her husband, who is 100 miles and several mountainous passes away in Jalalabad, but expected she and the other ladies should have been removed there several weeks ago.　　Mrs Sturt says it is too bad of the Company to leave them languishing in Kabul when the weather it starting to turn. Eleanor hopes the ladies won't blame her brother the Governor-General for the delay.

I am given coffee and we chat idly. Lady Sale is thinking of bidding for some of the furniture Elphie is auctioning prior to his departure. 'He has a lovely walnut bookcase which would go very nicely over there,' she says, indicating a blank space of wall. 'But if we are travelling home with him then it seems a bit pointless, doesn't it Drina dear?'

Her daughter says, 'There is really no point, mamma. The less we are encumbered with the better.'

Then Eleanor looks up from her embroidery frame and says, 'We may not be leaving yet, Major Pottinger, but as you are interested in Herat you may like to know Major Todd has passed through Kabul in recent days on his way back to Calcutta.'

'Todd? My successor there?'

'No longer, it seems. He has taken it upon himself to abandon his post and my brother is apparently not best pleased. Todd says he could no longer cope with the untrustworthy double-dealing of Shah Kamran and his Vizier.'

'No,' Captain Sturt says. 'They were taking lakhs and lakhs of rupees from us and negotiating with the Shah of Persia at the same time. Eventually Darcy could stand the deceit no longer and thought it was beneath the dignity of Her Majesty to deal with such thieves. It seems since Todd's departure Shah Kamran and his sons have been thrown into prison by that devil Yar Mahomed and the vizier has seized the crown.'

I cannot avoid a certain satisfaction in this news though it reinforces my view that Macnaghten's judgment is unreliable. He told Todd to save money and look what happens. I remember Macnaghten saying to me, 'Todd is an accomplished diplomat, Pottinger, not some adventurer.' Well, so much for diplomacy.

We do not discuss my immediate fears. I cannot bring myself to declare openly to the ladies that they would be safer far from this place, if not in India then with General Sale in Jalalabad. I wish to alert them to the coming danger and encourage them to leave but I cannot do so because, poor creatures, they are at the mercy of Elphinstone and Macnaghten. However much I might urge their departure, if the General and the Envoy are not prepared to take steps to protect our defenceless women, it would be wrong to create anxiety which might, after all, prove to be unnecessary. Perhaps I am wrong. Perhaps insurrection is not brewing. Perhaps we will be able to nip it in the bud if it shows its ugly head.

And perhaps not.

*****

I am only back at our paltry little fort a couple of days when Mir Masjidi Khan's deadline expires. The following morning we find almost 3,000 Afghans, most on horseback, armed with their long-range jezzail rifles, the rest kitted out with disconcertingly-sharpened swords, camped around us.

Nothing happens for a few hours and our small band of native infantrymen and Gurkhas waits nervously on our precarious battlements reviewing the enemy just a few hundred yards away. After a long morning in the chill of the autumn air, gazing across at this collection of bearded Ghilzais, who sit staring back at us, I collect my little band of officers – John Houghton, Dr James Grant and Charles Rattray – to ask for their advice. We agree to invite the Ghilzai chiefs into the fort for a parlay but they refuse to join us when I send Rattray out under a flag of truce. Instead they call for us to go out to them.

Unarmed, for it does not do to be provocative, I open the gate. Rattray and I slip out. There are about a dozen petty chiefs, drawn up in an orchard about 250 yards from the fort, though there is no sign of Mir Masjidi Khan. They call us foreigners and demand our withdrawal from Charikar. They say this is their land and they do not wish to submit to heathen invaders. They accuse us of lacking respect for Allah and their faith. I counter that we have only come into the country to restore the rightful King of Kabul to the throne and point out he is a member of their faith. We respect Islam and have no wish to disturb their religious rites in any way. They demand money; I say the truth, which is we have no money. They object to paying taxes; I say they would be required to pay money to the King whether we were here or not. The argument goes on as we stand around the rugs they have spread over the damp grass.

Lieutenant Rattray, an experienced hand, being older than me and fluent in the language, engages in a separate conversation with three of the lesser chiefs. They seem to be friendly enough. I overhear talk of water supplies and the three chiefs, all young men with dark eyes, lead him further away from the fort in the direction of the Kabul road.

My debate with the other chiefs carries inconclusively on until, ten minutes after Rattray's departure, we all hear a gunshot. I look at the chiefs, who stare in the direction of the shot as it dawns on all of us the lieutenant has been murdered. The first shot is followed by several more – clearly the enemy, having scented blood, is making the most of its grisly advantage over the British officer. Poor man, he had no chance.

I do not believe this attack was planned before we left the fort but don't wait to debate. If they will kill one unarmed British officer in cold blood, they won't hesitate to kill another. I turn and run towards the fort, where the men on the ramparts are preparing for an attack. I hear Houghton bellowing orders and Grant urging me to get back inside.

I'm close to the gates as the rebels' rifles ring out and volley after volley comes streaming towards the fort. I see shot punch holes in the walls close by as Grant ushers me swiftly inside and two men slam the gate shut, bar it and take position with their rifles in the gun-slits.

I cannot send a message to Kabul. It would be hard enough to get through to Codrington two miles down the road.

The firing continues sporadically for the next couple of hours but the enemy do not venture close enough to the fort for our guns to have much effect. The longer range of their weapons leaves us vulnerable while they are more or less untouchable. They kill and wound several of our native infantry and a couple of Gurkhas though we are generally in good shape when we hear firing coming from our right. Codrington has sent out a squadron of cavalry who are wreaking havoc. I call together the Gurkhas and, with Houghton, we rush out to join the fray. The Afghans, for all their bravado, are not so happy with cold steel in their guts and they quickly cut and run. The relief party has done its work and Codrington leaves a troop behind, bringing our strength back to 200. Codrington takes the wounded with him and promises to send up supplies tomorrow. By the time dusk turns to dark we are able to bury our four dead outside the walls of the fort and recover the terribly cut-up body of poor Rattray. Dr Grant, though a medical man rather than a doctor of divinity, leads the burial party and a moving little ceremony it is too. Only Rattray is officially entitled to a Christian burial but the Gurkhas don't object, given the reverence we accord to their comrades. The Afghan soldiers turn their backs on the ceremony, however, and retreat to the barrack block. This is worrying.

*****

The supplies do not reach us the next day, nor the following one. Instead we do what we can to shore up our defences and engage in brief skirmishes with the Afghans, who seem to be treading more carefully since they were surprised on the first day. We are low on food and water and ammunition is even more scarce. If they were to attack in force, I do not believe we have the resources to fight them off. We have no choice – we must withdraw to the castle and join the main force with Codrington there.

Houghton leads the first sortie out of the postern gate, leaving behind our few animals and the equipment, such as it is, that we cannot carry. The night is dark with thick cloud above and no moon. It is warm and sound is muffled in the heavy air. This allows his troop to steal away unheard. I lead the second group out of the fort an hour later and we slip into a little gulley which runs alongside the canal. One hundred men cannot move in complete silence and every so often we stop, to listen and look about us. We hear the voices of Ghilzais around a camp fire some distance from where we are. By crawling up the bank and looking over the canal, I can see their tents and horses and their smoky fires. The smells of wood-smoke and cooking drift towards us in the still air. I find myself involuntarily salivating – I haven't eaten for 48 hours and the strong aromas of the cooking remind me of what I have been missing. We cannot wait – on we press, step by stealthy step, until at last Codrington's castle comes in sight. It is lit with torches and busy with men – clearly Houghton's division has already arrived and we are expected.

From our vantage point, about half a mile away, we look down on the castle and, even in the dark, I realise how vulnerable it is to attack. Sited on low ground, overlooked by other buildings, with paltry battlements and roofless accommodation blocks – the rebuilding work has not been finished – we are swapping one death trap for another. The Company flag droops limply on its pole. I am surprised Charikar castle is so brightly lit, as if inviting a night-time attack.

The last 300 yards to the castle gates are across flat, open ground. If the Afghans are lying in wait, this is where we are most in danger. I give the order to leave the relative safety of our gulley and take the lead in heading towards the castle. I'm braced for gunfire, taut and itching to let off my pistols at the first sign of attack. But all is quiet. We trot across the field and into the castle where I am enthusiastically welcomed by Houghton and Codrington. The men are all gathered in. But we are certainly not safe.

We are just better placed to die together.

*****

Another lull. The Afghans are looting the fort which gives us some respite to prepare our defences but it is clear why Codrington never sent supplies – he has none to send. There is little food, less ammunition and a serious shortage of water.

We can see the canal, and beyond that the river, but the Afghans have moved up between the castle and our sources of water. Taking stock, some of the men have their own canteens of water, there is still some in the filthy, mildewed tank they built some months ago but this has to be filled by water-carrying parties and when Codrington sent out two dozen Afghans to the canal last night, none of them returned. He did not hear any sound of fighting which makes him suppose they fled or, in all probability, went over to the enemy. There are horses, of course, and a few sheep and goats but they need water too. Wasim, who is growing into a tall, strong young man and keeps at Hoosein's side at all times, is worried about whether Caesar, our dog, will survive long in this enforced drought.

At dawn we have men on the insecure ramparts and issue orders for them to make do with dew to refresh themselves. There is a lot of moaning but it doesn't last long because by the second hour of daylight we are under determined attack from Mir Musjidi Khan's rebels.

The castle is almost impossible to defend. It's got 100 yards of walls with one main gate and the postern but it is on low-lying land. The Ghilzais rain down fire on us from the top of the nearby minaret and another group stands along the battlements of a fort about 150 yards away. We are forced to rip down the tents where most of the officers and men sleep and sling them over planks of wood to provide walkways and cover. This takes several hours of hot, sweaty, dangerous work but at least they can't pick us off quite so easily when we finish.

During a lull in the fighting, around the time of the Call to Prayer, Codrington sends out a party of forty Ghurkhas to bring in water. We watch from the castle as they ride swiftly through the main gate towards the canal and the river, each with two empty water bags on the saddle. They are followed by another 20 men on foot, carrying buckets.

They get only 200 yards when the Afghans open fire from the cover of the trees in the orchard. A band of horsemen gallops round to cut off their retreat and another emerges from the far side of the canal. The fighting is fierce and many Afghans are slain but our men are overwhelmed by numbers and we are forced to watch as they are cut down. The Ghilzais slit throats, cut off heads, whoop and cry, exult in the slaughter and turn towards us to indicate we are next.

*****

Night brings some respite. We take stock. We have no water and ammunition is desperately low. The native troops slip away over the walls whenever they can. Occasionally one of our loyal Ghurkhas spots a deserter in the act and unceremoniously shoots him in the back. But it is no deterrent – these Afghans are divided in their loyalties and can clearly see the way the wind is blowing. We cannot hold out for long. Some of the men are slaughtering our remaining sheep simply to slake their thirst on the animals' blood. But there is not even enough blood to go round.

Codrington, Grant, Houghton and I have another council of war. We have lost two officers, a sergeant and 100 men killed, while twice as many lie groaning around our fort injured in the fighting. Many will die and there is little Grant can do for them. Wasim is acting as his assistant, fetching and carrying, binding up wounds and promising to bring water which, alas, he never delivers. Hoosein has taken up a post beside one of our three guns – two brass six-pounders which are reasonably effective and an old iron 18-pounder which was an antique when Clive was defending Arcot 90 years ago. It carries an inscription saying it was cast in the reign of George II. Why anyone thought it was a good idea to transport this unwieldy monster across the Hindu Kush all the way to Charikar I do not know.

Even so, and despite officially being the highest-ranking officer in the castle, I appoint myself captain of gunnery, while Codrington keeps overall command, concentrating on the outer defences and Houghton seeks new ways of obtaining the water we need if we are to survive even another couple of days.

'Why did they send us here unless it was to kill us?' Houghton complains.

'Macnaghten says the country is all at peace,' I remind him.

'What are we to do with the women?' Codrington asks. It's a good question – there are about 250 women and children, whole families, cooks and drabs with their brats slumped in corners, wailing and whining with fear and getting in the way. Can they even be trusted? They are wasting what little resources we have and may even be hoarding supplies, including precious water. We cannot care for them, protect or even feed them.

'We should expel them from the castle, this very night,' I suggest. 'They did something like that in Herat and, much as it pained us to watch them go, it helped the rest of us to withstand the siege.'

'No, we can't do that,' says Codrington, 'They would be cut down straight away.'

'They will die anyway,' I say, 'They would have a better chance outside these walls than remaining here. Perhaps their countrymen will take pity on them. Here they're just target practice.'

The others reject the idea and perhaps they are right to do so. The camp-followers will die whether they stay or go and it would go down in the annals of infamy if we were to turn them out only to see them massacred before our eyes.

Full of foreboding, we rest as much as we can under a wide, starry sky. In the distance we can hear the enemy camps, see their fires and smell their cooking. I lie awake thinking of Maparah while the bulldog, Caesar, lies at my feet with Wasim beside him. Is Maparah with God now and, if so, which God – my God, the one true God, or some Muslim alternative? The stars shine coldly down, each one a dead soul.

*****

251

We are woken from our fitful slumbers by the sound of vigorous drumming from what seems like a thousand hides. The enemy is now numberless – Houghton says 20,000 though how he can tell I do not know – and seems to delight in dancing around our small castle, careful to remain far enough away for our musket shots to be useless, though one or two of the men let off a defiant round from time to time.

I check on the guns and the men who are manning them. The two six-pounders are close to the postern gate, which is probably our most vulnerable position, while the 18-pounder is stuck aiming over the main gate.

After the drums, we are subjected to musket fire. The shot lands randomly on the canvas above our heads and causes little damage, though the noise is like a storm of hail and thunder. Several men are ordered to scramble around retrieving the shot in the hope we can turn it against those who fired it, though there is little lead in them. They consist mostly of mis-shapen pieces of rock and stone, primitive but still lethal.

The Ghilzais stay beyond reach of our muskets. We fire off a few cannon-rounds to little effect though it is good to offer some retaliation and each blast earns a half-hearted cheer from our parched garrison.

As the morning marches on, it is clear the Afghans are preparing to mount a frontal attack. We see horsemen mustering half a mile away, with many more on foot. They wheel and whoop for some time before an order seems to be given and they charge the castle. A new hail of gunfire descends from the nearby buildings and the minaret. We hold our fire until the signal is given – the first shot from the decrepit 18-pounder. There is a ground-shuddering boom as the old gun lets loose its first ball and we have to jump backwards to avoid the recoil. The gun does its job, though. The ball ploughs through the advancing warriors, cutting down several horsemen. Our troops on the ramparts start to fire and, here and there, a horseman or his steed plunges into the dusty ground.

With much effort we re-load the 18-pounder and fire off another volley into the circling, whooping cavalrymen. Again it cuts a swathe through their ranks and, as the men on the battlements take aim and fire at will, the enemy soon retreats leaving perhaps 100 dead and wounded on the battlefield.

'The bastards will be back,' growls Grant, who has been assisting me with the gun. The good doctor is sweat-soaked and dirty. I look at him and we both start to laugh because what I see in him, he sees in me – a big, red-faced unshaven Irishman filthy from the fray.

At night, we send out another party of Ghurkhas in search of water. They return bloody but more or less intact, though without that precious commodity. They fell on some of the Afghan outposts and slaughtered as many of the enemy as they could find. I dare say it will not be a pleasant sight in the morning but these men have been sorely tried. Their ferocity is understandable even if they have failed in the mission they were given and we are no better off than we were before.

After a dawn chorus of gunfire, our enemy falls eerily silent. The cavalry charge has not materialised. We send out a patrol, led by Houghton, which sets up an outpost on the way to the canal. If we can hold this, there is a chance we will be able to move on towards water without which we cannot possibly hold out. This is followed by a series of skirmishes with the Ghilzais as they try to prevent us from establishing a base outside the castle. By nightfall, however, Houghton's small force is still in place in a small tower a hundred yards from the castle. This is progress of a sort.

At night, though, the Ghilzais keep up a constant stream of curses and imprecations, threats and warnings. They scream and drum and yell and whistle, fire into the air and their mullahs can be heard bellowing they are carrying out the work of Allah in destroying the foreigners in their midst.

But still no concerted attack.

'If this is to be a long siege,' I tell Codrington, 'We must have water, we must conserve our ammunition and we must maintain some sort of discipline. Can we trust the native infantry?'

Codrington growls. Dr Grant sighs. Hoosein says, 'No Sahib, they are already deserting. They are not loyal.'

We summon their three officers, all good Afghan men loyal to Britain and to Shah Soojah but they shake their heads and warn there is unrest. The following morning Codrington orders a pay parade and we go through the long charade of pretending everything is normal and we have great confidence in the future by handing out rupees to all the men. This takes place even as a party of Afghans tries to blow up a corner of the castle wall and our Gurkhas fire volley after volley of shot down on them.

At midday three chieftains ride slowly across the field before the castle under a white flag of truce. All firing ceases and we open the gates to admit them. Codrington and I have both put on his full dress uniform for the occasion, to emphasise the Company's power and prestige.   Dr Grant has on a clean frock coat though some of the others are too weary and parched to maintain the pretence that we are unperturbed.

Two of the chiefs are bearded young men with fierce, dark eyes. They, too, have dressed for the occasion in the huge Afghan headgear with long greatcoats and apparently-new leather boots. They are unarmed. They are led by an older man with a long grey beard and a striking, intricately-wrought scarlet tunic and a head-dress of matching material pinned in place with a large emerald brooch.

They bow. We wait. Clouds roll overhead, the wind is chill but there is not a drop of rain. The castle is silent, our troops keep half an eye on our conference and half on the deserted fields without.

'Well?' Codrington growls. He is quite impressive, I admit, in his refusal to bow to these rebels.

The older man smiles, draws shapes in the dust with the toe of his boot, looks around him at our shambolic defences and the hordes of non-combatants we are saddled with. 'You foreigners,' he says, in a surprisingly civil tone, 'You will all die here I am sorry to say. You have invaded our land and brought your foreign God with you. You are heathens and you cannot stay.'

I step forward so I stand only inches from him. He smells of horses. I cannot say what he smells on me but I look him in the eye and respond in his own quiet tones. 'On the contrary, sir, we are rightfully here at the request of your rightful King, Shah Soojah-ool-Moolk Durrani, the rightful monarch and a good Mohammeden. We have restored your King to his Throne and restored your country to its true faith. You have no quarrel with us.'

The chief looks up at me and smiles. 'You speak well, foreigner, but like all foreigners, you lie. Our King is Dost Mohammed Khan not this Soojah. You act in the name of the usurper but he is your man, your puppet. He is not our King but yours. You will die here. Unless,' and here the chief looks around him at the nods of approval from his followers, 'Unless you submit yourself to Allah, throw away your false religion and embrace Islam truly and with your whole soul.'

Grant chokes in fury, Codrington cries, 'God damn you, man! Get out, get out, get gone.'

More politely, I say, 'I regret, sir, that Her Majesty's Army is an army made up of good Christians and we are not in the habit of abandoning the One True Faith at the request of a few faithless brigands. It would, perhaps, be desirable if you were now to withdraw and take with you the message that we would prefer to die here today as God-fearing Christians than live a thousand years as base Mohammedens.'

The young men reach for their sabres only to find they are not carrying them. Their elder smiles again and says, as politely as before, 'I regret we can find no accommodation between us, Major. You leave us no choice but to destroy you and your companions, whether it takes a day or a year. We will withdraw now, as you suggest. But the next time I stand here, I am sorry to say, you will be dead or dying.'

The trio is escorted back to the gate and allowed to ride away unimpeded while Grant mutters, 'Well, that's our last chance of survival gone, then, I suppose.'

'Unless they send reinforcements from Kabul,' Codrington points out.

*****

Reinforcements do not come. At one stage we see a cloud of dust on the Kabul road as a party of horsemen approaches Charikar. This leads to ragged cheers among the men. They think a relief force is on its way but it is only wishful-thinking – not a mirage, because the horsemen are real but they are not, after all, wearing colours of our own 5th Cavalry and, some distance away, they turn off the road into one of the enemy camps.

Grant, who is more anxious about his collection of ancient coins than he is about his life or that of others, constantly nags Codrington for the means to protect them. 'They date back to King Diodotus of Bactria,' he tells us constantly, as if this should mean something. Perhaps when we have the peace to discuss it properly, I shall ask Grant to tell me all about Diodotus and Bactria but for now I am content with my ignorance. Anyway, Grant has other duties to perform: the mass burial of our men in the pit which was supposed to be our water tank. The ceremony takes place at dusk and we are a melancholy party as we consign the souls of almost 100 men, as well as several women and a few children, to the care of Our Lord. We throw the dead bullocks and sheep over the castle wall rather than consign them to a Christian grave – a mistake as the furious smell of rotting carcases is added to our miseries.

After more fierce fighting, Houghton's outriders are finally forced to flee and we admit his depleted force back into the fort as the Afghan cavalry mount another charge. We deploy the 18-pounder to good effect – the balls cut through men and horses with indiscriminate anger – but this time it seems the attack is a decoy. A huge explosion in the north-west corner reveals a gaping hole in the wall. Houghton orders men to demolish the sheds used for their quarters and fill bags with sand to shore up this breach. We move one of the six-pounders to cover them and manage to keep out the invaders but it is clear we cannot hold out much longer.

Codrington takes a shot that opens up his chest. The poor man falls like a stone. Houghton rushes to his side and the old soldier groans, 'Take these, John, and give the buggers hell.' He hands Houghton his telescope and pistol, coughs, groans and closes his eyes for the last time.

There is another lull in the battle. The Afghans withdraw, allowing us to reinforce our defences further. Everyone is exhausted, parched, starving hungry. The native troops cannot be relied on, the camp followers seem to be dangerously invisible. Our injured now outnumber those who are more or less unhurt. Taking stock is a depressing business, especially as the stink of rotting animal carcasses is now unavoidable.

Towards evening, with the fields around the castle empty of our enemies, we see a white flag approaching from far off. It is being carried by one of our Afghan artillerymen. This one deserted a few days ago but here he is, approaching the main gate on foot under a flag of truce.

From 50 yards off, he calls out for Lieutenant Houghton. I have no idea who this young man is but Houghton recognises him and beckons him to approach. The youth stays where he is and plants the white flag in the hard ground. Again he begs conference with the Lieutenant.

'Go and see what he wants,' says Grant, turning his back on the scene and returning to the sick bay to tend the dead and dying.

'No, don't,' I say. 'This man is a deserter. By rights he should be shot. You cannot possibly trust him, John.'

Houghton, however, is nonchalant. 'These native boys are unreliable. He may be coming back to us with valuable information. And look, he is under a flag of truce.'

Houghton orders one of the gates to be opened. Grant and I take up our post with three other men beside the 18-pounder. We clean out the muzzle, stuff in another ball, prepare the fuse, ensure the match is lit and watch as Houghton strides with surprising energy for a man so sorely tried towards the youth with the white flag. A shaft of sunlight slices through the grey cloud, sharpening the scene. The young man wears a big white head-dress and a long brown coat. His hands are stretched out to either side and, as Houghton reaches him, he embraces the lieutenant like a long-lost friend.

Only as he does so do we see he has a knife in his right hand. He is attempting to stab Houghton in the back. The lieutenant yells and makes to grab the knife as the Afghan pulls a second one from inside his coat and slams it into Houghton's thigh. The two men grapple as the lieutenant tries to turn the knives on his assailant while on the battlements one or two men take aim but dare not fire for fear of hitting our officer. Three Ghurkhas race towards Houghton yelling in fury, their sabres flashing in the shaft of sunlight. Houghton falls to the ground, blood gushing from several wounds, but before the Afghan can deliver the fatal stab, the Ghurkhas are upon him and slash him to pieces in a matter of moments before taking up the body on the ground and staggering back towards the castle with Houghton in their arms.

As they approach, we hear the guns and cries of the Ghilzai cavalry as they follow up their lone deserter with another charge on our fortress. Grant and I are ready and fire off the first canon shot as soon as they are within 150 yards. By now the men are firing as rapidly as their muskets will let them, the gates are slammed shut and Houghton is dragged to the sick bay. I tell Grant to tend to him and take over his ram-rod duties as well as igniting the gunpowder. Two of our Afghans are on hand, one to clean the muzzle, the other to insert a fresh ball. But it all takes time. By the time of our second shot, most of the Afghans are out of our field of fire. Shifting this huge cannon takes too long but we fire off another ball anyway, then I order grapeshot because it will, at least, disperse more widely and should cause more damage to the enemy.

Behind the cavalry come men with scaling ladders. Our walls are not high enough to keep them out if they once set these makeshift steps alongside the building. The six-pounder at the breach in the north wall is going about its work effectively enough but the other one is silent. I look toward the postern gate and see its crew scrabbling over the wall, running away.

I take my two Afghans and two Ghurkhas and race towards the deserted gun. It's easier to manoeuvre so we haul it up beside the 18-pounder, point it towards where the men with ladders are making an assault on the castle walls and let rip the first of four volleys in rapid succession.

As the enemy turns to run, I hear a roar. It is an unnatural sound which, even in the fury of battle, seems to reverberate in my mind. It takes a moment before I realise it is my own voice making this roar. It takes longer for me to realise why I am howling like this. Part of my right leg seems to have been shot away. My britches have a big black hole in them and red blood is rapidly turning its dirty brown to something as crimson as a trooper's tunic. It takes another moment before I actually feel the seething pain which this wound has caused.

My body falls from the gun emplacement, collapsing onto the hard ground. I cannot break my fall or even work out what has happened to me. All I can now feel is a terrible pain, more fierce and cruel than anything I have ever felt before. I smell the sweat of my own fear and agony. I bury my face in the dust as if this will somehow alleviate the pain. I hear the intermittent reports of gunshot, the occasional boom of the cannon, the yells and cries of the combatants and look at a stone immediately before me as if I have never seen a roundish, brownish, hard-looking piece of rock before in my life. All I can focus on is the stone. How long has it lain here? Have I disturbed it or was it always here? Does it see my pain?

I cannot tell how long this lasts. Probably only a few moments but it seems like half a lifetime, the stone and me, staring at each other, blank and expressionless. Then I hear Wasim. 'Sahib, sahib,' he cries and tries to help me sit up. Hoosein is with him and grabs the shirt off the back of a dead Afghan who lies beside me – was he killed by the same shot which felled me? – rips it into strips and starts to bind up my leg.

'Tight, tight,' Hoosein mutters. 'Tourniquet,' he orders Wasim. The boy finds a stick and they apply it to the top of my thigh to stem the flow of blood. I try to make no sound, clenching my teeth as if this will somehow alleviate the pain that seems to run from my leg along my back and to my head. My whole body is on fire.

They take me by the shoulders and drag me towards the sick bay. I am helpless to resist though I want to know how the battle is proceeding. Wasim says, 'They are going, sahib.'

'For now,' adds Hoosein grimly as he takes a cloth and wipes some of the sweat and blood from my face.

I am parched. 'Water,' I groan.

'No water, sahib,' says Wasim.

They deposit me next to Houghton. Grant is amputating the lieutenant's left hand.

*****

Houghton is a brave man. His hand has been lost and he has terrible wounds to his neck and back but he will not give up. He makes me think my own pain is bearable. We sit under the canvas awnings and take stock. We have lost more than half our men, the native troops are deserting, the camp followers are rifling through our possessions and stealing whatever they can lay their hands on – though how they think they will fare when they fall into the hands of the enemy, I don't know. We cannot hold out any longer. Another attack and we shall be overrun. We agree the only reasonable course of action is to retreat this very night, despite our disabilities.

I get Hoosein to summon the remaining officers and we hold a council of war. I find myself not only the most senior but the most experienced officer here. I am mindful of Macnaghten's warning that I am just a diplomat, I am not to involve myself in military matters. I make this clear to the others and ask if they have any view.

The native officers are doubtful they can command their men

any longer. Several have already joined in the looting and others are surrounding the treasury, next to Codrington's quarters, no doubt planning a break-in and there is nothing we can do to prevent them – after all, going to war on natives who are supposedly our own men will just hand the castle over to the enemy even more quickly.

The other surviving British officers, and Hanrahan, the Sergeant-Major of the Ghurkhas, are more certain about their men but have no confidence that we will survive another concerted attack.

They complain about their inability to deal with the looters and camp-followers, who just get in the way, make demands on the men's scarce resources and cannot be trusted. I suggest the obvious tactic is to withdraw but say it is not my decision to make. Grant agrees it is the only option. Houghton says he would rather stay and fight but I point out to him he would not survive five minutes in his present condition. This he acknowledges. Sergeant-Major Hanrahan strokes his thick moustache and says, 'Major Pottinger, you are in command now, whatever your other orders may be. My boys would rather fight to the death than see themselves bested by these savages but I agree it is not the wisest course of action. In Kabul we can regroup.'

The others assent and so, like it or not, I am obliged to issue the order to retreat.

The looters will have to fend for themselves. We are only concerned with the men under our command. The bugler, Gabriel Peterson, will stay behind to sound reveille. It is probably a death sentence and his sacrifice will go unrewarded but the poor lad is already half-dead with fatigue, starvation, exhaustion and the flux so he is scarcely capable of taking part in a night-march in any case.

Still, we give Captain Codrington's pistol and telescope to Peterson, more as marks of respect than because we believe they will do him any good. He tells me that when I return to England I must look up his mother and sister in Coventry and give them an account of his deeds. I say I will, though we both know I am lying.

We hope the bugler will buy us a little time in our retreat. Tomorrow morning Peterson will do his stuff and pretend to rouse the castle's occupants to its defence and fool the enemy into thinking the siege must go on.

It's a feeble hope but our only hope.

CHAPTER 27

Fort William, Calcutta, December 1842

'Do you not think they will use this as proof of your cowardice?' Broadhurst asks gaily.

'Proof of cowardice?' I am aghast. 'Cowardice? How could anyone possibly accuse me of cowardice over the evacuation of Charikar?'

'Come on my dear fellow.' Broadhurst is pacing my small room, the lawyer now, preparing his case. 'We have to look at this from the point of view of your enemies.'

'My enemies? The Ghilzais?'

'No, I mean the people who wish to pin the blame for this whole obscene tragedy on one of the few men to have come through the ordeal alive and in pretty good shape.'

'Alive I grant you. But in good shape? Look at this leg. It will never be the same again. I shall always feel some pain, there will always be this confounded limp. I bear the scars, sir, I bear the scars.'

'Of course, Eldred, of course.' Broadhurst speaks more softly, with less of the arrogance of the courtroom about him, as he says, 'But remember, old man, Ellenborough wants someone to blame. He wants to make an example of someone. Our opponents will know very well the Governor-General is seeking a conviction. At least one head must roll.' I frown and Broadhurst quickly adds, 'Metaphorically speaking, of course. Heavens, this isn't France, man. The maximum sentence may be death but that's not what Ellenborough is looking for. Just a scapegoat. Someone to take responsibility, someone to demote and punish.'

Is Broadhurst right to say the Governor-General wants his human sacrifice and that sacrifice is to be Major Eldred Pottinger? It is bad enough to suffer this indignity at all, it is worse to realise how serious my position truly is. Cowardice? For quitting Charikar?

Broadhurst goes on, 'We have to recognise that some people might argue that you should have remained at your post and defended the castle to the last man. To attempt to slip away in the dead of the night, like thieves, is not in keeping with the prestige of one of Her Majesty's officers. To the casual observer…'

'Damn and blast the casual observer.' I am now angry and spittle sprays my only defender as I say, 'No-one in his right mind would have done any different. If the Ghilzais hadn't got us, I assure you thirst and disease would have done. Ask Houghton…'

'We may have to, though he was in no position to take responsibility for the decision to abandon his post, was he?'

'Of course not. The poor man could not stand or ride unaided. If we had stayed, he would certainly have died.'

'But while Houghton did survive, many more men did not. Many more.'

'But we were outnumbered. Out-gunned. Mad with thirst and hunger. We would not have held out another day. One assault more and it would have been the end anyway.'

'Maybe, but would it not have been better to die fighting than to slink away with your tail between your legs and canter back into Kabul as if you'd been on a Sunday outing?'

'Is that what it seems like to you?'

'It is how the prosecution will depict it, Major. An officer who saves his own skin and that of his fellow officer by abandoning his post and deserting even the men under his command. One dog, a couple of servants and Houghton at the expense of what? Sixty? Seventy men?'

'Not that many,' I say but he has a point. I have always seen the point. I am still alive when so many others are not. 'And it was a fair decision. You would have done the same; anyone with any sense would have done so.'

Broadhurst sits on the edge of the table and stares at his boots. We feel the breeze drift through the open windows. From afar we can hear the murmur of life from the city of Calcutta but the Fort itself is hushed into a warm afternoon daze. 'It was a fair decision,' I repeat, thinking back to the night we left Charikar. My words fall into the silence.

At length Broadhurst speaks, slowly and with a catch in his voice as if he is feeling a powerful emotion. 'My dear Eldred, I have no doubt it was and I have no doubt you have behaved honourably throughout. That is why I am proud to take on your defence. Proud, sir, and humbled by your fortitude both then and now. I have little doubt your judges will feel as I do. But we must prepare for all eventualities. We must address the charges laid against you and we must be ready for the worst the prosecution can throw at us. We do not know, Eldred, we really do not know what pressure Ellenborough may have brought to bear on the case. Lumley, Smith, Monteath and Wymer – all good men, all good men. But Clerk? The chairman of the tribunal? A career man in the service of the Governor-General? Clerk – I do not know the man and, not knowing the man, I do not trust him.'

*****

Broadhurst leaves me to think over what he has said. Was it cowardice to arrange a tactical withdrawal? Maybe it was. In the light of what happened afterwards, perhaps it would have won honour and glory to make a stand and die at our posts. At the time, it seemed sensible to try to preserve what was left of our force – don't they say 'he who fights and runs away lives to fight another day' or is the running away so abominable there is no credit to be gained from the preservation of life?

If we had stayed, we would have been of no service to Her Majesty or the Company. We would have been cut down and left to rot. That's what happened anyway, so perhaps it would have been the better course to take. At the time, retreat seemed like the right thing to do. Houghton could scarcely move, Dr Grant was so busy he had no time to think. I was scarcely any more fit for battle than Houghton because of the huge tear in my leg. I had lost much blood and, like everyone else, I was parched and famished. If we had stayed to fight we would have presented little or no realistic opposition to the enemy. We would have been wiped out in hours.

This was not like Herat where we had provisions, we had men and weapons, we had water, we had – moreover – strong defences. The seeds of the disaster at Charikar were sown months earlier when we were so slow to rebuild the defences, when we were apparently incapable of digging a well, when we recruited untrustworthy Afghan soldiers supposedly loyal to the new King but ready to switch their allegiances at the first scent of gunpowder. Oh and when we called for a show of strength which might deter the Ghilzais from attacking in force, that complacent idiot Macnaghten and that incompetent, sickly general Elphy were content to dismiss such suggestions as alarmist.

If only they had listened to me, perhaps everything would have been different. But these are complicated arguments which may not suit my judges in a Court Martial. Except that they are all soldiers too – almost all of them anyway – and they have seen the disaster at first hand. Surely they will not see our withdrawal by night as an act of cowardice but as a sensible strategic withdrawal.

No, I am happy I took the right decision. The Lancers may promise death or glory but that choice wasn't open to us. Death, certainly, but glory? Certainly not.

Still, perhaps I was wrong. Perhaps I should have chosen death. At least it would have been quick and clean and I would have escaped the ignominy upon ignominy that has been heaped on me ever since.

Though I would never have seen Eleanor again and that, for me, is reason enough to stay alive whatever the consequences.

CHAPTER 28

Charikar, October 1841

The walls of this castle are made mainly of sand. Waiting by the postern gate to lead the retreat, my fingers explore the stonework and it crumbles. I rub grains of sand between the fingers of my left hand while I hold onto the reins in my right. The sand is dry and warm, as I suppose it would be, though for some reason I expected it to be cold. Somehow, feeling these grains of sand crumbling between my fingers gives me a sense of normality, it seems to help distract my mind from the pain which shoots down my leg and up the entire right hand side of my body as the ache from my wound pulses like an agonising toothache demanding all my attention. I will not let it master me.

I look where Hoosein and Wasim are standing beside Houghton. They have wedged a cushion under his chin to keep his head from collapsing and prevent him from falling out of the saddle but they still stand either side of the Lieutenant's horse to keep him from tumbling off. Even in this gloom I see blood seeping from the bandages wrapped around the end of his left arm where his hand used to be.

I am not sure if Houghton is conscious. I doubt if we can keep him alive until we reach Kabul but we have to try. Wasim has both hands helping to hold Houghton upright; a thin rope is looped round his waist, the other end tied round Caesar's neck. The dog stands patiently awaiting his orders, his pale coat visible in the flickering lamplight. I wonder idly whether this coat will draw attention to us in our attempted escape but nobody is prepared to leave the dog behind so it's a chance we have to take.

Behind us, a long line of men, some able-bodied, most carrying wounds, a few on horseback, most on foot. In all, there are probably still 400 men awaiting orders but half of them are really not capable of a long, silent march through enemy lines. They have been told they are free to stay behind and take their chances if they would prefer. A few decide to remain though I am not sure this is wise because I don't believe we can trust them not to raise the alarm as soon as we are clear of the castle walls.

Grant and the Gurkha's Sergeant-Major, Hanrahan, command the rearguard. They will at least buy the advance party some time to escape.

'We will see you at the rendezvous an hour before dawn, Grant,' I say as he hands me two of his precious coins to secrete about my uniform. 'And don't forget to tell the men to cover their red coats as best they can.'

'We shall meet again, Pottinger,' says Grant, 'But let us not call it a rendezvous. I know things are a little difficult at the moment but that is still no reason to start using French words.' He slaps my back, we shake hands and I give the order to advance. The postern gate opens and our horses tread furtively out from the dubious protection of the castle walls, their nostrils scenting the open field and the distant river.

*****

Grant should have been here hours ago. We wait at the meeting point until long after daybreak but there is no sign of them. The night was cold but most of us were well-wrapped-up for a few hours in the Afghan night. We rode cautiously, every creak of leather sounding like a cannonade in the stillness. We avoided the obvious enemy camps, where fires were still smouldering, and reached the rendezvous without incident. Of the second group there is no sign.

The morning is clear and bright. It will be warm by this afternoon but Dr Grant's detachment should have been only half an hour behind us. What can have happened to them? We have heard no gunfire, no alarms or other sound of fighting.

The immediate vicinity of this orchard, where I wait with the men – those who are fit enough are stationed around the perimeter in case of attack – seems to be deserted. We stand here with pomegranate juice dripping down our faces as we pluck ripe fruit from the branches as if they were apples. I am not sure how this will affect the digestion of our empty stomachs but the seeds taste like Ambrosia. The horses eat them whole and make no complaint; the men are almost as undiscriminating. This is not food that satisfies our hunger but at least it quenches our raging thirst.

We wait and wonder. Should we send someone back to scout out what has happened to the rearguard, should we wait here and risk discovery, or should we press on? It is not possible to remain where we are for too long because it will not take much for a passing Afghan to stumble upon us.

There is really no-one to consult. Houghton, who is the most senior officer left alive with our party, is in no position to think about anything at all. He seems to lapse into unconsciousness and Hoosein, who is tending to him, is afraid his patient will not last much longer.

As we wait here, more men desert. They have no stomach for a fight and being native Afghans, they no doubt think their lives are at less risk if they give themselves up or simply return to their villages. There is not much I can do about this. I should order their execution but it would be unwise to start firing on our own men – that would bring further insurrection and alert the enemy to our presence. My injured and bloody leg aches intensely. All I really want to do is lie down, curl up and sleep. My head seems to swim and I find myself holding onto a tree to steady myself. It is like Houghton's hallucination a few days ago, when he declared he could see through Codrington's telescope the

5th cavalry coming up from Kabul to support us. The whole garrison was so relieved some of the men were reduced to tears. I think now I understand how the mind can play tricks on you.

Only Wasim has any vigour. He offers to go off and look for Dr Grant's detachment but I tell him not to. Instead, I have him pass on the order to prepare to resume our march. There is no point in waiting here indefinitely. Perhaps Grant has lost his way, or they have been taken by surprise by the enemy, or – most unlikely but possible, I suppose – the Gurkhas have mutinied and gone over to the Ghilzais. But no, surely Sergeant-Major Hanrahan would have put a stop to that.

We must go. The sun sets at half past six and we should make some progress during daylight. I conduct a head-count and discover our party of 200 has melted away; only 70 remain. All the native troops have gone. The sepoys are unhappy but they have nowhere else to go. I set out the route to take but I do not think most of them are listening to me. They mutter among themselves about the time we are wasting and argue over the best way back to Kabul if we are to avoid the main thoroughfares and settlements.

I give the order to depart but some of the men ignore me. The few remaining native officers are incapable of exerting any discipline. The rest slouch off at their own pace and there are perhaps only 35 of us still together. There is nothing I can do about the rest. It's now every man for himself, I'm afraid. My party makes slow progress through steep ravines and up mountain-sides as we try to stay off the beaten track.

The by-ways we take are intended to help us steer clear of the enemy. It is slow progress with Houghton in danger of coming off his horse at any moment. In the cold and darkness, I find Hoosein, Wasim, Houghton. But we have lost track of our companions and carry on alone, always alert to the danger of stumbling upon the enemy.

*****

271

We crouch in the long grass. I lie alongside my horse, trying to avoid the jagged stones, listening to the voices of cavalrymen about one hundred yards away. There is a terrible ache in my leg and I worry the dog might let out a bark even though Wasim is supposedly keeping Caesar muzzled.

Houghton manages not to groan. Hoosein is holding him gently by the neck with one hand while trying to lie on top of the lieutenant's horse muttering into her ear, to prevent her from standing and drawing attention to our whereabouts.

The rebels are combing the area. They shout at each other, announcing they have not found anyone in each of the places they are quartering. We are on the side of the hill, near the foot of the valley, within spitting distance of the river.

We have at least had a chance to gulp down some precious water. So have the horses. Hoosein has a flask which he administers gently to Houghton's lips from time to time but the lieutenant is barely conscious. He cannot know we are cowering from the enemy. I don't suppose he has any idea where he is or what is happening to him.

Perhaps that's just as well.

I stare up at the sky. Night has fallen but there is a clear moon and the dark, flinty mountains loom over us as we cower in the shadows trying to keep out of sight of the Ghilzais.

I don't think there are many of them. We might be able to make some sort of a stand of it but it wouldn't last long. I clutch my pistol. If I fired off a couple of shots, they would be down on us in an instant and we wouldn't last long.

Wasim has a sword which he can wield surprisingly well but I doubt Hoosein's prowess in combat. All he has is a knife; he's refused my entreaties to carry a sword let alone a pistol or a rifle. He says he can fend for himself; I am not convinced. He is such a small fellow, better suited to gossip and intrigue than he will ever be to armed combat.

It's difficult to lie still. The pain in my leg is not so bad when I am moving. Lying down here, I feel a regular thud of pain course through the entire right-hand side of my body. I want to groan but cannot. It's as well Houghton is so far beyond sensation because his injuries are enough to make any man scream.

I stare into the blackness, clouds scudding across the moon. The day was pleasantly warm but now it is freezing. This inactivity, the damp grass, the chill breeze make me worry my teeth will start to chatter even though I am warmed by the horse and wrapped in a blanket on top of various layers of uniform and Afghan woollens. Hoosein is murmuring to his horse. I gaze into the night sky and in my mind I compose angry letters to my father blaming him that I find myself here, on the edge of the world, in an agony of pain, wondering how God could have led us into this heathen hell-hole. Had my father not squandered all his wealth, perhaps I should never have joined the Company, never have endured the boredom and frustration of years in its service, never have volunteered to venture across the Northern Frontier… There is no point in this. I bring my mind back to the present and listen out, eyes staring across the valley into the gloom. The horses are breathing, Hoosein is murmuring, Wasim is stroking the dog – the two of them have not said a word but something about the way they are breathing indicates to me they think the immediate danger has passed. I listen more carefully. Houghton is silent. I cannot even hear him breathe. Perhaps he is dead.

Farther off, I can discern the sound of horses and the voices of the tribesmen. They are becoming more remote, fading away. The rebel patrol is moving on. We must lie here and wait. They may have left sentries behind them. Wasim makes to move. I quieten him with my boot. The dog grumbles a little and Wasim has to quieten him with a pomegranate, which is not something Caesar relishes but at least it keeps him occupied. The poor animal was fat when we found him, rolls of flesh around his neck and chest. Now he really is just skin and bones.

*****

273

We wait another hour, though the tension gradually lessens as we hear no sounds other than the slack water in the shallow river trickling down toward Kabul, the flicking-tongued repetitions of the nightjars and the eerie scream of a hawk. Otherwise all is quiet. The others of our party and those of the rearguard could be anywhere. It is deep night and we must get on.

We set off, though only with great difficulty do we manage to sit Houghton in his saddle. The man has to be constantly tended-to by both Hoosein and Wasim and even then, as we walk slowly towards the foot of the valley, where it seems to give out onto a wider plain, he slips off, first on one side and then on the other.

'Leave me,' Houghton says after he falls off for the third time. Each time he re-opens his hardly-healed wounds and you can see the blood seeping through his clothes and bandages as we set him back in the saddle. Hoosein declares he would rather stay and die with the Lieutenant than abandon him.

We make tentative, slow progress through the hours of darkness. Movement is preferable to the freezing agony of trying to lie still in the cold night. We are determined to avoid the main route into Kabul so we make for the by-ways and goat paths across the hills near the city. It is three o'clock in the morning, we have not slept and we have scarcely eaten for days. Our horses are as ready to give up as we are. And now we are lost.

Houghton says he cannot go on. We rest a while and I say I will see if I can scout out a route. After groping round in the darkness – there is a sliver of moon and the clouds rush past so it is not completely black – I come across what appears to be another track leading in roughly the right direction. I report back and we set off again, Hoosein, Wasim and I taking shifts with Houghton while the one not walking alongside his horse enjoys the luxury of riding my bony animal instead.

After half an hour, dogs start barking just off to our left and, in the gloom, we make out several black goat-hair tents belonging to a party of nomads. The hounds are tethered but their racket must have woken up the whole party. Perhaps they are accustomed to their animals setting a hue and cry because nobody emerges from the relative warmth of their tent to see what's going on. We increase the pace of our march and put a distance between ourselves and the camp. Happily Caesar, still on his lead attached to Wasim's waist, is not inclined to bark back – the poor dog is as exhausted as the rest of us and has had very little more sleep, and less food, than we have.

Walking makes my wound hurt keenly but on the other hand it becomes more of a sharp stab than a constant ache. I am not sure which is worse but the pain keeps me awake and alert rather than inducing the sort of lethargy it might be impossible to recover from. I feel my leg and my hand is sticky with blood. This is not a good sign but we are now approaching the outskirts of Kabul so perhaps our ordeal will end soon. This thought spurs me on.

Then it occurs to me the Ghilzais may be lying in wait to pick off anyone making his way back from Charikar. After all, if our entire force is dispersed, it's unlikely they will have killed or captured every man who evacuated the castle.

We do not know if Elphinstone and Macnaghten are aware of what has been happening. I have no idea if any of my messages to the General and the Envoy reached them. There has certainly been no sign of a relief force but it is possible our troops have been put on a state of alert and are even now securing Kabul. If they are, it is reasonable to assume the rebels have been dispersed from the outskirts of the city and we are therefore safe. But the failure of the General and the Envoy to come to our aid suggests we must assume the worst and they have done little to protect Kabul itself.

We proceed with caution.

At last we come to the edge of Kabul itself and are forced to take to the main route towards the bazaar. We will enter the narrow streets of the city, come close to Burnes's mansion, pass beneath the massive rock-pile walls of the Balar Hissar and onto the open road back to the cantonment itself where we may, perhaps, hope for medical attention, food and water.

As we trudge forward in the first stirrings of the dawn, when few people are about and the air is bitterly cold, a shout emerges from behind the stone walls of any outlying castle. 'Who goes there at this time of night?' he demands in Persian and I tell him we are weary travellers who lost our way. He bids us goodnight but the experience unnerves us a little and it is clear there are camps all around where more suspicious sentries may start asking more demanding questions.

We march on as quickly as the exhausted Houghton can manage and pass more or less unremarked through various makeshift camps where most of the inhabitants are still asleep. On the city streets we find no-one awake except one Muslim holy man sitting beside a water trough. He offers us the peace, blessings and mercy of Allah. I reply, 'And may peace be upon you.'

We are almost home. The camp is in sight. The Company flag flaps listlessly above the gatehouse. We pick up our pace at the sight of the cantonment, which is just as well for within one hundred yards of safety a shot rings out and we hear a cry from within the city calling on us to stop. We do the opposite and march on as fast as we can without upending poor Houghton again.

We are not given a hero's welcome.

CHAPTER 29

Kabul, November 1841

I am confined to the chilly sick bay, alongside Houghton and several other officers, and blessed by the personal attentions of Eleanor Eden. She is dauntless and brave in the face of human suffering and indignity, dismissing the native assistants and consulting on equal terms with Dr Logan, Dr Brydon and the other European medical men we have to minister to us. Eleanor herself cleans my leg and applies fresh bandages every day. She sits with me and chats about the comings and goings in Kabul.

She talks of potatoes and artichokes and says Lady Sale is taking a particular interest in Kabul cabbages which are, apparently, milder than the English red cabbage and therefore superior. Lady Sale's son-in-law Captain Sturt has acquired some pears from Turkistan, which Her Ladyship has pronounced delicious, and Lady Sale has herself bought the largest peaches she has ever seen for fifteen rupees. 'What else is there to spend our money on?' Eleanor asks, smiling and looking up at me from under a fringe of curly hair.

She is the most remarkable young woman and I could lie here all day listening to her chatter.

As for court gossip, Eleanor says it was a terrible mistake to return Shah Soojah to the throne. 'The man is mad,' she says. 'He kills anyone who crosses him. He complains we keep him short of money. He wants his own army. And as for his advisers. Well! Some of them are simply no good. That wouldn't matter if the others were honest or truthful or fair in their dealings with us and each other. But these heathens are cruel. They are malicious and line their own pockets at every opportunity. You should see the prices they're charging for food now.'

She says this with a laugh in her voice, as if none of it really matters. But she is shocked by what has happened at Charikar. She tells me several Ghurkhas have now made it back to camp. It seems the rearguard was ambushed within half a mile of leaving the castle. They were almost all killed though others have been taken prisoner and some have gone over to the enemy. 'Sergeant-Major Hanrahan says they are even now being sold as slaves to the traders from Tajikstan.'

'Dr Grant?' I ask.

'Dead.'

'How did Hanrahan survive?' I ask.

'The same way you did, Eldred. Sheer courage and determination. The man is a hero. There is scarcely a scratch on him though two of the Ghurkhas who came in with him are now dead of their wounds.'

'What does Macnaghten say about all this? Or Elphinstone for that matter?'

'Eldred, I cannot say.' She turns away from me and reaches for a water glass to bring to my lips. I see her flush red at the question. It is clear to me there is some news she does not wish to impart.

'Eleanor, you have to tell me.' I try to sit up but since I was transferred to the sick bay, I seem to have some sort of fever which leaves me with precious little strength.

'Here, drink some water.' She helps me sit up. 'You are so much thinner now, Eldred,' she laughs. 'It doesn't suit you, especially with that huge beard of yours.'

'You have to tell me.' I struggle to sit up. The effort leaves me short of breath and a hot sweat breaks out on my forehead even though, despite an open fire not far from my bed, the room is distinctly chilly because wood is now rationed.

She puts the glass back on the table and sits, hands together in the skirts of her dress, head bowed towards the floor because she cannot bring herself to look at me. 'Macnaghten blames you for the loss of Charikar,' she says. 'He seems more upset about the money than about the men. Thirteen lakhs of rupees, he says.'

'Nothing like that much,' I say. I am too tired to defend myself yet I fear more than anything being lowered in the esteem of Miss Eden. Wearily I say, 'I did warn Macnaghten.'

'I know you did, Major.'

'I did ask for reinforcements.'

'And none were forthcoming,' she says, 'I do know this, Eldred.'

'We held out for almost a fortnight with no food, no water and hardly any ammunition.'

'Eldred, the trouble is the Envoy needs somebody to blame and he won't blame himself.'

'Elphinstone? He's the military commander, after all. What does he say?'

'He listens to Shelton and the Brigadier-General says you were the wrong choice for the mission as you had not been in combat for so long.'

'Not been in combat? Shelton forgets about Herat, perhaps.'

'He does not, Eldred. He says defending a fortified city like Herat from an incompetent enemy is a very different proposition from protecting a British castle from marauding tribesmen. He says you should have exerted more discipline and control on your men and made a more concerted effort to defeat your enemy.'

I laugh bitterly and ask, 'And do Shelton and Macnaghten think the danger is now passed?'

'They do.'

'Then they are horribly mistaken. Charikar is just the beginning.'

'All the Brigadier-General is interested in is securing himself a new home. Do you know he wants to throw out Lady Sale, Mrs Sturt and me and take over our lodgings? Yet Shelton isn't even based at the camp, he's out in the Siah Sung hills with the 44th so he has no reason to make these demands.'

'Don't frown, Miss Eden,' I say, 'You look much prettier when you smile…'

*****

Burnes pays a visit the next day, bringing sweetmeats made in his own kitchens and Madeira wine which, he says, is an excellent tonic for the unwell. He is looking as smart as usual, in his diplomatic uniform, having been with Macnaghten for a conference with the King. The Envoy announced new fees for the use of the Khyber Pass.

'This is all about money, you know, Eldred,' says Burnes as he perches on the side of my bed and helps himself to one of Miss Eden's peaches. 'The Company says it is costing too much to maintain our establishment in Afghanistan and decrees we must save money. Macnaghten is desperate to do as he is told because he wants to get out of here and go back to Bombay as soon as possible. I agree – the sooner we are rid of that penny-pinching little clerk the better. I am confident we can keep the peace here but I have to say he is going the wrong way about it.'

'What has he done?' I ask.

'We pay a toll, a fee, to the Khyberees, the chiefs who guard the Khyber Pass and keep open our route back to India. Macnaghten is cutting their fees from 80,000 rupees a year to 40,000. They won't like it, they won't like it one bit. It was taxes which provoked the uprising you had to deal with in Charikar. We raise more with one hand and take more away with the other. This is not how to keep these people on our side. They are not well-disposed to us since we threw out Dost Mohammed Khan but, as long as we keep lining their pockets, they will tolerate our presence. If the money dries up, and we try to extort more, then I am not at all sure we can keep the peace. Cutting the tolls is a false economy. It will cost us more in men and munitions to maintain our position here. But Macnaghten won't hear any arguments against it. "Economy in all things," he says. "Economy, Sir Alexander, economy". I am worried, Eldred, I don't mind telling you.'

Burnes lights a cheroot and sighs. I say, 'But is he blind to what's happening?'

'I think he must be. I told him to be prepared for a wider insurrection. Told him to write for reinforcements. He seems to take this as a personal criticism. He doesn't want the Governor-General to think he is panicking unnecessarily and he thinks I am after his job…'

'Which you are,' I say with a smile that turns into a grimace as my leg gives one of its regular stabs of pain.

'Which I am,' Burnes acknowledges, 'But not at any price. Certainly not at the price of having to put down a rebellion. Macnaghten has been warned by our Afghan spies not to ride out in the early morning or late in the evening because his life is in danger but even this he treats as an attempt to undermine his position, not as a genuine threat. Three Afghans have sworn on the Koran to kill him and we have just lost a huge supply of munitions which Captain Moorgate left on the roadside because of a shortage of camels. A shortage of camels? Can you believe it?'

*****

Two days later I am drinking coffee when Brigadier-General Shelton marches in, his boots rapping on the wooden floor as if he were on a parade ground, his empty sleeve swinging out of time. He stands over me, threateningly, and barks, 'Malingering, Pottinger?'

I sit up and offer a weary salute. 'No, sir. I am injured as are all the men in this ward.'

'At least they got their injuries fighting for Queen and Company. Not simply saving their own skin, Major.'

'Sir, I resent the implication…' It is difficult to take up an argument when one is lying in a hospital bed wearing nothing but a night-shirt and covered in blankets.

'You resent the implication, do you sir? How is it that Eldred Pottinger manages to rescue himself from that inferno while leaving his men to die or be sold into slavery?'

This is a question I have been tormenting myself with since our return to Kabul. 'What else would you have had me do, Brigadier?'

'Fight to the last man. Fight to the last man.'

'And die anyway?'

'And die with honour, sir, not slink away in disgrace.'

I am too tired to argue and wonder if Shelton may not be in the right. Houghton, in the next bed, has scarcely spoken for days but now he croaks, 'We had no food, no water, no ammunition, sir. Couldn't trust the native troops. They were looting the stores and treasury. What should we have done?'

Shelton looks down at him briefly then back at me. 'Shoot the blackguards, of course. Shoot them dead and damn their eyes.'

'And hand victory to the rebels by destroying ourselves completely without any effort on their part?' I ask.

'If need be, yes. Better to die with honour than live on with dishonour.'

With this, Shelton turns on his heel and marches back out of the ward leaving me trembling and in a sweat of wrath, indignation and humiliation.

*****

John Sturt visits me later the same day. The captain looks harassed. He asks how I am and immediately blurts out, 'You need to get better, Major. Quickly. Someone's got to talk some sense into Macnaghten and Elphinstone. They won't listen to me and they won't listen to any of the other officers. Macnaghten insists all is peace and tranquillity; Elphie just bears the impression of the last bottom which sat on him.

He sends his best wishes, by the way, and says you are not at fault for the fall of Charikar. He says we should have sent reinforcements.'

'But he was asked to and he wouldn't.'

'You see my problem.' Sturt wrings his hands and as I look at this young, newly-married officer I see worry-lines creasing his forehead under his Bengal Engineers' cap. 'Elphie is a decent fellow. A fine fellow. A good man for a coffee house or a regimental dinner. But he hasn't got a clue, he is not capable of making a decision and he allows Shelton to bully him. The Afghan clans are gathering, Charikar won't be an end of it,' he says.

'And Macnaghten? Burnes tells me he will not take measures to secure our safety.'

'Macnaghten wants to get back to Bombay but he can't leave while the tribes are in an uproar. You know they've closed the Kabul Pass, do you?'

'Closed it?'

'By all accounts. As soon as the news reached them about the cut in their stipends they shot up our camps along the way, killed two dozen men and forced the rest to retreat to Jalalabad and join my father-in-law General Sale there.'

'And how are Lady Sale and their daughter, your wife?'

'In a state of some agitation, I don't mind saying so. This damned business is no place for a woman and with winter coming on there doesn't seem much hope of evacuating them even as far as Jalalabad. They will have to take their chances here, with us.'

'If it's really getting bad, we should make for the Balar Hissar. We can keep the entire nation at bay once we are inside that fortress.'

'I've already suggested that. Elphinstone, who says his gout is playing up and he really cannot move from his room, says it's up to Macnaghten; Macnaghten says it would disturb the King; Shelton says it's pointless because we should be leaving this God-forsaken country. Meanwhile we keep some men in the hills miles away, the Treasury in the city, our food supplies two miles from the camp and we pretend all is well. I tell you, Pottinger, it is very worrying.'

*****

This evening Hoosein arrives looking like he has been riding hard. Yet he can't have come from farther afield than the town. The little man almost tip-toes across the room to avoid disturbing my fellow patients. Most of them are already asleep. I hear a few snores and groans. Houghton's condition is still touch and go though Dr Brydon assures me he will live if he is allowed rest and nourishment.

'Sahib Pottinger sir,' whispers Hoosein with a breath which smells infernal. 'I have been in the city talking to the merchants. There is news, there is news.' I wait while Hoosein twists his hands together, rubs his arms, shakes his head and adjusts his turban. 'Taj Mohammed Khan, sir.'

'The melon hawker?'

'Maybe once, sir, not these days. Taj Mohammed is a great man in Kabul with his own followers. His man tells me Taj Mohammed wants to warn Sir Alexander, sir, that Sir Alexander is in danger.'

'Burnes, in danger?'

'Taj Mohammed says there is a plot to kill him, sahib.'

'There's a plot to kill Macnaghten. There's a plot to kill Elphinstone. There's probably a plot to kill me, too. And you, Hoosein.'

My friend frowns and falls silent. 'This is serious, Major. There will be an assassination attempt within the next 24 hours. They are planning a protest outside Sir Alexander's mansion.'

'They? Who are they, Hoosein?'

He shrugs. 'Who knows? These Afghans are only happy when they are killing someone. Foreigners are best.'

'And you take this threat seriously?'

'I do.'

'Why?'

'I have heard it's all to do with a slave girl. A very beautiful young woman who belongs to Abdullah Khan Achakazi. He's the leader of a tribe of shepherds and robbers but a big man here and he has sworn jihad against Burnes because Sir Alexander refused to give the girl back and hit Abdulla Khan's servant telling him to go to hell, the girl could go where she pleased and his chief was a wicked savage. There was a meeting. They swore on the Koran to be avenged on Sir Alexander.'

'Burnes knows about this?' I ask.

'I don't know. I came straight to you, sahib.'

'Then we must waste no time. Get to Burnes's house and warn him. Tell him to come into the camp and bring his friends with him. Get him out of there, Hoosein. Now. Take Wasim with you and take a note from me.'

With difficulty I sit up, pull a candle over to my bedside and find pen and paper. I write a quick note to my friend urging him to take the warning seriously and saying I trust Hoosein as a wise man and an expert at gleaning intelligence which may be of use to us.

*****

Two hours later, I have dozed off and the ward is quiet when Hoosein creeps to my bedside and shakes me awake. 'Sahib,' he whispers, 'I have seen Sir Alexander but he says this is all nonsense, he is not going anywhere. He says Abdullah Khan is an ignorant savage and the Koran is the book of the Devil. But as I was hurrying back here, a small crowd was gathering around Sir Alexander's house. I do believe he is still in great danger.'

Wearily, I haul myself up, slide my legs out of the side of the bed and reach for my clothes. 'Then we must go and rescue him, Hoosein. Go and wake Wasim, saddle up some horses. Come, we must leave at once.'

CHAPTER 30

Fort William, Calcutta, January 1843

New Year's Day but we are not looking forward, we are looking back.

I am scrubbed and shaved. I wear my blue, gold-braided uniform jacket with its scarlet collar, the white sash and the scarlet cummerbund, white trousers and a new pair of boots. I am not allowed to carry my sword – this is a court martial and defendants are prohibited from wearing any sort of a weapon in such circumstances, no matter what their rank or the crimes they are accused of. Instead I carry my sword in both hands. It is the sword presented to me by Lord Eden on behalf of the Monarch herself and is inscribed with the words: 'To Eldred Pottinger, first man to draw his sword for his Queen.' It is my most treasured possession and I trust, when it is laid before my judges, they will take due account of it.

I am allowed to wear my Order of the Bath insignia, awarded to me at the same time for my services in Herat. I am a member of an ancient order of chivalry, honour and nobility. This medal gives me some comfort and I am hopeful my judges will notice this too.

I suppose I should be grateful they have dispensed with a guard to march me into court, that I am not kept in a cell and I have not been manacled with chains. I don't feel grateful, though, just angry and tired of my own anger.

The day is hot and already I find myself sweating in this rig-out as Broadhurst – equally well turned-out, I am surprised to note – and I march across the parade ground to the court-room. I have been here already, to establish the lie of the land and examine the enemy dispositions. It is an adequately-sized stone room, with a raised platform where the high-backed red velvet chairs for the five judges are ranged across one end while the defendant and his counsel sit on one side of the court, the prosecution on the other, in dark-wood pews not unlike those in the nearby regimental church. Behind a small barrier, and in the gallery above, seats are ranged for casual observers as well as the men from 'The Bombay Times', the 'London Times' and, I have no doubt, other bloodsuckers from various scurrilous broadsheets. You would have thought they'd sated themselves on death and destruction by now but apparently not.

Broadhurst tells me yet again that today will be a preliminary canter through the charges. The prosecution will later set out his case and call whatever witnesses he can muster. The chief prosecutor, the Judge-Advocate-General, is someone I have not met before, called Captain Trevor Whistler, of the Bombay Artillery. I say this is a hopeful sign, as we are members of the same regiment. Broadhurst says Whistler is an ambitious young lawyer keen to make a name for himself and will not be swayed by such sentimentality. I dare say he is right.

We sit and wait as the courtroom fills up, various sentries are posted, Whistler makes his way to his desk with a pile of legal scrolls, a clerk in the inevitable wig chats with a native scribe who is supposed to take note of the whole proceeding. The clock on the church chimes half-past eight and at that moment a burly sergeant calls on the court to stand while the judges file in.

I look around and see Houghton in the public gallery, along with Mrs Sturt. There is no sign of Eleanor Eden, but why would there be? She is far away in England. Several others are also present, including Brigadier-General Shelton, I note, sitting with startling stillness, staring straight ahead.

Before I can think much about the weight the court might put on Shelton's evidence, the judges have reached their seats, nodded to the rest of us, we have nodded back, and the chairman has called for prayers. We bow our heads and ask the Lord to preside over our affairs and deliver justice. Amen to that.

The chairman is, of course, little George Russell Clerk. Broadhurst whispers during a lull in proceedings, 'They say Clerk is on his way to the North-West frontier to be governor there.'

'He'll be paying full attention to these proceedings, then, won't he?' I say.

Clerk is about six inches shorter than the military men around him and he wears a pen-pusher's standard-issue frock coat, waistcoat, white shirt, bow tie. He peers over a pair of spectacles and I note his thinning hair has been pomaded over to disguise his balding pate. Yet he has an amiable face. There does not appear to be any malice in him but who can tell?

Order is called and the court clerk, in his lawyerly wig, stands and, as everybody sits down, Broadhurst tells me to stay on my feet.

'Are you Major Eldred Pottinger of the Bengal Artillery?' he asks.

'I am.'

'Major Pottinger, you will present your sword to the court.'

I step forward and lay the weapon, in its scabbard, on the court clerk's desk. I salute the judges, who nod acknowledgement, and then retreat to my place.

'Major Pottinger, you are charged with the following offences: On the first count: Cowardice in that in October 1841 you did shamefully deliver up to the enemy the fortress and post of Charikar in Afghanistan, of which you were commanding officer, and which it was your duty to defend, and in doing so you did put at the hazard the lives of the men under your command, in order to protect your own person.

'On the second count: Cowardice that in December 1841 and January 1842 you did conspire with the enemy to agree a worthless peace treaty and thereby endanger the lives and liberty of the British garrison in Kabul.

'On the third count: Conduct disgraceful to the character of an officer, in having at Khoord Kabul, on January 9th, 1842, during the retreat of the British from Kabul towards Hindustan, in presence of the enemy, abandoned the said force, and sought personal protection in the camp of Mahomed Akbar Khan, the leader of the enemy.

'On the fourth count: Misuse of Company money, in that between the months of November 1837 and July 1838 you did disburse several lakhs of money belonging to the British East India Company without due authorisation and without accounting for said expenditures.

'On the fifth count: Misuse of Company money, in that between the months of September and October 1841 you did abandon treasure belonging to the British East India Company to the enemy.

'On the sixth count: Misuse of Company money, in that between the months of December 1841 and January 1842 you did disburse several lakhs of money belonging to the British East India Company without due authorisation and without accounting for said expenditures.

'On the seventh count: Misuse of Company money, in that between the months of February 1842 and September 1842 you issued promissory notes in the name of the British East India Company without due authorisation.

'Do you plead guilty or not guilty of the aforementioned offences?'

'Not guilty, sir.'

CHAPTER 31

Kabul, November 1841

Hoosein, Wasim and I ride across the fields to the edge of the city in the black night. Kabul is not asleep. Men, in pairs and groups, are making their way with a determined march towards the bazaar, their faces lit by fires from the makeshift camps which have sprung up around the city. The air is thick and filled with the smell of smoke. Most of the men carry weapons of one sort or another, long swords, knives, pistols, jezzail rifles, heavy clubs. They glower at us menacingly as we pass but make no attempt to impede our progress. My companions and I have swords and Wasim has a pair of pistols in his belt. My leg screams its pain throughout my body but I tell myself this is only because I have been lying in bed for some days and it is not used to being exercised.

We trot our horses down narrow streets to Burnes's mansion – to ride any faster might betray our concern and draw unwanted attention to ourselves. Outside the walls of the house a small group of people is milling around in flickering torch-light. We tell the four guards outside the house we have urgent business with the Deputy Envoy, we bang on the side door and are eventually admitted by a servant. A second man fetches the master of the house.

Eventually Sir Alexander Burnes strolls downstairs in a magnificent silk gown tied at the waist, his hair slightly dishevelled, his lower legs and feet naked.

'My dear Eldred,' he says, indicating we should follow him into the first reception room, 'What can I offer you at this hour – is it early morning or late night?'

'Burnes, you must leave,' I tell him with some urgency. 'Your life is in danger.'

'So Mohun Lal and your man Hoosein have been telling me,' he says with a smile and a flick of his hand, to indicate his nonchalant lack of concern. 'I have no fear, my dear fellow. I have my guards, my friend Chapman is here, my younger brother Charles – you haven't met Charles yet, have you? He's just arrived in Kabul. You must come to dinner, soon – so you can see we're all perfectly safe. And besides, I am well-known to the people hereabouts. They have nothing but respect for me. Is that not so, Sadiq?' he says, turning to his chief bodyguard, an ageing Hindu who has been with him for at least ten years. The guard does not react but stares across the room at the wood panelling. He does not indicate, even by a lowering of his head, any agreement and certainly does not confirm Burnes's assertion.

'There are people gathering outside here, Burnes,' I repeat, 'And even at this early hour the city is filling up with more men. They're all carrying guns and swords, Alexander. You must come back to the camp with us now.'

Burnes smiles and offers me a small glass of Madeira which I take in the hope it will help to numb the pain in my leg. 'My dear boy, there is really no cause for alarm. And you should not be here, Pottinger, dressed like that' – I am wearing a huge Afghan turban and a heavy woollen coat over thick cotton Afghan pyjamas, a pair of leather boots and carry a sword in its sheath strapped outside my other garments – 'You should be back in bed. You, sir, should have more of a care for yourself. I can take care of myself. Now, if you will excuse me, I must return to my bed, I have some unfinished business to attend to. Sadiq will show you out.'

We are dismissed and ride disconsolately back to camp as more men hurry into the city in groups of two and three, all armed and with grim expressions on their faces.

As we head back, other messengers overtake us, hurrying back to the army camp, carrying word of a possible insurrection. By the time we arrive, several other officers have already been roused. We gravitate toward the Officers' Mess where coffee can be found, weak beer and some brandy, to compare notes.

Nobody is sure what's afoot but Hoosein's intelligence is not far removed from the information others are receiving. An uprising of some sort is being planned with Burnes as the focus of the discontent. Some say it's all about taxes and tolls. Others claim Burnes has imprisoned an Afghan chieftain's son out of lust for the man's wife. Or it's about Abdulla Khan's slave girl. Others claim it is because Burnes cannot be trusted as the Chief Magistrate of Kabul to settle property disputes fairly. Whatever the reasons, the fact remains some sort of campaign against the Deputy Envoy is being mounted which is likely to end in violence.

After Charikar, I am more than ever convinced the only way to respond to this sort of action is by a determined and timely show of force. We must send troops into the city at once. Burnes only has a guard of a dozen men, utterly inadequate if his life is truly in danger. Another man, Johnson, points out the Company Treasury is just a few houses away, on the same street from Burnes's home, and it contains almost two hundred thousand rupees in hard cash as well as the Company accounts for the last three years. These need protecting as well as Burnes and his companions.

More messages come in from the city – a crowd is now filling the entire street outside Burnes's house.

We agree Captain George Lawrence, Macnaghten's secretary, must alert General Elphinstone to the threat. Lawrence, Sturt and I are among half a dozen officers who rouse the General from his bed and wait in the hallway as his servants wrestle to put on his uniform. By the time he descends the stairs, another messenger has arrived with a note for Sir William Macnaghten which, as Sir William is not yet awake, he has brought to the General instead.

Lawrence reads it and hands it to Elphinstone. 'It's from Burnes. He is asking for urgent assistance,' says Lawrence.

'Very well,' says Elphinstone, 'We shall ride to his aid gentlemen. Sturt, a troop of cavalry. We will leave in twenty minutes.'

'That does not give us time for breakfast,' one of the officers complains.

'This won't take very long,' says the General.

I am surprised by this decisiveness as it seems to run contrary to Elphinstone's usual habits of indecision but I welcome it and we disperse quickly to rouse the men and prepare for action.

*****

Dawn is breaking as the 11th light cavalry forms up on the parade ground. An orderly stands outside Elphinstone's quarters holding his mount, while several officers await the General's arrival. I ask Sturt where Brigadier-General Shelton might be but it seems he is back at his fort in the hills a few miles from here with the 44th foot.

There is a delay before the General, in full military uniform, finally emerges from his home, hobbles across the portico and down the steps to where his officers are waiting.

'Good morning, gentlemen, a fine morning,' he says in an attempt at levity though it is clear the pain in his legs is so bad he finds it hard to walk at all. 'Let us fetch this Burnes fellow back here, then, shall we?'

With that the General attempts to place one foot in his horse's stirrup and lift himself up onto the saddle. A couple of servants help to lift him onto the seat but it is a struggle and as the General seems finally to have come to rest in the traditional position, his foot somehow manages to come loose from the stirrup and, as he flails around to find it again, his weight shifts from left to right and he slips off the other side of the horse. Elphinstone grabs the saddle as he slips and this unfortunately disconcerts the horse as well. The General falls to the ground and the horse falls on top of him. The animal is swiftly pulled off but the General is clearly hurt and winded. He is ignominiously carried back to his quarters by six men while the horse is led away. Elphinstone goes quite white in the face, with shock I suppose, and he has probably cracked some ribs.

The poor man's humiliation means the rescue force is told to stand down. The horses are sent back to their stables, the men ordered back to their barracks, the plight of Sir Alexander Burnes forgotten.

'Can't someone else take command of the troop?' I demand of Lawrence.

'Several officers could do that, certainly,' he replies. 'But everyone is waiting for orders from everyone else.'

'Macnaghten?'

'We could go to him, he is probably awake by now,' Lawrence concedes and again a deputation of officers is sent to seek instructions while more messages come in from the city suggesting the need for even greater urgency. The great wooden gates to Burnes's home are said to be on fire and the Treasury down the road is under siege. Gunshots can now be heard carrying across the two miles or so between our camp and the town.

*****

'The Envoy is at his breakfast,' says the servant who opens Macnaghten's door.

'We will wait,' says Lawrence.

'We won't,' I say, and barge past the servant into the house and turn into the room where I last enjoyed an interview with Sir William Macnaghten and his wife Frances. He is just executing an egg as I enter, with my fellow officers more sheepishly following on behind.

'Sir William, Lady Macnaghten, good morning,' I say, and without pausing to allow him to respond, I continue, 'We are here, sir, on a matter of great urgency. Sir Alexander Burnes's house, and our Treasury nearby, are under siege and there is grave danger to life and property. I respectfully request your authorisation to take out a relief force as soon as possible. I should add,' I hurry on, as Sir William stares at me open-mouthed in his dressing gown, 'The General was planning to undertake this mission in person but unfortunately met with an accident and is even now receiving medical attention.'

There is a long pause. I can hear Lady Macnaghten breathing heavily as she considers whether to sip her cup of tea. She, too, is wearing her night-clothes and I imagine she is not pleased to be so rudely interrupted.

'I am sorry, Pottinger, that is out of the question. As I have had occasion to make clear to you more than once, you are employed in a political or diplomatic capacity. You are not in a position to lead any military men anywhere.'

'But, sir, our colleague Sir Alexander Burnes's life is in danger.'

'That's as may-be, Major. But I regret it is none of your business. Lawrence, is this true, is Burnes in danger?'

The lieutenant stands to attention. 'He is, sir.'

'Very well then. We must act at once. Captain Sturt, present my compliments to Brigadier-General Shelton and ask him if he would be kind enough to take a sufficient force into the city to restore order and protect the Treasury. And Burnes, of course,' Macnaghten adds as an afterthought.

'But, sir,' I protest, 'Shelton is miles away in the hills. It will take Sturt two hours to find him, it will take Shelton a couple of hours to get started and another two to reach the city. By then, Burnes may be dead and the money gone.'

'Those are my orders, Sturt. Will you be good enough to carry them out at once?' says Macnaghten, without looking at me. 'Now, gentlemen, you may leave me to my breakfast.' As the officers start to leave, Macnaghten adds, 'Not you, Pottinger.'

When they are gone, the Envoy stands, comes round his small

breakfast table and, at a distance of only a couple of paces, hisses at me, 'And don't you dare ever again lead a deputation like that into my private apartments, do you hear, Pottinger? I won't have it. You are supposed to be unwell; if you are no longer sick, you may resume your duties. Oh but you have none.' Macnaghten gives me a nasty smile. 'You deserted your post and fled back here to safety with your tail between your legs. Perhaps you might like to write up your report before you do any more damage. You may go now and, remember, I will not have Lady Macnaghten discomposed in this way no matter what the imagined crisis. Is that clear?'

It is all I can do not to hit the little man as he stands there before me, teeth clenched, blue-bottle eyes gazing short-sightedly into the middle-distance, his arms akimbo, hands on his hips, his dressing gown swinging open to reveal a thick cotton night-shirt and thin, pale legs.

I salute and say it is, turn on my heel and leave.

*****

I find Hoosein tending to our horses and tell him we are returning to Burnes's house at once. My servant is not happy. He shakes his head and sighs, 'We cannot, Major, it is too late. The streets are full of people and none of them is our friend.'

'And if we took a force of men?'

He considers the question, head to one side, right hand under his chin. 'We might break our way through,' he concedes, 'But will anyone follow us? We have no command here. We have no regiment of our own.'

'Sturt would help.'

'Captain Sturt is gone, sahib, to find Mr Shelton in the Siah Sung hills.'

'Lawrence?'

'He will not defy the Envoy, sir.'

'Who will, Hoosein? Who are Burnes's friends?'

'Everyone is Sir Alexander's friend, sir, everyone. Sir Alexander is a friend to every officer and woman. But they will not risk their lives for him.'

'Why on earth not?' I cry, somewhat desperately, as I try to mount my horse despite the pain in my leg.

'They know Sir Alexander has made many enemies, sahib, among the Afghans.'

'Enemies? I am astonished, I thought everyone admired him.'

'So they do, sir, so they do. But they see the way he looks at their women, at the Afghan women, at the chieftains' women, and they see why the crowd is demanding revenge. They are not surprised nor sorry. If Sir Alexander dies he would, as one of your officers said earlier this morning, get no more than he deserved.'

I am staggered. Nobody is willing to lift a finger to rescue my friend – their friend – and in so doing they expose our entire army to humiliation and the Company's Treasury to marauding plunder. How does Hoosein, my inoffensive Indian servant, know all this? Because he keeps his ear to the ground and he hears all the gossip. I trust him. 'Is there nobody?' I ask despairingly.

'The Ghurkhas might,' Hoosein concedes eventually.

'Then we shall ask them. At once.'

*****

We take a party of a dozen men and gallop into the city but we don't get very far. As soon as they see us, some of the mob turn on us and we are faced with the option of hacking our way through them or turning back. The Ghurkhas are more than willing to fight their way through but I do not think this will help Burnes. Instead we withdraw from the city, send the men back with our horses while Hoosein and I try to make our way through on foot. I hobble but at least I am not in uniform while Hoosein somehow manages to slip in and out of any situation without drawing attention to himself.

We can hear the crowd but we cannot see them and, as we come nearer to Burnes's house, we can hear men hacking at the walls in an attempt to demolish them and we can smell, though we cannot see, the fires which are now alight. One or two children follow at our heels and we don't bother to shake them off or bribe them to go away. I calculate that a little entourage of urchins might act as some kind of protection and draw less attention to us, though it would only take one of them to peel away and raise the alarm and no doubt a gang would be after us in no time.

We clamber over garden walls and pass through tranquil gardens where serving women stare at us without either hostility or apparent curiosity. We heave ourselves onto a roof and make our way crab-like towards the burning building. From this vantage point, Hoosein points out his friend Mohun Lal, Burnes's private secretary, and some others watching events from a nearby roof. We make our way towards him though by now the noise is deafening. The rioting can be seen in the streets as groups of men are trying to smash their way into Burnes's home and the Treasury building a couple of doors down on the other side of the street.

We are divided from Mohun Lal by the street but he signals warnings that we should keep out of sight. I am anxious to know where Burnes and his companions are and whether they are still alive. Can they be rescued? I shout across to Mohun Lal but he indicates either that he can't hear me or he doesn't know the answer. I determine to find out for myself and, telling Hoosein to stay where he is, I slide down the roof, re-opening my leg wound in the process, and clamber down the two storeys into a walled garden. I look around. This obviously belongs to someone well-to-do. There is a tinkling fountain and some well-tended roses which are only clinging on to life at this time of year but were clearly quite spectacular in the summer. Hidden behind a blood-red bougainvillea is a small door which gives out onto the street. I open it slightly and come close to the sweating body of one of the rioters as he yells curses towards Burnes's house. I slip out as he passes to find myself caught up in the crowd which is surging towards the great gates to the mansion.

The surge has been provoked by Sir Alexander himself, who appears at an upper window and throws down coins as he cries, 'My friends, my friends. Here is money, here is money. Disperse, disperse. Rewards, rewards.' His voice is almost drowned out by the shouts and threats yelled up at him from the street and the hammering on the gates and walls recommences with renewed vigour. Burnes is done up in his diplomatic uniform, complete with his sword, and beside him are two others. One is red-headed Will Chapman, his drinking companion, and the other I assume to be Burnes's younger brother Charles.

Shots ring out and Burnes is forced to withdraw from his window as glass is shattered there and elsewhere all down the street. Across the way I see a similar, if not even more determined, group of Afghans trying to force their way into the Treasury. Stones and bricks are being flung down, doors are being hacked open and muskets are being fired indiscriminately into the walls, into the air and at the guards.

I see it is impossible to enter Burnes's home. The poor man has been trying to turn it into a fortress but it is vulnerable at the front; no doubt it is more so at the rear. I fight and wrestle my way in the opposite direction from the furious mob, getting some punches and filthy looks as I do so, though nobody seems to realise I am a lone European. Eventually I reach an area where there is room to breathe and head off down an alley which, in due course, takes me towards the rear of Burnes's mansion.

The mob has got there before me and discovered the small gate into the garden. Men and young boys with knives and scythes are filing through quite calmly but in great numbers. I join them, taking out my knife to brandish in the Afghan fashion.

Burnes is there again, at a balcony, calling for help this time. Then Chapman appears on the patio with a pistol in each hand. 'Get back,' he yells as the tribesmen surround him, none willing to come close enough to do him any harm. A couple of Burnes's servants, armed with swords, appear by his side. The crowd retreats for a moment and I am almost suffocated in the crush before a shot rings out and, it seems, Chapman is hit in the arm. At the same moment he fires both his pistols and the crowd suddenly surges forward again yelling and cursing. The guards make a couple of thrusts with their swords but soon disappear under the wave of people while Chapman is brought to the ground and his poor body is surrounded by men and children thrusting knives into him.

Others surge on into the building and I can hear the noises of destruction as ornaments are thrown down, women scream, windows are smashed and the blaze, which seems to come from an outhouse, is used as kindling to light further fires inside the building.

Soon curtains are alight and flames flicker, pouring black smoke into the still morning air. I think I hear Burnes again and catch a glimpse of Charles at an upper window. They seem to be making for the roof in the hope of escaping that way.

The garden is still filling with people. I try to barge and shove my way into the house. I am taller and larger than most of these savages, which helps but means I am always in danger of drawing attention to myself. I take a discarded piece of cloth and cover my head with it, keeping my face down and pushing as best I can to make some progress.

Inside, it is mayhem. The mob has forced its way into the harem and the women are being killed or raped. I cannot stop it or protect them. The floor is slippery with broken glass, china and blood – I count the bodies of three servants and a guard as I try to force my way to the stairs. Some tribesmen are drinking Burnes's brandy, laughing and throwing it at each other in triumph. Others are intent on smashing his paintings. One or two are trying to set light to his books. Many are surging up the stairs in search of the Deputy Envoy. I hear a defiant cry which I take to be his brother's voice yelling, 'Get back you bloody heathens. Get back I order you.' This voice soon falls silent.

I reach the room with the balcony and look down into the garden only to see Burnes has somehow managed to get himself outside the burning building. I call to him but he cannot hear so I watch helplessly as the poor man makes one last appeal.

'Am I not your good friend?' he says, as a crowd of Afghans surround him waiting to strike. 'Are we not friends?' he says again. He receives nothing but jeers and insults. 'My friends,' he says, throwing his arms wide in appeal. 'We come in peace. You must go in peace.'

Someone throws a rock at him. He looks stunned but stands his ground. 'Very well, then,' he says, and deftly ties a black cloth around his eyes. 'I shall not see who strikes me dead,' he says, and wades into the mob wielding his sword and heading for the garden gate. He cuts several people, though I do not think he kills anyone, but it is only moments before his body is laid low by swords and knives. The frenzied mob will not stop. They start hacking Burnes's body to pieces and smearing his blood on their faces in triumph.

The building is getting hot. I do not wait to see what they do to my friend; instead I join the melee fighting to descend the stairs and escape the flames through the wide-open front doors. It is a slow flight, as I am jostled and elbowed by dozens of others with the same thought but eventually I stumble into the street and find myself grateful to be able to breathe the reasonably fresh air. It is a relief after the smoke-filled building but across the way paymaster Captain Hugh Johnson's treasury is being looted while his house is engulfed in flames.

I can't help thinking, if only it were Macnaghten not Burnes.

CHAPTER 32

Kabul, November 1841

'Why do they hate us?' asks Eleanor in genuine bewilderment. 'We have restored their King, we have brought peace – or we had done until now. I don't understand it. Is it just poor Alexander Burnes?'

We are crowded into Lady Sale's sitting room: Eleanor, Mrs Sturt, George Lawrence, several other officers and I, debating the terrible uprising and what we must do now.

'Elphinstone says he can't understand it,' says Lawrence, 'But then, the poor man is so laid-low I fear he is beyond all understanding.'

'Shelton? He's second-in-command isn't he?' someone asks.

'Says we should leave now before things get too hot to handle. He told Macnaghten this afternoon,' says Lawrence.

'What did Macnaghten say?' I ask.

'Said it was just a small difficulty. Said if Burnes had behaved himself in a more seemly fashion none of this would have happened,' says Lawrence.

'Well,' says Lady Sale, putting down her crochet-work and staring defiantly at Lawrence, as if it were all his fault, 'If the Envoy had a little bit of spine, the man would have ordered you all out of here immediately to put down this rabble before it got out of hand. But your officers are as weak as Macnaghten himself. And the General, a dear man I agree, most agreeable, is too far gone. It's up to Shelton to take command. The man's no duffer after all.'

We agree there is no doubt about Shelton's personal courage. He has shown that in the past. 'Trouble is,' Lawrence says, 'Shelton resents serving under Elphinstone and thinks Macnaghten is a pen-pusher. He refuses to take any initiative. He says he must await orders.'

'Knowing no orders will be forthcoming,' says Lady Sale with venom. She is not unattractive for a woman in her forties. Well-preserved, one might say, with a clear, relatively unlined skin and a winning smile which makes her popular among the officers. It is a pity her pregnant daughter Drina lacks her mother's vivacity though perhaps she is a little laid low by her condition. She looks forlornly up at Eleanor, who gives a reassuring smile. I am cheered by Eleanor's show of fortitude.

'Well, I for one would like to see Mr Pottinger take charge,' Eleanor declares. 'The hero of Herat would be equal to this situation, wouldn't you, Major?'

She smiles across the room at me, our eyes meet for a moment. I forget our predicament and find myself tongue-tied.

'Pottinger?' Lawrence laughs. 'I don't think Macnaghten would find that acceptable; I'm sorry Eldred.'

Miss Eden looks away with a laugh and I snap out of my reverie. 'No, Macnaghten would have none of it. But look, if we are to protect ourselves from these savages until General Sale can reinforce the garrison from Jalalabad – someone has sent word to him, haven't they?' I look around the room and nobody nods assent. 'In that case, we must get a message to him immediately.'

'Can't,' says one of the officers.

'Macnaghten won't allow it,' says another.

'We must send to him anyway. Perhaps Lady Sale can seek his help in a private letter. Madam?' I say, bowing to her.

'I shall consider the question, Major,' she says, slightly frostily, a frown crossing her high forehead.

'In the meantime,' I say, 'We should strike camp and move everything, especially our stores of weapons and food, into the Balar Hissar. The King might not like it but he was the only one to take any action to rescue Burnes and, if the insurrection succeeds, the best he could hope for is another period in exile. The castle's huge, it could accommodate our whole army, and it's more or less impregnable. From there we can command Kabul and protect our interests through the winter. Which, I need not add, can be horribly harsh in this part of the world.'

'He still thinks it's business as usual,' says Lawrence glumly. The young man looks exhausted from rushing around carrying messages between Macnaghten and Elphinstone, Shelton and the King. 'Why don't these people sit down and talk to each other?' Lawrence goes on, 'You know we had to attend a formal dinner in the palace on the night Burnes died. Everyone pretended nothing had happened but the pall of smoke from Burnes's house and the Treasury could be seen and smelt right up there in the Palace.'

Silence falls among our company as we think about the ridiculousness of this. Yet the King, Shah Soojah, was the only commander to try rescuing Burnes. He sent a regiment out from the Balar Hissar castle to fight its way through the mob. The men, mostly members of his own guard rather than our forces, came close to success, even though they met fierce resistance. But, before they could break through, the King ordered their retreat. It seems he was worried, after hours of waiting for news and watching from the battlements of the castle, that his son, Fatteh Jang, and the Prime Minister, Usman Khan, were in the thick of the fighting and might not come back alive.

At least the King tried to rescue Burnes. Shelton, as predicted, was not alerted to any danger until after Sir Alexander was dead and he was so slow to take action his regiment came nowhere near the city until sunset, by which time Kabul was seething with tribesmen and more were arriving all the time. Shelton simply repaired to the camp and declared he was awaiting further orders.

The silence is broken at last by Lady Sale. She looks at me, her face in shadow and her expression hard to read, but she takes her daughter's hand and squeezes it reassuringly as she announces in a somewhat regal fashion, 'I shall write to my husband, Major Pottinger. I believe you are correct in your assessment of the situation. We need strong military leadership and, in the meantime, we must make preparations for a siege.'

If only this woman were in command, I think to myself.

At that moment, Hoosein knocks on the door and rushes in, out of breath from running. 'Major, ladies, Captain Sturt.' He's so short of breath he can hardly get his words out. 'Injured,' he says, 'Stabbed. Outside the castle. Lancers…'

There is great commotion as most of the men rush from the room to find out more. In the gloom we see a party of about 50 lancers hurrying towards the house surrounding four men carrying a stretcher. We hurry to meet them and it's clear Sturt is in a very bad way.

The man's uniform is covered in blood. Attempts have been made to stem the bleeding which seems to come from his throat, arms and thigh, though it's not possible to tell. He is conscious but, apart from groaning a little, he is bravery itself. No screaming or panic though his face has turned a deathly grey.   Eleanor and Mrs Sturt rush out of the house and I send Hoosein to find a doctor as the stretcher is carried inside and eventually Sturt is laid down beside the fire in Lady Sale's sitting room with blood bubbling up from his mouth as he tries to breathe.

The general's wife issues orders and calls for servants, demands everyone leaves the room who has no specific role in assisting the captain and we are quickly banished from the house. My last glimpse is of Eleanor mopping blood from Sturt's mouth as she and Mrs Sturt encourage him to sit up as it would make it easier for him to breathe.

William Thain, a captain in the lancers, is waiting outside. He is filthy and exhausted and nursing a gash in his right hand which is not severe but looks painful.

Sturt was just leaving the Balar Hissar after an audience with Shah Soojah, he says, when a youth leaped out of a doorway swearing about 'foreigners' and proclaiming the greatness of Allah as he stabbed the Captain three times, in the throat, shoulder and left-hand side. 'It was the devil's own job getting him back to safety,' Thain says. 'Even with a party of lancers we were assailed from all sides. Two of my men are severely injured. I think we got half a dozen of the bastards but believe me they are dervishes. Screaming and grinning and calling us foreign devils. We had to take a long way back. It won't have done Sturt any good.'

*****

The next morning I call in on Lady Sale before Elphinstone and Macnaghten's 'council of war' which has been called for ten o'clock. The lateness of the hour indicates, I fear, their great lack of urgency. It is a cool morning with low clouds and a prevailing smell of burning which drifts towards the camp from the buildings of Kabul.

Eleanor comes to the door in a white linen dress spotted with blood, her hair held high above her head in a bun and her eyes pale with exhaustion. 'He's sleeping,' she says. 'Poor Drina. The doctor has sent her to bed with some laudanum to help her sleep. Lady Sale refuses to move from John's side and sits there with her crochet-work drinking cups of coffee and issuing orders.'

'How is Sturt?' I ask.

'Well he can breathe now, which is something.' Eleanor wipes her hands on her dress and smiles up at me. 'He is still in terrible pain but he doesn't complain. You could see the bone in his shoulder. He can't eat and can only sip water a drop at a time. Drina and I have been taking turns to wipe away blood from his mouth and drip water on his lips. His tongue was so swollen...' Her voice trails off in distress. I place an arm round her shoulder and hold her to my chest where she weeps quietly as I kiss her head and murmur how brave she is and what great service she is doing her friend's husband.

Eventually Eleanor breaks away and produces a bloody handkerchief from the folds of her dress, blows her nose and laughs, 'This is not very ladylike, is it?'

'My dear Eleanor…' I say without knowing what else to do but hold her to me again and protect her from this suffering.

'I'm alright, Eldred,' she says briskly, dusting down her dress. 'At least John can talk now. He said "bet-ter" after Drina helped him to more water. And Lady Sale cried.'

*****

Half an hour later I am in the General's headquarters. Elphinstone lies on a day-bed, pale and exhausted though it is early. His aides and officers sit at a long mahogany table where Macnaghten and Lawrence are also ensconced. I find a seat as far from Macnaghten as diplomacy allows while everyone waits in silence until the appointed hour is chimed by the large grandfather clock opposite the empty fireplace.

The room is cold. We can see our breath in the air. Everyone is wrapped up as if the meeting were to take place outside. Elphinstone is draped in rugs and furs though it is difficult to tell if he is awake at the moment.

As the clock chimes, Macnaghten says, 'Very well, gentlemen, let us make a start. Where is Brigadier-General Shelton?'

There is silence. Eventually Elphie asks, 'Has anyone invited Brigadier Shelton to this council?'

'We have received no orders to invite him,' says one officer.

'He is not in the camp, general,' says another.

'Lawrence,' hisses Macnaghten in a fury, 'My compliments to Brigadier Shelton and would he be kind enough to grace us with the pleasure of his company at his earliest possible convenience.'

Lawrence is dismissed. 'Take some lancers with you, Lawrence,' Macnaghten adds as his aide departs. 'You don't want to end up like Sturt. Now, gentlemen, to business. What supplies have we to hand?'

The meeting continues for an hour or more as Macnaghten asks perfectly practical questions and receives confusing answers. The supplies, food and ammunition, for instance, are stored in various godowns, warehouses and forts here and there across Kabul. Not one an adequate guard.

What intelligence we have about the enemy is confused and contradictory. Some say the uprising is led by the Duranni tribe, though as Shah Soojah himself is a Durrani that seems unlikely; others say it is the fault of the Barakzais, the family of the former King Dost Mohammed Khan. Still others say it's all Burnes's fault for abusing the women of the city. Nobody ventures the opinion, obvious though it must be, that the first cause of the revolt was the decision to increase taxes and halve the subsidies we provide the tribes of the Khyber to keep the pass open back to India.

Macnaghten still won't accept there is any cause for serious concern. Elphinstone suggests sending out raiding parties to secure our supplies. His officers debate the wisdom of this. Elphinstone says perhaps it is not such a wise idea. The general says we should meet the leaders of the rebels and find out what it is they want. Nobody seems to be clear who the leaders might be. Somebody says we should seek retribution for the brutal murder of Sir Alexander Burnes and punish the rabble with all the might Her Majesty's army has at its disposal; Elphinstone agrees this is a good idea but wonders how it might be accomplished.

The debates go round and round and no decision is taken. At about one o'clock we break for lunch and return at two as Shelton rides into the camp in no mood to enter into lengthy discussions.

Back in the General's office, everyone resumes his place as Shelton stands near the door and gives a little speech about the mad mullahs who are whipping up the Mohammedans against us and declares the time has come for us to depart from Kabul while it is still possible to retreat in good order.

Standing in his tight black uniform with his empty right arm swinging wildly, he declares, 'This is a vile and uncivilised country of no use to God nor man. We must quit it now or by God…'

'By God what, sir?' asks Elphinstone mildly.

'By God I shall not accept responsibility for the consequences, Elphie,' he says as insolently as he knows how. 'This is already a debacle. We must cut our losses and get out now, before it's too late.'

'Sir, your duty is to protect the interests of the Queen and the Company,' says Macnaghten, 'And I say, sir…'

'Don't tell me my duty, sir,' yells Shelton, grasping his sword hilt with his one good hand and taking a step in the Envoy's direction, his sharp-featured face contorted with rage.

'Your duty, sir, is to defend the interests of the Queen and the Company,' Macnaghten persists with quiet menace, 'And I am Her Majesty's representative in this country. Your duty, therefore, is to defend whatever I declare those interests to be. And I declare that the peace of Kabul must be maintained, we will not contemplate retreat and we must assert our moral and physical superiority over this rabble. General?' Macnaghten turns to Elphinstone for support.

'I suppose so, Sir William, but on the other hand…'

'On the other hand nothing,' Macnaghten says, banging his fist on the table. 'Now, gentlemen, tell me again who is leading this small disturbance and what steps we must take to quell it without further bloodshed.'

And so it goes on.

Shelton stands for a while with his back to the wall glowering on us all but as the chill deepens towards nightfall – with no decisions made, no actions ordered – he finds a space on the floor in front of the empty fire-place, rolls himself up in the rug and says not a word other than a few grunts of indignation as the 'council of war' turns into an endless debate.

This is my first conference with our leaders in Kabul and I am appalled by the confusion and indecision. Macnaghten wants to pretend nothing much has happened, Shelton thinks we should run away, Elphinstone has no idea what we should do. Most of the senior officers are elderly time-servers who bought their commissions, were very comfortable in India and have no desire to risk their lives in action. Their men, especially the native regiments, are unreliable and cannot be trusted. There is even some doubt about whether the King, Shah Soojah, can be relied upon. Few tears are shed for Burnes, despite the number of men who enjoyed his hospitality and delighted in his company. I keep my own counsel, knowing whatever suggestions I make will be slapped down by Macnaghten but eventually the Envoy turns to me with a sneer and asks, 'What does the Hero of Charikar have to say, I wonder?'

I stare at my hands, clasped in front of me on the table, and do not look up or catch his eye. 'Since you ask for my opinion, Sir William, I shall give it. The situation is dangerous but not desperate. Our first step must be to strike camp and move our entire army, together with our provisions, animals, ammunition, camp-followers – everything – into the King's castle.

'The Balar Hissar must be our headquarters for the winter. The King might not like it but it is safe, secure and strong.

'Then, once we have secured our base, we must impress on the Afghans our determination to remain here and defend ourselves. We must punish the rebels for the terrible murder of Sir Alexander and his friends, as well as for the looting and theft of money we have endured. We must take to the streets of Kabul, in force, and disperse all the armed groups which are gathering here. We must act as soon as possible and act decisively. As things stand, the only punishment is coming from the Balar Hissar where Shah Soojah's cannon have been firing into the city all day, though to what effect it is difficult at this distance to know. At least he is making a show of force even if we seem to be paralysed by indecision. If I were the General...'

'Mercifully, you are not, Major Pottinger, so we do not need to hear your dispositions,' Macnaghten interrupts though one or two of the younger officers now take up the same refrain and declare themselves ready to lead our men into battle as soon as the order is given.

Shelton rocks himself in his rug and groans. Macnaghten declares it is time for dinner. General Elphinstone says, 'Well, well, gentlemen, we shall just have to wait and see what tomorrow brings.'

CHAPTER 33

Fort William, Calcutta, January 1843

I am allowed to sit down beside my lawyer George Broadhurst, who stays very still as the case against me is outlined by Captain Trevor Whistler, the Judge-Advocate-General.

Whistler is young and bounces on the soles of his feet as he speaks. I find myself staring at his boots and trying to discern whether there is any pattern to the bouncing. I notice the cuffs of his trousers are slightly dusty, as if he has been too preoccupied to brush himself down before entering the court.

As Whistler emphasises a point, he seems to rise up on tip-toe while, when he is working his way through one of the more tedious passages of his speech, he rocks back onto his heels. Sometimes he stands on the sides his feet, his toes pointing towards each other. But mostly he rises onto the balls of his feet and lowers himself again, sometimes gently, occasionally with great enthusiasm. This performance mercifully distracts me from any close attention to the remarks he is making.

His voice carries hints of a North Country accent, perhaps Yorkshire, but glossed over by a more refined education. No doubt he's a younger son sent to India to make his fortune before returning with a wife and going into politics like most self-satisfied lawyers.

At one point, he proceeds to itemise the losses we sustained. 'Four horse artillery guns, three mountain trains, the Shah's second cavalry of 500 men...'

One of the judges interrupts him. Major General Sir James Rutherford Lumley, an amiable-looking man with thick, curly hair and humorous eyes, says to the chairman of the judges, George Russel Clerk, in a clear, clipped voice, 'I wonder if this is really necessary, Mr Clerk. Could we not dispense with this lamentable litany of losses? We are all only too well aware of what happened in Afghanistan, are we not?'

Clerk asks Whistler, 'Is this pertinent to the case, sir?'

'It is necessary, in my submission Your Lordships, that the court is fully appraised of the consequences of the decisions, of the decisions we submit were taken by the defendant, Major Pottinger, and the heavy burden of responsibility that rests on his shoulders.' Whistler says this while standing on the tips of his toes, one arm outstretched, the other, holding his notes, hanging down by his side. I wonder if he will tip over and, to my horror, I find myself smirking at the prospect. I draw a hand across my mouth to wipe away any suggestion of levity.

'I do think we can take all that as read, can we not, Mr Clerk?' persists Lumley. 'We all know the consequences of the decisions taken in Kabul. Some of us have only recently returned from that place ourselves.'

Clerk adds, 'It would save some time, Mr Whistler, if you were prepared to move on to the question of evidence.'

'Very well, sir,' says the prosecutor, falling back on his heels. There is a pause while he studies his notes. Broadhurst nudges me in the ribs and gives a small thumbs-up sign. I do not acknowledge him.

Whistler is thrown. He returns to his desk and shuffles through his papers. Everyone watches him. After a silence which seems to drag on interminably, though it probably lasts less than half a minute, the prosecutor resumes. His clear, confident voice is suddenly more hesitant. He has not enjoyed being interrupted in mid-flow and now stands on his heels, leaning back from the court clerk's bench as if reeling from an enemy onslaught. I tell myself this fragility must be a good sign.

'May it please the court,' he says in an ingratiating whine, 'I shall now turn to the specific allegations against Major Eldred Pottinger, late of the Bombay Artillery and the staff of Sir William Macnaghten, Her Majesty's Envoy to the King of Kabul, Shah Soojah-ool-Moolk Durrani.'

'Please do,' says Major General Lumley in a manner which suggests he is already beginning to feel the tedium of the trial even though it has hardly begun.

CHAPTER 34

Kabul, November 1841

'It is foolish and dangerous, Eldred,' says Eleanor, holding onto the baggy sleeve of my drab cotton coat. 'You must not go.'

'I must, Miss Eden.' I smile at her, take her hand, kiss it. She is standing outside Lady Sale's house, on her way back from another day in the increasingly-overcrowded sick-bay. She looks tired and anxious. Then she laughs, 'You do look ridiculous.'

That I know to be true. I am covered in Hoosein's Spanish black to disguise the colour of my skin, and I am dressed like some Ghilzai vagabond. So are John Logan, Wasim, Hooosein and Lieutenant Vincent Eyre. The five of us are going into the city, under cover of night, to find the remains of Alexander Burnes and give him a Christian burial.

It is a cold, star-lit night. I kiss Miss Eden's hand again and tell her we must go. 'Be careful, Eldred,' she says in a whisper. Her hand is chilly but her eyes are warm.

We leave the camp by a side gate which, like the whole cantonment, is now under constant surveillance by our enemies. Nobody tries to stop us. Merchants, traders, workers and other natives are permitted to come and go unchecked by the cordon of rebels set up just out of musket-range of the camp. For now, at least.

We head down the straight road into Kabul. The heights of the Balar Hissar glower down on us as we trudge slowly towards the town. We do not march quickly but shuffle as slowly as the bitter chill allows, to avoid attracting attention. As soon as we can leave the main road, Hoosein leads us through narrow alleys and by-ways until we reach the street behind Burnes's house. The air is still heavy with the smoke from smouldering ruins though the skeleton of his mansion, with its gouged out windows, can still be clearly seen in the bright night.

The back garden is deserted. Hoosein warned us he thought some Pashtun tribesmen had set up camp there but there is no sign. The body of Will Chapman lies where he was slain. Someone has had the decency to throw a cloak over his savagely wounded body. We lay three spades, which we carried hidden in our clothes, beside him, light a candle and, stepping cautiously, see if we can find the body of Burnes's brother or Sir Alexander himself. There is little left inside the building; everything has been eaten by the flames. There are no stairs to ascend, the library destroyed, the carpets, curtains and furnishings either consumed by the flames or stolen by looters. No bodies are to be found though maybe a dozen men died here and who knows what happened to Burnes's women?

We venture tentatively out into the street through the space where a door once stood.

Several people, women and children as well as men, are rooting around in the remains of what was Captain Johnson's treasury. The money and supplies are long gone but the fire did not completely destroy his office or his home and there may still be spoils to be had there, I suppose.

Between the door giving onto the street, and the treasury about fifty yards away, lies what is left of Sir Alexander Burnes. A mangy dog is chewing at his body, which is almost naked, stripped of its clothes and dignity. The people nearby ignore both the dog and the body. We are here to recover it and give him a Christian burial.

The five of us shuffle out of the house, trying to stay unobserved, and gather round the corpse of my friend. It has been hacked at by swords and knives, gnawed at by wild dogs, pecked at by crows. The dashing, debonair man I knew is unrecognisable. But this is Burnes alright. The same build, still with a kind of arrogant grin on his disfigured face; the same pale, Scottish skin. It is a shocking sight and for a moment I want to charge the looters and avenge my friend's death but that would defeat our purpose.

Instead, we wrap the corpse in a rug Hoosein and Wasim have been carrying with them and together we lug Burnes's remains back inside his burnt-out mansion.

Just as we think we have escaped unremarked, three youths cry out and rush over with drawn swords. Wasim steps towards them with a knife in his hand. 'What do you want?' he demands, as the rest of us hurry through the burnt-out building with Burnes's body.

One of the youths, about the same age but inches shorter than my lad, says, 'What do you want with that foreigner?'

'We are selling his corpse,' says Wasim.

'Selling?' The youths are taken aback. 'Where is the money in dead Christians?'

'Only the head,' says Wasim. 'Our chief, Mohammed Akbar Khan, has offered a reward. Now back off.' He steps towards them with a sharp knife in his hand and they draw back.

Wasim stays by the door to keep out intruders while the rest of us carry Burnes's body out into the garden and lay it beside his murdered friend. Dr Logan, Lieutenant Eyre and I start digging while Hoosein is posted at the garden door in case of trouble. We put our backs into the work but it is slow going. Despite the clear night sky, in the gloomy light of a single flickering candle it is difficult to see what we are doing especially as we want to avoid the noisy clash of spades and we have to work our way round large lumps of rock. We do not want to draw attention to ourselves and there is a risk too much noise will prompt inquiries from anyone who happens to be about.

After two hours digging, we consider we are ready to inter the bodies, which we lay as carefully as we can in the unforgiving earth. Before we cover them, Dr Logan conducts the burial service: 'I am the resurrection and the life, saith the Lord: he that believeth in me, though he were dead, yet shall he live: and whosoever liveth and believeth in me shall never die. I know that my Redeemer liveth, and that he shall stand at the latter day upon the earth. And though after my skin worms destroy this body, yet in my flesh shall I see God: whom I shall see for myself, and mine eyes shall behold, and not another....'

As Logan intones the words, I think about my friend and my own guilt. I could not save him. Perhaps I should have died with him. Should I have died with him? Should I have made more of an effort to rescue Burnes? I know it would have been fruitless but does that mean it should not have been attempted? It would surely be braver and more gallant to die at an enemy's hands than live with the shame of allowing him to die. I really do not know the answer but I am glad we at least saved his body from rotting in the street, mocked at by passers-by and gnawed by curs.

The service is quickly over. We do not wish to stay longer than necessary. Wasim reports all is quiet in the street though there are still people kicking through the remains of the treasury; Hoosein is not so certain the alley at the back is clear. He says he thinks he heard noises but cannot tell what they may be.

We emerge through the doorway with our hands on our sword hilts. No guns. If we get into a fight, must keep it as quiet as we reasonably can. We slip down the street and as we turn the first corner we meet a gang of eight young men, three of them the ones Wasim warned off earlier.

'Give us the head,' one of them says.

'No,' says Hoosein and draws his sword. 'Now go before we run you through. In the name of Allah go.'

The first youth lunges at Hoosein but Eyre is sharp and slashes away the knife with his sword. A second youth pulls out a pistol while the others now lay into us with knives and swords. I knock the pistol out of the youth's hand but it goes off as it hits the ground. Logan parries one thrust while Wasim brings his sword down on someone else's shoulder with such force he falls to the ground screaming in agony.

My leg screams with pain but I must fight if we are to get through this alive. Eyre wrestles one man while another bends to see how badly hurt his companion is. This creates an opening and, by swinging my sword wildly from side to side and yelling at my comrades to follow me, we manage to break through and run down the alley with three of the enemy in pursuit.

At the next corner, I usher the others past me then turn on the first of our attackers, stretching out with my sword to catch him just above the elbow. He yells in pain as blood gushes from his wound and the others hesitate long enough for me to catch one in thigh. He falls with a groan as the third comes on at me with a short, sharp knife. He lunges at my chest. I take half a step backwards and he loses his footing. As he stumbles forward, I slam the hilt of my sword down on the back of his head and he collapses, stunned, flat on his face. I hesitate, wondering whether to run him through with my sword, but decide on mercy. I turn and half-run, half-hobble to catch up with the others who are waiting for me by the next corner.

Panting and exhausted but unscathed, we walk hurriedly away as quietly as we can. 'A good night's work,' says Logan with a laugh, 'Better even than a game of cricket.' We reach a refuge where we pause for breath and take stock before emerging to slink back towards the camp and make our way innocently past the rebel pickets.

*****

This brief encounter is good for my morale but it does nothing to ease the plight of our garrison. After Burnes's death, the number of our enemies seems to double by the day. The longer we hold councils of war and take no action, the more emboldened they become. They taunt and mock us, firing volleys of shot in our direction, besieging our outlying quarters and slowly but surely tightening a noose around our camp.

Several times, officers defending some of these forts are promised reinforcements by General Elphinstone but find none is forthcoming. They fight to the last man and die at their posts when timely action would disperse the enemy and protect our possessions. Yet nothing is done. No orders are given or, if they are, nobody acts on them.

All is chaos and disaster. Not a day passes without our men being killed or so severely wounded they will die soon. We have lost our supplies. We send out raiding parties to glean a little food and, when some is found, even our own officers say there is no point in bothering because we shall not live to eat it.

Lady Sale is scathing. 'They are all croakers,' she says. 'Croakers. Croak! Croak! Croak! It's pathetic.'

Eleanor has turned herself into a nurse and constantly rushes between the sick-bay, now so full of wounded officers there is no room for other ranks, and Lady Sale's home where she is still helping Alexandrina Sturt and Lady Sale restore Captain Sturt to reasonable health.

The General and the Envoy only communicate by letter. Our 'councils of war' take place either with Elphinstone and Brigadier Shelton in one building or, a few hundred yards away, with Macnaghten in another. Neither the General nor the Envoy gives any orders. A few officers take it upon themselves to seek to secure our position but they cannot rely on support, reinforcements or even on the men under their command. It's clear the Mohammedens cannot be trusted to do their duty.

As for Shelton, Macnaghten sends him notes demanding action and receives replies saying Shelton is not subject to the Envoy's orders and will act only on the request of the General. Elphinstone is paralysed by indecision. The King, looking down on this confusion from the relative safety of the Balar Hissar, sends messages urging action and warning his own position is in jeopardy. He tells of plots and factions and warns no-one is to be trusted any more. Macnaghten insists the Afghans will soon see reason.

I take every opportunity to urge immediate action against the enemy and that the entire army decamps to the King's castle. I offer to lead the relief of one of our forts and Macnaghten, in one of his councils of war, declares, 'You, Pottinger, are a political. You are not a soldier. I expressly forbid you to take up arms in any capacity other than self-defence. Is that clear?'

The enemy seize the King's cannon and kill 200 of his men after they are sent out from the castle in a bid to regain control of the city. Hoosein says the King's attendants and servants are starting to desert him. He says the city is being colonised by a variety of different tribes, each with its own chieftain and its own designs.

'Nothing unites them, sahib,' says the little man with a sorrowful frown. 'But they have now declared a Holy War against us and their imams are going round the city making everyone swear on the Koran to fight for Allah against the foreigners. The imams are preaching against us, calling us heathen dogs, curs, less than humans. They hate us – not just the Europeans, all of us. Indians even more than English. And now they have a leader, sahib. They have Akbar Khan.'

'I know that name,' I say. 'It was his name Wasim used when he told those youths we were selling Burnes's head.'

Hoosein's frown deepens further. He looks weather-beaten and older than his years, which I guess to be only about 35. 'Akbar Khan, sahib,' he says, as if the name should mean something to me. 'Akbar Khan,' he repeats, slowly, as if to a simpleton. I look blankly at him though I know I should know the name. 'The fourth and favourite son of Dost Mohammed Khan, sahib. Dost Mohammed Khan, the King that was.'

'Of course, of course. I remember. And what do we know of Akbar Khan, Hoosein?'

'He has six thousand cavalry at his back and the other chiefs have acknowledged him as their leader. He is uniting the tribes against us.'

'Can they be united?'

'If anyone can do it, Akbar can, sahib. You know he personally chopped off the head of Hari Singh at the Battle of Jamrud when we were in Herat. They say he has been sent by Allah himself to free the people of Islam from the faithless foreigners and restore the rightful king to the Throne in Kabul.'

*****

I spend my time trying to negotiate supplies from the few friendly natives willing to do business with us. This is hard going because the prices rise by the day and the chances of bringing the food into our camp grow worse with every hopeless skirmish.

The native merchants, even the Indians from the bazaar, will only do business at exorbitant prices and as our Treasury has been emptied I must negotiate loans from the local bankers, who also know when they are on to a good thing, and demand usurious rates of interest. They point out they are running a grave risk they will never be repaid. 'What if your army is wiped out?' one of them asks, 'Then who will pay us? We are only helping you out of loyalty to the British. We risk losing our money or even our lives.'

We send out troops to bring food into camp but they are cut down and return with little or nothing. The weather grows colder. My leg aches permanently. It goes septic. From time to time, pieces of metal and wood emerge from the wound. The doctors are far too busy to bother with me and I am reluctant to ask for their help when men, women and children are dying every day – some the victims of enemy action, almost as many from pneumonia brought on by the cold and damp. We cannot even secure firewood to keep us warm any more.

I return from an expensive attempt to negotiate to buy some wheat. The price has gone up to three rupees for just one seer, which in this country is about a stone in weight. Three rupees! It is extortion but we are starving and food is hard to find. I agreed to pay 1,000 rupees for enough wheat to keep us in bread for perhaps a day and a half;

three days if it's properly rationed. Always assuming the grain is ever delivered.

As I trudge back from this secret meeting with one of the Indian merchants in a house down a back street, and pass unaccosted through the pickets of Afghans and into the camp, I am worrying away at the price of supplying 15,000 men, women and children with food when the cost rises almost hourly and the supply of goods shrinks at the same time. I am deep in calculations as I make my way towards Lady Sale's house to inquire after Captain Sturt when I see Eleanor Eden walking slowly in the same direction, also apparently deep in thought.

I stand and watch her in the gloomy twilight as she weaves her way through the men's tents from the sick bay and note there is blood on her skirts and she seems to be dabbing her eyes with a handkerchief. I hurry towards her as she makes her slow way home. 'Miss Eden, can I be of service?'

'Oh it's you Eldred,' she says flatly. Her eyes are red and bloodshot, her hair is drawn up in a bun on the back of her head under a little cotton cap, her dress is dirty with stains. She tries to brush down her clothes and adjust her cap, dabs at her eyes and sniffs away tears. There is no light in her eyes and she looks woebegone.

'You are crying.'

'How very perceptive of you,' she says defiantly and brushes past me.

'Eleanor,' I appeal to her and hurry to catch up. 'Tell me, tell me.'

She stops. 'Tell you what, exactly, Major Pottinger? Tell you that I have spent the whole day watching young men die in agony? Tell you that I have helped the surgeon saw off a man's foot? Tell you there is no room for all our injured men to have a bed each? That they can't bury the bodies fast enough? What should I tell you, Major? That Colonel Mackrell was brought in this morning with one leg sliced through at the knee, a deep wound in the thigh, three sword slashes in his back, two toes cut off and four cuts to his sword arm? Should I tell you the poor man is in agony and will certainly die?'

She looks defiantly at me but as I step towards her and put an arm on hers, she bursts into tears and I hold her close as the sobs burst from within and all the pain she has been feeling is at last released.

We stand like this for several minutes, even though several people we know walk past us. I don't catch their eyes; Eleanor's face is buried in my chest, her body heaving with anguish. There are faint flurries of snow as the night descends and the temperature falls further. Eventually I say, 'I must get you inside, out of this cold,' and lead her gently towards Lady Sale's house.

As we approach the porch, Eleanor's spirits rise a little. 'Don't tell Lady Sale about this, will you? She'll think I'm a croaker too. She thinks everybody's a croaker.'

'You are a brave young woman to endure day after day looking after our comrades, Eleanor, and I know how upsetting it can be.'

'But there doesn't seem to be any end to it, Eldred.'

'I know,' I reply. I do not feel able to offer any consolation – there does not seem to be any end to it.

And Akbar Khan is gathering his forces.

CHAPTER 35

Kabul, November 1841

Another 'council of war' with Elphinstone, on his chaise longue stationed by a roaring fire – where do they find the wood? – and Shelton, for once not rolled up in his carpet, saying nothing. This time, in front of about a dozen of his junior officers, he struts to and fro pointing vigorously with his one arm while the empty arm of his black coat swings about with a life of its own.

He has led a couple of fruitless sorties in the last few days, losing dozens of men, ammunition and supplies. 'I will not go out again,' he is saying, his small, furious face screwed up in anger, the lines of age deepening into furrows as he lays down the law, 'Not until I am found suitable accommodation, Elphie. These tents may suit the Indians and Mohammedens. They might even suit the other ranks but as the most senior active officer – active, I say, Elphie, active – I demand suitable accommodation. Lady Sale's house…'

Elphinstone, who flinches at each verbal assault, summons the strength to offer a mild word of reproach. In his quiet, clipped, upper-crust voice he says, 'Well, well, Brigadier-General, that is going too far. Ladies, you know, ladies.'

'Ladies be damned,' Shelton says, turning his back on the general and staring out of the window as a light fall of snow begins to settle.

'Lady Sale and her harpies should have been gone from here months ago, to her bloody husband who is cowering in Jalalabad and ignores our demand for reinforcements.'

'We can hardly turn them out now can we, Brigadier-General?' says Elphinstone mildly while we other officers exchange glances and raise eyebrows as our dire position is monumentally ignored while our commanders argue about tents.

'Bloody women should bloody bugger off,' Shelton replies before turning round, marching towards the prostrate body of out Commander-in-Chief saying, 'So should the rest of us. We must leave this benighted place. The weather's filthy, there's no food, the Afghans don't want us. Look what happened to Burnes. Look what happened yesterday. The sooner we quit this place the better.'

'In this weather?' murmurs Elphinstone, tugging tight the greatcoat wrapped around him.

*****

In Macnaghten's quarters the debate is, at least, a little more aware of our predicament. He, like Elphinstone and Shelton, consistently rejects the suggestion we should retreat to the Balar Hissar but Sir William is pursuing twin policies of his own.

A message has arrived from Elphinstone's adjutant declaring Shelton will take no further action against the enemy without written orders. Macnaghten says he is damned if Shelton should shiver in his tent like a lily-livered Achilles, the man should be giving these Ghilzai devils a damned good lesson.

He issues an order that, the following day, Shelton is to muster whatever strength is necessary and take the village of Behmaru, the site of a large rebel encampment not far from our own camp. The Envoy dispatches a message to this effect to the General and we await a response.

As we wait for an answer, Macnaghten tells his staff, of which I am, it seems, both the most senior and most unwanted member, that he is negotiating a truce with Akbar Khan. 'That man is at least capable of holding these tribesmen and savages to account,' says Macnaghten, adjusting his blue-lens spectacles and clearing his throat in an unconscious assertion of authority. 'So we have arranged another meeting with him.'

'Another?' I say, astounded that Sir William has been treating with the enemy behind the General's back.

'Of course another, Pottinger. You, my dear sir, need not be inconvenienced by these distractions. By all accounts, you already have your hands full.' There is a murmur of suppressed laughter at this sarcastic remark. 'And by the way, how is the Governor-General's sister?'

It is all I can do to remain calm but I do say, as icily as I know how, 'So what of this secret treaty, then, Sir William? May we all be party to the negotiations?'

Sir William leans back in his big, high-backed chair at the head of the table where a dozen officers sit waiting for one of our commanders to take the initiative. 'Tell him, Bygrave.'

Captain Bulstrode Bygrave is, contrary to his bullish name, a slight young man with the wisps of a moustache, an apologetic look and an embarrassed stutter, which make the delivery of what he has been asked to say so difficult he cannot look up from the table or meet anybody's eye, not even Macnaghten's. He mumbles and hesitates but the long and the short of it is he has arranged, through various intermediaries, three meetings with Akbar Khan and several other chieftains. This in itself would be a surprise given Bygrave's lack of forcefulness, if he had not been accompanied by George Lawrence, a bright and capable man wasted in the service of the Envoy. The pair arranged a meeting between Akbar Khan and Sir William Macnaghten where they were all treated with great civility and enjoyed a warm and friendly meal together. The aim was to create an agreement allowing Her Majesty's army to retreat with honour from Kabul taking the King, Shah Soojah.

In exchange, Macnaghten has given them a firm promise that Akbar's father, Dost Mohammed Khan, would be allowed to return from exile in India and restored to his place on the Throne in Kabul.

There were several sub-clauses still to be negotiated but, as an act of faith, Akbar Khan would ensure the garrison was protected and supplied with food and other necessaries through the coming winter before the army left with the first snow-melts of spring.

'This is all most satisfactory,' says Macnaghten when Bygrave has finished his mumbling recital but several other officers appear as unhappy as I am at this turn. 'How can we say we have departed with honour when this is mere surrender?' I ask. 'Especially when we betray Shah Soojah, the King who we chose to place on this Throne and are now throwing down to save our own skins? And if we are so sure of reaching agreement with Akbar Khan, why are we at the same time demanding a counter-attack?'

'To make assurance doubly sure, of course,' says Macnaghten dismissively. 'If we can weaken the enemy significantly, we can be confident he would not dare give up his side of the bargain.'

'Is it not dangerously provocative?' asks Vincent Eyre, the young officer who accompanied me on our mission to bury poor Alexander Burnes. Eyre has the look of someone who is happy to live dangerously which, of course, he is doing by questioning Macnaghten. 'Unless we succeed in wiping out Akbar Khan's forces, surely he will be bent on revenge not cowed into submission. There are many thousand more Afghans in and around Kabul than there are Company men. And they are fighting on home turf.'

'Home rocks,' somebody adds, provoking a slight chuckle which clearly irritates Macnaghten.

The Envoy bangs his fist angrily on the table. 'Akbar Khan must see we are not afraid to fight,' says Macnaghten. 'He must be taught the power of Her Majesty's Army of the Indus. These people lack the necessary respect. We can have our victory and still have our treaty.'

'And if we do not have our victory?' asks Eyre.

He is saved from Macnaghten's wrath by the arrival of a messenger from Elphinstone which begs to inform the Envoy that the General is unwilling to order an attack on the village of Behmaru because: the army is tired after several previous skirmishes and in need of rest; the men are hungry; the loyalty of the Mohammedens, and some of the Indians, cannot be relied upon; the army is short of weaponry and must conserve what it has; the enemy is too great in number and unpredictable; a large force sent out to meet the enemy would leave the cantonment dangerously exposed in the event of a counter-attack. The note concludes that General Elphinstone begs to suggest Her Majesty's Envoy to Kabul to curb his belligerence and await events.

'Who wrote this? Macnaghten demands of the messenger.

'It is signed by General Elphinstone, sir,' the man replies.

'But who wrote it?'

'I believe it was dictated by Brigadier-General Shelton, sir.'

Macnaghten immediately dictates a reply insisting inaction is tantamount to surrender. The General's reply, also apparently dictated by Shelton, says action will only be taken if the Envoy accepts personal responsibility for the decision and the outcome of any action he orders.

Macnaghten issues an order to that effect.

*****

The joke among the troops is that when a captain in the Bengal artillery called James Abbott asked the military board to send three 18-pounder guns to Kabul, some pen-pusher at the board, with the arithmetic of the habitual bureaucrat, responded by despatching six nine-pounders. It's 54 pounds in all, whichever way you look at it. The nine-pounders may be more manoeuvrable but they aren't half as much use as the 18-pounders would have been.

This helps explain Shelton's otherwise unaccountable decision to mount his attack with just one nine-pounder even though this is contrary to the army's ordnances which require at least two cannons to be taken into battle on every occasion. This is a wise rule because the guns get over-heated if they are fired too often without being given time to cool down between volleys. A pair of cannons ensures the artillery can maintain a constant barrage without rendering either weapon unusable. This is one of the first lessons we learn in the Bengal artillery but it is early morning, and Shelton's ragged army is well on its way, before it becomes clear he has taken only the one gun.

As dawn breaks, bitterly cold with frost on the ground and a strong wind blowing down from the mountains, we clamber onto the roof of Lady Sale's house to survey Shelton's progress. From this vantage point, wrapped in every warm item we can lay our hands on and fortified with brandy, Lady Sale, Eleanor Eden, Alexandrina Sturt, three of Macnaghten's staff including George Lawrence and I peer through telescopes and binoculars into the dawning day and listen to the explosions, cries and clash of battle.

Lawrence says excitedly, 'This is it, then, Major. Anderson's horse, the Envoy's own cavalry escort, the 5th native cavalry, the 1st, the 4th, Skinner's horse, Alexander's horse, the Shah's 5th and 6th, six companies of the 44th, two of the 37th. It's about time we took the fight to the enemy.'

The ladies are chattering nervously but do not seem alarmed when explosions three miles off make the roof shake and rattle the windows. I am some distance from Eleanor and cannot make out her reaction but as time goes on it starts to look as if Shelton has achieved an advantage of surprise and is pressing home his attack from the summit of the hill overlooking Behmaru. The nine-pounder is firing away into the woods surrounding the village though there are few signs it is having the devastating effect on the enemy one would hope to see.

Having reached the summit of the hill, all Shelton has to do is descend on the village and destroy the enemy. But he does not. We watch as he forms up his squadrons and despatches just a small raiding party which is quickly turned back. A second squadron is ordered into the fray and succeeds in penetrating into the village itself but by this time the enemy has regrouped. Some of their soldiers are now secure behind stone walls or inside stone buildings while many more have managed to slip away entirely.

There are skirmishes here and there for the next couple of hours. Our vantage point on Lady Sale's roof is not entirely safe. Occasionally a stray bullet from an Afghan rifle whizzes past our ears or lodges itself in the chimney. Nobody on the roof is hurt but, as we watch, we see more and more of our men cut down. The enemy is mounting a counter-attack. Some infantry advance cautiously towards Shelton's position but remain just out of range of our muskets. The cannon keeps on pounding them but what we see, and Brigadier-General Shelton does not, is a troop of maybe four thousand Afghan cavalry advancing along the Kabul road and heading towards the gorge which separates Behmaru hill from the Kabul lake.

Lady Sale takes her daughter and Eleanor Eden away at about ten o'clock saying it looks as if Shelton has won the day and her son-in-law Mr Sturt, still recovering from his wounds, will be wondering what has become of his breakfast. The rest of us stay on and watch as Shelton's advantage starts to disintegrate. He has formed his men into two squares – the sort of squares which served Wellington very well at Waterloo 25 years ago – but their muskets do not have the range of the rebels' jezzails, which, with their long barrels, carry over much greater distances. Our squares of red-uniformed infantry are more or less incapable of inflicting damage on the enemy but remain brightly-coloured standing targets. It is an unequal contest – the Afghans, hidden behind rock and walls, beyond the range of our muskets; our men standing stock still at the top of the hill in scarlet-coloured squares just asking to be picked off. Worst of all, the nine-pounder has fallen silent, no doubt overheated and in danger of exploding.

It is heart-breaking to watch. I feel the urge to scream from the rooftop at Shelton and tell him to take some positive action but my words would disappear into the noise and heat of battle.

Some of our men are brave and determined. I see, even from this distance, several heroic attempts to fight back. And certainly Shelton is no coward, standing there in the midst of it all, surveying the conflict and failing to issue any orders which might remedy the situation.

'Oh God,' says Lawrence. 'It's turning into a disaster. Look, they still don't seem to have seen the cavalry advance. Can't we get a message to them? Warn Shelton?'

We edge our way off the roof, down through the house and out into the camp in search of horses. Hoosein, waiting for me on the threshold, leads us quickly to where he has been stabling our horses and I find he has already saddled two animals. Lawrence and I set out as quickly as we can towards Shelton's two squares but it is impossible to find a way through the enemy lines on horseback. We abandon the horses and take to our feet though my wounded leg forces me to hobble some distance behind as Lawrence leaps over boulders and runs through orchards towards Shelton's position.

But we are too late. From three-quarters of a mile away, as we try to clamber over a wall, we see the Afghan cavalry descend on our comrades – hundreds of dervishes, screaming for blood, gallop down on Shelton's right flank and straight into the two squares of men.

There is a battle for the silent cannon and the artillerymen defend it to the last before they are run through, decapitated and the weapon is captured by the enemy. The infantry squares are cut down. Our cavalry, hemmed in beside them, has little room to manoeuvre. Even turning the horses round to face the charge, in that confined space, takes too long and creates chaos, if not panic. Yet all the while Shelton stands in the midst of it defying the enemy and issuing no orders.

Other officers try to rally their troops but, as Lawrence and I watch, the Afghan cavalry ploughs in amongst our men, the natives slashing their swords to and fro, giving far more punishment than they get. The squares waver, start to crumble and then disintegrate.

What starts as a retreat quickly turns into a rout. It's every man for himself as our broken army flees back to the camp.

Lawrence and I watch this disaster at close quarters but we are powerless to intervene and soon enough we have no choice but to join the rush for the dubious safety of the cantonment. And as we flee the Afghans – their faces distorted with fury, their eyes blazing with anger, willing to lose everything including their lives – I can't help thinking of Eleanor Eden's question when she heard the shocking news of Alexander Burnes's murder, 'Why do they hate us so much?'

*****

The gossip in Lady Sale's drawing room this evening is gloomy. Captain Sturt wants to know everything. The poor man is recovering from his terrible wounds but he's frustrated to be confined to barracks. He believes his duty lies with his men. The deep gashes he suffered are beginning to mend but only slowly. He can walk, after a fashion, but his tall frame is bent in pain and one arm is of no use to him at the moment. He sits with his feet up on a stool on the opposite side of the fireplace to his mother-in-law while the rest of us are spread out around the room perching on seats, the edge of Lady Sale's mahogany dining table or cross-legged on the carpets. There are about a dozen of us and we think of ourselves as the 'government-in-waiting'. There is a freedom to express an opinion here which would be regarded as insubordination if not insurrection elsewhere.

'Croakers, croakers,' Lady Sale complains, listing off the names of half a dozen officers who, from her vantage point on the roof in the early stages of the battle, failed to inspire her.

'Not all of them,' says Eleanor. 'Some of them were heroic. Did you see poor Sergeant Mulhall? He fought like a dervish, poor man.' I look at Eleanor and note she remains dry-eyed. Perhaps she is in shock. Perhaps she has grown used to blood and wounds during her time tending to the dozens – hundreds – of men who are injured or simply dying of pneumonia. From across the room I look at her eyes and there is no light in them; around those beautiful brown eyes she is blue with fatigue.

'As for Elphinstone and Shelton,' says Lawrence. 'When Eldred and I got back to camp I saw poor Elphie dragging himself across the parade ground and out to the main entrance to welcome the men home as if they were conquering heroes.'

'Yes but did you see what happened next?' asks Vincent Eyre. 'As a troop of the 44th dragged themselves back – they were exhausted and several were nursing wounds and carrying their injured comrades, Elphie yells "Eyes right" expecting them to salute him. And they look left. You'd laugh if it weren't so tragic.'

'I heard Shelton say how bravely the 44th had fought, how nobly they acquitted themselves,' I say, 'And I also heard Captain Troup reply, "Yes, right up to the moment they turned tail and fled like the coward dogs they are".'

'Good for Troup,' says Lady Sale.

'Shelton blames the rout on his Indian natives. He says they are too timid and it makes our European men timid as well.'

'They need proper leadership, that's all,' says Lady Sale belligerently. She then rises from her chair, as if to leave the room, but it seems it is to deliver some sort of speech. She stands with her back to the dimly-glowing fire where she has been trying to create some warmth in the room by burning the chairs from the servants' quarters now we are out of firewood. Lady Sale is a fine figure for a woman who must be 43 if she's a day. Her thick blonde hair and strong features, her angry blue eyes and her determined chin make her both a woman to be admired and feared. The room falls silent as she says, 'Gentlemen, I fear we have received some grave news. This afternoon I finally had a reply to my letter to my husband, the General, asking him to return to Kabul with his army and take charge. I fear the General is unable to oblige. I shall read the relevant part of his correspondence:

"As to your request, much as it would please me to ensure the safety of those I love and, indeed, of the army as a whole, I regret it is impossible. Our march to Jalalabad was dogged every step of the way by attacks from the natives. Our progress through the passes was constantly impeded by snipers high up among the rocks, picking off our men at every

opportunity. We lost dozens of good men, including several brave officers, before we finally reached our destination and I regret to say our enemies are now laying siege to the town and we are hard put to protect ourselves. Any attempt to break out and return to Kabul would be futile, my dear, we would be cut to pieces and with the winter driving in, I cannot see how it could be done for the next three months at least. I have, of course, passed on your intelligence and our own to the Governor-General with a warning about the state of affairs in Afghanistan but I do not doubt but it will be some time before we receive succour. In the meantime, I pray for you every day. We must trust in God – and keep our powder dry."

'He goes on at some length about other matters and the political situation but this is the nub of it. We are on our own now and can't expect any immediate help from elsewhere.'

With that, Lady Sale orders the servants to provide everyone with a glass of brandy while Dr John Logan, my old friend from Charikar, who has been sitting silently in a far corner no doubt shivering in the cold, suggests we say a prayer. Heads bowed, everybody listens reverently as Logan intones, 'Gracious Lord, creator of all things, Who hast placed us in the grip of Thine enemies, deliver us, we pray, from the depredations of these foes of the Word of the Lord and protect these Thy humble servants, delivering them safely to their homes or, if it pleaseth Thee to do so, take them to Thy bosom where they may enjoy the light of Thy salvation for ever-more. Amen.'

We all say Amen though Lady Sale mutters, 'Call that a prayer? I call it defeatism. We shall not be undone by these heathens.'

*****

As we are leaving for our freezing quarters, warmed only a little by Lady Sale's brandy, George Lawrence lingers on the threshold preventing me from any intimate farewell to Eleanor Eden. I kiss her hand and say, 'As Elphie would put it, "There's nothing to be done; let's see what tomorrow brings".' We all laugh dryly at Elphinstone's habitual indecision and Lawrence and I depart.

The night is bitterly cold, a thin layer of snow on the ground turning to ice, and the stars shining brightly down from a huge, cloudless sky. The bleak outline of the mountains is picked out clearly against the blue-black heavens. 'What is it, George?' I ask impatiently. My leg aches and I need to rest it.

Lawrence looks at Hoosein, who has been lingering just inside Lady Sale's house waiting for us to emerge. 'You can trust Hoosein,' I say.

'Well then,' says Lawrence, 'Macnaghten. Tomorrow he is meeting Akbar Khan. I thought you should know.'

Hoosein tugs my sleeve, seeking permission to speak, uncertain if he should intervene in a discussion with one of my fellow officers. 'Hoosein?' I say.

'Akbar Khan is not to be trusted, sahib, because he cannot trust his own friends. In the bazaar they say he is leader for now but not the real leader. They say they are united in hating the British but that is all. He thinks he commands; he does not.'

'Do we have any choice, Hoosein?' I ask.

'At any rate, Macnaghten is meeting him tomorrow,' says Lawrence, 'And we have our own intelligence. Osman Khan says they do not want to destroy us, they just want to see us leave the country. And Osman Khan spared several lives earlier today, restraining himself and his men when he had ours at his mercy. I've had this from two or three of the officers.' In the moonlight, Lawrence looks optimistic, even cheerful.

'Osman Khan works for Shah Soojah,' says Hoosein, 'If we go, the King goes too. He knows that. The power is with Akbar, not Osman.'

Lawrence persists, 'Macnaghten takes comfort from the assurances he has received. The Ghilzai chiefs say they will fight us but not very hard.'

'A sword is a sword,' says Hoosein sententiously. 'A bullet is a bullet.'

CHAPTER 36

Fort William, Calcutta, January 1843

The morning wears on, the day heats up. Even with all the windows and doors wide open, the courtroom is getting stuffy and my forehead is becoming clammy. Beside me, my attorney George Broadhurst is becoming red in the face and shuffling uncomfortably in his seat. The five judges, cooled a little by the fans above their heads operated by the punka-wallahs, have discarded their caps and hats. Trevor Whistler, my prosecutor, is still bouncing around on his feet like some bantamweight fighter looking for a scrap.

'We now come to the first charge relating to the misuse of Company funds, my Lords,' he says, halting his dance and rifling through a pile of papers on the desk behind him. 'You will see,' he says, waving a sheaf of them in his right hand, 'You will see the import clearly by perusing this set of documents, sirs, Exhibit A.'

'Are these admitted?' asks Mr Clerk.

'They are,' Whistler confirms, while Broadhurst gives a curt nod of agreement without really looking up at the judges.

'You will see from these admitted documents, my Lords, that the prisoner...'

Without warning Broadhurst suddenly jumps to his feet and exclaims, 'Your Lordships, I really must protest. Major Pottinger is not a prisoner. He is free to come and go. He has not been brought here in chains and will not be locked up in some dank cell when we are finished for the day. To refer to a gentleman of honour and distinction as "the prisoner" is discourteous, misleading and prejudicial to justice.'

Whistler is blown off course by this and sits while the chairman of the judges, Mr Clerk, responds. 'I agree, Captain Broadhurst, it is demeaning to refer to the defendant as a prisoner. Captain Whistler, you will show Major Pottinger greater respect if you please.'

'My apologies, your honour,' he says, rising to his feet again but without much of his former bounce. Taking up the sheaf of papers, he explains they represent the bills I signed while the army was in Kabul. 'These are promissory notes, Your Lordships, made out to various traders and middlemen, promising in the name of the Honourable British East India Company to repay certain debts incurred in the purchase of supplies for the Army of the Indus during its sojourn in Kabul. You will see, sirs, that the sum total of these notes or cheques is almost twelve lakhs of Indian rupees. I do not need to tell you, gentlemen, that is almost £15,000, a considerable amount of money and, we say, an excessive sum for the prison... err defendant... to take it upon himself to promise to anyone in the Company's name and without any official authorisation.'

Brigadier Wymer, at the far right of the panel, clears his throat and asks the chairman Mr Clerk, 'May I ask a question?' Given the nod, he goes on, 'Can you tell this court martial, Mr Whistler, whether these bills have in actual fact been honoured by the Company?'

'They have not, sir.'

'Why is that?'

'The Governor-General considers any thought of payment should await the outcome of this Court Martial. It is, of course, the case that the papers have changed hands several times since they were first signed by Major Pottinger and the holders are not the individuals from whom the Company first purchased the goods.'

'Yet those individuals will have traded in good faith in the reasonable belief the Company would honour its debts,' says Brigadier Wymer.

'It is reasonable to make that assumption, sir,' says Whistler, clearly irritated and wanting to get back to the main point of his address.

Wymer persists, 'What, sir, does this do to the reputation of the Company if it is prepared to renege on its debts?'

'If those debts were wrongly incurred, sir?' Whistler replies. 'Even Major Pottinger says that some of them were enforced under duress.'

'Does he?'

'He does, sir,' says Broadhurst, who adds, 'Major Pottinger has offered several times to go through all these bills, item by item, and identify those which he regards as true and fair and those which he sees as examples of extortion, money wrung out of him by usury and which he believes it would be dishonourable to meet in full, if at all. So far, the Company has rejected any offer, however.'

Wymer looks for support and General Lumley, in a growl of a voice which suggests anger suppressed with difficulty, says, 'Mr Whistler, sir. I think I speak for the Court when I ask you to present our compliments to the Governor-General and inform him it is our considered opinion that Company debts must be repaid when they fall due. To do otherwise is not only dishonourable, it jeopardises our entire relations with the moneyed sort across India. An Englishman's word is his bond, sir. Or at least it should be. If we forfeit their trust where money is concerned, we forfeit their trust altogether. Is that understood?'

The other judges nod their approval while Whistler writes down Lumley's comments and says they will be passed on to Governor-General Lord Ellenborough immediately.

Broadhurst nudges me and tries, unsuccessfully, to suppress a grin.

CHAPTER 37

Kabul, November 1841

Day after day the situation deteriorates. Brigadier-General Shelton insists we should retreat to Jalalabad. Sir William says all will be well. General Elphinstone is undecided what we should do. His senior officers pass occasional comments and suggestions but make no definite plans. Sir William, meanwhile, continues to negotiate with the rebels and, at the same time, talks via messenger with the King, Shah Soojah, who is firmly of the view that decisive military action would quell the rebellion and says if we retreat towards India he does not want to get left behind in the midst of several groups of hostile tribesmen.

I am required to attend meetings of Sir William and his advisers. Unfortunately these include a couple of Afghans who claim to know what is really happening in the city of Kabul and in whom he seems to have great faith. They say the hostility is 'nothing, nothing'. Hoosein says they are ignorant but Macnaghten trusts them implicitly, presumably because they tell him what he wants to hear. And then one of them, Mullah Khojeh Meer, slips away in the night.

A delegation of reasonably friendly chiefs comes into see Sir William and one of them even offers his son up as a hostage but their concerns are dismissed.

The idiotic Captain Robert Warburton comes into the camp with his

Afghan wife and an escort but without the two six-pounder guns he was responsible for. These are now being used against us in sporadic attacks on the cantonment and what remains of our outlying forts. The weather worsens and the men can no longer dry their clothes because there is no wood for fires.

The Ghilzai chiefs offer to kill Akbar Khan for a mere two hundred thousand rupees – a bargain in the circumstances – but Macnaghten says assassination is not the custom in Britain.

Our commissariat fort, with four hundred thousand rupees-worth of supplies is over-run. It contains all but three days' supply of corn, wheat and barley as well as our medical supplies and even our rum. The 44th Native Infantry flees as usual but when the 37th asks permission to re-take the building, Elphinstone will not give the order and the opportunity is lost.

Another fort is set ablaze and we discover it is our own men who have fired it. Our horses are now so hungry there is talk they are starting to eat each other's tails. We are forced to destroy some of them because we cannot keep them fed. A foraging party is attacked and wiped out. Supplies from the Kabul traders can scarcely be had at any price. Only the wild dogs, gorging on the corpses of our camels, have enough food.

Some officers claim the King himself, Shah Soojah, has called on all Muslims to rise up against the foreigners. Soojah insists the letters carrying his signature are forgeries. He has seven advisers blinded and a Mullah put to death to prove his innocence.

Fiorentina Sale is moved to tears when she hears the fate of Jan Fishan Khan, one of the few chiefs who still stands by us. His forts and property are destroyed and one of his sons is burnt alive. He does not know the fate of the others but when he urged the one wife still with him to flee from Kabul she declared, 'I will not leave you; if you fall, we die together; and if you are victorious, we will rejoice together.' 'Oh the nobility,' says Lady Sale, dabbing her eyes with her handkerchief and then saying, 'I will not cry, I will not. I am a General's wife.'

Every day more officers and men are killed if they venture outside the camp.

*****

Eleanor Eden waits for me to emerge from my tent. The morning is dull, a grey sky filled with snow that has yet to fall. The mountains are hidden in clouds. The ground is soft and muddy, the temperature seems to have risen slightly above freezing point but not for long, I fear.

I am in my Afghan rig-out, with one of their enormous head-dresses of scarves wound round and round. It keeps me warm and Macnaghten disapproves of British officers dressing like natives, which makes it all the more satisfactory. Eleanor is in a long, thick coat over her grey dress. She wears a pair of leather boots, necessary to negotiate these increasingly treacherous surfaces. Her head is covered by a felt hat which looks surprisingly becoming on such a dreary morning and I see she is smiling. After the daily traumas we are all subjected to, this is a pleasant surprise.

She curtseys deeply with a glint in her eye, like the young girl I remember from our first meeting in Simla, when she was carrying a bunch of roses. 'Major Pottinger,' she says, looking up at me with her large brown eyes, 'What an unexpected pleasure.'

I am not in the mood for flirtation. There is another tedious 'council of war' to attend and I am frustrated to the point of fury by the vacillations of our leaders and the slipperiness of our enemies. 'Miss Eden? How is Captain Sturt?'

'Improving every day,' she says with her unwonted cheerfulness.

'And you, madam?' I impatiently pull on my leather gloves. It's very cold.

'Today is my birthday, sir,' she declares, 'And I thought to celebrate it by holding a small party at Lady Sale's this evening.'

'My best wishes,' I say but I cannot unfreeze my cold demeanour any more than I can warm my hands.

'Eldred, you will come?' she asks, somewhat doubtfully.

'Eleanor, Miss Eden. You are aware of our situation, I assume?' I ask, as loftily as I can.

'That is precisely why we should enjoy ourselves,' she says. 'Eldred, this morning I shall work alongside native women and filthy sepoys tending to the vile ailments of young men both European and native. I shall be obliged to witness sights no well-bred young lady should ever have to endure, never mind a 19-year-old on her very birthday. I think I am entitled to a little light relief.' She pauses and adds, 'Don't you, Major?'

She is right, of course. She does not have to devote her time and effort to the welfare of our many dozens of ailing men. She is showing a true humanity which is all the more unexpected given her family's status. I sigh. 'I am sorry, Eleanor. You are right and I shall be delighted to attend, provided my duties do not detain me elsewhere.'

She laughs. 'Your duties, Major? I thought you had no duties? Neither the Envoy nor the General has any employment for you. Is that not what you told us all the other evening?'

'It is, you are right. But I do try to make myself useful nevertheless.'

'Well you can make yourself useful by coming to my birthday party. I shall expect you.'

*****

It turns out Eleanor Eden's birthday party is a small dinner just for the two of us. I arrive at Lady Sale's house to be greeted at the door by Eleanor herself who says, 'Come this way', takes me by the hand and leads me to a small room at the back of the building with a table laid for dinner, three servants to look after us, and a warm fire burning in the grate.

I am surprised into silence though the greatest surprise of all is Miss Eden herself. The dowdy young woman working in the infirmary has been transformed since we met this morning into a society lady of grace and elegance. This is not the young girl I met in Simla but neither is it the hard-working woman nursing wounded and dying soldiers in an army barracks.

Eleanor looks radiant in a full-length red velvet dress which shows off her shoulders and is cut low, inevitably drawing attention to her breasts. The dress has short, puffed sleeves but is tied tight at the waist emphasising her shapely body. Her brown hair is elaborately curled in loops and knots and she is wearing a triple rope of pearls with large gold ear-rings. Even more captivating is the sparkle in her eyes.

We have Champagne as the servants prepare our dinner. She sips from the glass, looks up at me and smiles. 'Why Major Pottinger, you have yet to wish me a happy birthday.'

'Eleanor,' is the only word I can say. It is a question, a statement, a term of endearment, a remark of astonishment.

She laughs again and says, 'Have some Champagne, Eldred.'

'Where is everybody else?' I ask.

'Oh I didn't invite them.'

'Lady Sale, Captain Sturt, Alexandrina?'

'Taken to their beds, I believe. Lady Sale has a headache and Captain Sturt is, as you know, still recovering. Drina is in need of rest herself, being with child. So it's just us I'm afraid. Are you disappointed?'

She laughs at me as I mutter my delight at finding myself alone with her. We sit down to our dinner. Eleanor must have been preparing this for some time. She seems to have procured not just the Champagne but some Claret wine, a bottle of brandy, some curried goat topped with fried raisins, slivered carrots and pistachios, naan bread and steamed rice. She has even got hold of some melons, grapes, pomegranates and oranges. It seems she has been bartering with one of the servants who has, in turn, been bartering with a merchant in the city who has obtained our little feast.

'We will not discuss the world outside this room, Major Pottinger,' she says. 'Instead, we shall discuss our families, our likes and dislikes, our impressions of India, our memories of home. We shall enjoy this moment. Do you agree?'

Of course I do and she tells me about her sisters, her childhood in Kent, her brother, his appointment as Governor-General, her own prospects for the future and she asks about my brothers. I tell her about my father, wasting all his money on racing yachts, and my stepmother whom I love. Sometimes we stray onto the prohibited subjects – Burnes is mentioned, and Lady Sale's husband – but only briefly before we return to more congenial topics.

Eleanor dismisses the servants once they have supplied us with brandy and we move closer to the fire, sitting side by side on a chaiselongue spread with cushions and pieces of patterned Persian silk and cloth. 'Where on earth did you find the wood?' I marvel, looking into the flames of the fire. 'There's none to be had now.'

'Well some of it has been supplied through the servants but some of it is from Lady Macnaghten's coach.' She giggles. 'Is that terrible of me?'

'My God, Eleanor, you never cease to amaze me. Lady Sale's coach?'

'Well I am reliably informed Sir William is being forced to give it up to Akbar Khan as part of their peace treaty. So Drina and I decided to visit it and see what could be salvaged before it is handed over to the enemy.'

'But you are not supposed to know about the negotiations.'

'Oh dear.' She giggles again, strokes my arm. 'You are not cross with me, are you Major?'

Eleanor moves closer to me. I take her hand, noting how pale it is despite the warm glow of the candlelight, and kiss it. I pull her head gently towards me and kiss her cheek. She turns towards me and we kiss on the lips, tentatively. She smiles and her eyes seem to sparkle. I kiss her again, this time a little more firmly and she sighs slightly. I wrap an arm around her waist and stretch along beside her on the chaise longue as she laughs quietly, almost a giggle, and she whispers, 'This is all going just as I had planned.'

'Really?' I ask, as I start nuzzling her neck and undoing the bodice of her dress. She nods and runs a hand down my back. I hesitate, move a little away from her and look at the attractively dishevelled young woman beside me. Her carefully curled and pinned hair is coming awry; her dress is a little undone; she has kicked her slippers off and wears silk stockings under the skirts of her red dress. 'Are you sure?'

She giggles and pulls me towards her. 'Don't talk, just kiss me.'

We close our minds to the world outside this little room. We see nothing but each other; we fear nothing; we think of nothing else. At this moment we are alone together in an act of celebration or defiance or hope. Slowly, passionately, intensely we make love and even though it is Eleanor's first time, I know she is happy.

CHAPTER 38

Fort William, Calcutta, January 1843

Did that night ever happen? I know that it did but it seems like a century ago. More than a year has passed since the two of us basked in the warmth of that room and enjoyed a celebration of life. I remember how we luxuriated in each other, how we kissed and embraced and laughed. There was no reason to discuss anything. It was such an obvious thing to do in the circumstances. It seemed inevitable.

We didn't care about her family or her brother the Governor-General's reaction. We did not discuss the possibility that Eleanor's chaperone Lady Sale, or her daughter Mrs Alexandrina Sturt, might somehow discover the truth. Nor did we discuss the prospects for the negotiations between Sir William Macnaghten and Akbar Khan any more than we considered the deaths and injuries, the privations and penury, we had been witnessing in the preceding weeks. We did not even discuss the cold though, as the fire died down and the night wore on, we were obliged to cling more tightly to each other and wrap ourselves in one of the carpets from the floor to keep warm.

For a couple of hours, it was as if the world of wolves howling on our doorstep was silenced, that there was nothing but the here and now.

Yet here and now, Eleanor is on a boat returning to England – she may be there by now, I do not know – and I am listening to Captain Whistler droning on about the ancient history of the collapse of the Honourable East India Company's presence in the city of Kabul and the destruction of the Army of the Indus. As if the judges need to be reminded of all this. As if anyone needs to be reminded of the dark days we went through.

And as if it were somehow all my fault.

'We will call a witness, Your Honours, who will show the prisoner… I apologise, Major Pottinger… was instrumental in completing the humiliation of our army at the hands of the rebellious tribesmen led by the usurper Akbar Khan, the son of Dost Mohammed Khan. Our witness will testify that it was on Major Pottinger's orders and initiative that the army was obliged to leave the safety of its cantonment and retreat through the rigours of the Hindu Kush towards Jalalabad in the depths of the merciless Afghan winter.'

It is hot and Whistler meanders on. His speech seems to last all morning and he will not say one word where a dozen would do. The five judges stare at the papers before them and I cannot be sure they are all actually awake. Certainly Major General Sir James Rutherford Lumley's eyes are closed and his head is resting on his right hand. If his elbow slips, I wonder if his head will fall with a thud onto the desk in front of him.

The crowd in the public gallery is becoming restless. The heat is growing and there seems to be much that Whistler wants to get through before he winds up his opening speech, never mind calling witnesses to support his allegations. I sit here thinking back on that night with Eleanor and wonder if we will ever see such a moment again.

I think I am falling into a daydream when suddenly George Broadhurst is up on his feet objecting to something Whistler is saying. The chairman of the judges, George Clerk, is almost as startled as I am and a flicker of interest runs through the room. Even the punka wallahs seem to put a little extra effort into their half-hearted attempts to breathe some air into the room.

'Mr Broadhurst?' Mr Clerk says.

'Your Honour, it is well-known that the treaty between the Army of the Indus and Akbar Khan was signed by General William Elphinstone and neither the agreement, nor its consequences, can be laid at the door of Major Pottinger. I submit to you, gentlemen, that this charge should not be pursued at any point and should be summarily dismissed by the court.'

Clerk looks at Whistler. 'Mr Whistler?'

'Your Lordships, it is the Crown's case that no agreement should have been entered into with Akbar Khan under any circumstances whatsoever and that Major Pottinger should never have entered into negotiations with this man. It is our case the contract between the Army and the rebels was forced upon General Elphinstone, entirely against the good gentleman's will, by the defendant here and that without the intervention of Major Pottinger, there would have been no treaty, no retreat and no massacre. This, gentlemen, is the crux of the Crown's case and cannot be dismissed simply because the treaty itself was signed by the General, not Major Pottinger.'

Clerk looks to his left and right as he says, 'I think this is a good opportunity for the Court to rise for the day. We will meet again tomorrow at eight o'clock. Meanwhile my colleagues and I will consider your submission, Mr Broadhurst, and announce our conclusion.'

CHAPTER 39

Kabul, November 1841

Akbar Khan strides into the officers' mess preceded by three tall, heavily armed Pathan warriors, and a rush of icy air from the wind-blown parade ground beyond the doors. He is followed by at least a dozen more of his men as well as six other chieftains. But it is Akbar we all look at. The man has a presence which eclipses those around him.

He is not tall – I am probably a head taller – and, at 25, he is five years my junior. He wears a long dark blue cashmere overcoat which sweeps the floor, knee-length leather boots, leather gloves and a thin metal helmet surmounted by a pair of small, sharply-pointed barbs. He carries a shield on his back and a sword at his side. He has a neatly-trimmed black beard; a pale brown skin and immodestly thick red lips which tend to contradict his warlike demeanour. Perhaps it is his greenish-blue eyes which make him so remarkable. They seem to be piercing and angry yet, at the same time, they appear soft and passionate.

He walks slowly, deliberately, taking in his surroundings with those shrewd sea-coloured eyes and an expression of arrogance, as if to say, 'All this is mine should I wish to take it; all of you are mine, should I wish to take you.' Akbar carries himself with the air of a man who is used to being stared at. It is as if he is so accustomed to command that he draws attention to himself without trying, as if it is second nature.

The chieftains following in his wake are by no means as impressive. They are older, thickly-bearded, somewhat unkempt though they all wear brooches and necklaces of diamond and gold. It would seem they are a little in awe of their leader.

Sitting at the head of this long table, Sir William Macnaghten does not rise to greet his guests. The Envoy wants to impose an air of authority by denying Akbar the usual courtesies. This does not work on Akbar Khan who, when offered a seat, says, 'We will stand, thank you. Our business will not take long.'

There is an awkward silence while Sir William removes his blue-tinted spectacles, wipes the lenses with a handkerchief and deliberately puts them back on again while Akbar's entourage gather around him at the far end of the room. Sir William and his closest advisers stay seated at the table. I stand opposite the fireplace where I may observe the proceedings; I am not a member of the Envoy's inner circle and I am therefore not invited to take a seat at his side.

George Lawrence, who is sitting near the Envoy, coughs diffidently and stands to say, 'Perhaps we should make some introductions, gentlemen.'

'That won't be necessary, Lawrence,' says Sir William firmly. 'Mr Khan,' he raises his voice and speaks more slowly than usual, on the assumption foreigners cannot be expected to understand Englishmen even when the Englishman speaks the foreigner's language. 'Mr Khan, in the name of Her Majesty Queen Victoria, I demand you call off your dogs.'

Akbar laughs dryly. 'Call off my dogs, is it?' He turns to his fellow chiefs and tells them, 'You are dogs, do you hear? Dogs.' They laugh along with him and one or two instinctively move their right hands to the hilts of their swords. Akbar gestures that they should not react and turns back to the Envoy. 'Sir William Macnaghten. Ever since you deposed my father, Dost Mohammed Khan, and replaced him with our sworn enemy, you and your men have been the dogs, the wolves, the curs.' Akbar speaks with quiet fury. He is in full control of his emotions but there is no doubting the passion of his contempt. 'You foreigners have invaded our country. You have debauched our women. That is why Alexander Burnes was taken from you. You have stolen our livelihoods – prices are now so high our poorest peasants cannot afford to buy food any more. Our people starve so your people can live off the fat of the land. Yet you impose taxes on us to pay the cost of your invading army. You wage war on us. You try to impose your religion on us. You steal, murder, rape and destroy. And you call us dogs.' Akbar spits contemptuously onto the floor.

Sir William looks through his spectacles at this angry man and frowns. 'Your father, sir, was a faithless traitor. We thought he was our friend but he was secretly dealing with our enemies. We were obliged to defend our own territories by preventing an alliance between Dost Mohammed Khan and the Tsar of Russia. We came in peace, offering the hand of friendship. But you and your fellow conspirators prove ungrateful. You spurn us, you defy us, you thwart us at every opportunity. I sometimes wonder why we bother to bring civilisation to these pagan places.'

'Then go,' says Akbar Khan. 'I will help you to leave. Or I will force you to leave. The choice is yours. Either way, you will have to leave. I offer you an honourable leave-taking. The alternative is war, Sir William. A war you know you cannot win.'

Sir William stares at a white sheet of paper on the table before him. He does not want this discussion but he knows it is necessary. He has little choice now. He will not meet Akbar Khan's eye. 'And if we were prepared to agree on a strategic withdrawal?'

'We would give you safe passage through the passes.'

'Not in this weather.'

'Not in this weather, no. In the spring.'

'In the spring,' Sir William repeats thoughtfully. 'And that is all?'

'Not all, Sir William. Not all.'

'The conditions?'

'Well, sir,' Akbar looks back at his supporters, 'The usurper Soojah-ool-Moolk Durrani will have to depart Kabul with you, with his whole entourage. In the meantime, he will be replaced by my relative Shah Mahommed Zeman and I shall be his Vizier. We also require you release my father, Dost Mohammed Khan, his wives, his court and his servants from captivity in Hindustan and grant them safe passage back to this country. And, against my father's safe return, you will leave certain gentlemen here in Kabul as our honoured guests...'

'Hostages,' murmurs one of Macnaghten's advisers.

Akbar ignores him and continues, 'You will pay us compensation for the expenses we have incurred so far, and will incur over the coming months. We believe 15 lakhs of rupees should just about cover it.'

'Fifteen? That's a million and a half,' splutters Sir William.

'So it is,' Akbar answers with a smile. 'So it is.'

'Anything else?' Sir William asks weakly. He looks like a beaten man.

'Only that, as a token of your good faith, you release into our hands some of the property and possessions that will encumber you on your march through the passes back to Hindustan. Your cannons, for instance.' Akbar Khan smiles again and turns to leave. 'We will give you two days to make a reply, Sir William.'

*****

And so we have more councils of war and peace and further indecision. Macnaghten condescends to visit General Elphinstone in person. The General says no treaty should be completed with Akbar Khan because he is not trustworthy.

Macnaghten replies, 'If the General will defend our honour, I am sure we can defeat them and we will not be forced into this surrender.'

Elphinstone mumbles: 'Macnaghten I cannot, the troops cannot be depended on.'

'So we have no choice then, General,' Macnaghten replies.

I am forced to comment, 'General, Sir William, we do have a choice. We can retreat to the Balar Hissar and defend ourselves from there.'

'Impossible,' says Shelton, who is sitting cross-legged on the floor beside the empty fireplace huddled up in a thick rug.

'Not impossible,' says Lawrence, and there is a murmur of approbation from several of the younger officers at the meeting.

'And the hostages?' asks Vincent Eyre. 'Are we to hand over our wives and children? Even if Akbar could be trusted, can we trust those around him? The Ghilzais don't take prisoners. They behead and dismember the bodies of the men. God knows what they do to women.'

'Goat-herds,' snorts Macnaghten with contempt.

'They may be goat-herds but they are accustomed to the slaughterhouse,' persists Eyre despite the Envoy's withering look. Eyre looks exhausted: filthy and wet, as well he might. Over the past few hours he has been fighting a rearguard action to re-take the commissariat fort where our supplies have fallen into the hands of the enemy. He was not given enough men and, worse still, he was supplied with insufficient ammunition. Eyre would have fought on but the General ordered a retreat even as it seemed the enemy was ready to turn tail. 'They killed one of our men and dismembered the body even though the fellow was waving a white flag at the time,' says Eyre. 'How can we trust them with women and children?'

'What would you have me do?' Macnaghten asks, a little less belligerently. 'The General tells me your men cannot be trusted to obey their orders. Brigadier-General Shelton failed in his attack the other day…'

'Failed?' says Shelton in his reedy voice. 'I do not call it failure to make a tactical withdrawal in the face of overwhelming odds.'

'If you had taken more than one cannon…' Macnaghten begins.

'Gentlemen, gentlemen,' says Elphinstone slowly from his recumbent position on the couch where he is wrapped in rugs, his cheeks sunken and flushing red with a fever. 'This will get us nowhere. Macnaghten will have to make the best arrangements he can with Akbar Khan, I suppose. But Eyre is right, the man is certainly not to be trusted.'

I am so incensed I cannot restrain myself. 'So we are to make a treaty with a man we do not trust because we do not trust our own men to obey orders and we are not prepared to take the safest course of action available to us which is to retreat – fight our way if necessary – into the Balar Hissar even though it is universally acknowledged as impregnable.'

'Nothing's impregnable,' pipes up Shelton, hidden from my view on the floor though I know his thin, imperious voice anywhere.

'Herat was not impregnable either,' I say, 'But we held out there for a year.'

'Herat, Herat, Herat,' says Macnaghten with a vicious laugh. 'The hero of Herat is turned into the coward of Kabul.'

At this, I leap to my feet and grip the hilt of my sword, stare at the clerkish Macnaghten where he sits at the head of the long table while my fellow officers wait with bated breath to see what will happen next. I stare at Macnaghten and hiss, 'Sir, if you were not my superior and Her Majesty's representative in Kabul, I would call you out for that. As it is, I shall withdraw from this discussion.'

Later, in the officers' mess, Lawrence, Eyre and several other officers gather round me, telling me they agree with me and even considering the question of some sort of mutiny against our leaders. 'For the sake of our womenfolk,' says Eyre vehemently.

I can see the temptation but insist, 'This is treason. We cannot even talk about such an idea.'

Nobody says much after that but it is clear we are all thinking the same thing.

*****

Over the next few days, messengers come and go with Akbar's new demands and suggestions from Macnaghten. Akbar promises us supplies and we issue promissory payment notes but the promised food arrives sporadically and in nothing like the promised quantities. The quality is beside the point now, much of it would be inedible but for the fact that starvation is an even less attractive option.

We send out foraging parties which return depleted and badly wounded or do not come back at all. Macnaghten gives one of the chiefs 50,000 rupees to create a diversion, though what the point of a diversion might be when our army is incapable of mounting a serious attack on anything, it is impossible to say.

I do not see Eleanor for several days; she is in the sick bay doing what she can for the injured men, those dying of pneumonia and other diseases. Every day there are more funerals. The Hindus are dying in greater numbers than the Europeans – they are ill-equipped for these conditions and seem stunned into a stupor by the severity of the cold.

Messengers are bribed, threatened and cajoled to take letters to General Sir Robert Sale in Jalalabad but nobody will go. In any case, we know from his letter to Lady Sale that the General cannot come to our aid.

Zeman Shah Mohammed is crowned in some ceremony in the central mosque even though Shah Soojah is still in the city, safe inside the Balar Hissar, where we should be too. Zeman writes to Macnaghten saying he has only taken the throne for fear that worse would befall Kabul and the British if the vacancy was not filled. Macnaghten replies that he does not recognise Zeman's authority – but is willing to negotiate with him through Akbar Khan, which is at least an acknowledgement of the true state of things.

Akbar now says Shah Soojah should be given up to the rebels, along with his family and harem. He demands our guns and ammunition and requires General Sale to retreat from Jalalabad to Peshawar before we can leave Kabul. Macnaghten points out no messages can be sent to Jalalabad. Akbar offers to facilitate such a correspondence. Sir William writes to the General setting out the latest demands. It will be weeks before we receive a reply and we know for sure what that will be.

Akbar Khan demands four hostages – I am to be one of them,

along with Trevor, who is already in enemy hands, MacGregor and Connolly – against the return of his father Dost Mohammed Khan. The personnel demanded change regularly. Brigadier-General Shelton is on the list one day; Captains Drummond and Skinner – also already a prisoner – the next.

The demands change. Shah Soojah is to stay and give his daughters in marriage to the chiefs and take theirs as wives in return. Soojah rejects this idea – he will not sacrifice his children to these savages who deserve to have their heads cut off, he says.

The native soldiers, their women and children are starving. There are fights over a small supply of rice which John Sturt manages to get his hands on. The rioters are beaten back with sticks otherwise the whole lot would have been stolen by just one or two gangs. We are starting to kill the horses to eat them.

Macnaghten orders the surrender of wagons and ammunition. There is a wailing scream of rage, heard half-way across the camp, when he breaks it to his wife that her personal carriage and horses are also being handed over. Lady M throws a vase at him in her fury.

Lawrence goes to the Balar Hissar to negotiate with Shah Soojah. The king rejects all the conditions set out by Akbar and refuses to leave the castle and retreat to India. Lawrence and his escort are shot at by the rebels as they ride from the camp to the castle and again on their return. One man is killed with a shot through his head. Soojah has the chief priest Mullah Shekoor blinded and thrown from the castle battlements to his death. He blames the Mullah for provoking the insurrection though there is no evidence to support the accusation.

Akbar offers a new deal. Soojah will stay as king with Akbar as Vizier as long as we provide him with a single payment of three million rupees and an annual pension of another 400,000. Soojah suggests a free pardon for all the rebels and a durbar where peace can be re-established. Nothing comes of it though we debate the pros and cons of the idea all night.

Every day I argue we should seek refuge in the Balar Hissar and every day Macnaghten ignores me while Elphinstone and Shelton say it is impossible, what with 700 people now sick and no provisions. How do they think we are in a fit state to retreat to Jalalabad, then, I demand, but they ignore my protestations. I will not give up though. There are now so many officers unwilling to offer a displeasing opinion I fear mine is almost the only voice standing out against the general agreement that Macnaghten's peace-with-honour treaty is our only option. 'If we were only in the fortress, we could quell this rebellion through canon-fire from its heights into the city. Shah Soojah is constantly firing into the city. If he had reinforcements we could quell this rebellion,' I say, and Macnaghten waves a dismissive hand.

Now Akbar Khan demands our muskets, bayonets, pistols and swords. He also says the hostages must be the married men, their wives and children. Several officers say they would prefer to kill themselves and their families than submit to this, especially as the hostages would probably end up being sold into slavery.

How can the Envoy and the General even entertain the idea?

*****

As the snow starts to fall in earnest, we are promised another negotiation with Akbar Khan himself rather than his envoys. A dozen of us, just the political officers rather than any of the men with direct military responsibility, meet Akbar's entourage in a fort half a mile from our camp. This was one of our great storehouses, sacked by the enemy. As we ride to the fort, I see the shapes in the drifts where several bodies have been left interred only in a shroud of Afghan snow.

'We should demand a proper burial for our men,' I say to Lawrence as we dismount and hand our horses' reins to Akbar's servants. Even as we do so, I wonder whether we have been lured into a trap, but Dost Mohammed's son has only a few attendants and just two of his closest advisers. We outnumber them. He must have come in peace, though our route back to the camp is lined by his men so if it comes to a fight there is little chance of escape.

Still, he indicates the shelter of a tumbling-down guard-house and we all crowd inside. There is little space to move, let alone draw a sword, which suggests we may be secure, but it is no warmer here than outside. Macnaghten speaks first.

'Mr Khan,' he says, 'You have treated us badly and we really must protest at this insolence.'

Akbar smiles wryly. 'You are under a misapprehension, sir, if you think I am responsible for everything that goes on here in Kabul. I can only control so much. It is not my intention to humiliate you or your British Queen. We wish to see you leave our country in peace and restore the tranquillity we enjoyed before your arrival.'

These preliminaries take some time, as the two men debate the whole question of our invasion, the restoration of Shah Soojah and so on. Eventually, after an hour of this, we reach the point of the meeting.

'You have surrendered much, as tokens of good faith,' says Akbar. 'We have some of your men as our guests and we wish to entertain others, especially those with wives and children. Children should not be exposed to the hazards of a long march.'

'The march will not be hazardous unless you make it so,' Macnaghten replies.

'As you see, sir, I cannot be held responsible for every accident that may befall you. But to the point. If you are willing to agree the terms set out in our recent discussions, then all shall be well.'

'The money?' asks Sir William.

'The King, Shah Sojah, remains on the Throne; I shall be his Vizier. You will return my father to Kabul on your safe arrival in Peshawar. In the meantime we shall retain your officers and their families as our honoured guests. To support their entertainment in the meantime you will, before your departure, provide me with a letter of credit for 30 lakhs of rupees and a promissory note in respect of an annual pension of four lakhs of rupees.'

'Three million now and four hundred thousand in perpetuity?' Sir

William sniffs. 'This is agreed.'

'Then, sir, we have an agreement. You and your army shall leave with the first signs of Spring, peacefully and as our friends.'

'And in the meantime you will have your men cease their daily attacks and you will guarantee our supplies of food?' asks Sir William.

'Of course, sir, of course,' Akbar smiles broadly and offers his hand to shake Sir William's. But the Envoy turns to Lawrence and snaps his fingers. Lawrence produces a box containing a pair of pistols – pistols belonging to Lawrence which were presented to him by his father and have accompanied him on his travels without ever being taken out of their case.

'Please, then, sir, accept this gift as a token of the high esteem in which I hold your Excellency.'

Akbar takes out one of the guns to inspect it. 'A handsome gift, Sir William, which I accept with gratitude in view of our high friendship and accord.'

The two men shake hands and turn to go. 'Tomorrow morning, Sir William, we shall sign a treaty together in front of witnesses. Agreed?'

'By all means,' says the Envoy, pleased with the progress he has made and the warm words on this bitterly cold day from Akbar Khan.

CHAPTER 40

Kabul, December 1841

Hoosein comes rushing over to the officers' mess where I am playing a game of billiards with Vincent Eyre. We've just had breakfast – though there was almost nothing to eat but some bread, the thin remnants of the army's supply of coffee and a drop of brandy to keep out the cold.

Hoosein pokes his head round the door and I can see he is in a state of great agitation. He is wrapped up in bundles of cloth topped off with one of those huge Afghan headdresses in an attempt to keep warm but his brown skin is flushed and he is out of breath.

'Sir William,' he says. 'The Envoy.'

'What about him?' Eyre asks with a pained expression. We are both heartily sick of Sir William Macnaghten and his ploys, plots and plans. He won't listen to any advice and he is convinced the Afghans are 'simple little people who need to be treated like the children they are'.

'He is dead, sahib.'

'Dead?' Eyre throws his cue in the air. 'Deliverance, at last,' he says.

'No, no, no, no,' Hoosein insists. 'Murdered.'

Now Eyre and I express astonishment. 'Murdered? Who by?' I ask.

'Akbar Khan,' he says plainly, as several other officers rush in, all agog at the news.

'But I only saw him this morning, insisting Akbar was our friend. He gave the man a pair of pistols yesterday as a token of his regard,' I say.

'It was one of those pistols Akbar shot him with,' Hoosein answers with an air of doom.

Over the next 20 minutes, as everyone who witnessed the event throws in his two-pennyworth, it becomes apparent Macnaghten arranged to meet Akbar Khan and a group of other chieftains half an hour ago on a hill about a mile from our camp. They were due to sign Macnaghten's treaty which he swore would deliver 'peace with honour'.

At the appointed hour, Macnaghten and three other officers, Colin Mackenzie, Robert Trevor and George Lawrence were ready to leave the camp but their cavalry escort was not. The cavalry needed another fifteen minutes to get ready but Macnaghten was impatient to depart so he and the others set off unaccompanied. It was a terrible mistake, though the greater failing is Shelton's in not demanding the escort was ready on time.

When Macnaghten's party arrived at the spot, Akbar was all charm, inviting them to sit with him on the rugs the Afghans had already spread over the snow-covered ground. The troop of cavalry was just leaving the cantonment when, apparently, Akbar said to Macnaghten, 'Sir William, are you happy to ratify the treaty we negotiated last night?' To which the Envoy replied, 'Yes, why not?'

'There, seize them,' Akbar said, pulling Sir William to his feet and shooting him with the very same pistol the Envoy gave the treacherous man just the night before. One shot, straight to the heart. Macnaghten had time only to say, 'What the Devil...' before he was dead.

Robert Trevor was taken by three other chieftains and hacked to death. Lawrence and Mackenzie fought back but our cavalry troop, which might have rushed to their aid, heard the sound of gunfire, turned tail and fled back to our camp.

*****

'We must take a proper force and ride out against them now,' I say. Several others agree. Eyre and I rush to the General's house for orders while Hoosein goes to saddle my horse.

Elphinstone is in conference, as usual. Shelton is there and several others. 'Ah Pottinger,' says Elphinstone as we burst in. Our agitation is not matched by his closest advisers, who are sitting around drinking coffee, smoking cheroots and looking at maps of Afghanistan – except for Shelton who has taken up his usual position wrapped in a rug in front of the non-existent fire.

'Macnaghten is killed,' Eyre declares, 'The others too.'

Shelton opens one eye. 'And have we actually seen any dead bodies?'

'It is certain,' says Eyre.

'Who says so?' asks Shelton.

'Witnesses. The cavalry escort which failed them. Everyone heard the gunfire.' There is general assent at this.

'But no bodies?' says Shelton, shrugging the rug back over his shoulders and turning towards the bleak fireplace with a groan.

'It cannot be so,' declares Elphinstone. 'No doubt the Envoy has gone into the city with Akbar Khan to continue their negotiations.'

'We must strike back, now.' I say this so vehemently that Eyre takes hold of my arm to restrain me from some violent act against the General and his advisers.

'Easy, Eldred,' he says.

'We must punish this outrage. Now. Now, General.'

Elphinstone struggles to sit up in his chaise longue and the rugs slip from his body. A servant rushes to restore them and hands him a glass of brandy. The General looks very ill, his cheeks flushed hot yet otherwise his skin is deathly pale, his eyes wet and rheumy, a cough constantly nagging at the back of his throat. 'This is all nonsense. Akbar Khan is our good friend; he is Sir William's good friend. Bygrave,' says Elphinstone, momentarily decisive, 'Go round the cantonment, see the officers and men in each regiment, and reassure them anything they think they may have seen this morning is almost certainly wrong. There is an innocent explanation. The Envoy and the others will doubtless return before the day is out.' With that, the General slumps back on his bed and wheezes as if the effort of this one command has exhausted him for the entire day.

From the floor, Shelton waves his one hand in the air and says, 'Goodbye Pottinger, you are dismissed. You may go. Now.'

*****

Eyre and I visit the main gates of the camp and question the men there to establish what they saw and heard. As we are making our inquiries, I see Eleanor Eden hurrying over. She is deathly pale and in tears. 'Is it true? Is it true?' she asks us as she comes closer and I say I fear that it is. Eyre tells her Elphinstone is convinced otherwise but adds, 'The man is deluded.'

Eleanor throws herself into my arms. In front of Eyre and the men. This is a rash and impolitic act but suddenly the niceties of convention do not seem to matter very much. 'What's to become of us all?' she asks.

'We must fight back,' I say. 'If Macnaghten truly is dead then this nonsense of a treaty with Akbar Khan must be dead too. We must hope, when they are convinced of the truth, that Elphie and Shelton realise we must fight for our lives and our honour.'

'I must go to Drina and Lady Sale,' says Eleanor. 'Oh Eldred, how did we come to this?' I hug her to my chest and kiss the little cap on her head, damp with snow though it is.

'We must be brave,' is all I can say, though it sounds so inadequate.

*****

All night we wait for confirmation of what we all, but General Elphinstone, know to be true. In the bleak officers' mess, with no heat and nothing to eat or drink, we smoke the dwindling supply of cheroots and drink thin tea. Eyre points out something I had realised but preferred not to think about – that I am now the most senior political officer in Kabul and therefore, if Macnaghten is dead indeed, I am in effect the Envoy, Her Majesty's representative. As such, it would be my duty to make a treaty with Macnaghten's murderer.

How am I to do that? How am I to retain my honour and reputation by treating with such an enemy? Can I persuade the General and Shelton to make a fight of it and seek refuge in the Balar Hissar?

We sit around and doze, play billiards and cards, smoke and speculate all night. Early in the morning a messenger arrives from the city with a note for the General, who summons yet another 'council of war' to discuss its contents.

The note is from Lawrence who confirms that he is safe, along with Captain Mackenzie, but that Macnaghten and Trevor are dead. It seems Trevor's body is hanging in the great central market while Macnaghten has been dismembered. His arms, head and legs have been paraded around the city and they are now on show, on pikes in the marketplace.

'How can we trust anything any of them ever says again?' I say to silence.

'They are devils,' agrees Eyre. Several other officers make similar outraged comments while Elphinstone lies on his chaise longue looking more fatigued than ever, his face crumpled in shock and disappointment while Shelton is up on his feet, for once, standing before the empty fireplace, a fierce look in his sharp little eyes.

'We must be away, away at once. We must be gone,' he says. 'These people are savages. There is nothing to be gained from remaining here a moment longer.'

'We can't go,' I tell him. 'We can't possibly make our way through the passes in this weather. Everyone says they are impassable in winter and there is no certainty the Afghans won't come after us and harass us every step of the way.'

'Then you will have to arrange a treaty, won't you Pottinger?' he says with a look of gloating and triumph in his voice. 'After all, you are the

Envoy now, sir. Do your duty.'

'General?' I appeal to Elphinstone but he just shrugs and says, 'Of course we must go. We have no fight left in us, none at all, what? What? No fight?'

There is a murmur of dissent around the room and Eyre pulls out his sword, slams it down on the table and says, 'Well I for one have fight left in me. We cannot let this slaughter go unavenged. We must re-capture the city and drive these people out. Let us do it. Now.'

Several others slam their swords down on top of Eyre's and I add my own, saying, 'There General, there is fight left in us after all.'

Elphinstone struggles to his feet, to get a better view of the crossed swords on the heavy teak table. It is an impressively warlike sight, more than a dozen weapons piled one on another as a declaration of war against Akbar Khan and his chieftains. 'Dear, dear,' says Elphie when, after some grunting and the support of two servants, he is standing at last. 'Dear, dear, gentlemen. I admire your pluck, I really do, but I am afraid it cannot be. Can it, Shelton?'

The Brigadier-General shakes his small head. 'You will all follow your General's orders or you will never see Bombay again. I shall see to it. Mutiny is a capital crime, may I remind you? And this is verging on mutiny.'

'Verging on mutiny?' I explode with contempt. 'Here we have the pride of the Army of the Indus, what's left of it, ready to do battle to save the honour of our nation and you call us mutinous.'

'Ah, the coward of Kabul,' says Shelton. 'Isn't that what Sir William called you? The coward of Kabul. What is it you are afraid of, Paddy Pottinger? Afraid of a little snow and a bit of cold weather? Hungry for your doxy, perhaps?'

'How dare you?' I reach for my sword from the table but Eyre and a couple of others restrain me.

'Just obey orders, Pottinger. Or aren't you capable of that?' says Shelton with a sneer.

CHAPTER 41

Kabul, December 1841

That evening a few of us convene at Lady Sale's. She is as shocked as the other ladies at the fate of Macnaghten and Trevor. Our dilemma is simple – can we take matters into our own hands or must we follow the orders of General Elphinstone and Brigadier-General Shelton?

'You know even talking about it is mutinous?' says Lady Sale. She, Mrs Sturt and Eleanor are busily sewing together rugs and sheets to become makeshift panniers big enough to sling from the side of a horse and capable of carrying some of the wounded if we have to withdraw from Kabul. Alexandrina Sturt is pale and silent, her pregnancy now showing clearly. Eleanor is also pale and subdued but Fiorentina Sale is flushed and angry. 'This morning I had to tell Frances, Lady Macnaghten, that her husband was indeed killed. The poor girl…' Lady Sale breaks off for a moment in contemplation then resumes, 'And to think we will just sit back and accept it. To think we will take no action, seek no revenge, exact no price. Macnaghten, for all his pompousness, was Her Majesty's representative in Kabul. His death is a grievous insult to our Queen and country. Yet we sit back and take it.'

Sturt asks, 'So should we take matters into our own hands, mother-in-law? What would your husband say?'

'Sale? He would say you must obey orders. If you do not obey orders, all discipline breaks down and then where would we be? If you officers disobeyed General Elphinstone, why should your men obey you?'

'Loyalty?' suggests Eyre.

'Are they loyal?'

'They can't be relied on,' admits Eyre, 'Especially the Muslims. They are torn. Akbar has declared a jihad against foreign invaders – a holy war. And the mosques are full of mullahs preaching the blessings of destroying the foreigners. Akbar Khan is boasting he has slain our chief with his own hand.'

'We can expect no reinforcements,' says Sturt.

Eleanor looks up from her sewing and gives me a wan smile. She says, 'Major Pottinger is the most fit to take command and lead us to the Balar Hissar. He has experience of withstanding a siege, do you not, Major?'

'I do, madam, and I firmly believe safety is only a couple of miles off. But how can we convince Elphie?'

'Tomorrow is Christmas Day,' says Mrs Sturt. 'We must pray for our deliverance.'

*****

I wonder if I shall see another Christmas. It seems Akbar Khan is now demanding our immediate withdrawal from Kabul. This Christmas, when we celebrate the birth of our Saviour, is the bleakest I have ever endured. Wet, cold and miserable, we convene in the parade ground, the troops supposedly in their best uniforms, native as well as European; the officers and their ladies seated at the front of what I imagine to be an open-air cathedral vaulted by the low ceiling of a louring sky which is silently dropping its white petals of snow across the whole landscape, the hills shrouded in the distance, the rebels firing their rifles into the air and circling the camp menacingly. If they were to attack now we would all be massacred. Instead we listen to Dr John Logan preach a sermon on patience and love. 'Ye have heard that it hath been said, An eye for an eye, and a tooth for a tooth: But I say unto you, That ye resist not evil: but whosoever shall smite thee on thy right cheek, turn to him the other also. I say unto you, love your enemies, bless them that curse you, do good to them that hate you, and pray for them which despitefully use you and persecute you.'

I look around me. Hundreds of dispirited and angry soldiers, shivering with cold, many unwell or nursing minor injuries, all famished, filthy and frustrated. The Europeans are bitter; the Indians bemused by the turn of events. Everyone is fearful.

Behind the ragged ranks of the regiments assemble our army of camp-followers. Wives, mistresses, doxies, whores, servants, cooks, cleaners, stable-lads, labourers – and, of course, their ragged, sullen children.

At our head stands poor, ineffectual General Elphinstone, a kind and jovial man, who in other circumstances might have made a revered commanding officer but who, here and now, is condemning us all to God knows what fate. Certainly to the most dishonourable and foul, if not downright cowardly, capitulation in our nation's history. We plan to walk away from Kabul, through thick snow, knifing winds and narrow passes like humiliated barbarians passing under a yoke of Roman spears.

I see the General standing almost to attention, servants on either side to hold him upright, as he gazes with rheumatic eyes into the middle-distance towards the hills hidden in snow-clouds and see a frail, old man with sunken cheeks and shrunken frame over which his dress uniform hangs like an empty sack. Shelton stands nearby, little eyes darting around looking for offence.

After the service, Elphinstone calls another 'council of war'. This is my last attempt to dissuade him from a course almost everybody thinks is cowardly and doomed. 'Sir,' I say as soon as Elphinstone is settled back on his chaise-longue, 'Are we seriously proposing to accept the enemy's terms of surrender?'

'Oh come now Pottinger, you can't call this surrender. It is a strategic withdrawal,' says the General, turning to Shelton for support. The Brigadier-General merely snorts with indignation. The General signs heavily and says, 'We have no choice but to accept whatever terms Akbar Khan offers us, eh? What? Is that not so, gentlemen? Is it not so?'

Elphinstone looks exhausted. He falls back in his seat and waves for a servant to bring him some Madeira. Elphinstone's other senior officers Brigadier Thomas Anquetil, at 58 almost as old as Elphie himself and almost as tired; and Colonel Sidney Chambers, another relic aged 53. These two are his senior staff officers and we have no choice but to obey them. Elphie, Shelton, Anquetil and Chambers are of one accord: there is nothing to be done but to treat with Akbar Khan and secure our urgent retreat before the situation deteriorates further, the men mutiny or desert or we are simply overwhelmed.

I am obliged to negotiate on behalf of a parcel of fools bent only on their own destruction. But short of leading a mutiny, I have no option.

*****

Messengers arrive from Akbar Khan in the early evening. There are three of them and they sit, without invitation. They pull out some papers and issue their demands. We are to leave immediately. We are to abandon all our money and cannon. They require us to surrender to them all our married officers and their families. They wait in a well-appointed, though chilly, tent while I relay their message to the General and Shelton.

I tell them we should reject these demands and I am over-ruled. Elphinstone agrees to hand over several hundred thousand rupees and 130 hostages, including Lady Macnaghten, Lady Sale, Mrs Sturt and my own Eleanor Eden despite constant warnings from Mohan Lal, poor Burnes's man, and my own Hoosein, that Akbar cannot be trusted.

'We don't need to listen to wogs,' says Shelton.

Elphie sends a man round the camp asking for volunteer hostages.

He says anyone willing to go over to the enemy will receive a bonus of 2,000 rupees each. Captain William Anderson says he would rather shoot his wife and children than hand them over. Sturt says his pregnant wife Alexandrina and mother-in-law Lady Sale will only be taken at the point of a bayonet. Vincent Eyre, however, says, 'I will stay with my wife and child if it is productive of the greater good.'

I tell Akbar's negotiators I cannot sign promissory notes for money; that job belongs only to George Lawrence so they will have to set him free and come back tomorrow. And I remind them that, in return for handing over hostages, we are supposed to receive some food as we make preparations for our retreat.

A little food arrives in the morning, inevitably much less than we have been promised. Meanwhile some of the ladies, their children and some wounded officers, are taken to the Khoord Kabul fort. Lady Sale, Mrs Sturt and Eleanor are not among them though those who reach the fort are at least given some food. One little boy, a sergeant's son called Robin Dekker, is stolen away along with his mother Mary. He is rescued by some of the Afghans who remain our friends but there is no word of Mrs Dekker. I fear the poor woman is now dead, or worse.

Akbar now demands the withdrawal of our troops from Jalalabad and Kandahar as well. I am required to write to the commanding officers there setting out this requirement but I add a message using Greek characters to the contrary, saying it was against Her Majesty's interests for them to comply with these demands and trusting they would be received with the contempt they deserved.

I tell the General and his officers yet again we should fight our way into the Balar Hissar but there is no point in making the attempt unless everyone – especially the senior officers – are prepared to travel light. That means abandoning all their libraries, furniture, silverware and plates, all their wine and even their cheroots. They dismiss this as impossible and Shelton laughs, 'You don't give up with this incessant demand to hide under the skirts of the King's harem, do you Pottinger?'

I turn on him, as he lies rolled up in his carpet beside the empty fireplace. 'You do not seem to understand. They have declared jihad and will massacre every single one of us. We will never see Jalalabad, let alone India again. We have only one chance of survival and that is to withdraw into the protection of Shah Soojah's citadel. Why do you not understand how grave the situation has become? You call me the coward of Kabul, Brigadier-General, but I say we should fight – it is better to die in battle than have the stigma of cowardice fixed on us for ever.'

Shelton climbs slowly to his feet, throwing off the rugs with an air of menace. He is wearing his black dress uniform with a sword hanging by his side. 'Are you calling me a coward, sir?'

'I am not, sir. But the stigma of cowardice will hang over you, as it will hang over me and over everyone here, if we meekly march away into the snow and our certain deaths.'

'I should hope not,' says Shelton. 'We are not doomed, sir, but this kind of talk does nothing for the morale of our men. We must have no more of it, is that clear? Your task, Pottinger, is to fulfil the instructions given to you by General Elphinstone here and secure a peace treaty for us with Akbar Khan. Nothing more. Now, if you would be so kind, perhaps you would like to get on with your work.' Shelton calls a servant, 'Brandy, boy, brandy for the officers. Now.'

*****

They send George Lawrence back to sign the promissory notes. He looks haggard and has aged ten years since he saw Macnaghten murdered. He says he was reasonably well-treated in his captivity but was afraid for his life all the time, having seen the Afghans parade the limbs of Macnaghten and Trevor outside the house where he and Mackenzie were being held. Mackenzie is also allowed back as several officers and their families are taken hostage instead. He says he saw Akbar Khan kill Macnaghten with his own eyes and yet Akbar protested vehemently, and for several hours, that he was not responsible for the Envoy's murder. To prove his sincerity, Akbar even managed to produce tears of remorse. Yet Mackenzie saw Akbar draw out the very pistol Macnaghten had given him and fire it directly into the Envoy's chest. 'These people are very convincing liars,' says Mackenzie. 'We must never trust a word they say.'

With that in mind, I make it a condition of the payment that the notes will only be honoured once the army – including all the camp followers – are safely the other side of the Khyber Pass in Peshawar. That might at least afford us a little protection, though Hoosein says Akbar Khan is not in sole charge of the rebels and cannot answer for how they will behave once we are on the march.

I visit Lady Sale's in an attempt to persuade the ladies that they would be safest remaining in Kabul rather than retreating with the army. Hoosein is with me and promises he and Wasim will look after them. The ladies will have none of this. Lady Sale says her husband would expect her to take her chances with the men; Mrs Sturt will not stay without her husband and he is determined to play his part with the army; Eleanor says she cannot desert her friends.

We have a few moments alone where I beg her to take my advice and stay in Kabul. I say I may be able to persuade Shah Soojah to find her somewhere in the Balar Hissar itself. 'What and join his harem?' she asks with a rueful smile. She places a hand on my arm and I kiss her quickly on the lips.

'My dear love,' I say, 'I am afraid for you. I am afraid for all of us. And I will not be able to protect you every step of the way as I should wish to do. Stay with Hoosein and Wasim – they are under my orders to remain and do what they can to help those we leave behind. Please, Eleanor, I beg of you.'

'I cannot, Eldred. I am the Governor-General's sister. I cannot desert my post. I cannot.' I look into her eyes and see a flicker of fear and a bright light of determination. Her lips are taut, her jaw is set, yet her touch is soft and vulnerable. This young woman is anxious but she will not allow her worry to conquer her. 'My duty, Eldred.'

'Duty. I know,' I say dully. I want to throw my arms around her and protect her from everyone and everything to come. Instead I take her left hand in both of mine, raise it to my lips and kiss it gently. 'We shall have another day, Eleanor. We shall have another day.'

*****

Akbar Khan's messengers demand the surrender of our cannons. I allow them to take only two every day. Somehow it feels less like complete capitulation, though that's what it is. How can we give up our most potent weapons to an enemy? Yet that is what we are doing.

In one of our meetings I demand safe passage to the Balar Hissar and, somewhat to my surprise, I am given it. I take George Lawrence and a troop of 60 cavalrymen with me and as we trot down the snow-covered street to the citadel's main entrance, our every move is scrutinised by hundreds of rebels who lean on their jezzails or stand sharpening their sabres as we pass. We are accompanied by two dozen of Akbar Khan's men to ensure we are allowed through but even so it feels as if we are running the gauntlet.

We are admitted to the Balar Hissar, though Akbar's men are required to stay outside the walls, and we ride up towards the King's palace. Lawrence and I are led through empty corridors not to the King's stately reception hall but to a small room with windows looking out over the city.

There is no ceremony today. The King sits on a bench with his back to us, gazing over Kabul. 'I know every street, you know,' he says without turning to look at us. 'I know most of the people too. They are my people, this is my city, my kingdom,' he says. The King rises and turns; Lawrence and I bow. 'Get up gentlemen. In the Sight of Allah all people are equal, and the only superiority anyone can have over anyone else is his fear of Allah and faith in Him.'

Shah Soojah holds a telescope which he has been using to survey the city. He is wearing plain robes without jewellery or any display of ostentation or power. His long beard is white, his eyes are puffy, his eyelids flicker nervously. 'So you are abandoning me,' he says with a bitter laugh. 'I, who was so valuable to you, I am to be left to my fate. You know they will blind me? That is why I spend my time looking out over my city. To remember it.'

'Did you not blind your own brother?' asks Lawrence.

'That was years ago,' says the Shah dismissively. 'Besides, he was a traitor. Have I betrayed the English? I have not. Have I betrayed my own country? I have not. Yet you blind me by abandoning me. You blind me, gentlemen, you blind me.' Soojah sits wearily, puts the telescope aside and rubs his eyes, opening them wide when he is done, as if to remind himself to make the most of every sight that comes into view.

'Your Majesty,' I say, 'You are welcome to accompany us back to India. You are assured safe passage by Akbar Khan...'

'Akbar Khan? Do not talk to me about that son of a whore. His father has raped many women, you know. Even princesses. It was an evil day when he first sat on my Throne; I will not give it up again to him or his bastard offspring.'

'Shall you be safe?'

'Here, in the Balar Hissar? Of course. They can't blind me here. But I can never leave and I can admit no-one. I am trapped, a prisoner in my own palace. They will find a way, eventually. They will find a way.' The King strokes his beard slowly, deep in contemplation. 'And my wives, my wives. What is to become of them? And my daughters?'

'Akbar Khan would have you marry your daughters to his allies, Your Highness.'

'I would rather kill them myself,' says Shah Soojah and I believe him. He has executed so many people in this savage country that the slaughter of his children would not be the worst thing he could contemplate. We are abandoning him to whatever Fate has in store for him but I do not consider this is either a good man or a good King. Our retreat is shameful but so was our advance, putting this man on the Throne as our puppet and turning a blind eye to the vengeance he wrought on his enemies, pretending it did nothing to stir up resentment against him and against us as the agents of his tyranny.

Soojah cuts a lonely figure now, though. His Court is emptying. Every day more courtiers slip away to join the rebels, abandoning their King because they can see the tide has turned decisively against him and there is no loyalty, even among half-brothers. Soojah may well fear for his harem, though most of the women will be safe – assuming they do not mind being parcelled out among the victors.

This is not my problem now, though. I make a sort of speech to the King, as he sits shaking his head at us, 'Your Highness, we are here as representatives of Her Majesty, Queen Victoria, and in the place of Sir William Macnaghten and Sir Alexander Burnes, both of whom you have known well, to take our leave of you as we have contracted with Akbar Khan to quit Kabul and retire to Hindustan. In our negotiations for our departure, we have been at pains to preserve the position of Your Majesty and we have assurances as to your safety and as to Your Majesty's position on the Throne. Akbar Khan has suggested he might become your Vizier but we have agreed that decision rests with Your Majesty alone…'

'That shall never be,' the King mutters.

'However, Your Majesty also has the option to leave Kabul under the protection of the British army and return to Ludhiana with your entire court and resume your life as guest of the Honourable East India Company.'

'You mean swap back with Dost Mohammed Khan? I move out, he moves in; he moves out, I move back in?' The King gives a sorrowful laugh. 'Gentlemen, I have seen enough. My eyes are already blinded by tears. What can hot irons do that grief has not already performed? Your Queen, your Governor-General, your Generals, your army – you Major Pottinger, and you Lieutenant Lawrence – you have all betrayed and abandoned me. Go, gentlemen, go. I leave you in the hands of Allah in whose protection nothing can be lost by those in his merciful care.'

With that, the Shah takes up his telescope again and scans the horizon.

CHAPTER 42

Fort William, Calcutta, January 1843

The morning is cool, though it will heat up soon enough. My attorney George Broadhurst already looks uncomfortable in his thick woollen dress uniform. He is a big man and he is forever wiping away the sweat from his forehead with one of the handkerchiefs he keeps about his person. As we walk across the parade ground to the court house, he is telling me of his exploits in the back-streets of Calcutta last night. 'The women,' he says, 'So cheap and so accommodating.' I say how pleased I am for him and he looks at me.

'Eldred, I know this is a strain but don't frown so much. This is not the end of the world. This Court Martial – what's the worst that can happen?'

'Dishonour, Broadhurst,' I say. 'There is nothing worse than the loss of reputation. I do not want to go to my grave as the Coward of Kabul.'

'You won't, you won't, dear boy. You will be completely exonerated, old man,' he says seizing my arms in his big fists and squeezing hard. I feel disheartened and when he adds, 'Trust me, Eldred, trust me' it does not buck me up. My instinct, when someone tells me to trust them, to assume they are hiding something.

George Russell Clerk, the chairman of the bench of judges, looks ready for business; keen, alert and eager to get on with it. There is no time-wasting here. Before either my attorney George Broadhurst or Trevor Whistler for the prosecution has time to stand and make any comment, Clerk looks to his left and right, receives nods from his colleagues and announces, 'We have considered the latest submission that, because Major Pottinger did not sign the treaty with Akbar Khan, he is therefore not implicated in the surrender but we cannot accept this argument. If Major Pottinger represented the interests of the Honourable East India Company and Her Majesty in Kabul which, following the death of Sir William Macnaghten, he indubitably did, then no treaty could have been entered into without his agreement or, at the very least, his acquiescence.'

'Your Honour…' Broadhurst is on his feet protesting.

'Allow me to continue, Mr Broadhurst,' says Clerk with a grim little smile. 'While we acknowledge the subordinate position of Major Pottinger in the strict hierarchy which applies throughout the Indian army, we therefore accept that there may be circumstances where he has little choice but to follow the commands of his senior officers. We have yet to discover to what extent Major Pottinger was acting on his own initiative or at the behest of the army's commanders, notably General Elphinstone who is, alas, no longer with us to testify one way or the other. We conclude, therefore, Mr Broadhurst, that this court martial must proceed.'

Broadhurst sits, agitated, while Whistler leaps to his feet. 'Thank you, Your Lordships.' He is back jigging about as he was at the start of the case, his confidence now fully restored. I glance sideways at Broadhurst. Did he know in advance what the judges' ruling would be? His big, round face glistens but gives nothing away. I suspect he did.

Whistler, meanwhile, is going through the details of the treaty Sir William Macnaghten entered into with Akbar Khan. 'This document,' he says, waving the actual treaty, 'Is complete with the seals of no fewer than seven of the rebel chiefs, the Afghan noblemen – though I use that term loosely – Akbar Khan, his half-brother Sultan Mahommed, his cousin Mahommed Osman Khan, Akbar's half-brother Mahommed

Shureef of the Kuzzilbash tribe, Mahommed Shah Khan and Khoda Buksh Khan of the Ghilzye tribe and Aminullah Khan Logari. This document, sirs, brings shame on the Honourable East India Company, it brings shame on the British army, it brings shame on Her Majesty the Queen. This document, sirs, represents the cowardly capitulation of the Army of the Indus and brings shame on all those involved in this abject surrender.

'And this document, my lords, was negotiated by Major Eldred Pottinger, the Acting British Envoy to Kabul, and by none other.'

Whistler pauses after this rhetorical flourish and there is a stir among the spectators, an intake of breath, a shuffling in their seats, a whispering of comment. There is no doubt Whistler puts on a good performance. I glance at Broadhurst and he just sits there, his plump stomach spilling slightly over his trousers, his eyes gazing into the middle distance for all the world as if he is contemplating last night's triumphs rather than defending my character. He does not look at me and I wonder if he knows I am looking for some sort of a reaction.

The five judges look alert, as if suddenly conscious of the gravity of the allegation against me.

Whistler holds the treaty before him. Speaking more quietly now, as if to emphasise his regret at the turn of events, he says, 'That document is the original treaty. It is written in Persian, a language Major Pottinger speaks fluently. It cannot be said, therefore, that he was at any point unaware of its contents. In translation, sirs, it consists of just thirteen articles. I shall remind the court of its contents.

'Article one calls for immediate supplies to be furnished to the troops, to any extent required, as also carriage cattle; article two, British troops to evacuate Afghanistan; three, an offensive and defensive alliance to be formed; four, Dost Mohammed Khan and all his family to be released.

'Article five relates to the treatment of His Majesty Shah Soojah-ool-Moolk Durrani. It states he is to have the option of remaining in the country as a private individual, to be treated with all honour and respect, and have a guaranteed stipend of a lakh of rupees annually, or, if he so wishes it, to be allowed to accompany the British troops to Hindustan, taking all his property and family with him, only giving up such effects as had formerly belonged to the Dost Mohammed. It further states that, in the event of carriage not being procurable for his family, they are to remain in the Bala Hissar, and be treated with all honour and respect; and on the return of Dost Mohammed Khan and other Afghans from India, Shah Soojah and his entourage are to be transported with safety to India. I should note here, gentlemen, that this is perhaps the most dishonourable article in the entire treaty. It was the Company's policy to place Shah Soojah on the throne of his Durrani ancestors yet this treaty all but abandons him to his fate for, as we know now and knew at the time it was signed, there was no carriage procurable for the King and his family. He would not be hounded once more into exile; he had no choice but to await his fate at the hands of murderers and rebels.

'Article six states that all the sick and wounded were to be left under the care of the nobles in Kabul and to be treated as guests. Article seven demands all our ammunition, guns, and small arms, if the means of transport are not procurable, to be made over to the nobles; eight, that all the surplus property of officers, for which carriage might not be procurable, is to be left in charge of Zuman Khan, and be forwarded to India the first opportunity. Zuman Khan, sirs, is a chieftain who, as we know now and knew then, was one of the most duplicitous, dangerous, two-faced, untrustworthy, ambitious, greedy men in the whole of Afghanistan. And our officers were supposed to place their property in his hands for safe-keeping.

'Article nine say no man is to be molested on either side for his actions during the war. Such chiefs as had stood staunchly with the King, Shah Soojah, were to be allowed either to accompany his Majesty, taking with them all their property, or were to be allowed to remain in Afghanistan, to be treated with every respect. As we now know, this, like every other clause in this worthless treaty, was regarded with contempt by the seven rebels whose names are appended to this document.

'It goes on. Article ten says any British subject wishing to remain in Afghanistan, for the purposes of trade, is to be in no way molested. Eleven, that the troops at Jalalabad were to evacuate that fort, before the Kabul force commenced its retreat – but, as we know, this was neither desirable nor practical, any more than the requirement for our forces in Ghuznee and Kandahar to quit those places as soon as the season would admit of their marching.

'Article twelve required that Mahommed Akbar Khan, Osman Khan and any other chiefs wishing to do so were free to accompany our troops on their march to Peshawar. This is all very well, but accompany did not mean attack at every opportunity, rob, kill, maim and murder our troops every step of the way.

'And finally, article thirteen required that we allow four hostages to be given over to Akbar Khan for the full performance of the above articles, to remain in Kabul until Dost Mohommed Khan arrived at Peshawar.

'This, my lords, is the shameful treaty Major Pottinger arranged with the enemy. The most infamous humiliation in the Company's history. The articles are not disputed; the role of Major Pottinger in negotiating this treaty is not disputed; all that is in dispute, gentlemen, is whether, in securing this agreement, Major Pottinger acted under orders or on his own initiative. If the latter, we say he is plainly guilty of cowardice and should be condemned for his crime. If the former, then we must ask, under whose orders did he proceed? As we know, on the death of Sir William Macnaghten, Major Pottinger became Acting Envoy to Kabul and the most senior political officer in Afghanistan. He was not subject to military orders and therefore he was able to disregard the orders of officers who might, in other circumstances, have been his superiors, namely General Elphinstone and Brigadier General Shelton. We say, therefore, that Major Pottinger cannot have been acting under orders for there was no superior officer to issue those orders. He was, therefore, acting on his own initiative and is therefore guilty of cowardice in the face of the enemy.'

CHAPTER 43

Kabul, January 1842

We leave tomorrow. Tonight I make one last attempt to persuade the General and the Brigadier General we should not leave but seek sanctuary in the Balar Hissar, especially as we receive a plaintive message from Shah Soojah offering sanctuary to the wives and children and asking, 'Is there not one officer who will stand by me in this, my hour of need?'

There is a long, detailed argument about whether it is possible to retreat to the castle without being massacred. Lawrence and I suggest we could establish a battery of muskets, rifles and our remaining canon on the Siah Sung Hill overlooking the route to the Balar Hissar. But of course the General's advisers, led by Brigadier General Shelton, look for all the disadvantages and dangers that would involve.

'How are the men on the battery to be protected?' asks that buffoon Bulstrode Bygrave, though Vincent Eyre and Captain Sturt speak in favour of the plan.

'There may be no answer to the question of what happens to the men in the battery,' says Sturt, 'They may lose their lives. But surely it is better to die fighting than march out into this winter and perish of cold and surely it is preferable to protect the vast majority of the army by seeking the succour of the Balar Hissar than it is to march every man, woman and child to their doom.'

'Ridiculous,' is all Shelton will say while Elphinstone just groans and wafts a pale hand in the air saying, 'Well, well, there it is, there it is.'

Short of a mutiny, there seems to be nothing more to be said or done. I salute the general and depart to find Hoosein and Wasim making preparations for our departure tomorrow. They are loading sacks with possessions but I tell them to abandon everything. There is no point in being weighed down with goods. More to the point, I say to Hoosein, 'You are not coming with me.'

He looks up from his packing and frowns. 'Sahib, you will need us. We both want to go home, don't we Wasim?'

The youth is adjusting a pair of stirrups and nods. 'India is home for me now, sahib,' he confirms.

'Gentlemen, may I have your attention please? Put these things down a minute and listen to me. You have been true and devoted servants for three years. We have been through much together but now we must part. I will not have you lose your lives on this expedition. You have friends here, Hoosein, you know people, you can live safely. If you join in this retreat, you will probably die. Stay and live. That is not a suggestion or a request, it is an order.'

Hoosein smiles wryly. 'I have a wife and children at home, sir.'

'All the more reason to stay here, Hoosein. Stay and one day you will be free to make your way home; leave and join the army of the doomed. For we are surely all doomed. You have told me so yourself. Your own contacts say there is a holy war against us. You have told me Akbar Khan's promises of safe passage are nonsense. Admit it, you know he is not to be trusted and, even if he were, he does not have the power to control all the tribes now licking their lips at the plunder they are about to descend on.'

'It is true,' says Hoosein, looking down on the muddy ground of our outer tent.

'But who will care for your horse, sahib? Who will pitch your tent and prepare your food?' asks Wasim.

This tall, thin lad looks close to tears. 'We may be parted, Wasim, but not for all time. We will be reunited.' I take his arms firmly and squeeze them affectionately. 'I promised your mother I would look after you and this is the best way to preserve you. In Hoosein's care, you will be alright. Now, take anything you want or anything you may be able to sell and slip away into Kabul, tonight. Both of you. Go, go.'

In the dim half-light of a guttering lantern, I take out a piece of paper, sit at my desk, sign it and hand it to Hoosein along with some rupees. 'This is a promissory note from the East India Company,' I tell him. 'When you need money, find a trustworthy merchant and negotiate. The Company will honour this paper up to 10,000 rupees, more if you have to. Here, I have signed it. Make out the sum when you know what you need. But wait as long as possible; it's value will rise.'

I take the little man's two hands in mine. There are tears in his eyes. 'Thank you, Hoosein, for your true and faithful service. Now go. And take the dog with you. It's a wonder Caesar has survived this long without being killed for his meat. Take him and go.'

Hoosein shakes his head from side to side and wipes his eyes. 'We shall go, sahib, as you order. But God bless you and keep you safe. God bless you. Come, Wasim, we must go.'

From the chill of my rug-lined tent, I step out into the night again and listen to the sounds of activity as the entire garrison prepares for departure. There is much shouting and swearing, a few gunshots; there are fires burning and men round braziers trying to keep warm. There is little food and most of the cattle has long since been slaughtered. Several officers ridiculously insist on loading up bullock carts with their possessions – furniture, clothing, books, even ice-skates and cricket bats – though it should be obvious to the meanest intelligence that the struggle we endured getting all these goods through the narrow winding passes of the Khoord Kabul and the other gorges between here and Pesharwar in mid-summer will be as nothing compared with the impossibility of getting them through in mid-winter.

It is snowing heavily and freezing cold. Tonight, though, Lady Sale's house is as warm as it has ever been. She has had her mahogany dining table chopped up for firewood – 'well we can't take it with us, can we?' she points out – and the whole house is almost too hot to bear for those of us who spend most of our time in and around the chilled camp wrapped up in greatcoats, scarves, boots and thick layers of Afghan turbans.

Lady Sale is in the hallway supervising the packing with the same relaxed imperiousness she might adopt if the family were leaving Bath for their London home. Her servants rush hither and thither under her command while Mrs Sturt and Eleanor are seated in the drawing room sewing for all the world as if they were back at home in England awaiting their carriage though they are actually making hammocks to help transport the wounded. They both seem surprisingly calm and untroubled by the prospect ahead of us. I remark on this and Mrs Sturt laughs bitterly, 'How would you have us behave, Major? Are we to rush around panicking or should we, like so many of the servants, throw ourselves on the tender mercies of the Afghans?'

I try one last time to persuade them to seek sanctuary in the Balar Hissar. 'I do believe Shah Soojah would be warm in his welcome. Your husband John is not fully recovered from his wounds and you, madam, are scarcely fit for the arduous journey ahead. Let me make the arrangements, I beg of you Mrs Sturt. And Miss Eden.'

'Oh Eldred,' says Eleanor, putting down her work, 'You do try hard, don't you?' She rises and walks across to where I stand, places her delicate hands on my bearded cheeks and rises on tip-toe to kiss my nose – all this in front of Mrs Sturt. I am shocked by this but do not protest.

'My dear, I really do wish…'

'We have been through this, Major Pottinger,' she says, sounding formal but speaking with a smile, 'Mrs Sturt will not desert her husband and John will not desert the army. Nor will Lady Sale and neither shall I. We all have our duty and our duty is to serve our Queen. As you, Major, know well enough yourself. No doubt you could seek sanctuary with the King should you choose to do so. But you choose not to do so. You know your duty, sir, and we know ours. Besides, Drina's baby is not due until long after we arrive in Peshawar, isn't that right Drina?'

The poor woman nods and tries to smile. 'May,' she says and rises slowly to her feet. 'I think I shall see if I can get some sleep, Eleanor, I'm feeling a little weary this evening and I suppose we will need all our strength for tomorrow. Goodnight my dear. Goodnight Major Pottinger.'

Once Eleanor and I are alone, she throws herself into my arms. 'Oh Eldred,' she mutters breathlessly as, without further discussion, we start to kiss with growing passion and desire. We are both thinking the same thing – this may be the last time we hold each other. Ever.

Eleanor's modesty is abandoned and we throw ourselves down onto the rug before the fire and make a kind of desperate love which abandons all propriety and caution, though we are in Lady Sale's house, visitors are likely to turn up at any moment, and it is filled with servants.

We do not have a moment to discuss what has just happened or share our fears for the morrow before we hear someone at the front door and rush to adjust our clothing and settle ourselves into seemly poses as George Lawrence and Vincent Eyre enter the room with Colin Mackenzie and Robert Waller in tow.

Eyre holds aloft two bottles of port which he says he has been hoarding for a special occasion and he can think of none more special than this. The port is passed around and we sip slowly, sparingly, to eke out this last drop of pleasure. There is some rowdy conversation about the journey, the snow, the horses, the Afghans – all bravado, of course, but what else can we do? We find ourselves laughing at jokes about whether Elphinstone will manage to stay on his horse and how Lady Macnaghten will fare without her carriage. We wonder if Brigadier General Shelton will insist on being saluted by every soldier he passes when we are in the narrow confines of the Khoord Kabul as he does around the camp.

Then Lady Sale bustles into the room. 'Listen to this,' she says, 'I just found it among Captain Sturt's books which, I am afraid, we are now burning in the bedrooms. It's called The Battle of Hohenlinden. Listen:

> *"Few, few shall part where many meet,*
> *The snow shall be their winding sheet;*
> *And every turf beneath their feet*
> *Shall be a soldier's sepulchre."*

There is an appalled silence.

CHAPTER 44

Kabul, January 1842

It is the most dismal sight I think ever beheld. An entire army creeping away from our camp in snow a foot deep and temperatures well below freezing, the mountains clouded and dark, the road lined with jeering enemies shaking their swords and jezzails at cowed and beaten men in what passes for their scarlet uniforms as they struggle with wagons and starving animals, dogged at every step by hundreds of hangers-on and dispirited by weather, hunger and the prospect of worse to come.

The great Army of the Indus, which set out with such glory and hope only four years ago, is reduced to trudging away through a gauntlet of screaming mockery as our enemies celebrate by firing their guns into the air, throwing rocks at us and dashing out to steal any stray piece of baggage or food. The flags and banners which once waved joyously in the breeze now hang limp and damp on their standards, some of them ragged and torn as a result of the skirmishes of the past few weeks.

On the parade ground in the camp, even though we are running away, a young Indian sepoy is being flogged on the orders of Brigadier General Shelton. The poor youth failed to salute Shelton with due deference when their paths crossed earlier and he was ordered to be lashed 24 times, thus delaying the departure of the 54th native infantry while the command is carried out under Shelton's indifferent gaze.

Eleanor is with the other ladies, surrounded by servants, on the best available horses. Some women are being carried in panniers slung across our remaining camels. They are all wrapped up tightly in sheepskin coats, leather boots and leather gloves with thick turbans on their heads but that will not be enough to keep out the creeping cold as the animals make their way at a slow walk down the road and across the new bridge over the Kabul River which the sappers had to erect during the night because the enemy destroyed the original bridge the other day.

I stand at the Kabul gate and watch the ladies, including Mrs Sturt, Lady Sale and Lady Macnaghten file out. Eleanor, frowning in concentration as she settles herself into the side-saddle and guides her large brown mare over the small bridge across the defensive ditch, does not notice me. Lady Macnaghten, who is furious at the loss of her carriage and complains bitterly about being humiliated by travelling in a camel pannier with her three cats, is unhappy about something and two servants rush off to find whatever it is she is demanding. Lady Sale is trying to encourage her daughter as their horses slip a little on the packed snow.

I look to my left and discern through the constantly-falling snow the outlines of Shah Soojah's castle, the place where we would be safe if only the Generals were willing to put up a fight to reach its sanctuary. Its grey walls stare back and I imagine the Shah himself watching our departure through his telescope. 'Will not one officer stay with me?' he has asked and the answer is no, we will abandon him along with all our hopes for this country.

A messenger from Hoosein comes into the camp. He says there are still some Afghans who do not wish us ill, though they are increasingly hard to find and unwilling to risk their own necks to help us. Hoosein warns yet again that Akbar Khan has vowed to destroy the whole army. Hoosein writes that Akbar has told his followers they must 'kill every man except one who is to have his hands and legs cut off and placed at the entrance of the Khyber Pass to deter all foreigners'.

George Lawrence and I wait as icicles form on our beards, listening to our angry, bitter soldiers grumbling as they pass by. Our four thousand five hundred able-bodied men are encumbered with about twelve thousand servants, women, doxies and children, most of them ill-equipped for the conditions and lacking all discipline or purpose. Already the camp followers are jostling with our marching men, getting in their way, disrupting what's left of military discipline and delaying the whole army.

We wait for hours in the freezing cold for the arrival of the two thousand men we have supposedly hired to protect the army on our march to Jalalabad. It is clear they will never arrive long before Shelton's rearguard, composed of the 54th Native Infantry, the 5th cavalry and our last two six-pounder guns, is ready to depart. Another waste of money – non-existent reinforcements ordered by General Elphinstone and paid for in 40,000 rupees of hard cash, not even bills we can repudiate later.

A message eventually arrives from the chiefs regretting the absence of their men. They fear the two thousand cannot be raised at this time of the year. The weather is too inclement and, besides, they cannot weaken their own forces by parting with such a large contingent. My anger helps me to keep warm, standing here in this terrible weather watching our ramshackle army trudging towards its destruction, but my head is aching as if a blacksmith is hammering behind my eyes, and my leg wound, which has still not properly healed, hurts constantly.

At last Lawrence and I set off. Progress is slow. The bullocks have difficulty dragging the guns, carts and planks of wood we may need to build bridges. The camels are more cantankerous than usual because they have not been fed for days. The camp-followers straggle along in no order, stumbling into the ranks of the infantry and even falling among the cavalry horses. The advance guard can still be seen from the cantonment hours after its departure, wending its way in the direction of the Khoord Kabul pass. We are circling round the city. Even now it would be possible to change the plan and race for the Balar Hissar.

Not everyone would make it – but then not everyone will make it to Jalalabad anyway. I discuss this with Lawrence who is as enthusiastic as I am but how could we convince the General and his senior officers? We have no authority over the army and, though I am convinced the men would follow us if we took a lead, we have our orders, no matter how suicidal they may be, and it is ours but to do or die.

As soon as the rearguard has crossed the defensive ditch around the cantonment and set out on the road, Afghans swarm into the camp searching for anything we have left behind. Lawrence and I try to trot through the chaos to reach General Elphinstone in the forlorn hope he may listen to reason. The advance has only travelled three or four miles from the camp and night is already drawing in. We will be spending it exposed to the blast of an Afghan winter within sight of the Balar Hissar.

At our back, smoke and flames rise from the cantonment as the Afghans rip the place apart. We see swirls of yellow, orange and black against the dark snowy skies, we hear the shouts of glee and the gunshots of triumph as they tear down buildings and make off with anything that could be of use or value.

As Lawrence and I make a slow progress, we see servants disappear to left and right bearing away whatever goods they can carry. We should shoot these deserters but there is no point – they will be lucky to last long at the hands of the Afghans anyway. Lawrence does take aim at one woman dragging a trunk into a ditch but I suggest he saves his ammunition for later.

As we pass, it seems more and more people, men as well as women and children, have already given up the struggle, throwing themselves down in the snow and accepting their fate. There is little we can do to help or say to encourage them. They are so scantily-dressed they must already be disabled by frostbite and we have nothing to offer that might alleviate their misfortune.

I see one young Indian girl, no more than four years old, lying face up with the snow settling over her little corpse. Soon she will disappear from view but not from my memory. I mutter a prayer but realise if I were to do the same for every dead and dying body I pass, I would be repeating the same incantation over and over again. To what effect?

Before we reach Bagrame, just five short miles from Kabul itself, where Elphinstone has chosen to stop for the night, we hear the sound of more sustained gunfire. It seems some of the Afghans are already attacking Shelton's rearguard.

*****

The General has a tent. He has hot soup and brandy. His officers are similarly provisioned. He lies, exhausted, on a camp-bed with rugs piled over his ailing body. The others are sitting round a small fire just outside the tent itself which is, miraculously, glowing with warmth but it is little consolation as the icy night descends. The sky is clearing of clouds but the wind is getting up, reaching inside our layers of protection to dismember our minds from our bodies like a knife stabbing first at the feet, then the hands, then the face, then deeper into the heart. Nearby, exhausted men lie down on the frozen ground, curl themselves up and make the best of what they have about them to retain some life-saving warmth. There is nothing for them but they are too woebegone to protest let alone organise an insurrection against their officers enjoying comparative luxury only a few feet away.

Lawrence salutes smartly; I feel obliged to do the same. The General groans. 'Gentlemen?' he says.

'General,' I say, 'It is not too late. We are still in sight of the Balar Hissar. If we turn towards it now – tonight, under cover of darkness when the ground is easier to travel over because the snow is packed hard by the freezing cold – we can be at the castle gates before dawn. Some of the army, at least.'

'If we do nothing, we will all die of the cold sir,' says Lawrence.

'I know,' groans Elphie. 'But what am I to do? The army is spread from here to Kabul. Brigadier Shelton is with the rearguard. He cannot lead the army from there.'

'No sir, but some of us could – Waller, Sturt, Eyre, Waller, Skinner as well as Lawrence and I. The King would welcome us. We would be secure there. We could regroup, send out sorties for supplies, re-assert our sovereignty.'

Elphinstone groans. 'Perhaps tomorrow, Major. Perhaps we can discuss it again tomorrow. For now, we need rest.'

*****

The ladies are camped together, a couple of lanterns providing a faint warm breath. They are drinking sherry and wave me away; they do not wish to be disturbed. They are tired and cold but they still have faithful servants around them and, in comparison with the army, they are well looked-after. Eleanor smiles at me from her spot on the ground which she shares with Drina Sturt, but she is disinclined to move, I assume because she has managed to retain some warmth and does not wish to risk exposing either of them to another blast of cold air, though the wind is seeping in under the tent and I doubt they will manage to remain tolerably warm all night.

Tomorrow we must brave the Khoord Kabul. A regiment will be sent up before first light to prepare the way but we should have pressed on this evening. It's only six miles or so from where we are and if we can reach the ravines first, it is possible the enemy will not be prepared for us.

The Khoord Kabul is a long, extremely narrow pass between mountainous rocks. In places it is only about six feet wide between sheer cliffs. Travellers have to cross and re-cross the river dozens of times on the ascent. Even in summer, it is a dangerous route. Now, filled with snow and possibly infested with hostile Afghans, it will be treacherous.

*****

I lie beside my horse hoping to benefit from some of the animal's heat. Next to us lie Lawrence and his horse. Like everyone else, we scarcely sleep but the night is eerily quiet. A few wolves howl but our cattle make little sound, our men are frozen into silence and, though we can see the fires of Akbar Khan's camp and the glow of the burning cantonment back in Kabul, we hear nothing of the enemy. Even the wind seems to have stilled itself. As I lie, trying not to think of the pain and hunger crawling through my body, I wonder what has become of the rebels. I cannot believe they will leave us unmolested.

As day dawns bright, windy and frozen, I see lifeless bodies, children, women and men – including our own European soldiers – who have simply died of cold during the night. One man from the 44th lies with icicles clinging to his beard but no sign of life comes from his body. Another has perished leaning against a wagon. A couple of servants are stripping his body of its clothing in the hope it will keep them alive. I should shoot them for looting but as they will probably die anyway there does not seem much point in wasting good ammunition – especially as it is unlikely either my pistol or my hands will function properly in this cold.

The horses look for water and fodder. We have none. Lawrence tries to melt some of the snow but makes no progress and ends up feeding balls of it to his horse in the hope it may help. The horse snorts in disgust and kicks out irritably but they let us mount and we move onward, trying to reach the vanguard of this long, snaking trail of misery.

The bright sun glares at us across the snow, its light so strong it is blinding if I look in its direction, yet it brings no warmth. Our clothes are now almost solid, thickly frosted white pieces of wood offering no comfort or warmth. I cannot feel my toes or my fingers. Towards the horizon the mountains of the Hindu Kush are sharply etched against the icy blue sky.

Raiding parties of Afghans harry us at every step. Shelton's rearguard is constantly attacked. They make a stand, stave off the worst of it, then turn to re-join the rest of the army, every time leaving more of their comrades turning the white snow crimson with their blood.

Everywhere the weak and vulnerable are cut down and robbed of anything they possess as Afghan raiders on horseback charge into the retreating throng and lay about them with their sabres. It is no wonder many of the servants and the Shah's troops are deserting. Some simply dump whatever they are carrying and wade into the snowdrifts in despair, others try to bargain for their lives. One or two are allowed to live – but stripped naked of all their clothing, which is as good as running them through with a sword only, perhaps, more cruel. Lawrence and I have a couple of encounters with these savages and manage to beat them off. On one occasion I think I severed a man's hand from his arm but I can't be sure.

After marching only five miles, Elphinstone calls another halt at the mouth of the Khoord Kabul. Bulstrode Bygrave has apparently convinced him attempting the pass in the afternoon, with night closing in, would risk the whole army.

As Lawrence and I reach the General's tent, Mackenzie is pleading with Elphinstone, 'General, we have reports the Ghilzais are preparing an ambush. The longer we give them, the worse it will be. Please, sir, we must press on.'

'Well, well,' sighs the General. 'Yet you see about you, gentlemen, how grave our losses have been. So many unfortunates have dropped, benumbed with cold. His Highness Akbar Khan is our friend. He wishes this delay so he may send his troops on ahead to clear the passes for us.'

'To ambush and massacre us, more like,' says Mackenzie and, in a fury he adds, 'You forget General, I was at the Envoy's side when Akbar – in all good faith – shot down Sir William. I do not expect to escape with my life again this time.'

'Come, come, sir, have some soup while there is some left,' says Elphinstone patting the ground beside him and holding his bowl out to the furious Scotchman.

There is yet another inconclusive council of war. Elphinstone sends a messenger to Brigadier General Shelton for his opinion. We wait for a reply but it never arrives, possibly because Shelton treats it with his usual contempt or, more likely, because the man Elphie sent has been murdered. Either way, no decision is made so the army once again grinds to a halt, does what it can to pitch camp, sets up pickets in a vain attempt to keep out raiders and prepares for another freezing, foodless night.

CHAPTER 45

Khoord Kabul, January 1842

Akbar Khan sends two messengers and a troop of 30 cavalrymen into our camp. I am summoned to attend on His Highness along with Lawrence and Mackenzie. The rebel chief seems to think we are diplomats, not soldiers, and are somehow more important or influential. Elphinstone says we must go. I protest we should defy him, he will hold us hostage and further deplete our army. The General says we must go. 'We have to trust him, Major,' he says and I wish I could defy my orders.

'We have to go,' says Lawrence.

We are escorted from the camp, where some semblance of order still persists, sentries are posted, guns are in place, a few tents are pitched. As we ride through the exhausted rabble and hear the agonised cries of women, children and the swearing fury of the men, I wonder if there is any hope for the army. How many of us will return to Pesharwar?

We ride about two miles, in the twilight of a bitter day, away from the main route to the pass and towards a hilltop castle near the Khoord Kabul where Akbar Khan has set up his base to oversee the retreat and slaughter of our army.

This fort is a small and unimpressive building, with low walls and a couple of modest towers, which could have been destroyed in an afternoon by a determined and well-led division with a couple of 18-pounders. Yet here we are, virtual prisoners, entering its meagre defences, being led by rebel soldiers into the presence of the great man who presides over the destruction of our friends and comrades. We are relieved of our weapons: swords, knives and guns. But we are too hungry, cold and tired to react to this indignity. As we reach his Royal presence I feel a burning anger rush through me.

The first thing I notice is not Akbar sitting on a carpet cross-legged drinking tea with his cronies – these people call themselves chieftains; they are nothing but vagabonds and thieves with their ludicrous turbans and their greasy beards. What strikes me immediately is the warmth of the room. A huge fire is burning in the chimneypiece and it is all I can do to resist the desperate desire to rush over and attempt to thaw my frozen body. Instead, at the entrance to this low-roofed hall, I cry out, 'Where is our escort? Where are our supplies? Why are you attacking our men, women and children incessantly, hour after hour? What do you want with us?'

Akbar looks up, smiles and says, in terms of perfect civility, 'Come, gentlemen, you must be cold. Sit, drink some tea with me, warm yourselves up.'

'While your henchmen murder our friends?' I cry out and turn away, though the door to the room is closed now and blocked by a couple of burly guards.

'Mohammed Himself, peace be unto him, says: "Be in the world like a traveller, or like a passer on, and reckon yourself as of the dead",' Akbar says with a warm smile as he orders the servants to present us with glasses of piping hot tea. They are irresistible. First Lawrence succumbs and takes a sip, then Mackenzie and finally I do so too. An oasis in the desert, warmth and strength in a glass, tasteless to our benumbed senses but like liquid gold. Akbar watches us with a smile of satisfaction. He says: "Honour the guest, oh son, for though he be an infidel, open the door".'

What are we to say? Are we to feel gratitude to our tormentor, give thanks to our captor? I cannot reply though neither can I put down my glass until I have enjoyed every last drop of tea. It is so miraculous I fear I may actually burst into unmanly tears. I look at Lawrence, who maintains a straight and dignified demeanour, and at Mackenzie, who uses the glass to thaw some of the frost from his red beard. Akbar's savages stare at us with unfeigned curiosity – I know what they are thinking: Here are the great British men from India, the foreign invaders, reduced to desperation and gratitude for a simple glass of tea which no Afghan could deny a visitor however much he was disliked.

'More,' Akbar orders and the servants refill our glasses. We cannot fight him. 'Come, gentlemen, sit,' he says reasonably. 'Let us discuss our predicament.'

The fight has not quite gone out of me. 'Our predicament? It seems to me only one side is in difficulties and one side is in control. You, sir, have brought this bloodbath down upon us, you are the cause of all our suffering – we have the predicament, you have the power over life and death.'

'Oh then you misunderstand the nature of my country, Major Pottinger,' says Akbar, smiling ruefully. 'We are not one nation, as you should know by now. We have our territories and our loyalties, our hates and our vendettas. We are many different people. These people, my friends, are loyal to me. Today. But tomorrow? Who can tell what tomorrow brings? And some people have no loyalty to me and no loyalty to that usurper Soojah-ool-Moolk either. No loyalty but to their own clan. These tribesmen harassing your party, they are not doing my bidding, gentlemen. They are masters of their own fate. I have no control over them.'

'You could stop them,' Mackenzie spits this out with contemptuous fury, his thick Scottish accent accentuated by the trembling shivers which pass through him as his body adjusts to this unaccustomed warmth. 'You do not have to sit here drinking tea and breaking promises.'

'Captain Mackenzie, Captain Lawrence, did I not protect your lives and release you after the cruel murder of Sir William Macnaghten?'

'You murdered him,' Mackenzie cries, agony as well as suffering give his face a contorted fury. His high cheekbones protrude more than usual, thanks to days without food, and his melting beard is wild. I find myself stroking my own into some semblance of order as I watch him go on, 'You killed him in cold blood, you broke your faith, you are a liar, sir.'

Akbar sits calmly, looking at Mackenzie with an air of regret. 'You are mistaken, Captain, you are undoubtedly mistaken. Sir William was my friend. He was attacked by others – as I say, others I have no control over.'

'You lie, sir, damn your eyes,' insists Mackenzie, leaning menacingly towards his enemy while the chiefs around us instinctively reach for the swords they have laid down at their sides but Akbar does not react, merely signals to his servants to place before us bowls with warm rice and some sort of spiced meat which might be lamb or goat. It is impossible to resist – we fall on this food as if we have never eaten before in our lives, feeling shame for our hunger and weakness.

As we eat with greedy fingers, Akbar rocks to and fro, smiling at us and announces, 'You three gentlemen are now my honoured guests. You will stay with me for the time being. You will not return to General Elphinstone and Brigadier General Shelton. This is for your own protection and also for the protection of my father, Dost Mohammed Khan, and his court, who are now held in captivity in the place of the usurper Soojah-ool-Moolk. Once my father is restored to Kabul and his rightful place on the Throne, you will, of course, be free to leave and I shall provide a suitable military escort to secure your safe passage through the passes to Peshawar. In the meantime, we will do what we can to make your stay with us as comfortable as we can, in the circumstances.'

I do not listen closely, knowing anything Akbar says cannot be trusted. I think about protesting but the food, greasy and unappetising as it might at other times be, commands my full attention.

'Tonight, gentlemen, you will remain here. Tomorrow, Major

Pottinger, you will take an escort of my most trusted friends – all gentlemen, I assure you – and you will invite the General and the ladies in his party to join us. Major?'

I look up at the fat little toad squatting on his embroidered silk cushions and resentment stirs me to anger. 'How can you possibly know if the ladies are even still alive, Mister Khan? I do not know if they are still alive, do you, Mister Khan? No, of course you don't. They could all be dead as far as you're concerned and you really don't care. Do you plan to add them to your harem, sell them as slaves or keep them as hostages? They would do better taking their chances in the Hindu Kush than with a cold-blooded murderer such as you.'

'Well said, Eldred,' comments Mackenzie gruffly while Lawrence just pats my back.

Akbar Khan is unperturbed. His chieftains just chuckle. One says, 'Sell them as slaves? Now there's a thought,' while another says, 'They aren't fit for a harem' and both men chuckle at their little joke.

Akbar Khan calls for more tea for himself, his chieftains and for us, his prisoners. He says, 'They will be safer here, with me, than they will be out on the mountains in this weather. As I have said several times, Major, I have no power over your tormentors. The Ghilzais are a race of hereditary robbers. They are going about everywhere, and will do all the mischief they can. I am powerless to prevent them. But I can protect my friends. Will you not allow me to protect my friends, Major Pottinger? Will you not?'

'Protect your friends?' You, sir, are a cold-blooded murderer. We do not, we cannot, trust you and your protection is worthless.'

All Akbar does is chuckle. 'You have two options, Major Pottinger. I shall release you tomorrow to meet General Elphinstone but only on your honour as a gentleman that you return here and remain here. Your mission will be to invite the General to surrender up to me all the married officers, their wives and children. Should the General decline to do so, you must return alone, Major. You do have the option of refusing to carry this message, of course, but should you refuse to do so, and should neither Captain Lawrence nor Captain Mackenzie offer to carry the message instead, then I fear for the safety of the ladies and their children. As you know, Major, I cannot control the actions of the rapacious Ghilzais and your ladies may suffer severe consequences.'

I suddenly find myself completely exhausted. Food, hot tea and the warmth of this room overwhelm me. I consider Akbar's proposal and look at Lawrence and Mackenzie only to find them both gazing towards the fireplace with expressionless eyes as if they, too, are mesmerised by this soporific atmosphere. 'I shall report to General Elphinstone,' I say, 'And I shall urge him to commit the ladies into your charge as the lesser of two evils – evils, I say, for their surrender places them at your mercy, Mister Khan, and we all know where that is likely to lead. But I shall give no undertaking to return here with or without the ladies. I take my orders from the Commander of the British Army, General Elphinstone, and from no other. I shall urge the General to let me remain with the army and fight you and your blood-soaked tribes every step of the way back to Peshawar.'

To my annoyance, Akbar just chuckles again, gets up and leaves with his retinue. At the door, he turns again and says, 'By the way, Major Pottinger, you will kindly address me as Emir Akbar Khan or Prince Akbar or Your Highness as I am the son of the rightful king of Kabul and not some lowly Mister. I trust it will not be necessary to remind you of this for, while for myself I can bear any insult, these, my loyal friends, may find it a little tiresome.' The thugs cackle at this and rattle their swords.

Lawrence, Mackenzie and I are left alone without rush-lights or candles but with some food and the illumination – not to mention the heat – of a roaring fire. I think of my friends, and my beloved Eleanor, shifting as best they can in the freezing night and shrink inwardly, disgusted at myself for this comfort and safety.

'Can we escape?' Lawrence asks, trying the heavy wooden doors and attempting to reach the one small window high up in the wall.

'We'd do better to rest and prepare for the morning,' says Mackenzie.

I have to agree. We remove most of our outerwear, including our disintegrating boots, and lay it all out in front of the fire where it steams in the heat.

*****

Before dawn I have no choice but to join a dozen of Akbar's men, wearing bright blue tunics which stand out even in this snow and carrying the Prince's standard. It is a luxury to be wearing dry clothes, to be rested and to have a full stomach. I find myself sick with guilt – why should I enjoy these privileges when hundreds of my countrymen have nothing but freezing cold, hunger and thirst to accompany their march? Yet I have no choice. I am under orders to act as the liaison officer between the army and Akbar Khan. I did not wish this for myself and I did everything I could to persuade the General not to succumb. Am I at fault? It feels so dishonourable to avoid the hardships of the army, however involuntarily. Yet, I ask myself, what else can I do?

This guilt torments me as we wait on horseback in the courtyard of the castle, while thick snow deadens sound and blankets the country, for the arrival of a larger force – the chieftains Akbar has promised, who will supposedly protect the officers and wives on the arduous trek through the gorge itself. Any warmth is soon lost as a biting wind gets up again. Eventually a larger force of chiefs arrives at the castle gates and we trot down to the mouth of the gorge.

We pass camps of Ghilzai savages who acknowledge our presence and allow us to pass on unmolested. They squat by fires eating or sit on rocks sharpening swords and cleaning their rifles. As a surly light starts to appear above the mountains in the East, it is clear they are preparing for another day of bloodshed.

Our troop reaches the army rearguard, which still resembles a disciplined military unit. I see they have managed to drag our two remaining field guns this far and the gunners are preparing for action. We are challenged and I have to present myself to the commanding officer before we are allowed to pass through. We trot towards the General's tent and I see dozens, perhaps hundreds, of dead bodies – men and women who have frozen to death during the night. Baggage litters the entrance to the pass: cases and casks, thrown open and looted; weapons and ammunition plundered by our own servants before they deserted or perished; camels and cattle slaughtered or dying of exhaustion. At this hour, a ghostly silence has fallen over the plain where thousands of men, women and children step slowly one way and another searching for warmth or food, stepping over the frozen bodies of the dead without giving them a second glance. They are concentrating on the ordeal ahead, attempting the long, narrow pass between almost sheer rock faces, white with frost and black with granite. The day is dark and the looming gorge is bleak. We have to ford the deep, fast-flowing river perhaps 50 times in six miles before we can escape the pass and reach higher, safer ground.

The frost clings to men's beards. Those who are alive and ready for today's march look like yeti, blanched and iced by a night of severe frost and covered with snow, clothes stiff with cold and damp, their fingers and toes frostbitten and dying.

We reach Elphinstone's tent, where the General is being given coffee by his faithful manservant Elwyn Evans. The old man looks wretched. His fat face is now gaunt, haggard and care-worn. His eyes are glazed and rheumy. He stares ahead as if he were blind and I wonder if he wishes he were so he could avoid the sight of the destruction of his army. Evans has to help Elphinstone sit up and holds the coffee cup to the General's lips, offering him sip after sip as if he were an invalid. I explain the rebel chiefs are here to provide an escort for the officers, their families, the General and his staff.

'How very thoughtful,' says Elphinstone. 'There, Pottinger, haven't I always said Akbar Khan is a decent man? Honourable, what?'

'General, he is offering to protect the officers and wives because he knows the army will be massacred and he wants some survivors to hold as hostages. Even now, sir, we should regroup and make a stand here rather than try to force the pass.'

The General's old friend Brigadier Thomas Anquetil stumbles into the tent groaning and announces, to no-one in particular, 'By God it's bloody cold. The men are in no mood for anything much. Bygrave reckons there's over two thousand natives dead. No wonder in this bloody cold. We really should get going, Elphie. Set an example, lead the way, that sort of thing, don't you think? Oh hello Pottinger, looks as if you were right old man, we should have stayed put. Still, can't be helped now. Just got to soldier on, ain't we Elphie?'

'His Highness has sent us an escort for the pass,' says the General.

'That's very decent of him.'

'Gentlemen,' I say, 'This escort is a ruse. Akbar is keeping Mackenzie and Lawrence as hostages. He demands I give myself up to him as well. He is not trying to help us, he wants to increase his stock of hostages to bargain for the freedom of his father.'

Anquetil, a red-faced, jovial man from Jersey who spent the last decade on half-pay living in Calcutta with, so it's said, three young native girls, is not perturbed. 'Well, anything to get out of this cold, eh Elphie?' he says, taking a long slug from a flask before offering it first to the General, who refuses, and then to me. I accept and find myself swallowing some sort of firewater which heats my mouth and throat and numbs my lips.

'Local brandy,' says Anquetil with a chuckle. 'These tea-total Muslims know a thing or two about the warming properties of alcohol, eh Pottinger?'

*****

Most of the women and children are gathered together as part of the advance party heading into the gorge. They have been there since before dawn in the perishing cold, Eleanor on an elegant grey stallion which was not the animal she left Kabul on. 'He died,' she tells me mournfully, 'And this animal, which I have called Major, after my own Major, lost his owner on yesterday's march, Eldred.'

I am astonished at the lightness of Eleanor's tone. She and the other ladies spent the night in a couple of thin tents, struggling for warmth and comfort, deprived of food or protection, while men, women and children were dying all around them. Yet Eleanor looks defiant, as do her friends Lady Sale, Drina Sturt and Emily Eyre, Vincent's wife. Akbar Khan's escort party is assembling the whole group and preparing to press on. Other ladies, with their small children, are accommodated in pannier baskets slung across some of the sturdier remaining camels. They are passing round sherry to fortify themselves for the ordeal ahead, even the children are encouraged to take a sip. It seems to have no ill-effect.

'Eleanor, this escort of our enemy, it is too good to be true. Stick close to Akbar's men, do not let them fly from you,' I tell her.

At that moment, we hear guns. Our gunners are firing one of the cannon. As the rearguard closes up on the entrance, and the rest of us edge slowly forward caught between sheer cliffs, on a narrow path filled with soldiers, cattle, horses, baggage of all kinds and thick with snow, the Ghilzais at our rear charge towards us forcing a greater panicked rush into the mouth of the pass creating a crush which kills many women and children, crushed underfoot by the stampede for the false security of the rocky pass.

The men defending our retreat are almost incapable of fighting. Their ancient muskets will not spark and, in any case, their hands are too numb to manipulate them. There is desperate hand-to-hand fighting with our men using swords, bayonets or knives – whatever weapon they can lay their hands on – while the crowing Afghan cavalry pass among them hacking to left and right and, with every blow, crushing the life out of another man. It is slaughter but I cannot retreat through the crush in the pass to reach the fighting.

The fighting alarms everyone and there is another surge towards the mouth of the pass. The surge becomes a rout, pressing in on the chieftains and their party of officers and wives who are now hurried into the pass whether they will or no. The press of panicked humanity cannot be resisted, the only choice is to press on into the Khoord Kabul with its sheer cliffs extinguishing even this pitiful daylight.

The walls of black rock loom above us now. The mouth of the pass narrows from a hundred yards or so at the outset to a matter of feet. It twists and turns alongside the water of the Kabul River, now in full spate. We cross it every few hundred yards, slippery, freezing and knee deep. We are in the vanguard. The snow is almost virgin here, white with a dark gash where the river runs. The animals struggle to keep their footing and we move slowly, the press of humanity, the clash of swords, the screams of women, the shots from rifles, all fill the air.

And then, as we turn another corner, the gunfire begins from above as well as behind us. I look up and see two men perched on a crag way up in the rocks re-loading their weapons, the clouds of smoke from their last shots still hover about them. A little further, on the other side of the ravine, I see a third Afghan shoot his jezzail into the throng. One or two of our men try firing back but their muskets are not good for sharpshooting and they are, in any case, jostled and thrown about by the terrified crowd.

One of Akbar Khan's chiefs yells up at his countrymen, calling on them not to fire, they are friends. This cry is taken up by several others in the escort party but it does not seem to have any significant effect. The deeper we go into the pass, the more we come under fire from Ghilzais, stationed in ones and twos, high up in the cliffs, pouring down destruction on our heads.

The cries and chaos worsen. A camel carrying two ladies and their babies is hit. Another bullet ploughs through the trooper in front of me and I feel his hot blood on my cheek as he falls from his horse and my own animal stumbles as it tries to step over his body. The chieftains yell at their party, calling on them to pick up the pace. The Afghans urge their horses into a trot and the rest of us follow suit. Soon we are cantering up the pass, regardless of the dangers underfoot, for fear of the destruction raining down from above and racing up behind us.

My horse is hit. He stumbles and throws me to the ground where my fall is broken by the body of an Indian from the native infantry. His blood seeps into the snow and for a moment I find myself staring as the white crystals are slowly dyed red, absorbing the warm life of the dead man. The horse struggles to stand but a bullet has gone through one of his forelegs and his blood, too, is turning the snow a dark crimson. There is nothing I can do but put the animal out of his pain. I seize the musket from the dead soldier but with freezing hands it is difficult to raise the hammer let alone get the powder into the pan, ram a ball down the muzzle and hope it fires properly.

Eventually the gun is ready and I'm tempted to aim it at one of the snipers up in the rocks but my horse is still struggling and in pain. I must put him out of his misery so I fire the old Brown Bess into his head, turn my face away from the bloody consequences, throw down the musket beside his lifeless body and join the hundreds staggering through this terrible valley of death.

Every step now is over or around a body, dead or dying. One or two rebels are in among us, stabbing and robbing as they pass. I pull one away from a servant and stab him with my knife. He grins maniacally at me for a moment but his arm slumps to the ground and his corpse is added to the crush beneath our feet.

I walk on, bullets and cries all around me, expecting pain and death at any moment. I must soon die. Knowledge of a death which will take place at some point in the distant future is not the same as certainty the moment has arrived. Now, not tomorrow or next month or next year but now, in the next few hours… minutes… in the teeth of this filthy gale, in this squalor and damp and confusion.

I watch my countrymen, some of them my friends, all of them my comrades, struggle upwards, leaning into the snow as it whips their faces, crouching down for fear of the next rifle assault or cavalry attack or knife in the back. There is no hiding place.

I am going to die. Now, here, in this gully between these grey rocks under this grey sky. Unshriven. Unshriven? What do I mean by that? Is this faith or am I using a phrase to take my mind off my imminent end?

The idea of a soul, a heaven and a God disappears in this freezing fear and impossible misery. How can there be a God, any God? My soul, if such a thing exists, will melt away like this snow in the spring. I shall be nothing.

I don't want to be nothing. I don't want to disappear. I don't want to succumb to this extinction. To cease would be to ease the pain and suffering. Perhaps the grave is warm – it cannot, surely, be any colder than I am now. I have never known such perishing purgatory. The grave, under warm earth, baked by hot suns, perhaps this is the heaven we hope for, not annihilation after all, but a warm bed to rest in.

I am tired. I need a rest. I would enjoy some warmth. I am going to die and yet I do not feel ready for death.

Death is now my enemy, not Akbar Kahn or his chieftains, not his father the King of Kabul, not poor dead Macnaghten, not even Shelton. Death is my enemy. Am I to surrender? Do I have a choice? He can take me any time he likes but I shall not give in to him. I shall soldier on. He shall not have me without a fight. I might despair and I know I am on death's threshold but he will have to come for me, I shall not seek him out. I will not give up without a fight.

The blizzard assaults my face once again. I wrap my scarf as tightly around my face as I can and stare down onto the ground to discern where it is safe to step, avoiding the bodies in my path. I dismiss death, I dismiss fear. I do not have the strength to look around me to spy out danger. I must simply do as everyone else does, place one foot in front of the other and struggle slowly on towards nightfall in the hope the Afghans leave us alone for a few hours and let us get out of their wretched, cruel country.

I do not think. I do not think of death. Or my family. My brothers, my sister, my step-mother. My father. I do not think of my uncle Sir Henry. I do not think of you, my dear Eleanor.

Every time I tell myself I will not think of them, I realise I am thinking of them and I try to dismiss these ghosts from my mind. I do not think of why I am here or the disasters which brought me to this pass. I do not think of the suffering around me. I do not think of death or the possibility of life after death. I do not think of all the experiences of life I shall miss. I do not think how wonderful a good meal, a beef steak or a glass of beer, would taste on a warm Irish afternoon. I dismiss all these things from my mind as soon as they present themselves. And I know I shall have to dismiss these thoughts again and again because they return step after step, unbidden, even as I try to shut down my mind, which should be as numb with cold as the rest of my body. I concentrate on the pain. The aching feet, the pangs in my hands, the freezing blood on my wounded leg, the dislocated shoulder, the stinging eyes. If I walk fast enough I can retain a little warmth. I step up my pace. If death comes for me, he will have to be quick.

CHAPTER 46

Khoord Kabul, January 1842

I can't believe it – Eleanor is laughing. Laughing. Her head is thrown back and she is smiling like a happy young girl with her friends at a summer party.

She stands by her horse in the freezing blizzard with dead bodies around her, gunfire and screams coming up from the gorge below us and she is laughing. With her are Emily Eyre and Drina Sturt. All three of them are pink-cheeked, their eyes sparkling and giddy. They are passing round a flask of something, it smells like brandy. Nearby, Lady Sale is receiving attention from Dr Brydon, who is wrapping bandages round her left arm but she, too, seems to be in good spirits, almost exhilarated. I can hear her saying, 'It's nothing, doctor, nothing.'

'Eldred, Eldred,' says Eleanor excitedly, 'Look, we made it. Emily won but Drina and I ran her close and poor Fiorentina would have beaten us all if she hadn't taken a beastly bullet in the arm.' The women start laughing again. 'You should have seen us,' Eleanor continues, 'We just flew. We flew. And we were riding properly, like men. I'm renaming this horse Pegasus, aren't I Pegasus darling?' She says, nuzzling closer to the horse's head.

'You should have seen us,' says Drina. 'We left them all standing. It was like the Epsom Derby.'

'Only with bullets,' says Emily Eyre, and they all burst into giggles again as Eleanor hands me the flask. 'Here, Eldie, try some of this. It'll warm you up' and again they start laughing.

'This is all very unladylike,' I say sternly, handing the flask back to Mrs Eyre without tasting its contents. 'And where is your husband, Mrs Sturt?'

'Oh John's gone back down the pass to rescue Captain Thomas. He'll return soon enough.'

'Eldie, Eldie,' says Eleanor with a grin on her face that, at any other time, might have looked attractive, 'Don't look stern – you don't mind me calling you Eldie do you? – it was so thrilling,' says Eleanor. 'The pass was getting more and more crowded and the enemy were firing down from the heights.'

'They didn't need to take an aim,' says Mrs Eyre, 'Every shot found a target.'

'Look,' says Eleanor, holding an arm out for inspection. 'If this coat was any thinner then, who knows, they might have killed me?'

'But they didn't did they, Ellie?' says Drina Sturt and the three women start laughing again and passing round the flask.

'Oh look,' says Mrs Eyre, 'Empty. Poor Lady Sale.'

'She's got her own sherry,' says Drina.

'We were half way along the pass,' continues Eleanor, 'With our noble escort' – more amusement – 'When Fiorentina says, "We must make a charge, ladies. Tally Ho!" and off we went, hell for leather...'

'Pell mell,' says Mrs Sturt.

'Lickety-spit,' suggests Emma Eyre.

'Full-tilt,' continues Eleanor, 'Up the pass, through that terribly nasty narrow bit, up and up, through the snow and over the stream, higher and higher.'

'And even the Ghilzais and their jezzails couldn't stop us,' says Mrs Sturt and yet again the three young women start laughing and throw their arms around each other.

'I haven't had so much fun since we rode out with Lord Southampton's

Hounds,' says Mrs Eyre.

As they continue to enjoy their survival, a rabble of soldiers plods dejectedly up the final yards of the pass as it opens up onto the high, flatter ground were a camp of sorts is being established. They spot a group of comrades gathered round a small fire, which is being fuelled by clothing stripped from the dead bodies of Hindu troops and camp-followers who have not made it this far. The new arrivals have with them a barrel of wine which they offer to the others in exchange for places closer to the fire. There is some shouting and scuffling but most are too shattered with exhaustion, cold and hunger to argue. The cask is broached but the wine is frozen solid.

A few moments later I see a horse stumble onto the higher ground with a body draped across its back, led by the baggage Sergeant, George Wade. The body appears to be lifeless but as soon as he realises he has reached what passes for safety on the plain above the pass, Wade calls for help. I rush over with a couple of others to discover it's John Sturt, who has at least three deep sword slashes, two on his back and a third, where he is losing most blood, on his thigh. I call over Brydon, who has just finished patching up Lady Sale, and the four of us lift the almost-lifeless body off the horse and place Sturt as gently as we can on a blanket. Eleanor notices what's going on and alerts Alexandrina. There is a wailing cry of agony as she rushes over to where her husband lies gasping and she kneels in the snow at his side trying to staunch the flow of blood from his wounds with her coat.

*****

Night is already falling under a snow-filled sky, the evening bleak and dark, the temperature well below freezing and the army, as it emerges onto safer ground above the pass, exhausted, bloody, filthy, perished and utterly demoralised. Some attempts are made at military discipline – the camp, such as it is, has men on guard duty all round it, though their hands are too stiff with cold to pull a trigger. The camels have almost all died, the cattle have been stolen or slaughtered, the goats have been eaten. Camp followers disappear into the snowdrifts or sit down to die. The officers are as dispirited as their men though some try to maintain an impression of discipline. Brigadier General Shelton is with the tattered remnants of the 44th, issuing commands and making demands of his junior officers which they all know cannot be carried out. Shelton was with the rearguard all day, in the thick of the fighting. According to Waller he was successful in beating off some of the most ferocious attacks and, with his one arm, was ready and willing to thrust his sword at anyone who came too close. The action did little good, though. The complete massacre of the army was only prevented because the gorge becomes so narrow even the fanatical Ghilzai horsemen could not find room to manoeuvre and choked the pass, hacking away at their victims until they, too, were hacked down or shot by their comrades on the rocks above.

Shelton is now in one of the remaining tents, with General Elphinstone and a few other officers. Elphie is prostrate on a makeshift bed, exhausted, almost snow-blind and so unwell he can scarcely sit up to speak. Shelton is on a small camp chair, head in his hand, a couple of other officers share a small flask of rum. The two guards outside the entrance to this tent nod me through without a word. Evans, Elphie's manservant, acknowledges me briefly as he hurries in with some bread and brandy for his master. 'General's in a bad way, sir,' he says briefly.

I wait as Evans helps Elphinstone to sit up and persuades him to nibble on bread and sip on the brandy. Shelton looks up. 'Ah Pottinger. I'd heard you had already fled and gone over to the enemy,' he says with a bitter smile.

'Under the General's orders, I was required to visit Akbar Khan yesterday, Brigadier-General, but, as you see, I have returned. Akbar offers safe haven for those officers with wives and children still alive. I am here to pass that offer on to the General.'

'And you get to secure your own safety as well, I assume?' Shelton demands.

'Not at all, sir.' I raise my voice to attract the General's attention, 'General Elphinstone sir, Akbar Khan has taken Captain Lawrence and will not let him go, and Captain Mackenzie. He says he will provide safety and shelter for those officers with wives and children among our party and I am here to convey the message.'

Elphinstone looks up at me with glazed, expressionless eyes. 'Can he be trusted?'

'No sir, he has proved that time and time again.'

Shelton pipes up, 'Of course he can't.'

There is a pause. Exhaustion is the enemy of debate. At length, I say, 'I shall send a message back to Akbar saying the women and children will stay with the army, as will I. He will have to content himself with Lawrence and Mackenzie.'

'Now, now, Pottinger,' says Brigadier Anquetil, who seems to have taken on the task of speaking for the General. 'Let's not be hasty. The ladies are in danger. Their children also. Their husbands, those still living, would not wish to be parted from them. They can do little good remaining with the army – the women are a mere encumbrance, the children more so, while the husbands are so anxious about the safety of their families as to be prejudicial to good military discipline. In the circumstances, I recommend we accede to Akbar's request and surrender the officers and their families to his care. General?'

Elphinstone has not heard a word. Evans is coaxing another drop of brandy down his throat while the poor man seems scarcely alive. Anquetil, who is almost the same age as Elphie but is far more alert, raises his voice and repeats what he has just said for the General's benefit. Elphinstone nods, though whether in assent or not is hard to tell. 'There you are then,' says Anquetil, while Shelton nods, as if in agreement, though again it is hard to tell.

'I shall remain here,' I repeat.

'Someone must lead the party, Pottinger,' says Anquetil. 'Akbar is expecting your return?' Reluctantly I admit he is. 'Then you must accompany them.'

'I cannot desert the army, sir.'

'You must, Pottinger. You are the Queen's envoy and must remain with what passes for a Government in this country. You have your diplomatic responsibilities I'm afraid.' Anquetil turns to Elphinstone. 'Pottinger to accompany the officers and wives into captivity, sir?' he says slowly, in a loud voice, as if speaking to an imbecile.

The General groans. 'Captivity? Well yes, yes, I suppose so, I suppose so.' He sighs and closes his eyes, shivers and Evans throws another rug over Elphinstone's body.

'Is that an order?' I ask. I do not want to go. I should share the deprivations and dangers of the army. Whatever fate Akbar has in mind for his hostages, it cannot be as bad as the fate in store for the rest of the army. 'General,' I say, 'Seeking shelter with our enemy is so utterly dishonourable I cannot do it except under the specific orders of my commanding officer.'

'You heard the General,' says Anquetil. 'General, that is your order, is it not?' he says slowly and loudly, as if Elphie were deaf and stupid.

'Oh for God's sake,' Shelton interjects, 'Of course it's an order, Pottinger. Get the officers and wives together and get them out of here at first light. They are no use to us here. You are no use to us here. Get gone, man, just get gone, damn you.'

*****

Sturt is dead. Drina, his wife, is beside herself with grief. Eleanor is trying to comfort her while the doctor is telling her to be calm for fear of damaging the child she is carrying. Lady Macnaghten is complaining one of her cats has disappeared and accuses her two remaining servants of selling it for food. Lady Sale is demanding a proper burial for her son-in-law and insisting we must find John Logan to perform the last rites. She has commandeered a couple of men to dig a grave for Sturt and sends me off to find Logan. The chiefs who led the ladies through the pass all survived the ordeal unscathed, quite an achievement considering they ran the same risks as everyone else, and are anxious to depart with their hostages.

It is dark now and we agree we must wait until dawn. The chieftains make their own arrangements for the night and disappear from the camp, promising to return. I help Sergeant Wade and a couple of others dig a grave for Sturt. It is not deep – there is little soil here and a great deal of rock beneath the thick snow – but it is at least a Christian burial. Logan conducts the service by the light of some of the few remaining torches we have, which help to keep the ice from our hearts as Sturt's wife, his mother-in-law and his many friends give him as decent Christian burial as anyone could hope for in the circumstances.

Lady Sale insists on paying tribute to the dead man. 'He would have made a fine General,' she says. 'If our leaders in Kabul had listened to his wise counsel he would not have died on this bleak plain. He would have made a fine father as he made a fine husband, a fine son. He has been cut down in the prime of his life, one among many to have died today but John was our beloved and a brave young man. – I will not cry,' she pauses, gathers her strength again, and goes on '"As for man, his days are as grass: as a flower of the field, so he flourisheth. For the wind passeth over it, and it is gone; and the place thereof shall know it no more." But here rests Captain John Sturt and we honour him for his courage and self-sacrifice. And remember the words of our Lord, "for he will avenge the blood of his servants, and will render vengeance to his adversaries".'

Now here, I think, is at least one person who still has the stomach for a fight.

*****

We descend the Khoord Kabul in the company of Akbar's chieftains. It is no longer snowing and the sky above is bright blue, though the gorge is still dark with shadows. The snipers have gone and the army which passed through yesterday is no longer scrabbling up the steep path. Instead the whole route is crowded with the bodies of the dead. Our horses cannot step safely without the risk of stumbling or even crushing some piece of destroyed humanity. We descend a valley of corpses, some half hidden by fresh falls of snow, some muddied and half drowned in the river, some lying at contorted angles with expressions of horror or desperation on their rigid faces.

A few Ghilzai women strip the bodies of anything they can loot. Everywhere there are signs of massacre. I look behind me to see Eleanor staring ahead with blank eyes. Drina Sturt is nursed along by Emily Eyre and Lady Sale, who ride as close as they can either side of her, though the rough terrain separates them much of the time. The rest of our ragged party is strung out over a quarter of a mile as we descend the precipitous pass, in and out of the streaming river, around and over the bodies in our path. The chiefs who lead us do so with an impressive military bearing, as well they might, being the victors in this one-sided battle, heading for home with their human prizes.

There are about three dozen of us in all. As well as Eleanor, Lady Macnaghten and Lady Sale, Drina Sturt and Mrs Eyre, our party includes Captain Walter Boyd and his wife Mary, whose youngest boy Hugh was carried off by an Afghan raider; Mrs Matilda Mainwaring, who preserved the life of her three-month-old child despite an Afghan's repeated attempts to steal them both away from the army; Captain Sampson Anderson and his child – his wife is missing and we fear the worst; Captain Robert Troup, Lieutenants Robert Waller, Vincent Eyre and George Mein, all wounded; the conductor of the army band, Thomas Ryley, his wife and three children; Mrs Mary Trevor, whose husband was killed last month, and their seven children; Sergeant George Wade, his wife Grace and their three children. We also have about a dozen Hindu servants to assist the ladies.

I had expected Lady Sale to protest at being handed over to the enemy. She would have called it croaking, I suspect. But she and her daughter were still shocked by the loss of John Sturt and in no frame of mind to do anything but as they were invited. Eleanor offers what comfort she can, which is scant, but agrees captivity with Akbar Khan must be preferable to another day's retreat.

I look at her usually-flirtatious eyes and see nothing in them but a desire to blank out their surroundings and a loss of hope which is more heartrending to me even than the sight of so much humanity hacked down by our enemies. Eleanor has an air of resigned helplessness and there is nothing I can offer to restore her spirits. We have nothing to look forward to but captivity among a dangerous and unpredictable enemy who would as happily slit our throats or sell us into slavery as he would treat us with hospitality and respect. All we can reasonably hope for is to stay alive and trust the future offers something better than the present misery.

*****

We arrive at Akbar Khan's headquarters to be greeted not by the rebel king himself but by his young cousin Sultan Jan. This boy of about 22 makes a little speech to our ragged troop after we are ushered into the great hall where Lawrence, Mackenzie and I spent the night. These two are there to greet us and usher the women and children towards the fire, where roaring flames offer consolation for the horrors of our journey.

When everyone is crowded into the room, Sultan Jan stands at the doorway and declares, 'You are most welcome here. You are our friends and our honoured guests. We are here to serve you and ensure your stay is as comfortable as we can make it. I apologise for the accommodation, which may not be of the standard you are used to, but please feel free to enjoy what poor facilities we have available to you. There are three rooms for accommodation and, of course, I leave it to you to decide who should go where. For now, what can we do to assist you?'

Eleanor turns defiantly towards him and says, 'Isn't it obvious? Water, clean clothes and food?'

Sultan Jan looks hurt. He is a handsome man, tall for an Afghan, lean, with eyes which suggest a sensitive disposition. 'Water,' he says, rubbing his hands and turning to his servants, 'Water. To drink?'

'And to wash,' says Eleanor. 'We are all filthy.'

'Hot water?'

'Of course hot water.' I want to tell her to modify her belligerent tone but I am so pleased to see some life coursing through her veins once more that instead I watch in admiration. 'Hot water for washing, cold water for drinking. And we have nothing to wear but what we stand up in. And we have scarcely eaten for three days.'

'We are at your service, madam,' says Sultan Jan as he withdraws, clapping his hands and ordering his servants to do what they can to meet Eleanor's demands.

At midnight some mutton bones and greasy rice are brought to us.

CHAPTER 47

Fort William, Calcutta, January 1843

Whistler adjusts his uniform with unnecessary care, consults his papers, looks up at the panel of judges, waits for Mr Clerk to say 'Mr Whistler?', coughs to clear his throat and, shuffling from one foot to the other as if he were dancing at a ball, declares, 'I am grateful, your honour. The prosecution wishes to call its first witness, Major General John Shelton of the 44th Native Infantry.'

'Major General?' I whisper to Broadhurst who scribbles me a note: 'Promoted two weeks ago. I thought you knew.'

Shelton marches with clicking heels to the witness stand where he strikes a dapper figure in his tight-fitting black uniform. He removes his cap, takes the oath, smiles an acknowledgement to his brother generals and looks in anticipation at Whistler.

'Major General,' he says with an ingratiating smile, 'Thank you for taking the time to join us today.' Shelton nods. 'You know why we are here, I believe?'

'I do,' he says gravely, in his piping voice.

'Major Pottinger is accused of cowardice, among other crimes, and it is this, above all, that which we are here to address. The question for this court martial to determine is whether Major Pottinger was the architect of the downfall and ruin of the Army of the Indus. There are, as we know, very few surviving witnesses to the events of one year ago so your testimony will be of crucial importance, General.'

'I am aware of that, sir,' Shelton says with a slight air of irritation in his voice.

'Let us go back to the death of Sir William Macnaghten. Were you aware that Sir William was negotiating the terms of the army's withdrawal from Kabul at the time of his brutal murder.'

'I was, sir.'

'And were you in agreement with his proposal?'

'I was not, sir.'

'And why was that, General?'

'Because I took the view we should not negotiate with the enemy, we should make our own decisions without promising anything in return. We were flattering them and encouraging them to think they were our equals when these Afghanis are a Godless, brutal, uncivilised, uncouth race without an ounce of humanity among the lot of 'em. We should have just left 'em to rot. We should never have negotiated anything.'

'After Sir William's death, was that still your view?'

'It was. We had no need to try bribing that vile, greasy wop Akbar Khan with hundreds of thousands of rupees. We should have departed, defiantly, all guns blazing and given the bastards what-for as we went.'

'So you agreed with the ends but not with the means?'

'If you mean did I agree we should quit the abominable place, sir, you are correct. I was damned if we should stay a moment longer. We were under siege. They were taunting us, they were starving us, they were undermining the men's morale. We had no choice but to quit as soon as possible. The negotiations delayed the inevitable and gave the enemy time to make his dispositions.'

'And what was your view of the talks between Major Pottinger and Akbar Khan?'

'Waste of time. Couldn't trust either of 'em. Akbar, known murderer and rebel; Pottinger, known trouble-maker and Irishman.'

'In your opinion, was it cowardly to enter into a treaty with Akbar

Khan?'

'Craven cowardice, sir, craven cowardice to negotiate with such a foreigner.'

'Thank you, Major General.'

Whistler sits down and Broadhurst struggles to his feet. It is a warm day and I am sweating heavily in my uniform. This is it, this is the moment of truth. If Captain George Broadhurst cannot extract the truth from Shelton – Major General Shelton – all may be lost.

My attorney is sweating as heavily as I am. He wipes his brow with a red handkerchief and looks at Shelton.

'Let us be clear, Major General,' says Broadhurst, 'Are you saying to this court that you agreed with the idea that the army should abandon Kabul and march back to India in the dead of winter?'

'I am saying that, sir.'

'Perhaps you would be kind enough to explain your reasoning, Major General,' says Broadhurst, as politely as he knows how.

'We could not hold the place. We were surrounded by a hostile and numerous enemy. We had no clear strategy. General Elphinstone was incapable of making a decision. It was costing us a fortune in men and treasure to stay at that uncivilised outpost. My firm view, which I had held for several weeks, was that if we did not retreat, we would perish.'

'But that is precisely what happened.'

'It is.'

'Do you accept now that your judgment was mistaken?'

'I do not.'

'But General Shelton,' Broadhurst is calmness itself, though he wipes his brow again as he asks, 'General Shelton, are you saying you concurred with the negotiations between Sir William Macnaghten and Akbar Khan.'

'No sir.' Shelton stands stock still in the witness box, back straight, shoulders to attention, the empty right sleeve neatly tucked into his jacket pocket; a small man in a General's uniform, the unimpeachable symbol of military authority and dunder-headed stupidity.

'You would have retreated even without an agreement?'

'I would have done so, sir, yes. Securing an agreement was a waste of time and allowed the enemy time to prepare his attack.'

'You would have retreated from Kabul whatever the prospects for the army?'

'Whatever the prospects.'

'Were you aware of the treaty eventually signed by General Elphinstone?'

'I was, sir.'

'And what was your opinion of this treaty, sir?'

'Waste of time. No point negotiating with these people. Can't be trusted.'

Broadhurst pauses, thinking. Is Shelton walking into a trap? Broadhurst continues, 'This treaty is regarded in some quarters, including some in this court, as an abject surrender and evidence of cowardice on the part of the defendant, Major Pottinger, and yet you are telling us you were a party to this cowardly capitulation.'

Shelton waits a few moments, staring at his inquisitor, before he replies, in his high-pitched voice but with an air of menace nevertheless, 'I should say, sir, that withdrawal from Kabul was the only practical step we could take in the circumstances. I reject completely the accusation that this represented a cowardly capitulation. Indeed the accusation is deeply offensive and I call on you, sir, to withdraw it.'

Broadhurst looks at Judge Clerk and the others on the bench for support. Clerk looks down at his papers while the military men, Major General Sir Lumley, Major General Smith, Brigadier Monteath and Brigadier Wymer stare out of the windows, look into the depths of the courtroom or stare straight at Shelton – none of them offers Broadhurst a lifeline. 'I fear, sir,' says my attorney carefully, 'That my task is to defend Major Pottinger against the heinous charge cowardice. It follows, if he is guilty, that those officers who advocated and supported his negotiations must be regarded as having demonstrated that very same vice.'

There is a shocked silence in the court. I look behind me and notice the newspapermen are busy scribbling away.

Broadhurst tries another tack. 'Major General Shelton,' he says, 'You and Major Pottinger have not seen eye-to-eye. Is that correct?'

'It is.'

'And why is that?'

'He is a jumped-up Irishman assuming powers and authority that were not rightfully his. He is insubordinate and contumacious.'

'And how did this show itself?'

'He fled Charikar without authorisation, taking it upon himself to lead the garrison there to its doom. Yet somehow Major Pottinger was among the only survivors and later, in Kabul, he would not take no for an answer.'

'Sir?'

'Kept trying to muscle in on military matters, as if he knew better than we did.' Shelton emits a short, bitter laugh and looks at the judges for sympathy. They remain, for the most part, glassy-eyed.

'So, a coward then?'

'Well... Above himself, certainly.'

'A coward?' Broadhurst insists.

Shelton straightens himself up even more, if that is possible. His eyes narrow and he stares at George Broadhurst with a look of loathing and contempt. 'Mr Broadhurst,' he says, slowly and deliberately, 'It was not cowardice to wish to withdraw from Kabul, it was a considered military judgment. The cowardice, sir, was in seeking to negotiate an agreement with an implacable foe. The cowardice, sir, was in placing any faith in the word of Akbar Khan.'

'And this, you say, is what Major Pottinger is guilty of.'

'It is.'

CHAPTER 48

Jagdalak, January 1842

The ladies are hysterical and inconsolable. Their 17 Indian servants, mostly young women, have been taken from them and murdered. They were simply herded out into a back yard and their throats were cut. Sultan Jan wrings his hands and says there was nothing he could do; Akbar Khan says we are lucky it's only the Hindus. He blames the Ghilzais.

These servants have shared and suffered, stayed loyal and kind, especially to the children. All the ladies are in despair, made worse because we have been moved on as part of Akbar Khan's entourage, following in the footsteps of the retreating army.

At every step, we see more bodies frozen in attitudes of horror and pain. Everywhere there are men we recognise. There is a powerful smell of blood and rotting flesh, which can never be forgotten. For many miles, the white snow is stained with smears and pools of red. The Ghilzais scurry among the corpses stealing whatever they can find or cutting the throat of anyone still showing signs of life. As our ragged band passes, guarded by heavily armed followers of Akbar Khan, the savages jeer and spit, wave their trophies in the air and occasionally throw severed limbs at us.

We reach Akbar's new camp near the Jagdalak pass. It is visible from some distance as a result of the pile of corpses he has had created near his tents. The number of captives is swollen by the arrival of several more officers including Lieutenant Henry Melville, who was taken defending the colours of the Bengal Artillery, which he had wrapped around his body. Several of our party do not believe Melville put up much of a fight as he has only suffered a few sword cuts to his right arm. I can't say it makes much difference now.

Lawrence and I are summoned to Akbar's tent, a large marquee-sized construction where he is enjoying a meal with most of the leading Ghilzai chieftains. We are astonished to discover General Elphinstone and Brigadier General Shelton, with Captain James Skinner who, it seems, has been carrying messages between the two sides.

Akbar is offering Elphinstone and Shelton tea and some new deal. He stands to greet us and declares, 'My friends Major Pottinger, Captain Lawrence, I trust you had a pleasant journey. Tea for my guests. I was just telling the Generals here how honoured we are to have been graced with their presence and how delightful if would be if they could see their way clear to instructing those officers still out there to join us here in the warmth. What do you say, Major?'

'I say you have murdered our servants and are like to murder the rest of us and I say to the Generals that you are not to be trusted.'

Akbar ignores this, sits down again cross-legged on his rug and starts eating from the communal bowl of lamb and rice. 'You shall stay here tonight, General Elphinstone.'

Elphie seems to have rallied a little. Perhaps it is simply warmth, drink and food which have revived him, for he is sitting up straight, unaided, and tells his host, 'Only on condition you fulfil your pledge, Your Highness. Water and food for the men and call off your dogs.'

'Dogs?' Akbar laughs and encourages his allies to laugh with him. 'Wolves, more like,' he says. 'But it shall be done. I shall send food and water to your men and I shall escort your army all the way to Jalalabad in safety.'

'It is very noble of you, Your Highness,' says Elphinstone though

Shelton scowls and grunts his dissent.

*****

The night is spent in thin tents which let in the freezing cold. The ladies and children are crammed together in just two. Lady Macnaghten demands a third for herself, her cats, and Lady Sale but does not get one. The officers and men are equally cramped and it turns out we have to pay for our food – a couple of women are selling chapatis. They start out costing three for a rupee but in no time, demand being so high, they become a rupee each. Luckily most people still have money which has not been stolen yet.

The following morning, Elphinstone and Shelton demand to be allowed to return to the army. Akbar Khan smiles his refusal and says it is vital for the safety of us all that they remain with him. Shelton shouts and swears and would, I do believe, have risked his life in defying the rebel leader if he had a weapon to hand. Despite his nature, I find myself admiring his belligerence. Elphinstone says, 'Your Highness, I cannot abandon my army and abide here in comfort and safety when my men are enduring such hardship. I must go back to them or die of shame. I must, sir, I really must.'

'Let him die here,' says one of the chiefs with a grin as the others begin to debate what is to happen to the hostages. They want to murder us. One of them, Mahommed Shah Khan, who appears to be Akbar's father-in-law, tells him, 'What did we tell you when Alexander Burnes first visited this country? We begged your father Dost Mohammed Khan to kill him and send a message to the English that we are not to be trifled with. But what did he do? He let Burnes go and when he returned it was at the head of a great army. Let us now do what your father should have done then, while we have the chance – let us kill these infidel dogs.'

Akbar argues the hostages must be allowed to live because the English hold his father in Shah Soojah's place at the palace with Mahommed

Shah Khan's own daughter, among others.

Elphinstone interrupts. Strangely, the man has become decisive, almost forceful, 'Your Highness, I really must insist on being allowed to return. If you require a hostage in my place, I feel sure I could persuade Brigadier Anquetil to return in my stead.'

Akbar says this is not possible. Shelton asks if the troops have been supplied with food and water, as promised. Akbar admits they have not yet received any supplies. Shelton asks if the promised cease-fire has been put in place. Akbar says that, alas, it has not. He says his father-in-law and the other Ghilzai chiefs have refused his requests for mercy.

'Mercy?' laughs Mahommed Shah Khan, 'We show these infidel mercy? Why should we when they invade our country, seize our King, replace him with that slippery snake Shah Soojah? When they steal our money, rape our women and raze our cities? We will not be satisfied until every last one of them is cut down. They shall never see India again.'

Akbar shrugs and says to Elphinstone, 'You see what I have to contend with, General. No, you are safer here with me. You see, we wish you had come among us as friends, and not as enemies, for you are fine fellows one by one, though as a body they hate you.'

I cannot resist reminding Akbar what the Koran tells him. 'Does it not say "Feed the hungry and free the captive if he be unjustly confined; assist any person oppressed, whether Muslim or non-Muslim", Your Highness?'

He smiles and his fat lips smirk. 'Ah yes, Major Pottinger, but does it not also say, "kill the unbelievers wherever you find them, and turn them out from where they have turned you out"?'

*****

Over the next few days we are moved from one camp to another. I have been designated as the leader of the hostages, for General Elphinstone has once more fallen into despair while Brigadier General

Shelton says it is beneath his dignity to bargain with barbarians.

Food is scarce, the weather abominable, everyone is frozen, wet, unwell and unhappy. There is a look of shock on Eleanor's face all the time now. She does her best to struggle on through these deprivations, caring for several motherless children and Alexandrina Sturt, but abject misery is never far from the surface.

We snatch brief conversations when we can. I tell her I love her and will do everything in my power to protect her but she knows as well as I that my 'everything' is very little at the moment. I try to reassure her that, though we may be prisoners of war, Akbar Khan will not lightly kill us or sell us into slavery because we are valuable to him. We represent the safety of his father and his father's court-in-exile. While Dost Mohammed Khan is in British hands, his son cannot afford to lose the power that holding our lives in his hands represents.

Eleanor is not convinced – and she worries that, if her identity as the sister of the Governor-General of India is made known, she could be singled out in some way for special treatment.

'You are a companion to Lady Sale and Mrs Sturt,' I say, 'You must remind them not to mention your brother Lord Eden, for that would, indeed, complicate matters.'

We are taken to another fort, somewhere off the route to the Khyber Pass and the ladies and children are crammed into a grain store while we men have to shift as best we can in doorways, on winding staircases or in the unreliable shelter of the castle walls.

*****

The Army of the Indus is no more. It has been wiped out entirely. We learn this from Captain Thomas Souter, when he is captured and brought in by the Ghilzais who assumed he was a senior officer because he had the 44th regiment's colours wrapped around him. The remnants of the army reached the village of Gandamak, exactly half way between Kabul and Jalalabad, where, Souter says, the Afghans offered to take them prisoner but one of the sergeants shouted 'not bloody likely' and the remaining 22 officers and 45 men fought to the death even though few of their muskets would fire and they faced an overwhelming enemy. Souter thinks everyone else is dead. He did see Dr Brydon make his escape but assumes the enemy caught up with him and cut him down.

As the days progress, our privations get no worse. There is much coming and going. Akbar Khan has returned to Kabul, presumably to stake his claim to the throne.

We receive messages from the outside world almost every day but I have difficulty with Lady Sale, who constantly assails me with new facts which turn out to be misplaced rumour and gossip. When she is told there is an army half a day's march away, she believes it. When this fabled army fails to materialise, she seems to think it is my fault.

'You are our senior officer,' she says, 'You are responsible for our safety.'

That may be true but I cannot conjure an army out of thin air. I wish I could. Fiorentina Sale is no more weary of this than I am. It is an exhausting business being responsible for an irregular army of children, women and fellow officers, all of them dispirited, most of them very unwell, some of them dying, all of them under-nourished, bored, virtually penniless, ragged and lice-ridden.

I shout at our guards. I cajole. I bribe when I can. I deliver ultimatums and demands, I compromise and debate but I have no power over them other than the possibility there really is an army on the way and that, in the long run, it is not in their interests to treat us like slaves. The problem is our guards would willingly take the Bokara slave-traders' money and run away now, while there is still time. They reckon if they stick with us, they will probably be executed for holding all these Englishmen, their wives and children, as hostages so they may as well exploit us while the going is good.

I argue Her Majesty is a merciful, Christian Monarch who understands forgiveness. I tell them the Company, far from seeking retribution, will be much in their debt if they keep us alive to be re-united with our kith and kin.

There is some truth in this but I am not sure I'm convinced so it's unlikely I can persuade these nervous Afghans they would be safer and richer if they stuck with us than if they abandoned us to a fate which, it is true to say, would be far worse than death.

The tales one hears of slavery in Bokara do not bear thinking about. Wretched creatures kept in cells, forced to labour in all weathers with little food, shelter or warmth in the freezing winters; the women condemned in some cases to an even more appalling fate, passed from one stinking native to another and then discarded; the children, too, treated as labourers or worse. Poor Stoddart, who was such a friend in Herat, has been trapped there by the Mad King for four long years.

On Sundays we hold a church service, which is much-mocked by our captors. But it is necessary to assert our Christianity and it helps ward off despair. It even gives some shape to our shapeless lives.

John Logan preaches Psalm 79:

> *"Oh God, the heathen are come into thine inheritance.*
> *The dead bodies of thy servants have they given to be meat unto the fowls of the air.*
> *Oh let the sorrowful sighing of the prisoners come before Thee...*
> *Pour out thy wrath upon the heathen that have not known thee, and upon the kingdoms*
> *that have not called upon thy name."*

Luckily our captors do not speak English.

CHAPTER 49

Budeeabad, April 1842

The roof wobbles. I feel as if I am standing on gelatine. My legs swing away from my body and back again. My head feels dizzy. The earth seems to shake and twitch, like the skin of a dog dreaming in his sleep. I watch a series of shudders descend the valley, throwing up clouds of dust and debris as if mortar shells are landing at irregular intervals.

We run for the stairs to get off the roof before the whole thing collapses. Vincent Eyre is the first to descend but Shelton roars after him, 'Lieutenant, damn you man, do you not wait for your senior officers?' He turns to me and says, 'Put this man on a charge, Pottinger.' I ignore him and wait while the Brigadier General slowly descends the stone steps as the trembling continues.

There are cries of dismay as a wall collapses. Lady Macnaghten yells, 'My cat! My cat!' though everyone ignores her as the upheaval seems to roll in a wave all along the valley and we hear the sound of crashing masonry close by. Our guards are probably more frightened than their prisoners. We have grown used to disaster, they still think their God is protecting them from His wrath.

Lady Sale disappears under falling stones. She was hanging out some washing when the tremor began. Eleanor is first to begin scrabbling through the stones calling her name. It is not long before we discover Fiorentina has been protected by a falling beam, which, far from crushing her protects her from serious harm. One of the children, an orphaned soldier's son called Seymour Stoker, who has turned himself into Lady Sale's little helper, has broken his arm.

The walls, towers and turrets of this small fort shudder and shake, parts of the building collapse but, as it is the middle of a mild spring day, most of us are outside in the courtyard and escape unharmed. It is a pity, though, to see parts of our prison come down because this fort, built quite recently by the Ghilzai chieftain Mahommed Shah Khan to house his wives, is the most comfortable place we have been imprisoned in.

We've been here some weeks now and fixed things up tolerably well. The ladies have no fewer than six rooms between them while the men have been allocated part of the cellars underground. There are no locks on the doors and we are free to come and go as we please.

Communications are now open with the army in Jalalabad – General Sale has not retreated one inch and nor has he been thrown out by Akbar Khan or his allies. Supplies of all sorts are making their way here: dresses for the ladies, sweetmeats, sugar, books, writing materials and boots for the men, our own being worn out. An entire chest of drawers arrives for Lady Sale, much to Lady Macnaghten's annoyance, as there is no-one in Jalalabad to provide her with the accoutrements necessary for the maintenance of her dignity. Eleanor and the heavily-pregnant Drina Sturt are provided with changes of clothes by Lady Sale. She also, grudgingly, offers a few items to an entirely ungrateful Frances Macnaghten, who makes a point of screwing up one proffered dress and placing it in a corner of their room for her two remaining cats to sleep on.

'Fiorentina was spitting,' Eleanor relates with some glee. 'The two ladies do not like each other and Fiorentina says if she catches one of those cats out at night she will personally strangle it. You know they keep getting stolen, don't you? Lady Macnaghten has twice paid a reward of 20 rupees to the same guard. I think he steals the cats, hides them for a day, and miraculously finds them again.'

Some of the old sparkle is returning to Eleanor's eyes. She sees the absurdity in our position without allowing it to drag her into despair. 'Poor Emma Eyre,' she goes on, 'Fiorentina really put her in her place the other day. She was trying to mend her dress, which has been badly torn, and wanted to borrow a needle so she asked Fiorentina. And do you know what? Fiorentina said "My dear, a General's wife deserves a degree of deference and that undoubtedly includes not being asked to give over her needles to the wife of a mere Lieutenant." Emma was livid and I am not surprised, especially as Fiorentina is having her portrait taken by Vincent Eyre.'

Eyre passes his time sketching fellow prisoners. He has some idea they will become valuable mementos when we are eventually released. Lady Sale is writing her diary and Eleanor has established a little school for the children, where she teaches reading, writing and the Scriptures. Some other ladies are trying to fashion dresses out of the yards of cloth sent up from Kabul by Akbar Khan himself, though this material was undoubtedly looted from our own stores some months ago.

The chief's wives have opened up communications with our ladies and entertain them from time to time to what, at home, I suppose we might call afternoon tea. Eleanor finds these occasions amusing because of the mutual incomprehension both of language and of habits. She says the English ladies could scarcely contain their hilarity when it became clear they were expected to drink their tea straight from the spout of a tea-pot and eat hot radishes.

Eleanor goes on, 'The chief's wives are terribly common, Eldred. They show off their breasts to keen advantage but their clothes are of the coarsest materials, inelegant and held together with pieces of chintz. They look like common night-dresses with little pieces of silver or gold tacked onto them. Some of them wear necklaces of coins strung together – altogether laughable. These are all silver except for the favourite wife, whose chains are of gold. She had a nose ornament with a few common pearls and a very flawed emerald. And their hair. Such a mess. And their hands! Painted red right up to the wrists as if they were plunged in blood – disgusting.'

Our daily diet consists of lamb, rice and chapatis doled out as fairly as possible every day by George Lawrence. Eleanor says, 'Lady Sale says the rice is rendered nauseous by the ghee butter poured over it. She says she wouldn't put it in her lamps in India. The rice gives her heartburn, but she eats it anyway.'

*****

This morning my old friend Hoosein arrives at our prison. He looks well and beams with pleasure when we embrace. He has ridden here from Kabul and says he has witnessed some sorrowful sights on the road. I ask about Wasim, Mahparah's son whom we rescued from the clutches of Yakoob Beg, the Khan of Wardak, what seems like a lifetime ago. The smile disappears from Hoosein's face. 'He died,' he says simply. 'Of a fever.'

'But he was such a strong lad,' I say.

Tears swell in his eyes. 'I did all I could, sahib. I cared for him, mopped his brow, fed him with my own hands, gave him water to drink. But he could not be saved. Ah sahib,' Hoosein goes on mournfully, 'We are all weaker than we once were. You, yourself, are but a shadow. Your eyes are ringed in dark shadows, you must weigh half of what you once did, you walk with a limp because of you injury, your beard – your beard,' he says decisively, 'Your beard must go' and he whips out a sharp shaving knife. 'Come, we will remove it now.'

As Hoosein sets to work trying to civilise me – I have no idea how I look but he assures me I resemble a savage – he fills me in on the Kabul gossip.

Hoosein has been sheltering in Kabul with other Hindus, working when he can at their business, which is the financing of commercial transactions, but he says there has been little trade recently because of the turmoil in the country. There is much debate in the bazaars over the merits of destroying the British army. Many agree the foreigners deserved it but others are fearful for the future. What if the British return seeking vengeance? This is something all Afghans understand only too well – it can take many years but eventually an Afghan will have an eye for an eye. Do the British not think the same way?

Most talk is about the fate of Shah Soojah, the King of Kabul, the man we placed on the throne in the stead of Dost Mohammed Khan. Shah Soojah is dead – murdered at the gates of the Balar Hissar by his own godson. 'They say he refused to leave the castle but the chiefs told him he must show leadership and take an army to Jalalabad to get rid of General Sale,' Hoosein says. 'The Prime Minister, Usman Khan, himself guaranteed the King's safety and eventually Shah Soojah agreed to this and came out into the city. He reached the main gates of the fortress in his best ceremonial robes to be greeted by the Prime Minister's son Aslam, his own godson, who took out a pistol and shot the King's brains out. Usman Khan has disowned Aslam and vowed never to let him set foot in his house again but, as you can imagine, there are many new candidates for the Throne.'

'Not Akbar Khan?' I ask, somewhat surprised. 'Surely he must be in charge, at least until his father returns, assuming he does.'

'No, no. They say Akbar has become too lordly. They say he does not know his place. They say there are others with greater claims to the Throne. Akbar is Vizier only at the moment and Soojah's son Fatteh Jang is King. But it can't last.'

'Why not?'

'You know, Fatteh Jang is a Durrani; Akbar is a Barakzai. The two tribes hate each other. Some people say it goes back to the time Dost Mohammed Khan raped a Barakzai's wife but there is more history to it than that. Fatteh Jang cannot trust Akbar, the man he believes was behind his own father Shah Soojah's murder and we all know Akbar plans to place his own father back on the Throne. If he doesn't take it for himself. There will be no peace in Kabul for a while. But if Akbar can throw General Sale out of Jalalabad then he will have the power to throw Fatteh Jang out of the Balar Hissar as well.'

'And they say the recent earthquakes have destroyed much of Jalalabad's defences,' I say.

*****

Life and death are our constant companions. Three of the ladies have now given birth, all to daughters. Alas only one of them has a husband who is still alive, the others having been slain. There is much commotion when one of them goes into labour and the Afghan women, whose own living conditions are little better than our own, are anxious to help. Everyone is ailing. Malaria has taken three men already and several others are languishing. The flux is a common problem and the latrines are vile. My leg injury is causing great pain – small pieces of metal and wood continue to emerge from the flesh from time to time and there is nothing to clean the wound except brandy, which is too precious to use for medicinal purposes.

Eleanor is a pale shadow, suffering not just from the privations we must all endure, but an overwhelming apprehension that the loss of our army will destroy her brother's career and bring disgrace on the whole family. I try to console her but she is probably right – with Burnes and Macnaghten dead, the responsibility has to fall on Lord Eden's shoulders. He was, of course, responsible not just for the invasion but for the penny-pinching that provoked the revolt and for the appointment of dear Elphinstone, an old family friend, as the General responsible for the Kabul garrison.

I say 'dear Elphinstone' because, despite everything, it is hard to despise him. I visit him every morning and the poor man is broken and dying. He remains polite, kind, interested in the world around him as he lies on his bed while Evans tends to his needs as best he can. Elphie was never a strong man but now he is thin and drawn, his big eyes are bulging and watery, his thin hair is pasted to his head as a result of the night-sweats he suffers, he is constantly cold even though the season is advancing now and spring is upon us.

Meanwhile Akbar Khan comes and goes, issuing orders, threats and demands amid rumours of a new army on its way from India. One day, there is one army; the next, there are two. One day, the single army has been defeated in the Khyber Pass and General Sale has surrendered Jalalabad because the city walls have been thrown down by the earthquake; the next, one of the invading armies has raised the siege at Jalalabad, beaten back the Afghans and is on its way toward Kabul.

The mood of our guards varies accordingly. They are wary, possibly frightened. One minute they threaten we will be sold into slavery at the first opportunity; the next they beg for written testimonies of good-treatment which they can present to the invading English army in exchange for their lives.

Akbar's mood swings as wildly as anyone's. On each visit, he demands a private audience and we tend to walk out into the surrounding orchards in a companionable-enough fashion. This afternoon he is in high good humour. He is Fatteh Jang's Vizier, the Prime Minister of Afghanistan and in charge of the whole army.

'This is only temporary,' he assures me, taking my arm and escorting me through trees just coming into blossom. 'Fatteh Jang knows it is only temporary, until my father returns and is once more installed in the Balar Hissar. Then,' he says with a beaming smile and an intimate squeeze of my arm, 'I will personally escort you to Peshawar and see you safely on your way back home. The only problem is my father-in-law. He says we should take advantage of our freedom to manoeuvre and exploit our hostages while we still can.'

'Exploit?' I ask. We stop in the shade of an apple tree. The day is bright and clear, the weather warm, the mountains in the distance are almost purple under this blue sky. We hear the birds chirping in the trees, full of the joys of spring, and somewhere not far off a rivulet tumbles down towards the Kabul River.

'Well, you know,' says Akbar evasively. 'I am your saviour Eldred. I am keeping you free and alive.' He smiles at me rather ingratiatingly. 'I did not mean to kill Sir William Macnaghten, you know, just to take him hostage,' he goes on. 'And I did all I could to stop the massacre of your army. You heard me order my men to spare them.'

'I heard you tell them that in Persian,' I agree. 'But I also heard you speak in Pashtun, Your Highness.'

'Your Pashtun is not good, Eldred.'

'I understand "Kill them all, show no mercy", sire.'

Akbar lets go of my arm. We stand on a rise in the orchard with a view down the valley south-westwards, where the ground descends in a mist of blossom and birdsong towards a village where smoke rises lazily towards the sky. Somewhere a dog barks and children shout.

'Of course, of course,' he says, and changes the subject. 'Now as to your accommodation, are you well provided for?'

'The ladies could do with more clothes, the men with new boots. We would like to enter into correspondence with our friends in Jalalabad. We have a great need for more medical supplies, cloth, linen, bandages, quinine, new latrines further away from our prison cells. We have seen three babies born now and there is at least one more on the way. Better food would be welcome.'

'This all costs money, Eldred.'

'As you know, Your Highness, we have very little ready money. But we can sign promissory notes on the Honourable East India Company which will be readily honoured. Assuming we survive, of course.'

Akbar laughs. 'Assuming you survive? But of course you will survive, my dear friend.' He seizes my arm again. 'You are my guests. I shall not allow my father-in-law and his brigands to take your lives, though nothing would delight them more than to slit your throats. And I shall not allow you to be sold to the Bokara slavers. Trust me, my friend, trust me.'

CHAPTER 50

Fort William, Calcutta, January 1843

Broadhurst pauses again and looks down at his desk. There is nothing there. Major General Shelton waits impatiently, tapping his switch-stick on his boot in irritation. Whistler looks over towards where I sit and our eyes meet. I think I see a moment of doubt in my foe's gaze, as if he is troubled at the way the cross-examination is progressing. I smile at him and try to look confident.

At length Broadhurst takes a step across the courtroom towards where Shelton stands in the witness box and says, slowly and carefully, 'May I be absolutely clear, Major General? In your view, the retreat itself was not a cowardly act. Is that correct?'

'It is,' Shelton snaps irritably.

'The cowardice was in opening negotiations with Akbar Khan? Correct?'

'Correct. The man was not to be trusted.'

'So in your view the late, much-lamented Sir William Macnaghten, was also guilty of cowardice in seeking a treaty with Akbar Khan.'

'Sir William had the authority to do such a thing.'

'His authority is not in doubt, sir. But was it a cowardly thing to do?'

'It was certainly not conducive to maintaining the authority and prestige of the Crown, sir.'

'But cowardly, Major General? Cowardly? This is, as you will know only too well, a serious accusation to level at any soldier or servant of Her Majesty. The worst crime of all. And yet you say entering into talks with Akbar Khan was a cowardly act?'

'I do,' says Shelton defiantly and looks at the panel of judges for support. They fail to meet his eye, each of them preoccupied in one way or another. In the public gallery there are whispers of surprise, if not outrage. I hear one lady burst into tears.

'Very well then, Major General,' says Broadhurst. I can see the sweat glistening on his forehead and imagine it running down his back, encased as he is in his thick uniform. He must be feeling even more uncomfortable than I am. But he seems somehow to dominate the courtroom, standing on the flat of his feet, his sturdy frame and strong arms making him look a little like that imperial portrait of King Henry VIII. Even his voice seems to have become deeper, more authoritative. 'Very well then. So what do you say to this, sir?' he asks and holds up what appears to be a handwritten note which he has removed from his jacket pocket and unfolded.

'What is that?' asks Shelton while the senior judge, George Clerk, leans forward and holds out a hand asking to see it.

Broadhurst hands it to Clerk but speaks to Shelton. 'You will see, sir, it is a note from the then Brigadier General Shelton to none other than his sworn enemy Akbar Khan begging – I say begging because that is the precise word used in the note – begging the Afghan for fodder for his horse. To remind you, Major General, the note, dated December 4, 1841, reads:

'To His Excellency Prince Akbar Khan. Greetings Your Majesty. In view of the parlous state of our Company stores at this juncture, may I beg your grace and favour to look kindly upon the case of my own animal, a splendid Arab stallion called Borak and permit the supply of fodder to restore him to health? I remain Your Majesty's honourable servant, John Shelton, Brigadier General.'

'It is very understandable, is it not,' Broadhurst tells the judges,

'That an officer should wish to care for the welfare of his horse? Major General Shelton's motives in corresponding with his enemy show a degree of compassion I am sure we can all admire. However, Major General, is this not the kind of cowardly act of which you have just now accused Major Pottinger?' There is a pause. Broadhurst turns to face Shelton, walks up to the witness box, and, with his face only inches from the Major General's, he says, quietly but with force, 'If Major Pottinger is a coward, sir, does this note not prove, in your own assessment, that you are a coward as well?'

There is a commotion in the public gallery. George Clerk bangs his gavel. General Lumley snorts indignation though I cannot tell if he is outraged at Shelton's actions or at the accusation of cowardice.

Shelton carefully rests his stick against the side of the box and strokes his moustache. 'Sir, no man has dared accuse me of cowardice. My military record speaks for itself. Why, even on the retreat from Kabul, I commanded the rear-guard and we…'

'Nobody doubts your bravery in combat, Major General. But you did say that anyone – even Sir William Macnaghten himself let alone Major Pottinger – who entered into negotiations with Akbar Khan was a coward. Surely, sir, you are damned by your own evidence.'

'This is outrageous,' Shelton booms, staring at his fellow generals for some support. 'A note asking for horse-fodder is not the same as a treaty with an enemy determined on humbling the British army.'

'No sir, it is not. But it is indicative. Does it not reveal that, at the time you wrote this begging letter, nobody in the British garrison at Kabul had any option but to negotiate with Prince Akbar Khan for was he not, at that time, the lord of all he surveyed?'

'He was,' says Shelton reluctantly.

'And what of Major Pottinger then, sir? Is it not the case that, of all the officers stationed in Kabul, he was a lone voice in calling for stout resistance to the Afghans? Did he not argue on several occasions that the army should fight its way out of the cantonment and find shelter behind the walls of King of Kabul's castle, the Balar Hissar?'

'He did make that argument. Several times. But he was over-ruled. Wiser heads prevailed.'

Broadhurst looks astonished. 'Wiser heads, sir? Where was the wisdom in the course of action the army took thereafter? The course of action was, as we now know, the fatal decision for the army to leave Kabul in the dead of winter and try to make its way through the passes as far as Jalalabad. Was that the view of General Elphinstone, of yourself Major General Shelton, and of the senior officers on your staff?'

'Yes, sir, it was,' says Shelton, clearly and defiantly. His small face is screwed up in anger, his one hand grips the lip of the witness box as if it were itching to strangle my attorney, his eyes stare fiercely towards the windows and out to the sunlit parade ground.

'Well then, sir, can you tell this court martial whether Major Eldred Pottinger, the man accused of cowardice for signing the treaty with Akbar Khan, can you tell us whether Major Pottinger himself concurred with this general view that retreat to Jalalabad was the only course of action open to the army?'

The court is almost silent. I can hear the steady flap of the punkawallah's rugs as they try to circulate the air. Shelton commands everyone's attention. Even the judges sit up and await his answer with grave frowns on their faces. George Clerk holds a pen, ready to note down the response. This is the moment we have been waiting for. Shelton is almost the only living witness whose testimony would carry weight in this courtroom. He can clear my name. But will he?

CHAPTER 51

Budeeabad, June 1842

Akbar Khan commands Lawrence and me to attend on him in the great hall of the castle. This is no friendly chat in an orchard, this is an official conference with the man who holds our lives in his hands.

The earth is still trembling, as it does almost every day at the moment, and rocks fall from the walls. I hear Lady Macnaghten screaming she has lost her cat.

Akbar sits on what passes for a throne, a wooden chair carved with fantastic beasts raised on some kind of dais only about six inches above the floor. Seated on carpets around him are about two dozen chiefs, some so young their beards have scarcely grown, others older, all of them weather-beaten and fearsome. Soldiers line the walls. At Akbar's shoulder stands his father-in-law, the Ghilzai chef Mahommed Shah Khan, wearing a frown of hatred as he stares threateningly at us through his piercing black eyes.

Lawrence and I are marched in by six guards. We bow low and remain standing. Akbar toys with a knife as he slouches on his throne. He holds the knife by the point, as if he would throw it across the room at one of us.

'You are causing me endless heartache, Major Pottinger, Captain Lawrence. Endless heartache. What are we to do with you? What are we to do?'

We have nothing to say.

'You know, of course, that your Major General Pollock has forced his way into our country at the head of yet another army?'

Are we expected to reply? I do not know this, though we have been hearing rumours for several days. Lawrence says, 'Has he?' with an eager curiosity which does our cause no good.

'He has, Captain, he has.' Akbar continues to hold the knife by its point and stare at its gold hilt. He tests its sharpness with his delicate fingers. He holds the point to his cheek as if he wishes to draw his own blood.

'Tell them,' says his father-in-law.

'Very well.' Akbar sits up straight and announces, 'We are marching on Jalalabad to turn back these infidel. We shall not send them back to India, we shall leave them on the field of battle just as we left your comrades. We shall meet them and we shall defeat them and we shall show them no mercy. No mercy.' There is a grumble of support from the chiefs. One or two talk about infidels and dogs.

'These earthquakes, Major, these earthquakes are given to us by Allah himself. He throws down the walls of Jalalabad. The city is at our mercy. But we shall show no mercy as your own armies showed no mercy. At Ghunzee you raped our women and slaughtered our children. And when we have done with this impertinent Pollock, we will have done with you too.'

*****

Later Akbar takes a different tack. He seeks me out and walks me towards the precarious ramparts of this fort. He wears a frown of friendly concern and again takes my arm. 'You see my dilemma, Major. My father-in-law wishes me to kill you all now. I say we must keep you alive. You are worth more to us alive.' He smiles.

'I am pleased to hear it, your majesty.'

'Do not take everything I say at face value,' he says.

'Your majesty.' I bow my head slightly in acknowledgement of his politically tricky position. I don't wish to tell him to his face that I know him for a liar.

'You must write to General Pollock, Eldred my friend. You must tell him to advance no further. Tell him I shall accept a payment of 200,000 rupees in ransom for my hostages and you will all be free to leave. Provided he also makes an annual payment to me of a further 50,000 rupees, offers a truce in this war and ensures the return of my father, Dost Mohammed Khan, the rightful King of Kabul.'

I write a long letter to Major General George Pollock at Jalalabad setting out Akbar's demands. This is read to Akbar and meets with his approval. Colin Mackenzie agrees to make the precarious journey to deliver it. I send a second, secret message telling Pollock that, in my view, paying a ransom for prisoners is improper and contrary to our long-term interests. If we are once known for buying back hostages, nobody will ever be safe. 'Ransoming prisoners for money is very objectionable,' I tell him.

*****

A week later Akbar is back and in a fury. He marches me out into the surrounding fields and holds a knife to my throat. 'You fool, you fool. You have written to Pollock telling him not to pay any ransom, haven't you?'

'How do you know that?' I bluster.

'I have spies in his army, Eldred. I know everything. I know what Pollock is planning before he knows it himself. You fool. I could have saved you. I could have saved you all.'

To my astonishment, Akbar Khan bursts into tears and falls to the ground. 'Woe to you all, Eldred. Woe and woe. I have done my best, I have tried to protect you. To keep you from harm. And how do you repay me? Secret messages, Major, secret messages. This is too much.

Too much. How am I to keep control? How am I to maintain my power when you are working against me? Do you not understand even now? Nobody else – nothing else – stands between you all and utter destruction. How can you do this to me? Am I not your good friend?'

*****

Eleanor is preoccupied. Drina Sturt has gone into labour and all the women rush round to do what they can for her. They do not want any men interfering. Eleanor kisses me lightly on the nose and says, 'Go away. Go and see the General.'

Evans sits beside Elphinstone's bed staring at the floor. The General gasps for breath. All he can manage are short sucks of air but it is a losing battle. The poor man has been more or less insensible for several days. Evans tends him devotedly and cares for his every need but the General has given up the fight. It's just as well. If he were to survive he could look forward to nothing but ignominy and disgrace. He is a decent man. He should never have been left in charge of the army of Kabul; he was never capable of the task. I look at his pale face, his thin grey hair plastered with sweat over his head, his eyes closed, his every breath filled with agony and I know easeful death is the best fate for him.

Even now the Afghans will not let him be. A delegation comes from Kabul demanding we honour various supposed debts we owe in exchange for their promises we would be allowed to leave the country unmolested. Naturally I cannot prove any individual in this delegation of merchants, charlatans and petty-chiefs was not involved in the massacre of the army but as the entire country was up in arms against us, I tell them the General is too ill to grant them an audience and suggest they apply in writing to the Honourable East India Company in Calcutta.

This does not please them. One of them takes out a knife and makes a throat-slitting gesture. I grab his arm, twist it hard until he is forced to drop the weapon and I pick it up with a smile. Our guards look on without reacting. I could kill this blue-eyed heathen here and now. But what's the point? The others would only stab me to death. I look at them, clutching their own weapons and smile. 'Gentlemen,' I say, returning the knife to my enemy, 'Kill me and you will never see any money from the Company. I offer you no guarantees but every legitimate claim on the Company, which has been truly and honestly fulfilled, will be honoured in due course. But you see how we are situated. You will have to trust the honour of the British Government, a name renowned throughout the world for its honesty, truthfulness and plain-dealing. If we have promised to pay you for your services and those services have been faithfully rendered, you can rely on us to honour our debts.'

They retreat, muttering. I cannot understand what they thought they might gain or why they have applied to us for money which we cannot pay at the moment and, in most cases, have no reason to pay as they have plainly failed to fulfil their side of the bargain. I cannot say they won't get the money because that would, indeed, jeopardise all of us. But I shall make sure the only bills we eventually pay are those for services truly rendered, and there are precious few of those.

While this fatuous audience takes place in the declining hours of a rainy evening, General Elphinstone finally dies and Alexandrina Sturt gives birth to a fatherless baby girl. Eleanor emerges from her friend's confinement to kiss me and announce the child is to be called Victoria Fiorentina.

A small crowd gathers round General Elphinstone's quarters amid murmurs of regret. His servant Elwyn Evans is weeping. 'He didn't deserve this, he didn't deserve this,' Evans keeps saying. 'He was a good man, a decent man, a fine Christian.' I see Hoosein raise one sceptical eyebrow.

Brigadier General Shelton shoves his way through the crowd, telling people irritably to get out of the way. He has been on his hookah again – he seems to spend his entire time attached to the hallucinatory pipe. But now he is all business. 'Evans, for God's sake stop that blubbing man. Get this body out of here. Get it dressed for burial. Get the women to help. Get Elphinstone out of here and then, when you are done with him, move my belongings in here man. Is that understood?'

John Logan emerges with a Bible and starts to intone: 'The beauty of Israel is slain upon thy high places: how are the mighty fallen. Tell it not in Gath, publish it not in the streets of Askelon; lest the daughters of the Philistines rejoice, lest the daughters of the uncircumcised triumph. Ye mountains of Gilboa, let there be no dew, neither let there be rain, upon you, nor fields of offerings: for there the shield of the mighty is vilely cast away, the shield of Saul, as though he had not been anointed with oil…'

Lawrence takes me to one side. 'We can't bury him here among these heathens. We must arrange for his body to be sent to Jalalabad. He must have a memorial we can protect, not some plot these savages can desecrate.'

Akbar Khan is in the great hall with his chiefs, planning, so it seems, a march on the same city. He agrees very readily to the idea. I realise, too late, that taking the body to Jalalabad will give him an opportunity to spy on the enemy.

As we are leaving, Akbar calls after us, 'Be warned, my friends. If the British advance on Kabul, I will make presents of you to my chiefs.'

*****

Lady Macnaghten demands to be sent with Elphinstone's body to Jalalabad. 'I am the Envoy's wife,' she insists, as if that somehow made all the difference.

'Come now, my dear,' says Lady Sale, 'You know your husband would have wanted you to stick by his men.'

'I know no such thing,' declares Lady Macnaghten indignantly. 'And my cats. My cats. How many more of these earthquakes until the poor things are buried alive?'

I suggest to Akbar Khan it would be easier for everyone if we were rid of Frances Macnaghten but he just smiles and shakes his head apologetically.

We all gather by the fort's eastern gate to watch Evans and a couple of others, accompanied by half a dozen of Akbar's men, depart for Jalalabad with General Elphinstone's body. I feel tired and relieved the poor man's anguish has come to an end. There was nothing left for him in this life; I hope and believe he will have better fortune in the next.

Eleanor stands by my side, takes my arm and rests her head on it. 'People will see,' I whisper.

'What does it matter now, Eldred?' As we watch the little funeral cortège stumble along the stony track away from us, I hear exhaustion and despair in her voice. 'We know Akbar means to kill us or sell us as slaves.'

It is my duty to offer hope so I say, 'Yes perhaps. But perhaps not. He could have murdered us at any time in the last six months but he has not done so. We have to ask ourselves why. It could be we are worth more to him alive than dead. He might even feel that if he preserves our little lives then he is somehow not responsible for those thousands of deaths. Or perhaps he is using us to impress his superiority on the other chiefs – while we are alive because he insists on it, we prove his power over death and life. Perhaps, I don't know. I cannot fathom the man. At any rate, we are alive and where there's life, there's hope.'

I turn to Eleanor and realise we are now alone at the fortress gate. The others have drifted off. I indicate to the guards that she and I will be taking a walk in the surrounding orchard. They nod and let us through – they know there is no escape from this remote spot.

The countryside here is at its spring best. The orchards are in blossom and we can hear the murmuring of the nearby stream. Clouds scud by overhead and the sun is warming as we pick our way through the trees, Miss Eden holding my arm as if we were a courting couple on a perambulation about Hyde Park. 'I regret, madam, my carriage and servants are not with us today,' I say.

'My dear sir, think no more of it,' she says. 'My brother's house is quite nearby. We shall repair there for tea, I think.'

'A splendid notion, my dear. Come, here we shall sit ourselves down and prepare for that essential interlude.'

'Do you take sugar, sir?'

'But of course. Do you?'

'Naturally.' Eleanor smiles and takes an imaginary sip from an imaginary china cup. 'Ah delicious,' she declares.

We continue in this vein for a while and I succeed in making her laugh again. She lies in my lap and looks at the sky. I kiss her softly on the lips. 'You are so delicate,' I say.

'Emaciated, you mean,' she says, but with a laugh in her voice and a smile on her lips.

'When we get home again…'

'Home?' she asks, 'Do you mean India or England? Or Ireland, my fine Irish friend?'

'I am not sure where I mean by home,' I say. 'I suppose home is wherever you might be for that is where my heart will reside even if my body lies elsewhere.'

The warm spring day, the isolation of this orchard, the intoxication of each other's company, the brief sense of life and hope. It is here, in this foreign field, where we grasp desperately at love.

CHAPTER 52

Tezeen, July 1842

We have our marching orders. We must be ready at first light. All the men have been searched and our weapons, a few swords, a pistol or two and several knives, have all been taken from us. Lady Sale is in a rage because they have even taken poor Captain Sturt's sword, which Drina sleeps beside every night.

Eleanor is also in a fury. She marches up to me with a look of thunder on her face. 'Sergeant Wade,' is all she can say.

'What about him?'

'They have robbed him.'

'They have robbed everybody, my love,' I say and put a tentative hand on her arm.

'They have strangled him.'

'Strangled him?' She leads me into the men's quarters, where the European hostages have been sleeping. Wade's body is stretched out on the old rug that was his bed, warm blood still flowing from his throat. I check if there is any life left in him and ask the other men gathered round, 'How do you know he was robbed?'

'Saw it,' says one truculent Londoner. 'Bastards marched him in here, asking "Where is the gold? Where is the gold?" George wouldn't say, so they stabbed him in the leg, here – look. Then he scrabbled under the rug, pulled out a little bag of coins, give it them then one of these bleedin' savages slit his throat anyway.'

'And you just watched?'

'They was armed. What could we do?'

Another body to bury tonight before we are made to leave, I think wearily. 'How did they know he had money still?' I ask.

Eleanor leads me outdoors again. 'Look,' she says.

Across the courtyard, where our guards are also preparing to depart, stands a woman in a long Afghan shawl, her face almost obscured, talking quietly with one of the soldiers. With most of her face shrouded, I do not recognise her though the skin of her hands looks European to me. I turn to Eleanor questioningly.

'Mrs Wade,' she says bitterly, spitting out the words, her face grimacing as if in pain. 'She has been fraternising with the enemy for days now, weeks probably. We have all seen it. Now it is out in the open – a traitor to her husband, to her friends, to her country, to her Queen. How could she?'

'We don't know she betrayed him,' I say. But of course we do. Mrs Wade, a young woman who was not, apparently, particularly happy in her marriage and therefore somewhat dismayed to find her husband survived the massacre as well, has thrown in her lot with the enemy. Eleanor's indignation is understandable but, if we look at things from Mrs Wade's point of view, she is at least taking a course of action to secure her survival. Which is more than can be said for the rest of us.

*****

Lady Macnaghten is in another fury. Mohammed Shah Khan has taken all her jewellery and her shawls. How she managed to keep them this long is a wonder but there is no doubt behind her apparent helplessness there is a shrewd and calculating young woman. She says they were worth 150,000 rupees and is in tears, stroking her cats for consolation.

Lady Sale has no sympathy. 'That woman is no lady,' she has been heard to say on more than one occasion. Lady Sale does have a look of grim satisfaction on her face, though, as we chat before our party is forced to leave. 'You know that bottle of nitric acid we were keeping in case you had a chance to make a rocket, Major? The Afghans have found it and taken possession of it as well as a bottle of lunar caustic we used to cauterize poor Sturt's wounds. I do hope they decide to drink it.' She chuckles grimly.

We leave before dawn. The sky is overcast but it is still warm. We are also leaving two ladies. There is a faint hope they might survive the terrible fever afflicting them if they are not moved while it is sure long rides curled and cooped up in camel panniers, going who knows where, will kill them. The child Seymour Stoker is remaining with them and is supposed to be tending to their needs. I fear this is the last we shall see of any of them.

We are being moved at Akbar Khan's orders. Rumours and stories abound. The repeated earthquakes have reduced Jalalabad to rubble; the city walls have remained intact despite the upheavals. Our army has been defeated; Akbar's army has been defeated. Our army is turning back to India; Akbar has fled for the hills. We are being moved to keep us safe; we are being moved so we can be sold to the slavers from Bokara. Nobody knows our fate, not even our guards, though they are less friendly towards us now, partly because of the murder of Sergeant Wade, partly, I fear, because they think they will soon be ordered to slaughter us all. It doesn't do to become too friendly with prisoners you are about to murder.

Mrs Wade rides behind her new husband, her arms clasped tightly around his waist. The other ladies will not look at her.

Lady Sale complains, 'We are being forced to ride like men. What have they done with our saddles?'

I have no answer, though I doubt whether side-saddles are of much value to Afghans.

We ride single file along tracks which seem scarcely to have been used for some time. We cross a cultivated valley with forts every couple of miles, some of them in a state of collapse because of the earth tremors. The landscape is disconcertingly beautiful with yellow briar-rose in bloom and asphodels in yellow, pink and greenish-brown. There is borage, red sage and blue sage. 'It is five years since I first set foot in this country,' I say to Eleanor, 'And I still don't understand how it can have so much beauty yet be so savage.'

At last we come to something resembling a real road. It seems to lead to the Huft Kotul pass, where the remnants of our army were forced to march during that terrible massacre. How different it seems on a sultry summer's evening from the dark depths of misery our army was forced to endure only a few months ago. We pass with as much care as we can over the decaying bodies of our comrades. The bodies of Major Ewart, of the 54th, and Major Scott, of the 44th, are still recognisable. We were not allowed to stop to give them a Christian burial or even say a few prayers over them, though we collectively recited 'The Lord is my shepherd...'until our guards ordered us to keep silent.

*****

I feel like the Wandering Jew, condemned to walk the earth for the rest of time. One day we are pitched in tents beside a fast-flowing river in an orchard with forget-me-nots and cranesbill, with good food to eat; the next we are stuffed into a couple of ramshackle barns with no food at all and no way of finding any.

Day after day, we are forced to move on. The weather worsens and it pours with rain. We are all riddled with lice and plagued by fleas. Our days are tiring and dispiriting but from time to time Hoosein appears as if by magic, bringing news from Kabul. It seems the temporary king, Shah Soojah's son Fatteh Jang, has fled the city leaving it in Akbar Khan's hands. According to Hoosein, Fatteh Jang has escaped through the lines of Akbar's undisciplined army and reached General Sale in Jalalabad. The General is still holding out there against Akbar's army. It seems that, despite all the earthquakes and Akbar's hopes, the city walls have not been thrown down. Worse still for our captor-in-chief, there is more talk about invasion from India. Hoosein tells me the gossip is there may be not one army but two on the march into Afghanistan to avenge the humiliation of Elphinstone's forces.

There is no doubt our guards seem nervous. Our chief jailer is one of Akbar's secretaries, Saleh Mahommed Khan. Saleh is a nervous young man, prone to taking instant decisions and then thinking better of them. He is kind to the ladies but off-hand, or downright rude, to the men. He insists we are not prisoners, merely Akbar Khan's honoured guests. I point out that honoured guests are free to come and go as they please. Honoured guests are not forced to live 25 to a room, sleep on straw or dirt, fed only occasionally and obliged to tramp from place to place in pouring rain. He smiles sorrowfully and draws up a document we are all asked to sign, saying that in his custody we have all been well-treated.

'He is worried,' Hoosein insists. 'He is afraid. He hears the stories of invading armies and the might of the English and he fears for the future. This is good news.'

Hoosein says the armies are under the command of two generals, Sir William Nott and Sir George Pollock. Pollock is in Kandahar and is said to have won a victory over the Afghans, he says, while Nott is close to Jalalabad. Akbar is going, in person, to confront him.

Hoosein is optimistic. 'Don't worry, they won't kill you all nor sell you into slavery. If the generals succeed – and I am sure they will – your captors will need you alive to preserve their own lives.'

It is true even Akbar Khan has changed yet again. We meet him a few days later. He is sitting alone on a rock, weeping. He hails us as we pass, smiles a wan smile. Perhaps stories of his defeat at Jalalabad are true. We do not know for sure but he watches us pass by without any conference or discussion. 'That man is evil,' hisses Lady Sale. 'Evil, evil, evil. If he weeps, it is not for all the lives he has taken, it is for himself.'

It turns out later it is because one of his little sons has died but this sign of weakness is heartening. Our jailer Saleh Mohammed Khan has noticed his weeping master too and I think it unnerves him even further. I can see him ask himself, as he chews his bottom lip – if his commander is in despair, what does the future hold for rebels who put an English army to the sword?

I confront Akbar. 'I am sorry about your child but you are making war on women and children so it is no surprise your God punishes you. These ladies, these babies, are being treated disgracefully. They are ill and ailing, close to death, yet they are slung into bags and dragged across stony paths hanging from camels which are themselves near to death. They are wet, filthy, tired and hungry. Is this any way to treat "honoured guests"?'

The warlord throws his hands in the air and drops them to his sides in a gesture of despair. 'I am keeping you safe, Eldred. I am your protector. You know this.'

'Your forts are a sea of mud, your food is inedible, your quarters infested and disgusting. Why can we not return to Budeeabad? Why must you drag us all over this country?'

'Eldred,' he says with a sigh, taking my left hand in his right and stroking my fingers, 'I am your protector. Fatteh Jang, the usurper Shah Soojah's son, was coming with an army of 400 men to carry you away to your deaths.'

'That I doubt,' I say, 'He has gone over to General Sale.'

'I swear this is the truth. That is why I had to move you. And you know my father-in-law would slit your throats. And while he is in Kabul and I am on my way to Jalalabad, your lives hang in the balance. I am keeping him from you. And as for the conditions, they are no worse than those my poor father and my wife must endure as your prisoner in India.'

'That, sir, is a gross lie. Dost Mohammed Khan has guards, yes, but only to protect his person. He has food, he has a palace, he has money, he has his friends and his ladies. He goes hunting most days, he lives a gilded life at our expense.'

'I will do what you wish, when I am in a position to do so. But while Mahommed Shah Khan is in Kabul he commands the very bread in my mouth. Trust me, Eldred, I am your friend, am I not?

*****

A party of slave traders newly arrived from Bokara joins us this evening. These people are not friends of the Afghans but they are here to negotiate the purchase of the prisoners. First, three of them are conducted round our party. I can see them sizing up each individual. They are particularly attracted by the children who will apparently fetch a good price in the market. The younger white women are also seen as attractive commodities. The men, especially as most of us are injured or unwell, are not considered such attractive merchandise though we would sell for 46 rupees each even when the women fetch just 22 and the children a mere ten. This does not make much business sense to me but I decide not to point out these discrepancies between price and saleability. Presumably the slavers know their business well enough and I have no wish to encourage them in their trade.

Saleh Mohammed Khan tells them they would have to purchase everybody as one job lot. He is not prepared to split up the goods into smaller batches. If he is to disobey his orders, he needs to be rid of his entire burden in one transaction so he can escape Akbar's wrath.

The ladies refuse to look at them and hide the babies as best they can. The men threaten violence while our jailers look on with indifference. If it came to a fight, I doubt if they would protect us or prevent us from taking on the slavers.

The traders withdraw without anybody coming to blows. I watch them now, squatting round a fire in the twilight, debating the pros and cons – not just the price or the health of the prisoners but whether it is in the interests of our captors to conclude a deal, hand us over to the traders and make off with their money.

After some laughing and frowning, spitting and muttering, Saleh

Mahommed Khan excuses himself and makes his way over to where George Lawrence and I are sitting against a stone wall having our likenesses drawn by Vincent Eyre. So far no-one has offered to try creating a likeness of Eyre himself, lacking the necessary skills to do so.

Saleh squats down beside me. He looks doubtful, almost afraid, certainly nervous. 'Major Pottinger sir,' he says. 'They are offering a good price on your heads.'

'Then take it, Saleh. Take it and disappear into the mountains. It is your only chance.'

'But if I do, what will become of you?'

'You know the answer to that, sir,' I say slowly, staring down into the dirt at my feet while Vincent sketches on, showing no interest in the conversation. Lawrence looks over his shoulder with a frown of concentration, watching the progress the artist is making and offering no comment. 'Samarkand. Some of us will be put to work. The children will be sold on. The ladies will become servants. Or worse. We will all be beyond rescue. You know all this. What, though, will become of you, my dear sir, if you were to take the money and run?'

'I know,' says Saleh mournfully. 'Your fate would be sealed.'

'And so would yours, sir, so would yours. If you sold us, your commander Akbar Khan would lose one of his most valuable assets, a bargaining chip for his father's life. And he would not be happy to find us gone.'

'No, he would not,' Saleh admits. 'He would find us and kill us.'

'He would,' I say matter-of-factly.

'And if the talk of invasion is true, which I believe it to be?'

'I cannot believe our British generals would be pleased to discover that you have sold your hostages into slavery – a fate worse than death. I have seen men blown apart by a cannon for less.'

'Yes,' says Saleh unhappily.

'So you are stuck with us, my friend. We are your only hope. You know this, don't you?' He nods and spits on the ground.

'I shall send them away,' he says decisively and returns to the campfire where the men engage in further debate and expostulations but Saleh remains firm in his decision.

CHAPTER 53

Ghoolghoola (City of Screams), August 1842

Lady Macnaghten screams. My immediate thought is it must be her cats again but this time she's crying about her diamonds. They have been stolen. She emerges from her tent and marches across to where our captors are camped with their own womenfolk and cries out: 'Grace Wade. Grace Wade. Come out here you filthy thief.'

Our guards are startled but soon start chuckling as Her Ladyship stumps through the mud around their tents crying out for Grace Wade. 'You thief, you thief,' she calls out.

Eleanor emerges from one of the ladies' tents, looking thin and unwell but smirking a little as she says, 'Oh dear.'

A small crowd assembles as Sergeant Wade's wife finally emerges from one of the tents, her face hidden completely, but for her eyes, by her hijab, and stands with her head on one side as if looking quizzically at the late envoy's wife. 'You little trollop,' says Lady Macnaghten. 'Betrayed your husband. Had him killed. Now you rob me of my jewellery. You filthy traitor.'

'You're just a whore yourself,' Mrs Wade yells back at her. 'Only married him for his title. Serves you right your stuff got stolen. Anyway, didn't you say it was stolen weeks ago?'

'Not my diamonds,' Lady Macnaghten screams. 'Not my diamonds, you bitch, you filthy thief.' Lady Macnaghten spits at her. She actually spits and then goes to slap the woman but her arm is seized by one of the soldiers who remonstrates vehemently in a language Lady Macnaghten does not understand. She has made no effort to learn Pashtun or Persian and cannot communicate in anything other than English. She is used to having servants and deference – she is not accustomed to being robbed with impunity by young Englishwomen, always assuming Mrs Wade is actually responsible.

'Grace Wade knows where all the money and valuables are,' says Eleanor, as if reading my thoughts. 'For once I feel sorry for Lady M.'

'But I thought she had already had her jewellery stolen,' I say.

'There is always more,' Eleanor whispers with a smile.

The soldier marches Lady Macnaghten back towards the other prisoners, still telling her to be quiet and denying anyone has stolen anything from her, only to be met by incoherent assertions of Grace Wade's guilt and treachery.

'Mind you,' Eleanor continues in a whisper, 'Mrs Wade is right about Lady M marrying the Envoy for his title. She told us one evening, "Now he's dead," she said, "I'm going to marry me a Lord. Higher and higher, that's my motto," she said. And it's true. Her first husband was only a colonel.'

Mrs Wade is screaming across the campsite at Lady Macnaghten, who is being comforted by Lady Sale and a couple of other women, while she cradles one of her cats and kisses it with great fervour.

Our plight is certainly trying and everyone is fractious. We are all riddled with mosquito bites which, if they have not reduced us to sickness, at least keep us occupied in scratching ourselves all the time, which, of course, only increases our discomfort. My leg is still not healed. I change the dressing as often as I can, and wash it when there is an opportunity, but shrapnel – small pieces of wood, mainly – continues to ooze from septic wounds.

Our captors are becoming more unpredictable. The remaining Indian servants have been stripped almost naked, searched for money, and turned away to fend for themselves as best they can in these mountainous fastnesses. I imagine many of them will not survive. Luckily Hoosein was not with us at the time. I sent the little man on a mission to Jalalabad to discover what he can about the prospects of our rescue, though as we are forced to move on almost every day, I do wonder if he will be able to find us again.

One guard, whether he is issuing idle threats or not, I cannot tell, announces the officers are to be put to death. We will be blown from field guns, starting with the most junior of us. Meanwhile Colonel Thomas Palmer, who surrendered Ghazni under Elphinstone's orders, has been dragged to our prison. The poor man was most brutally tortured with a tent-peg and a rope because he had custody of 400,000 rupees of the Company's money, which he had hidden away. We assume Mrs Wade was the informant but we can't be sure. I think one or two of the soldiers' wives would kill her if they could. I am not sure I would try to stop them.

*****

Akbar Khan arrives. He carries three wounds, to his left arm, his right thigh and across his back. He looks exhausted and in pain. Plainly he has fought a battle and lost. He is angry and dispirited which seems to make him vengeful – he orders the soldiers to torture one of the messengers who brought money and notes for Captain Colin Troup. We hear this young man's screams as his fingernails are ripped out. Akbar tells him he must pay a fine of six thousand rupees and throws him into a small cell where he will stay until a member of his family furnishes the money.

Around twilight, Akbar limps across to where Lawrence and I are talking to Captain Hugh Johnson about the rumours of invading armies. Our tormentor-in-chief scowls and cradles one arm in the other to ease the pain from one of his wounds. 'Pottinger, Major,' he says in an affable-enough tone, but with a smile which somehow manages to look concerned and threatening at the same time, 'Are my men looking after my guests?'

I do not respond and Akbar looks at the other two. 'Well gentlemen? Am I not keeping you safe? Did I not promise this?'

Lawrence laughs and replies, 'Your Highness, in our country we do not starve our guests, threaten to sell them into slavery, shift them from one tumbledown fort to another, force them to shift for themselves in cattle-sheds and goat-pens.'

Akbar laughs but it is not his humorous chuckle; it sounds both bitter and full of contempt. He frowns deeply, flings his arms wide, winces and declares, 'Your friends have marched another army into my country. What can I do but bring these foreigners to the same state as before?'

'Do I take it you have suffered a reversal, Your Highness?' I ask as gently as I can. We all want to know more. Is there a chance of rescue? I don't want to provoke him.

'We can return you to your countrymen,' Akbar admits, changing tack. 'With a number of conditions. The ladies and children, and the men, they can go. The officers must stay.'

'They can go?' exclaims Lawrence excitedly, looking to see if anyone is listening in to our conversation. 'Do you really mean it?'

'Two hundred thousand rupees,' says Akbar.

Lawrence is crestfallen. 'We do not have any money, as well you know. Your men have robbed us of all we had.'

'Two hundred thousand. To start with,' says Akbar.

'To start with?' says Johnson incredulously. 'A down-payment?'

Akbar ignores him. 'I have done so much for my countrymen. They called for an end to foreign rule. I gave it to them. I killed the envoy and destroyed his army. Now I have drawn down vengeance upon me and the mullahs, the tribes, the mosques, they desert me. Desert me.' Akbar pounds his chest as he goes on, 'I would draw their guts out and feed them to the kites.' He spits on the ground, pauses, smiles and adds, 'I do not want your money, gentlemen. I wish only for the friendship of your nation. And perhaps eight hundred thousand rupees. To reimburse me for all the expenses I have incurred on your behalf.'

'Eight hundred,' declares Johnson, ever the financial quartermaster. 'What happened to two hundred?'

'A down-payment, I said,' says Akbar. 'You know they tried to trick me into the Balar Hissar where they planned to kill me?'

'Just like they killed Shah Soojah. At your behest,' says Lawrence without much sympathy.

'Anyway, I am King of Kabul now,' says Akbar. 'King, gentlemen.'

'And what of this talk of an armistice?' Johnson asks.

Akbar spits into the dust. 'Armistice? Armistice? Never. Your generals wanted me to give up my guests and all my guns. Can you imagine? These foreigners, will they never learn?' Akbar looks at us with big, round eyes as if seeking our sympathy; as if we are on his side in the struggle with these 'foreigners'.

'Did they say anything about your father, Dost Mohammed Khan?' Johnson goes on.

'They might release him if I perform everything they demand. But I have told them the closer they get to Kabul, the further from that city my guests will go. Here we are safe. They will not venture this far into Afghanistan. Genghis Khan was the last man to conquer these lands.' Akbar laughs and points from this castle in Bamyan towards the ruins half a mile away on a rocky outcrop. 'Ghoolghoola,' he says grimly. 'You know its other name? The City of Screams. Do you know why? That is where Genghis Khan avenged the murder of his favourite grandson. Jalal-ud-din, the Sultan of Delhi, killed the grandson but Genghis couldn't bring down the castle until Jalal-ud-din's daughter betrayed him. She showed Genghis the secret passages into the city because Jalal-ud-din had murdered her beloved. Genghis's army slaughtered every man, woman and child in the city – every animal as well – even the daughter who had betrayed her father. That is why it is called the City of Screams, the pain of slaughter could be heard up and down the valley.' Akbar grins. 'That is how things are in this country. That is how things are…' His voice trails off and he stands in thought.

I watch the last of the sun disappear behind the mountains and listen to the bleating of goats and the sounds of domesticity around us. Lawrence kicks a rock gently with his boot. Johnson is consulting a pocketbook, perhaps working out how to raise 800,000 rupees. After much thought, Akbar goes on, speaking with a new vigour, 'One of your generals is threatening to reduce Kabul to ashes. We shall have to reduce him to ashes, shall we not, gentlemen?'

✦✦✦✦✦

The following morning, a sultry but warm day, as we are walking with Mrs Sturt and her new baby in the orchards outside Bamyan castle, Eleanor tells me, 'Lady Sale calls this place not Ghoolghoola but Golgotha. It's much the same – city of screams or valley of skulls. She says she is haunted by those huge Buddahs carved in the rocks down the valley. She says they are symbols of all the men who have died. I think she is beginning to flag now. After all, the poor woman is quite elderly and she has suffered as much as anybody. It is her birthday tomorrow and she says she doubts if she will live to see another one.'

'Tomorrow? What date is it?' I ask. It is difficult to keep track of time when every day slides into the next with no change other than pain or privation.

'Tomorrow is August 13.'

'Then today,' I say with a smile, 'Oh how astonishing, today, my dear, is my birthday. August 12.'

'I have been meaning to ask you, Eldred, how old are you?'

'Today I am 31 years old.'

'Congratulations, my dear Major,' says Drina Sturt with a shy smile as she soothes her baby over her shoulder. 'Many happy returns of the day.'

'I shall kiss you,' says Eleanor, as if this is the first time she has ever done such a thing. She stands on tip-toe and places a gentle kiss on my cheek.

Drina says, 'Eleanor,' and laughs. Eleanor giggles and kisses me on the lips. 'Your secret is safe with me, my dear,' says Mrs Sturt.

'Let's not keep it a secret any more, Eleanor,' I say with a burst of enthusiasm. 'You have seen me at my worst as I have you...'

'What do you mean by that?' she asks with mock-indignation.

'Why should we not be married?'

'Married? Where? Here?'

'Here.'

'When?'

'Today. To celebrate my birthday. To celebrate life.'

'Oh how lovely,' says Mrs Sturt with a smile. 'John Logan could perform the ceremony.'

'Oh I don't know, Eldred. I would not have my family's permission.'

'You are of an age, are you not my dear?' I ask, wondering now whether Eleanor is, indeed, over 21 years old. 'I know I have nothing much to offer you – nothing at all, at the moment, but my honest devotion and love – but when we are freed...'

'If we are freed,' she reminds me.

'Indeed, if we are freed. But if we are not, should you really wish to die an old maid?'

She laughs at this and considers the question for a moment before jumping up and down with delight. 'Yes, why not, yes, yes, let us be married. Do you think Dr Logan would be willing?'

'Let's ask him.'

*****

Logan asks for 24 hours' notice, to prepare, he says. Eleanor applies to Lady Sale for permission to marry, as she has been under Fiorentina's protection for the last three years. Lady Sale is reluctant, worried about what Eleanor's brother Lord Eden, the Governor-General, might say of the match. But she concludes that we could both be dead by now and may yet be slaughtered or sold into slavery. 'In the circumstances,' she says, 'Who am I to deny us all this pleasure? Of course, my dear.'

The ladies spend the evening trying to find respectable clothes to wear on the morrow. Lawrence, who is to serve as my best man, is seeking out a suitable ring for me to present to my wife. Johnson is negotiating with our guards for the purchase of some food for the wedding breakfast. Vincent Eyre is creating a makeshift altar for the service while Colin Mackenzie says he will find something to drink; he thinks the Afghans have some wine they may be prepared to sell. I ask him where the money will come from but he says that is none of my business.

When he hears of our plans, our jailer Saleh Mahommed Khan insists on attending the ceremony and promises us a dozen of his finest men to form a guard of honour for the ceremony. He sports a very smart blue frock coat which must have been obtained from a European, probably a dead Englishman, but he offers it to me to wear at the ceremony. It is velvet with gold braid with newly-polished brass buttons and appears almost new. Better still, though Saleh is a smaller man than I am, the frock coats fits me well, especially as all this privation means I have lost a great deal of weight.

Johnson has found apricots, grapes, apples, pears as well as some small fish, lamb and goat which will be cooked and served after the ceremony. Mackenzie, after lengthy negotiations, produces six bottles of locally-made white wine which, he insists, is sharp, clear and dry. This is such a luxury he, Eyre, Lawrence and I secretly agree to a private tasting to make sure that it is, as the Afghans claim, tolerable. After drinking from earthenware mugs, we conclude happily that it is – the taste of wine after all this time is intoxicating, both physically and spiritually and Eyre produces some opium which we smoke to keep the optimistic mood going a little longer.

As we are chatting, Johnson declares Saleh Mahommed Khan, our jailer, to be 'a jolly good fellow' and points out that our guards are largely made up of deserters from the deposed King's regiments. They are used to British military procedures and, indeed, they are using our drums and fifes to prove it. The noises they make are excruciating – they have never been trained and the local music is nothing like the fine tunes we make at home – but Johnson says, 'These boys are not our enemies, Eldred. Watch them tomorrow. You will find them surprisingly compliant.'

'Especially now they know we are back in the country with some real generals in charge of a proper army,' adds Mackenzie, laughing as he draws deeply on the pipe.

*****

By a happy chance, little Hoosein arrives this morning, a couple of hours before the appointed time for the ceremony. I tell him the news and he reacts with horror. 'No, no, no, you cannot marry like that,' he declares. He insists I must have a proper shave and sets about the process, chattering away all the time.

The news he brings from Kabul is that Akbar Khan has been heavily defeated in a battle near Jalalabad by Lady Sale's husband, Sir Robert. Even better, an army under Major-General George Pollock has forced the Khyber Pass and reached Sale in Jalalabad while a second army under Major-General William Nott is marching on Ghazni, the city poor Palmer gave up to the enemy without a shot being fired. 'They call them the armies of retribution,' says Hoosein with a grin, 'And all the Afghans are trying to get out of Kabul before it's too late. Every day, hundreds are on the move. But Akbar has made everyone in the city swear on the Koran they will stand by him. The mullahs demand loyalty. But the Qizilbash Persians are Shia Muslims and refuse to take the oath. In fact, I think they are happy if Akbar falls. My friends in the city are laying low – they are not Muslims and will not side with Akbar; they want the English back. But they are frightened. You never know from one day to the next who will be in charge there.'

All this Hoosein expounds as he dexterously wields his cut-throat razor. Johnston interrupts this lecture by reporting back on another conversation he has had with Saleh Mahomed Khan. Always cautious, Johnson suggests Saleh might be open to negotiation. 'I think we may be able to engineer our freedom, Eldred,' he says.

We agree to hold a conference with Saleh later in the day. But first, I point out, we have a wedding to attend.

*****

I don't know that I ever imagined what my wedding day would be like but if I ever have done, it is nothing like this. Here we are, imprisoned in a tumbledown fort overlooked by the ruins of the 'city of screams' half a mile away and watched in fascination by our guards as almost the full complement of prisoners makes the effort to appear on parade for the ceremony. Several ladies, a couple of children and three officers are all too unwell to join us, while Shelton chooses to absent himself from the ceremony declaring it to be illegal because the make-shift altar is not on consecrated ground.

Logan says that, in the eyes of God, Eyre's makeshift altar is as good a place of worship as any other and he is of the belief that it is in line with both God's and man's laws. Either way, everybody looks as respectable as they can, given that the officers no longer have wearable uniforms, the ladies are obliged to clothe themselves in the cloth we persuaded Akbar to supply a few weeks ago, and the children are filthy street urchins.

Every effort has been made to dress Eleanor in a style fitting a young bride, however. She wears a garland of flowers created by Mrs Sturt and Mrs Eyre out of wild roses, marsh marigolds and jasmine. Her hair has been shaped into short curls and she wears a simple high-waisted, off-the-shoulder dress of red and white-striped cotton which reaches almost to the ground. On her feet, to my astonishment, she wears a pair of satin slippers.

None of this makes as much of an impression on me as Eleanor's beautiful smile and the shine of delight in her brown eyes. It is a warm morning, there is no rain, the clouds drift high above us, suddenly I am at peace as my bride and I go through the ages-old ceremony of marriage. Logan delivers a little homily. He recalls the time he and I helped to bury Alexander Burnes and, without referring to more recent events, he says the love of a man for a woman offers hope for the whole of mankind and represents defiance of the Devil, the infidel and all their heathen works.

Afterwards, we sip the rare Afghan wine. It is warm and slightly bitter but Lady Sale, who has made a great effort to get off her sick-bed for the occasion, declares it the best wine she has ever tasted. Lady Macnaghten, however, says it isn't fit for her cats to drink and it is as disgusting as everything else about this vile country. I tell Eleanor she looks beautiful and smells of roses and make a short speech thanking our fellow Christians for their good-wishes and hoping we can one day hold a more appropriate celebration when we go home to India, which I hope and believe will be in the near future.

We are provided with our own private tent for the night, at a discreet distance from everybody else.

*****

Was it a foolish thing to do, get married in the middle of hostile territory with no certainty of freedom? When we are half-starved and filthy? When so many people are dead or dying? When we do not have the sanction of Eleanor's illustrious family?

We discuss it half the night – the first time we have really had a chance to talk about it. 'When you are close to death every day,' Eleanor says, in between kisses, 'It is easy to despair. But it really does make you appreciate how precious life is and how fragile it is. When I was a girl, I never thought about it. But now…'

'Now,' I say, 'Our duty is to create new life.'

CHAPTER 54

Fort William, Calcutta, January 1843

The court is so quiet I can hear the punkah fans flapping backwards and forwards. The judges are all attention, even Major General Lumley is peering at the witness box. Shelton merely gazes at Broadhurst as if he has not heard him.

'Shall I repeat the question, Brigadier-General?' he says with a hint of impatience in his voice.

'Major-General, Captain,' spits Shelton. 'And there is no need to repeat the question. You ask if Major Pottinger concurred with us that a strategic withdrawal from Kabul, under the protection of the forces of His Highness Prince Akbar Khan, was the correct response to the situation. My answer is that, to the best of my recollection, he did not concur.'

'Let me be clear, Major-General, because here we hit on the nub, the point, the very heart of the allegation against Major Eldred Pottinger, do we not? He is accused of cowardice in treating with a faithless enemy. But you are telling us now – and you are, sir, the most senior military officer and witness to these events to have survived this great ordeal – you are telling us now that, far from being a coward in the face of the enemy, Major Pottinger did not agree to signing a treaty with Akbar Khan. Is that correct?'

'He did not agree, sir. He wanted to withdraw to the Bala Hissar, the King's palace-fortress in Kabul.'

'And why did you not follow this eminently sensible strategy, sir?'

'It was dangerous folly. We would have lost many lives and most of our treasure and equipment.'

'Whereas, by retreating under the protection of your enemy Akbar Khan, you lost everything, sir, everything.'

George Clerk interjects. He taps the desk with a gavel to draw our attention and frowns. 'Mr Broadhurst, you will not be impertinent to the Major-General.'

Broadhurst bows courteously and turns to Shelton. 'A thousand pardons, Major-General Shelton, if aught I may have mis-spoken were to be construed in any way as an impertinence or a calumny.'

It is difficult to avoid the thought that my attorney is laying it on a bit thick. Clerk frowns down at him but allows him to proceed. Brigadier Wymer makes a note, I can hear his quill pen scraping on the paper because the courtroom is still unusually silent. Broadhurst has not finished yet.

'Major-General, sir. Nobody would ever doubt your personal courage.'

'I should damned well hope not,' says Shelton gruffly.

'However, would you be kind enough to explain to the court why you and the military high command in Kabul considered it wiser, safer, more in keeping with the maintenance of British honour and dignity, to flee from Kabul in the depths of winter rather than take the option of a short, concerted effort to make for the safety of a citadel which is, according to all who have seen it, one of the most secure bastions in the whole of the East Indies?'

Shelton glares at Broadhurst. His small, balding head scowls and frowns. His little eyes seem to sink further into his emaciated cheeks. His hand balls into a fist which he begins to tap on the ledge of the witness box in agitation.

Whistler, the prosecutor, rises slowly to his feet and drawls out in his upper class voice with its taint of Yorkshire, 'My lords, must we endure any more of Captain Broadhurst 's insubordination? It is not for Major-General Shelton to justify his decisions, or the decisions of other senior officers and generals, to this hearing. Mr Shelton is not the one on trial here for cowardice. The Major-General's personal courage is well-known. His stout rearguard action on behalf of the entire army before the Khoord Kabul deserves to be celebrated for its bravery, resolution and honour.'

Three of the judges, including Mr Clerk, nod in agreement and I begin to worry Broadhurst has gone too far. Shelton, however, speaks up anyway. 'Thank you Mr Whistler,' he says, 'But I do not need any support. The fact is, Mr Broadhurst, you were not in Kabul at the time. You were not aware of our weak military position. You did not know our dispositions. Even now, sir, you are not in full possession of the facts. We made decisions as we saw fit at the time and required Major Pottinger only to play his part in putting them into effect. It was not his business to question our orders and we did not tolerate it when he did.'

'You did not tolerate it when Major Pottinger questioned your orders?'

'No, Mr Broadhurst, we most certainly did not.'

'Thank you, Major-General, for your testimony. I have no further questions, sir.'

Broadhurst sits down. Mr Clerk thanks Shelton and tells him he may step down. Surely now they will agree I am no coward. I feel a strange euphoria sweep over me, it is a physical surge of relief which makes me almost grateful to the dreadful man for his arrogance and stupidity. At least he told the truth. He could have contrived to bring about my utter disgrace; instead, he exonerates me. I trust the newspapermen, as well as the judges, have absorbed the importance of Shelton's words.

I look over my shoulder at the people in the public gallery and see Lady Sale arrive. I did not know she was in Calcutta let alone that she would deign to present herself at these proceedings. I haven't seen her for some months and, while she has regained much of the weight she lost during our ordeal, she now looks like an old lady rather than the attractive woman so beloved by the men serving under her husband. With her are Alexandrina Sturt and Mrs Eyre. I suppose they have been told today is the day when I am being called to give evidence in my defence.

CHAPTER 55

Ghoolghoola (City of Screams), August 1842

We are woken at dawn by the roar of cannon. The whole valley, from the City of Screams through the town of Bameen and on, down past the vast ancient monuments to the Buddha, the sound of gunfire echoes and reverberates. It is as if the ground itself is shaking. From high in the mountains we see the flash of explosions.

At the same time fat drops of water start to rain down on us from the dark clouds in the sky.

After a first surge of optimism that our army is here to rescue us, we realise it is only the start of another thunderstorm we've had lately. But I am up and dressed, ready for action and Eleanor has drowsily followed me out of the tent. Several others have been invigorated by a brief burst of hope and we rush for the shelter of the cattle shed where we usually gather to eat whatever Saleh Mahommed Khan has procured for us. Today there is only one servant supervising a cauldron from which tea is dispensed in dirty cups but Saleh himself is in attendance. I thank him for the use of his blue frock coat and rush through the rain back to our tent to retrieve it.

By the time I return, Saleh is deep in conversation with Captain Johnson. They are laughing but they seem to be discussing money. Johnson, who has become quite friendly with Saleh and declares him to be a fine, jolly fellow, says, 'Eldred, we need a conference with my friend here and Captain Lawrence. Somewhere private.'

Lawrence emerges from the men's quarters looking as if he has not slept – but I suppose none of us is looking well-kempt at the moment, what with the fleas, the mosquitos, the lack of food, water and sanitation. Every morning Lawrence does his rounds, as if he were a doctor, to see who is too sick to leave their bed today. But before he has a chance, Johnson brings him over to where Eleanor, dressed in a long Afghan coat to keep the rain off, and I are standing sipping cups of tea and thanking various well-wishers.

'Eldred, George,' says Johnson, 'Saleh has news for us.' Our jailer stands beside him and grins happily as Johnson goes on, 'It seems certain General Nott is advancing on Kabul and he has undoubtedly taken Ghunzee, where poor Palmer was tortured and robbed. The rumour among Afghans is that Nott has not simply dispersed the defending army there but his army has killed every man, woman and child in the place. At the same time, it seems Akbar Khan is nowhere to be found, rumoured to be in Kohistan. He has apparently fled before the advance of General Pollock and General Sale from Jalalabad.'

Lawrence smacks the palm of his hand with his fist. 'At last!' he declares and turns to announce the good news when Johnson pulls him back.

'No, George, no. Not yet. Saleh has a problem.' Johnson looks at our jailer.

Saleh pulls a piece of paper from inside his cloak. 'I have orders from Akbar Khan,' he says, 'See.' He offers us the paper but carries on, 'You are all to be sent to Uzbekistan. And those who cannot travel are to be put to death.'

'We will never return,' says Captain Lawrence.

'No,' I agree. 'Sold into slavery.'

'The good Saleh, whose men were once in the service of Shah Soojah, does not want to obey his order,' says Johnson with a smile.

Saleh talks rapidly, he is excited, 'You are all most honourable gentlemen and ladies and it has been a burden and a pleasure to have you as our guests. Not our prisoners, our guests. I have done my best to make your stay as comfortable as the circumstances allow.' He looks at us for a reaction; we smile and nod. 'Gentlemen I have no wish to remain in the service of Akbar Khan or his father-in-law. I wish to put myself and my men at your service instead.'

He pauses. There has to be a 'but'. And there is.

'But there is the question of necessities. There is the question of the men's pay. There is the question of compensation. There is the question of the future.'

'So many questions,' I say, ironically. 'Perhaps we should discuss them more closely.'

'We already have discussed them,' says Johnson, ever the practical man.

'And?'

'Saleh will turn himself, his men and this castle over to us. But for a price – a payment of 20,000 rupees, a monthly pension of 1,000 more plus the command of a regiment in the service of Britain.'

I have argued strongly that our Government should not pay for the release of hostages as it would set a dangerous precedent and leave every European in the East Indies at the mercy of kidnappers. But perhaps there is a distinction to be drawn between the Government buying our freedom and our buying it for ourselves. I'm not sure, in the long run, there is any difference so Johnson, Lawrence and I retire into an outhouse where, to the sound of rain beating down and dripping into the building, we debate the case. And whatever point of principle may be involved, we are all agreed the desire for freedom is overwhelming. And despite the success of our armies, we have no certainty they will be swift to come to our aid – if Saleh pursues his orders promptly, we might be long gone before a rescue party can be sent for us. We are so close to being released and yet, still, so far from it.

There is also the question of where we could get the money from. And in any case we cannot promise Saleh a position in the army.

'He might overlook that,' says Johnson. 'They are now frightened the army will slaughter everyone who stands in their way. Saleh wants to save his own skin. He will negotiate.'

'We cannot issue bills on the Company for this,' I say. 'It would contrary to everything we stand for.'

'But we could all subscribe towards the 20,000 and promise the monthly payments for his lifetime,' says Johnson. 'I think if we asked our fellow captives for a contribution, according to rank and means, we would easily find the sum.'

'Would he accept a promise of money?' I ask, 'Because we certainly don't have any ready money lying around.'

'If we swear on the Holy Bible, apparently,' says Johnson, 'He will be content. He says he has seen us at our Church services and knows we are pious, God-fearing folk who would not act contrary to the will of our God.'

We agree to consult our fellow prisoners but meet with some resistance. Shelton says we are simply making matters worse and our friend Akbar Khan may turn against us; Palmer says he has already been tortured into handing over 400,000 rupees and if we go ahead with this nonsensical plan he wants it on record that he dissented.

Lady Sale imperiously dismisses the idea when we consult the ladies. 'How can you assume one lady is worth more, or less, than another?' she asks. 'And where is this money to come from? The Government in India will not pay it. From our own pockets? Poppycock.'

Lady Macnaghten is even less impressed, complaining that her contribution is greater than any of the others because of her rank.

Neither of these ladies is very well. Lady Macnaghten has spent the last five days in bed with a fever; Lady Sale is also incapacitated. Mrs Sturt and my own Eleanor talk them both round in the end but Lady Sale is still grumbling.

By lunch-time it is all settled. Dr Logan holds out a Bible and Lawrence, Johnson and I each take an oath pledging to furnish Saleh Mahommed Khan with twenty thousand rupees and one thousand rupees a month for life and promising to pay over the money at the earliest practical opportunity. We sign a pledge 'in the presence of God and Jesus Christ' and, in front of his men, Saleh hands his sword over to me, invites me to inspect his troops and declares to them all they are now under the orders of the British.

Those officers and men who are fit enough take up arms and we divide the Afghans into three small troops, each with its own British commander. The rain has stopped, the sun comes out through the clouds and reveals a big blue sky while the Afghans, who were once taught a little drill under one of our Sergeant Majors, march up and down across the parade ground playing the fifes and drums they may once have been issued with or may have stolen at some point in the last few months from the dead bodies of our comrades. I try not to think about it as I order Saleh to take a dozen men to dismiss the Chief of Bameen and find a loyal replacement.

We decide the town must supply us with money and over the next two days the local merchants are surprisingly willing to demonstrate their loyalty by handing over taxes as well as new clothes for the ladies. Eleanor and Drina Sturt stitch together a makeshift Union Jack which we fly from the castle flagpole and I issue a proclamation declaring the whole valley is now under British control and all administrative issues will henceforward be dealt with by me or my representatives.

One by one the local chiefs come to our court where I sit on a high chair, made to look like a throne, and issue a proclamation in the name of Queen Victoria demanding they state their subservience to the British Crown. To our delighted astonishment, this reappearance of imperial authority seems to be working, at least in our valley which is more or less cut off from the outside world.

We post guards from among the Afghan troops, though commanded by British officers, and the ladies are invited to take tea with the wives of Saleh and the other chiefs. Eleanor returns grimacing, complaining, 'All we had to drink was water – poured out of a teapot.'

My wife laughs and I kiss her lightly on the forehead.

CHAPTER 56

Fort William, Calcutta, January 1843

The weather is close, the afternoon somnolent. Broadhurst says this won't take long, he will quickly run through the charges, I will deny them and then he will leave it to Whistler to do his worst. I am looking forward to this. I am keyed up and angry, full of anticipation and eager to get the ordeal over with.

The courtroom is packed. Hoosein has arrived with his wife and two of his children and is forced to stand at the back with the other Indians. Lady Sale is seated in state beside Mrs Eyre and Mrs Sturt. It is kind of these ladies to attend. I am grateful for their support though Lady Sale scowls at everyone and scarcely acknowledges me when I smile at her.

The judges are arrayed in front of us looking bored. This court martial has gone on too long already, they seem to be thinking. Perhaps they have already reached their verdicts. Is there anything I can do to sway them in my favour or, if they are already inclined to acquit me, is there any pitfall I must avoid that might make them change their minds? Of course, I cannot tell but the very thought sends a shiver of fear down my back while at the same time I become clammy with sweat inside my dress uniform which is, in any case, not designed for these climes.

I take the oath, give my name, rank and regiment and then Broadhurst gets straight to the point. He looks at me with a serious frown, as if warning me with his expression what is at stake here – my honour, my profession, my reputation, my whole world.

'Major Pottinger, am I right in thinking the sword you have surrendered and which now lies on this table here was awarded to you by Her Majesty Queen Victoria for your bravery in her service?'

'It was not awarded by Her Majesty in person, sir, but yes sir, I was given that honour.'

'That was after the siege of Herat, was it not, when you stoutly led the defence of the city against the Russians and the Persians?'

'It was, sir.'

'Well then, Major Pottinger, what do you say in answer to the charges of cowardice which are the subject of this hearing?'

'They are shameful and humiliating. And I do not believe any of the actions I have taken over the last two years have been cowardly in any way. I have always held in the forefront of my mind, even in the most extreme circumstances, the knowledge that I was acting on behalf of Her Majesty, her government, the Governor-General and the honour of our great nation, sir.'

'And yet you signed the peace treaty with Akbar Khan which led to the destruction of our army.'

'I did, sir.'

'Why was that?'

'I had no choice. As the senior political officer it was my duty to negotiate with our enemy. As an officer in the Indian Army, it was my duty to obey the orders of my senior commanders. I therefore had no option but to carry out their wishes.'

'Yet you disagreed with this course of action.'

'I did, sir.'

'So why did you not refuse to sign the treaty?'

'I did my utmost to persuade General Elphinstone, Brigadier General Shelton and the other senior officers that a better course of action would be to withdraw to the Kabul castle, the Balar Hissar, rather than retreat to India in midwinter with only vague promises to reassure us. But they were adamant my proposal – a proposal, I should add, which was supported by most of the more junior officers – was impracticable. Short of leading a mutiny, I had no choice but to follow the directions of my superior officers.'

'Thank you, Major. I think that clears up that matter. Now let us turn to the other accusations.' Broadhurst turns to the judges with a smile and says, 'I will take them all together to save the court the hardship of dealing with each charge item by item if I may. Now, Major Pottinger, you are accused of misusing funds drawn on the Honourable East India Company. It is certainly the case you signed a great many promissory notes and bills during your time in Kabul after the death of Sir William Macnaghten and during your months in captivity, is it not?'

'It is, sir.'

'Can you explain to the court what right you had to do such a thing and why your expenditure of the Company's money was so lavish, if not profligate?'

'As before, Captain Broadhurst, when I was required to assume the responsibilities of Sir William, they included the need to make payments for food and other necessities. The prices rose day by day for fewer and fewer provisions and our treasury had been raided and destroyed. We had very little real cash. We traded on the Company's good name because we had no choice.'

'We, Major? It is you who are accused of misusing the money.'

'My fellow officers were frequently aware of these transactions and often demanded further payments to various Afghans for food or by way of bribes for one thing or another. Captain Johnson, who was responsible for the finances in Kabul, concurred with all my actions. And when it came to payments for our safe passage out of the country, I was clear in my own mind that none of these bills would be paid unless and until the army arrived in Jalalabad or even in Peshawar unmolested. As this did not occur, the money should never be paid and the bills should be repudiated. I have tried, on several occasions, to go through these bills with Company officers to establish which were for genuine services rendered and should in all honour be paid in full, or in part, and which must in all honour be repudiated.'

'But the Company prefers to put you on trial for misuse of public funds, Major?'

'So it would seem.'

'Thank you, Major, that is all.'

I haven't really studied Captain Whistler properly until now. He is a small, not very muscular man wearing a lawyer's grey wig and a lawyer's gown. I assume he has some qualifications to justify this display of judicial one-upmanship. He wears long whiskers and glasses, which he whips off from time to time, though when he does so he squints painfully, suggesting he is woefully short-sighted. I hear the county of Yorkshire in his voice but it has been glossed over by a more respectable London accent. Rather like my own somewhat Anglicised Ulster brogue, I suppose.

He squints now as he stands and pauses for a moment, looking at me. I try not to stare back with excessive hostility. The man is just doing his job, I tell myself, but it is difficult not to loathe him. He turns and picks up a piece of paper, replaces his spectacles, peruses it for a long time and eventually declares, 'Major Pottinger, Captain Broadhurst has glossed over the specific charges against you. May I remind you exactly what they are? There are in fact not one but two charges of cowardice: surrendering Charikar; signing a treaty with Akbar Khan; there is a charge of conduct disgraceful to the character of an officer in seeking the protection of Akbar Khan;   and no fewer than four charges of misusing Company money, first in Herat in '37 and '38; abandoning Company money in Charikar; misusing Company money in Kabul between December '41 and January last year; and finally the same offence during your time as a guest of Akbar Khan. Your advocate seeks to gloss over the specifics but if I may I shall take each of these charges one at a time.'

By now, Whistler is bouncing around in his usual over-excited manner. My natural instinct is to deliver him a knock-out blow but I know I must try to stay calm. It was one of Broadhurst's repeated demands, so I say nothing while Whistler pauses, apparently waiting for me to speak.

'Well, Major?'

'I am sorry, Captain Whistler, I did not realise you had asked me a question.'

There is a little giggle at the back of the court, which clearly irritates my adversary. 'Then let me ask you a question, Major. Why did you abandon your position in Charikar leading to the destruction of our forces there, and why did you abandon the Company's treasure?'

'We were over-run, sir. We had no choice but to retreat. I had repeatedly called for reinforcements to protect our position and they were not forthcoming. I still believe that, had we seen the cavalry we were hoping for, the situation in Charikar could have been remedied and it is possible the entire Afghan disaster might have been averted.'

'Oh so you consider your tactical wisdom superior to that of your elders and betters, do you sir?'

'That is not what I said.'

'It is what you implied, sir.'

'Well, we shall never know now,' I say, wishing to avoid a confrontation.

'That is certainly true. So you say you were over-run and had no choice but to flee the city? Is that not an admission of cowardice? Why did you not stay and fight?'

'To the death?'

'To the death if necessary.'

'Because, sir, I considered it in the interests of all concerned – the men under my command, the Company and the reputation of our nation – to avoid complete capitulation if at all possible.'

'And yet that is what you achieved in Charikar,' says Whistler with a smirk.

'It is true, to my infinite regret, that the withdrawal was a disaster and many, many lives were lost.'

Broadhurst stands up and appeals to the judges. 'Your honours, it is well-known that Major Pottinger risked his own life several times in Charikar and on the retreat from the city and that he was personally responsible for saving the life of Lieutenant John Houghton.'

Clerk looks at his fellow judges when he says, 'Do we doubt the personal courage of Major Pottinger, gentlemen?'

'This is surely what this hearing is all about, sir,' says Broadhurst with more animation than I would have given him credit for. 'If you gentlemen do not doubt his personal courage then I fail to see how he can be found guilty of cowardice. Military mistakes were undoubtedly made during our possession of Afghanistan by many senior figures. I do not cast any blame but I do say, gentlemen, that if the defendant's personal courage is not in doubt then – even if he were guilty of making mistaken decisions for the best of reasons – he cannot, he must not, be branded a coward.'

Clerk frowns and runs a hand across a perplexed forehead. 'Thank you, Captain Broadhurst, but these comments are better left to your closing speech, do you not think?'

'As Your Lordship pleases,' he says, resuming his seat and looking across at Whistler, who is waiting to take up his cross-examination again.

There is a sly grin on his face, as if he has won a point. He says to me, 'Saving the life of one officer, sir, may be a sign of courage of a sort, I accept. However, the destruction of an army of 750 Gurkhas as well as 200 women and children scarcely compares with one small act of heroism. Major Pottinger?'

I sigh as I listen to this. 'Mr Whistler,' I say, slowly and carefully, 'There is, after all, some truth in the accusation that my decision led to the destruction of this force. A destruction I shall regret to my dying day. However, by the time we came to abandon Charikar, the force was already heavily depleted, the camp-followers were abandoning us and turning to the enemy, we were besieged by what Lieutenant Houghton reckoned were 20,000 Afghans, we had no food, no water, two elderly cannons and no cavalry. We could, I admit, have stayed on and awaited our own destruction but I considered the alternative, of trying to escape the enemy's clutches, to be a preferable and viable alternative. It is true our plans for the retreat were thwarted by the enemy. And if taking a calculated decision to withdraw means my decision was cowardly, sir, then I plead guilty to cowardice. I do not regard it as cowardly. However, if this Court Martial thinks otherwise then, of course, I will have no option but to submit to its judgment. I still believe the decision was the right one in the circumstances and that it gave us all – us all, sir, the remaining force, not just Lieutenant Houghton and me – a better chance of survival than sitting in a ruined fort awaiting complete destruction.'

There is silence in the court.

Have I just admitted to cowardice? I cannot tell. I think I have given an honest account of the situation and it is for the court to judge whether my decision was cowardly. I have agonised over it myself many times and still do not see what other action I could have taken.

Broadhurst will not catch my eye. Major-General Lumley looks out of the window, as if to disassociate himself from what I have said; George Clerk is busily writing notes; the other judges sit with their heads bowed over their court documents. Have I signed my own death warrant?

During this pause, Whistler rifles among the papers on his desk, extracts what looks to be a letter, studies it carefully for a moment, and resumes. 'If I may change the subject for a moment, Your Honours, I have here a letter which casts the defendant's reputation for integrity and honourable behaviour in a new light. This letter claims, and perhaps, Major Pottinger, you are in a position to help this Court Martial with a simple question, this letter claims,' he pauses, grins, bounces on the balls of his feet, waves the paper in the air, 'This letter, sir, claims that during your captivity under Akbar Khan you debauched a young woman. And not just any young woman, sir, but the sister of Lord Eden, our late Governor-General of India. Is that true, Major?'

My indignation knows no bounds. I bellow, 'That, sir, is a lie, a calumny. How dare you? I should call you out for that, sir.'

There is an animated buzz around the courtroom. People are whispering and even laughing, exclaiming in fascination or outrage. Clerk bangs his gavel and calls for order. Eventually something like silence falls and Mr Clerk says in a quiet but menacing voice, 'Mr Whistler, I do not know the meaning of this but I do suggest you tread very carefully if you are proposing to traduce the reputation of a young woman of birth and position who has, as we are all too well aware, suffered the privations of incarceration at the hands of the Afghan savages.'

Whistler is taken aback at this. 'Your Lordship,' he says, at his most fawning, 'I am merely seeking to demonstrate to the court the true character of the defendant on trial before you. Far from being the 'hero of Herat' as he was once called, he is in reality both the coward of Kabul and a cad, a bounder, a rake, a debaucher of young ladies and, if he can stoop so low, of what else, sir, is he not capable?'

My fists are clenched. My teeth grind in impotent fury. I have not hated any man, not Akbar Khan or his vile father-in-law Mahommed Shah Khan, not even Shelton himself, as much as I loathe and detest Captain Whistler at this moment. It is all I can do not to yell and curse him. Broadhurst crosses the courtroom and places an arm on mine, whispering, 'Keep calm, Eldred, keep calm.'

Mr Clerk says, 'Captain Whistler, if you feel it is necessary to impugn the integrity of a noblewoman and cast aspersions on her character then you must proceed but I warn you, sir, that you are treading on very dangerous ground here and we fail to see how this line of inquiry promotes your cause.'

'Thank you, Your Lordship,' says Whistler, 'But perhaps Major Pottinger can clear up this little matter and allow us all to move on. Major?'

I am hot with sweat and indignation. I dig my right thumbnail into the forefinger of my left hand in the hope that the pain it causes will help me to avoid losing my temper. I say as quietly and evenly as I can, 'You are mistaken, sir, in believing that I have behaved in any way dishonourably. I do not know the source of your information, Captain, but if you were to make any inquiry at all before presenting this calumny before the court, you would know that I have the honour of calling Miss Eleanor Eden my wife. We were lawfully married by the Rev Dr John Logan in the presence of many Christian witnesses in an honourable ceremony at Bamyan on August 13 last year. It is true that Miss Eden – Mrs Pottinger, I should say – did not have the permission of her brother, the Noble Lord, though as she is of age that was not a necessity. However, she did have the permission of her guardian and friend, Lady Fiorentina Sale, who is in this courtroom today and can vouch for these facts if you feel it necessary to pursue this line of inquiry any further.'

Before Whistler can respond, Major General Lumley frowns and in a severe voice asks the prosecutor, 'Can you explain the meaning of this approach, Captain? I fail to see how this affects Major Pottinger's actions in Afghanistan in any way? We are surely prepared to accept his marriage was lawful and, far from debauching the lady in question, if anything it is your accusation which has sullied a young woman's spotless reputation.'

Whistler is chastened. 'I apologise both to the court and to Mrs Pottinger, gentlemen, if I have made unwonted accusations or inadvertently sullied the good lady's reputation.'

He is retreating and as he prepares his next line of attack I think about that letter he flourished. I think I know who wrote it and it isn't Brigadier General Shelton. I think it comes from Sir Richmond Shakespeare, a Captain in General Pollock's army.

CHAPTER 57

Ghoolghoola (City of Screams), September 1842

No sooner have we established some sort of makeshift administration in our secluded valley than Hoosein arrives to break up the party. It is hard to tell whether his information is true or not but he declares he has been told by several sources in Kabul that Akbar Khan has not fled the country but is heading out here to regain control of his hostages because we can still serve as a valuable bargaining chip in his negotiations with the invading army. Hoosein, who has ridden almost non-stop to deliver this news, and is filthy and exhausted, seems seriously worried. He says he has also heard that the two generals have no orders to secure our release. 'Their orders are to cause havoc and retreat again as fast as possible,' he says, a dark frown across his forehead. 'General Pollock and General Nott more worried about which one gets to Kabul first than they are about your fate, sahib,' he says.

'But surely rescuing the women – Lady Macnaghten and Lady Sale at least – would be important wouldn't it?' I say as we sit in a corner of the courtyard beside an open fire drinking cups of the tea Hoosein has brought with him from his friends in Kabul.

It is early evening. The muezzin calls the Mohammedans to evening prayers as the sun descends rapidly behind the black mountains and shadows rush across our valley, plunging us into darkness but for the brands which Saleh's men have lit. Hoosein says, 'We must move to Kabul as soon as possible. You are still not safe. Akbar could descend at any moment, or his allies and friends – of which he still has a few.'

'The locals are very friendly,' I say, 'We have fortified the site, purchased what weapons are to be had, and Saleh's men have sworn oaths of loyalty.'

'Maybe they have and maybe they haven't,' says Hoosein enigmatically. 'You can never tell with these people.'

'Yesterday they threw the Mullah of Kabul off his horse and threatened to kill him,' I say, laughing at the recollection. 'The Mullah and his entourage were running away but Saleh's men blamed him for the rebellion. They said he had encouraged the revolt and now he was fleeing from the result, leaving his followers at the mercy of the British.'

'What happened to him?'

'Saleh let him go in the end. But I did have to laugh at the way they treated this great prelate. Of course the locals are Hazara Shias and the Mullah is a Sunni so there's not much love lost there.'

'The Mullahs may be running away now but they will never give up,' says Hoosein. 'The Shias may hate the Sunnis but they all hate foreigners even more than they hate each other. Hindus, Sikhs, Christians – everyone.'

I know he is right and when, during the night, we are kept awake by rumours that an unfriendly party of about 100 cavalry are in the vicinity – we are forced to spend hours on the castle walls awaiting an attack which never comes – it is clear we must take steps to ensure our safety. Staying here, two hundred miles away from Kabul, will guarantee neither our rescue nor our security. If our armies will not come to us, we must go to them.

*****

Two days later we are on the march. We have bought horses locally, at ridiculous prices, paid for with the local taxes we have levied, and we have acquired further weapons. Some of our own men refuse to carry guns or swords. They are so disheartened they would prefer to stay where we are than summon the strength for yet another march through hostile territory towards an unknown fate. I tell them they can stay here and trust to the mercy of God, but we will leave them no weapons or provisions. Reluctantly, they change their tune.

Saleh's men make a show of military discipline, with their fifes and drums emitting a tuneless, rhythmless cacophony as they shoulder arms and try to march in step. The ladies are reduced to travelling in the usual bags slung over camels though Eleanor insists on riding by my side on a pony which is too small even for her. She, Lady Sale and Drina Sturt have all demanded their own jezzail rifles. Eleanor says it is to 'humiliate those feeble creatures who call themselves British soldiers if they see mere women are prepared to shoulder the burden'.

The locals crowd the roadside as we depart. They are friendly and wish us well. Is this because they are genuinely well-disposed towards us or because they know our invading armies are not far away and have wrought revenge on the towns and villages which were involved in the massacre of Elphinstone's army? I cannot be sure but suspect the latter. Johnson insists these people are our friends but George Lawrence is among the many who will not trust any of them under any circumstances.

Hoosein, who has procured a fine Arab from somewhere, rides at my side with a worried frown on his face, muttering that 'these people will smile today and slit your throat tonight'.

Eleanor, on the other hand, insists they are not universally untrustworthy. 'Some of the women have been kind to us,' she says, 'And the soldiers are comical not just because of their silly show of discipline but because they are truly friendly. They say, "If you hadn't come here as our enemies, you would certainly be our friends" and when you thank them for some small service, they are always quoting the Prophet by saying, "Kindness is a mark of faith: and whoever hath not kindness hath not faith".'

It is a beautiful, sunny morning with high clouds slipping across a bright blue sky. There is a taste of autumn in the air but the day is hot without being stifling and cool enough to make this a very pleasant ride. Or it would be if we were not worried that at every twist and turn in the route we might meet Akbar Khan and his henchmen determined to take us back into captivity or murder us where we stand. We are still three or four days away from safety and, though we have sent messages to the Generals, we have no certainty they have even received them, let alone sent a detachment to our rescue. After so long, the fear that freedom may be snatched from our grasp at the last moment is enough to dispirit many of us, especially those suffering from various maladies and injuries as well as lack of nourishment – which is, in fact, all of us.

There are almost 200 in all. Over the months, prisoners have been added to our number, like Colonel Palmer and others from Ghunzee. A quick head-count shows that as well as Saleh's troop, we have a dozen ladies with 22 children in all, 37 officers and 51 men. That includes Mrs Wade, though whether she will stay on here in the guise of an Afghan wife once we are at liberty is a matter for some speculation.

Mackenzie and three others have been sent on ahead to scout out the ground and from time to time one of them rides back in a state of anxiety because horsemen have been spotted. These are all false alarms so far but every scare gives rise to more speculation that Akbar Khan is coming to get us.

*****

We make camp in the valley before the Kaloo Pass and, after scratching together some rice and lamb for supper, Eleanor takes my arm and we wander away from the others into the twilit countryside. It has been a warm day and heat lingers, giving rise to a sweet scent of cut hay in the fields, where recently-harvested stooks stand like sentries. The sun casts long shadows across the wide valley, which is green and fertile, with a small river of clear water running through it. The air is filled with swooping swallows and the rolling landscape, despite the mountains in the near distance, reminds me of Ireland. 'No, it's more like Kent,' says Eleanor, who has never been to Ireland.

She puts an arm in mine and we wander slowly across a cut field, feeling the first chill of night. Eleanor shivers. 'I am tired, Eldred,' she says. 'And I want to go home.'

'Home? To Kent?'

'I want to see my sisters again. And spend nights in clean sheets with normal weather and good food and country rides. I want to see England again.' Suddenly she is crying and I look at her in the descending gloom. Her face is worn and thin, her eyes are blurred with tears, her lips are pursed, her clothes are little more than rags while her feet are shod with a dead soldier's boots.

'I am sure we shall be safe now,' I say, as reassuringly as I can. But I know that isn't really what she is worrying about. I think she would prefer to be in England without me than in India at my side. 'I shall have to resign my commission,' I say, hoping she will at least agree that is a good idea but she doesn't reply.

I go on, 'I should have a good lot of back-pay stored up. We can go wherever we want. Kent, Belfast, London – you decide.' I smile and hold her face between my hands, try to kiss her lips and though she lets me it is clear her heart's not in it.

'My brother,' she says at last.

'What about him?'

'He may not approve of what we have done.'

'It's too late to worry about that now, isn't it?'

'My allowance,' she says. 'My allowance comes from him. I have to see him, talk to him.'

'Without me?'

'It would be easier,' she says with a sigh.

I step back and contemplate the young woman I am married to. She is looking intently at me now. She is not sure how I will react; I am not sure how to react. She wants to make her peace with Lord Eden but as for going home, surely that is not necessary unless she wants us to part. 'My dear Eleanor,' I say with a formality which I hope will conceal my confusion, 'You need only visit Simla to explain the situation to your brother and I have no doubt he will be delighted to see you again. You won't have to sail home to do that. We can review things at our leisure when – if, if, if – we escape this terrible place.'

She steps towards me, puts a hand on my arm and looks up with something like alarm. 'You haven't heard, have you?'

'Heard what?'

'My brother has been sent home. They've replaced him with a Conservative, Lord Ellenborough. The Whigs are out; Robert Peel is in and they are blaming poor George for everything.'

'How do you know all this?'

'Hoosein. He told me. He said he thought I ought to know. He told me this morning.'

It is dark now and we turn back towards the camp, where half a dozen fires are now burning, betraying our position to any enemy in the vicinity. I worry we should extinguish them all, though we have posted guards all around, but at the same time I am trying to make sense of what Eleanor is telling me. Her brother, the Governor-General, who ordered the invasion of Afghanistan in the first place, has been sent home and been replaced by Lord Ellenborough, someone unknown to me. 'Are you saying you need to go home to seek your brother's approval?'

'Well, I can't just abandon George and my sisters, can I, Eldred? You see that, don't you?'

I am not sure what to say.

*****

We strike camp early and we are heading towards the top of the pass – which is, mercifully, wider and not as steep as many – when two of Mackenzie's men come galloping towards us warning they have spotted an army some distance away. They are swiftly followed by Mackenzie himself who says, 'I am sorry, Eldred, but I think we have visitors.'

I call a halt and immediately insist every man – even those who are desperately unwell – takes up arms and gets into position to fight off these raiders, whoever they may be. Some of the ladies, too, insist on taking rifles and positioning themselves in readiness for an attack. Eleanor, Mrs Eyre and Mrs Sturt say they will form up around a rock, with the other ladies in the party as support. Lady Sale, who is scarcely able to stand now because she is so feverish, is propped up and given a rifle. The children are told to issue ammunition and run around from man to man handing out bullets. Saleh says, 'We are ready to die for you, sahib. We will show our loyalty to your Queen' and orders his men to take position at the top of the pass but remain just out of sight of the enemy.

Some of the men are reluctant to cooperate, including Brigadier General Shelton. He trots over to me and says, 'I told you this act of defiance against Akbar Khan was a mistake. I told you he would not tolerate it. I told you he was our friend and our only hope.' With that he trots towards where the ailing Colonel Palmer sits with the baggage, dismounts, finds his hookah pipe and starts to smoke.

Those men on horseback are turned into a makeshift cavalry. We wait behind Saleh's men and our own infantry for a proper sight of the enemy but after half an hour of frustration I trot to the brow of the hill where I see, in the distance, the dust rising as a cavalry troop makes its way towards us, but only about half a mile away rides a single horseman in what looks extraordinarily like a British uniform. I call Lawrence and Mackenzie forward and, squinting across the rocky mountain, we become more and more sure the man whose horse is cantering in our direction is not brown-skinned but is dressed in a British officer's uniform with a crimson jacket and gold epaulettes.

Is this our liberty? Are we to be freed? Our excitement becomes infectious as we call back to our companions that we think the force heading towards us is friendly. But everyone is still suspicious until it becomes very clear the approaching horseman is, indeed, one of our very own.

He arrives to a cheer from our party, dismounts, bows deeply to the ladies, and says, 'Richmond Shakespeare, at your service.' He is immediately surrounded and everyone fires questions at him at the same time, asking if it is really true, if the army at his back is our own and whether we are truly free at last. I look for Eleanor and she is among the ladies greeting this saviour, a broad smile on her face and – I cannot help but notice – a look of admiration at the tall, fit, smart young officer with his neatly-trimmed moustache who has ridden to our rescue.

I stand back and listen to the chatter a while. Shelton, however, rises from his makeshift seat among the baggage, relinquishes his hookah and stalks over to where Shakespeare is still surrounded by people and demands they part before him. 'Make way there, make way,' he says as he pushes aside men and women until he stands before Shakespeare and everyone falls silent. 'You sir, who are you sir? It is customary for an emissary to present himself to the most senior officer, is it not? And yet you have seen fit to ignore this common courtesy and make no effort to appraise yourself of the situation or go through the proper formalities. For your information, sir, I am Brigadier General John Shelton and it should have been to me, and to me alone, that you reported.'

Shakespeare grins. He doesn't care for Shelton's formalities. Yet he straightens up, salutes and declares, 'Captain Sir Richmond Shakespeare, sir, sent on the command of Major General Pollock to secure the release of you and your fellow prisoners and to escort you back in safety to the city of Kabul, which I am pleased to declare has now fallen to our army. General Pollock presents his compliments and begs to inquire whether the Brigadier General and his fellow former prisoners would care to accompany us at their earliest convenience.'

Shelton grunts in disapproval, salutes half-heartedly, says, 'Carry on' and turns away.

*****

We march for Kabul the following day. Our scouts report at least two bands of rebels in the vicinity but with Shakespeare's 600 cavalry, and in reasonably good weather, well-supplied and heading for safety, we don't feel excessively vulnerable. Even so, it is still a relief when a messenger meets us, sent up by General Sale himself, announcing he is proceeding at the head of the Third Dragoons and is only hours away from us. Perhaps that's why the rebels have restrained themselves – for once, the boot is on the other foot.

Shakespeare is very liberal with his charm and light heartedness. He tells Lady Sale her husband has been struck by a spent ball, which travelled through his tunic but did no lasting damage. He says General Sale has been made a Knight Grand Cross of the Order of the Bath for his victory at Jalalabad. He tells Lady Macnaghten her husband is deeply mourned and how the tragic news of his death was received with outrage not just in Calcutta but in London. And he seems to spend an inordinate amount of time describing to Eleanor and the younger ladies the triumphs and travails of 'the army of retribution'.

It seems both General Pollock and General Nott have reached Kabul, which has been subjugated. Their men are in a fury from advancing on the city over the skulls and ruined bodies of their dead comrades. The generals' orders are to lay waste the country and show no mercy. 'Some of the faces have been preserved in ice all this time,' says Shakespeare. 'They call on us for revenge.' Nobody disagrees though I do tell Shakespeare I am worried our vengeance will be so indiscriminate it will hurt our few faithful friends as well as our undoubted enemies. 'My dear Major,' he says, 'When you have hauled a gun carriage for five miles over the skeletons of your countrymen, you will not feel much like discriminating between one Afghan and another.'

Soon we come face to face with General Sale himself, flags flying and the pennants on his men's lances fluttering in the breeze. The old man waves his salutes and slips from his saddle as he sees daughter running towards him. The officers and men of his party follow suit and there is a general rejoicing as we hostages believe we are finally secure in our freedom.

Sale's camp is only a few miles away and he leads us back. For the first time in all our months of captivity, Lady Sale is so overwhelmed with emotion she cannot speak. Her daughter, Drina Sturt, is less restrained and tears roll down her face as she introduces her son, born in captivity after his brave father's death, to the grandfather he has never met. Eleanor is equally tearful and all of us are overcome by strong emotions. It is as if the tension and fear we have been living with all this time is suddenly released like a dam collapsing and pouring water into the arid valley below. George Lawrence and Vincent Eyre march arm in arm smiling and waving as we enter Sale's camp. I try to martial the men into some sort of respectable military unit so we can put up a decent show but it is difficult to do when the men of the 13th are cheering and clapping and firing guns into the air, offering us food and drink while the Captain of the Guns, Tom Backhouse, is firing a royal salute from his mountain train.

Eleanor whispers, 'Food, quiet, safety, a good night's sleep, a wash, clean clothes... Oh what bliss, what heaven.'

CHAPTER 58

Fort William, Calcutta, January 1843

This morning there is a chap outside the court-house declaring to the gentlemen of the press that they really do not understand anything. This turns out to be Lieutenant Henry Crawford of the third Bombay Native Infantry, who was imprisoned when Palmer surrendered Ghazni. Crawford has buttonholed the man from The Times of London and will not let him go before he's had his say.

'It was a pleasant sort of life to lead, never being certain of life for 24 hours together. I think a little similar experience would do some of the newspaper editors a great deal of good and render them not quite so prone to lavish their criticisms on the conduct of unfortunates like ourselves; they sit under their punkahs, drink gin, and write leading articles laying down the law and talking as familiarly on military matters as maids do of puppy dogs. You and your like are the self-selected, self-constituted judges of mankind,' he declares.

We are back today so I can finish giving my evidence and we can get this thing over and done with. Broadhurst says it's going well. More or less talking to himself, as we march into court, he is muttering, 'Whistler did himself no good introducing Eleanor into the proceedings and some of the officers on the bench are sympathetic to us, especially Brigadier Wymer. And you can tell Harry Smith doesn't think much of

Whistler – jumped-up little twerp, I'm sure that's what he's thinking. Lumley looks a bit more stern and unforgiving; I can't make out Monteath at all, though as he was at Jalalabad too he must understand how chaotic it all was out there. It's Clerk who matters most and he sits there looking inscrutable. I wonder if he is under orders from Ellenborough to secure a conviction…'

That's a nasty thought to be handed just as I am about to return to the witness box. This is clearly some sort of show trial – they obviously want scapegoats – someone must take the blame and most of the real culprits are dead. Could Ellenborough, who has consistently refused to meet me and still denies me the pay I am owed, could this great man have ordered George Clerk to bring in a guilty verdict whatever the evidence? And would Clerk, a pen-pushing civil servant with a career to build, be the sort to do his master's bidding? My stomach churns in apprehension as the judges return to court and Whistler takes up the cudgels again.

'Major Pottinger, let us turn to the question of money if we may. You assumed the responsibilities of the Envoy upon his lamentable murder, did you not?'

'I did.'

'And you began issuing bills of exchange, payable at a number of British treasuries throughout northern India, did you not?'

'I did, payable when and if the army returned safely to Peshawar and not before.'

'Are you aware of how much these bills came to? In total?'

'I am not, sir, though I believe it is in the region of nine or ten lakhs of rupees.'

'Nine or ten lakhs, Major? Will you accept that it was actually 13 lakhs or one million, three hundred thousand Company rupees you promised to pay to our enemies? And do you accept that these notes have changed hands many times since you issued them and that the banking firms in the North of India are refusing to honour these notes?'

'Sir, these notes were only payable if the army was given safe passage. It wasn't, so they should not be paid.'

'Yes, Major, but do you not realise these notes change hands and ultimately depend on the honour of the British East India Company for their conversion into hard currency? Are you not aware that any failure to honour these promises undermines the Company's entire trading position throughout Hindustan?'

'I am not responsible for the uses to which these bills have been put, sir. My responsibility was to try, by whatever means had available, to purchase the safety of our army. I failed and so the notes are worthless.'

'Worthless to Major Eldred Pottinger, perhaps,' persists Whistler. 'But not to the bearers.'

This is tedious. I feel my temper rising. 'Then they should have tried harder to secure our safe passage back to India, shouldn't they?' I say.

'Perhaps,' Whistler says, 'Perhaps. Nevertheless, the unauthorised issuance of so many bills of exchange has succeeded in undermining the Company's relations with all the bankers in Northern India. Because the Company will not turn them into cash, three banks have so far collapsed and the Company's reputation for financial integrity has been severely undermined. Do you accept personal responsibility for this, Major?'

'No, sir, I do not. I am sorry if these bills have caused such difficulties but, as this courtroom has heard before, some bills should be paid and others should not. Most of the 13 lakhs you refer to now were to be paid if we achieved a safe passage home. We did not. They should not be paid. And any middleman who purchased them and has now lost his money deserves his ruination – to lose money is not the same, sir, let me remind you, as to lose a life let alone to lose 15,000 lives.'

Major General Lumley stirs. He raises a hand to restrain Whistler from his next question and says, 'But you are alive though thousands are dead?'

'Yes, sir, by the grace of God I am, sir.'

'And what quality does Eldred Pottinger possess that preserves his life while those about him are dying?'

'Good fortune, sir. Nothing more than great good fortune.'

'Not cowardice then, sir?'

'Cowardice? Sir, I recognise this is not the first time I have heard that hated word in reference to my name but every time it has the same effect. Incredulity. Disbelief. The rage of a soldier whose every action has been in furtherance of the interest of Her Majesty, the East India Company, his comrades and his fellow men. I am no coward, sir. I am no coward...'

I find I am thumping the rail of the witness box with my fist. George Clerk says mildly, 'That will do, Major Pottinger' turns to Whistler and asks with a heavy sigh, 'Mr Whistler, how much more of this accountancy must we to endure?'

'Not much more, sir. I feel we have established that Major Pottinger did, indeed, issue these bills with the serious consequences I have mentioned. I have just one further question and then we are done. Major Pottinger, who authorised you to sign these bills of exchange?'

This is a trap, of course. I look at Broadhurst who just leans back in his chair and smiles reassuringly. I look at General Lumley and he raises his eyebrows, as if to say, 'Go on then, man, answer the question'. I look to the back of the courtroom at the spectators and notice the journalists waiting, pens poised, for an answer.

'Who authorised me to sign these bills?' I start cautiously.

'Yes, sir; who, sir?'

'Well, Sir William Macnaghten had the right to sign them.'

'But Sir William was dead.'

'He was. I was required to assume his responsibilities. Required by the Commander in Kabul, General Elphinstone. So the answer is the General authorised me to make these payments.'

'The General? Did he give you such authority in writing, sir?'

'He did not.'

'Did he specifically say to you, "Pottinger, you must pay money to our enemies"?'

'He did not. Though he was aware of what was going on and at no point did he suggest we should not attempt to pay for a safe passage back to Hindustan.'

'Yet, despite having no written authority to make any payments and in the full knowledge you were promising vast sums of money to the Company's enemies, you went ahead and signed these bills in any case?'

'I did, sir.'

*****

I am dismissed from the witness box. Mr Clerk looks at Whistler and says, 'In summary, then?' and Whistler is on to his closing argument almost before I can resume my seat beside Broadhurst, who pats me on the leg reassuringly.

Whistler, his Northern accent becoming quite pronounced as he becomes more and more excited during his speech, reminds the judges of the charges. 'It is clear from his own admission that Major Pottinger abandoned Charikar and doing so left hundreds to their fate. An act of cowardice by any definition of the word.

'He admits also that he entered into a treaty with the enemy – another plain act of cowardice. Major Pottinger's argument that he had no choice in the matter does not withstand scrutiny. He was at liberty to refuse to treat with the enemy and yet he went out of his way, expending vast sums of money in the process, to secure a cowardly flight from Kabul in the middle of winter, jeopardising the entire army.

'He further admits he deserted that army in its hour of need and surrendered to the enemy rather than fight on which, by any reasonable definition, is conduct disgraceful to the character of an officer, as the charge says.

'As for the misuse of Company money, Major Pottinger admits he spent hundreds of thousands of rupees trying to buy off the enemy – without success, I might add – without any authorisation. He abandoned Company treasure to the enemy in his flight from Charikar and at no point did the defendant make or keep proper accounts of these payments, to the utter confusion of the Company clerks.

'The facts, my lords, are simple. The terrible tragedy in Afghanistan – one of the most humiliating passages of arms in the entire history of Great Britain – was precipitated and hastened to its end by the way this man connived with the enemy to save his own life and sacrificed the lives of so many thousands of his comrades. If any one person is to blame for all this, it is the man once known as the Hero of Herat and now, rightly, christened the Coward of Kabul. Gentlemen, there can only be one set of verdicts in this case – Major Eldred Pottinger is guilty of misusing Company funds, he is guilty of disgraceful conduct in an officer and, above all this, he is guilty on three separate occasions of utter cowardice.'

Whistler sweeps to his conclusion in a volley of words and flamboyantly resumes his seat while gasps and chatter fill the courtroom. I know I have been expecting this but even so, to hear such accusations expressed with such vehemence in public is shameful whatever the outcome of this court martial. And, again, I am consumed in self-doubt – were my actions cowardly? Was I trying to save my own skin? Am I guilty? Do good intentions count for nothing?

Broadhurst takes his time before slowly rising to his feet, adjusting his uniform to brush away the creases in his trousers. He looks at me, then at the judges, whose grave faces are full of frowns as they absorb Whistler's accusations.

'Gentlemen,' he says at last, 'Captain Whistler would have you believe a brave and honourable man – a man of great reputation, well known for his true and trustworthy nature – has turned into a cringing, snivelling wretch prepared to take any step, no matter how perilous to his friends, in order to save his own skin. Sirs, nothing – nothing – could be further from the truth. Eldred Pottinger acted as I hope and pray we would all act in similar circumstances. He was courageous, noble, self-sacrificing and obedient to his superior officers. Rather than heaping blame and contumely on this sterling fellow, this court should be holding him aloft as an example of stoicism, resourcefulness and resolution unparalleled in the history of the great British East India Company.

'Eldred Pottinger is no coward. His actions at Charikar were based on reasonable and sound judgment. He organised a retreat from that city, yes, but knowing that to remain would mean the entire force was wiped out. He believed withdrawal gave the men he found under his command – and remember, sirs, that the command fell to him only because the original commander was already dead – a better chance of regrouping and taking the fight to the enemy than remaining under siege, to be massacred, would have done. The outcome was not what anybody would have hoped for but Major Pottinger cannot be blamed for the consequences of his decision. Sometimes the best decisions, taken for the best of reasons, do not result in the best of outcomes. This is one such example.

'As for signing a treaty with Akbar Khan, we have heard from Major General Shelton himself. Major Pottinger argued strenuously in favour of more positive military action but was over-ruled by his superiors on several occasions. What is any obedient officer to do in such circumstances? He can make his case but when his superiors overrule him and order him to carry out their instructions, he must do his duty. That is army discipline. The army would not survive for long if the orders of Generals and Brigadiers were ignored or countermanded by junior officers. It is every man's job to carry out his instructions to the best of his ability – and that is exactly what Major Pottinger did. If the treaty with Akbar Khan was a cowardly act, the cowardice was not on the part of the man ordered to negotiate that treaty but with others.

'As for falling into the hands of Akbar Khan during the retreat from Kabul, while we could plead Major Pottinger was by no means the only officer to submit to such a fate, he did so again under orders from General Elphinstone, to protect the ladies of the party and to provide liaison between the rebel leader and our retreating regiments. He had no choice but to become a captive. His was not conduct disgraceful to the character of an officer, as the charge claims. He was carrying out an order and, even if he were not, his presence among the hostages ensured their survival for many long months of deprivation and terror. Without Major Pottinger it is doubtful if the prisoners would have lived to tell their tale. Sirs, his courage is without parallel.

'As for the charges relating to money, you have heard already how easily they can be rebutted. Major Pottinger was obliged to offer bribes to various Afghans in the vain hope they would abide by their word and provide the army with a secure escort through the passes all the way to Peshawar. If you accept that retreat was inevitable – something, as you know, which Major Pottinger does not accept – but if you believe retreat was inevitable, it is not unreasonable to try to secure safe passage by paying Afghans to provide an armed escort or to call off their raiding parties.

'Please note, gentlemen, that most of these promissory notes and bills of exchange were only payable on the safe arrival of the army in Hindustan. That did not occur, therefore the money is not payable. And Major Pottinger has made repeated offers to the Company to identify those few bills which should be honoured and those many others which should be repudiated. All his offers have been rejected.

'Why should this be? Why should the Honourable Company have turned its back on this loyal servant? For the same reason, gentlemen, that he finds himself hauled before this Court Martial and subjected to these wounding accusations. The truth is the Government in London needs someone to blame for the whole Afghan disaster. And Major Pottinger has the misfortune to be its chosen scapegoat.

'Gentlemen, Major Pottinger is not to blame for the invasion or for its consequences. His conduct throughout this ordeal has been exemplary and I urge this court to do its duty, as Major Pottinger has done his duty throughout, and clear his traduced name and reputation once and for all. Thank you.'

Broadhurst seems carried away by his own vehemence in my defence. His voice is loaded with emotion and spittle sprays from his mouth as his voice rises to this conclusion. When he is done, he seems almost light-headed and has to place a hand on the desk in front of him to steady his large frame. He turns to look at me and smiles, almost apologetically, before returning to his seat.

I have no idea whether his rhetoric will work but I am pleased with this forceful defence of my good name. I shake his hand, a little awkwardly as we sit side by side, and the courtroom is again filled with talk. George Clerk looks at his fellow judges who nod in unspoken agreement before he announces, 'We will now withdraw to consider this case.'

We all stand as my judges file out in silence to decide my fate.

CHAPTER 59

Kabul, September 1842

'These people stink. They never wash. Their food is filthy, their manners are worse. The men hold hands in the street – disgusting. I must go, Eldred. I must go home and see my sisters and my brother. Richmond says he will escort me to Bombay.'

'Richmond?'

'Shakespeare,' Eleanor says, all big eyes and innocence, 'Sir Richmond Shakespeare.'

'Since when have you and Sir Richmond been so intimate?'

'Oh Eldred but you have been so busy, reporting to the Generals and writing reports and attending conferences. We ladies are to leave at the earliest opportunity and Lady Macnaghten has demanded Sir Richmond leads our escort. She says he is a brave and handsome soldier.'

'She does, does she?'

Eleanor places her hand on my arm and looks up into my eyes. Hers are glistening with tears. 'Sir Richmond likes cats,' she says with a wan smile.

'And will you return?' I ask.

'Of course I will. You are my husband and I love you. We have been through so much together.'

'And the dashing Sir Richmond?'

'He is not the Hero of Herat,' she says.

*****

Saleh Mahommed Khan is treated as an honoured guest, given clothes and his own tents. His servants and men are welcomed into our camp on the Kabul racecourse but he is told he will not be given any command in the British army. He will receive his money, which the Company has agreed to pay, and his pension. And he is given the opportunity to withdraw with us to India rather than remain in the country once we have gone again – for the Generals have no intention of staying here a day longer than necessary and there is no plan to resume our occupation of Kabul. Saleh says he will stay in Kabul and offer his services to the new King, Prince Shahpur, a younger son of Shah Soojah, even though nobody seriously expects his occupation of the throne to last many weeks after we have gone. Fatteh Jang, Soojah's eldest son, has resigned the Throne in favour of Prince Shahpur and decided he and his entourage of wives, servants, relatives and hangers-on – all 500 of them – will accompany the army into exile in India. It is certainly the safer option with Akbar Khan still somewhere around and doubtless champing at the bit to return once we are out of the way.

I explain this to Saleh but he says he cannot imagine living anywhere else and he knows his countrymen well; they are not to be governed by anybody and, if the new King is overthrown, he will return home to his own castle as he believes he will be able to live there in peace. 'Nothing will ever unite us,' he says with a sigh, 'But our hatred of foreigners. Yet this is where I live and where I shall remain.' I wish God's blessings on his house but I fear for his future.

We all attend a christening organised by Lady Sale, who seems to have recovered from her prison fever and is bustling about quite as if nothing serious has befallen her. Her grand-daughter and three other children born in captivity are all admitted to the Church of England by Dr Logan, while the Generals and most of the officers in Kabul gather for the celebration. 'The ladies and the children look lovely,' says George Lawrence as we toast the day in Champagne carried over the Hindu Kush with our invasion force.

There are only two questions on everybody's lips: What reprisals should the army inflict and when should it retreat?

It seems the Generals are agreed. Sale will take a substantial part of the army and march back through the Khyber Pass at the earliest opportunity with most of the hostages, long before the weather starts to deteriorate. The main body is to follow within weeks. But first there is talk of scorched earth. 'We must give these savages a lesson they will never forget,' says General Nott. 'A lesson they will never, ever forget.'

As the service finishes and the ladies retire towards their tents, one of them spies Grace Wade skulking among Saleh Mahommed Khan's troops, who are cooking over a large camp fire. Lady Macnaghten abandons the dignified gait of a churchgoer and marches as swiftly as her skirts will carry her towards the fire crying, 'Grace Wade, Grace Wade. Come here you thief, you murderer.'

Several other women scurry after her while the rest of us wait to see what will happen.

Grace Wade, whose husband George helped me bury Sturt as the army was being massacred and who was later murdered, marches towards Lady Macnaghten, trying ineffectually to roll up the sleeves of her Afghan clothes while the best part of her face is covered by some kind of shawl. 'You bitch,' she screams, as Lady Macnaghten grabs onto the shawl and pulls it from her head.

By now half a dozen soldiers' wives have joined the redoubtable Lady Macnaghten. One of them reveals she is carrying a knife and orders her companions to hold down Mrs Wade. She then proceeds to hack off her victim's hair amid much screaming and abuse on all sides. The Afghans in Saleh Mahommed Khan's contingent stand back and watch as Grace Wade is abused as a traitor, whore, thief and murderer, her hair is shorn from her head and her clothes torn from her body.

Nobody intervenes to defend her though by now half the camp

seems to be watching the spectacle. Lady Macnaghten retreats from the scene sooner than the rest, leaving Grace Wade to the mercies of the others.

Eventually she is kicked, thrown and pushed back toward the Afghans, one of whom finally walks over to her and drapes her nakedness in a cloak.

'She got what she deserved,' says Drina Sturt, kissing her baby's head tenderly. 'If you ask me she deserves to be hanged.'

*****

The ladies depart the next day with General Sale. It will be a difficult journey with no certainty they will get through. But the area has been subjugated and Sale is an experienced and reliable commander. Eleanor and I, who have spent little time together since our wedding night, are rather cool with each other.

'Shall you write?' I ask.

'Of course I shall,' she says with a laugh. 'Eldred, you must have faith in me as I have faith in you.'

'And your special friend?'

'Drina Sturt?'

'No, Richmond Shakeshaft.'

'Oh Eldred, don't be silly,' she giggles. 'We shall be re-united soon enough, I promise. You are my husband, you must trust me.'

She stands on tip-toe and gently kisses my lips. She carries with her the scent of roses, the scent I first noticed so long ago in Simla when I first saw her carrying cuttings in her arms. How is it the scent still lingers? I feel tears sting my eyes. 'I shall miss you, my dear,' I say. I never trust anybody who tells me to trust them.

'I shall miss you too, my Hero of Herat.' She strokes my cheek with a gloved hand.

It takes three hours for Sale's army to depart from Kabul but at least this time there are no hostile Afghans to dog them every step of the way. How it will be in the treacherous passes we cannot tell but the weather is fine and the party is in good spirits.

*****

I am asked by Pollock to join four divisions setting out in search of Akbar Khan. Pollock seems to think I will enjoy the chance of exacting revenge on our tormentors though, in truth, I have had more than enough of this whole business of slaughter.

We don't go far. About 30 miles from Kabul we reach the town of Istalif, which is really only a collection of houses on a hillside, surrounded by a fertile valley of orchards beside a clear stream. Burnes used to say it was one of the jewels of Afghanistan. I stand eating very sweet plums straight off the tree a few hundred yards away from the houses as our soldiers set light to them, slaughtering men, women and children with swords and bayonets, pillaging what they can lay their hands on and destroying everything they cannot carry away. I see one European seizes a small child by the arm and throws her over a wall, dashing her brains out on the rocks below as her mother screams. It is nauseating but it is no worse than the Afghans did to us and we must maintain British prestige to teach these heathens we are not to be treated so lightly in future. And we must impress this on our own people in India – we cannot afford to lose our reputation for power and success because, once lost, who can tell what misfortunes may follow? Even so, the sight of women and children being so badly treated is distressing. The same fate has been bestowed on the rebel town of Charikar as well and I cannot but feel a sense of triumph that the massacre of our garrison there is being avenged.

A cry goes up. They have discovered 500 of our Indian sepoys kept prisoner in cellars under some of the larger houses. These poor wretches are led blinking into the sunlight, chained, nearly naked and starved almost to death – they must have been there for weeks. It seems the Kabul chiefs have moved all their most valuable possessions here in the hope of escaping the wrath of our army but when they abandoned Istalif as well they left behind what they couldn't carry – including these men.

These captives now round up about 150 of the local Afghans and throw them into a building which they set alight. Those who try to escape are shot, the rest are burned alive. The men play dice to divide up the women among themselves. Some are just raped; others are raped and then put to death.

I am sickened by this cruelty. It makes us as bad as our enemy. It besmirches the reputation of our nation. It is disgusting and yet the Generals seem happy to wreak as much havoc and cruelty as possible while many of the Indians in the army are fired up with religious fervour against the Muslims.

*****

There is no sign of Akbar, of course. The wily Prince will be far away by now, biding his time, waiting either for our departure or the arrival of another devastating Afghan winter. We cannot afford to delay many days in our search and hurry back to Kabul firing every dwelling we come across on the way and putting to the sword any Afghan foolish enough to show his face.

General Pollock orders the destruction of every house in the street where Alexander Burnes was murdered. Any local who complains or protests is instantly killed but most of them know better than to challenge this new, fearsome version of the British army – so uncompromising and so unlike the force which previously occupied the city.

Four days before we leave, Pollock takes a walk through the city's market. It is quiet now, almost deserted but for a few people selling vegetables and one stall hawking rare birds. 'So this is where they displayed the head and limbs of Sir William Macnaghten is it?' he asks me as I lead him up and down the deserted streets.

'They say this marketplace is the most beautiful building in Afghanistan – some say in the whole of Asia,' I tell him. 'It was built in the reign of the Mughal emperor Shah Jahan, who built the Taj Mahal, almost 200 years ago and is the centre of commerce for thousands of miles around.'

'It must be destroyed,' the General says and turns one of his officers, 'Go on man, get dynamite. I want to leave this place a heap of rubble.'

'But, General,' I say, 'We are reducing ourselves to the level of our enemy.'

'Pottinger, I should have thought you, of all people, would realise the necessity of giving these people a lesson they will never forget. A lesson they will never ever forget.'

The next day the Kabul bazaar is torn down as house after house is set on fire and the new Mosque, built to celebrate the destruction of Elphinstone's army, is itself demolished. To our eternal shame, the troops are allowed to rampage through the city bringing terror and death wherever they go. Kabul is almost devoid of Afghans, so it is our Hindu and Quizilbash friends who bear the brunt of this brutality.

As their homes are looted and their people murdered, Hoosein protests, 'These are the people who took me in, who gave me shelter, who nursed poor Wasim through his illness. These people lent us money and gave us food. These people are my friends. Save them, Sahib, save them.' Hoosein is weeping uncontrollably as we watch from the racecourse, outside town, while flames and smoke engulf old Kabul. Shots of rifle and cannon are heard, the screaming of women and the cries of men carry across to us on the breeze.

'This is worse, this is worse,' Hoosein keeps saying. 'This is worse. Terrible, terrible. Betrayal. Cruelty. Oh Sahib, the injustice, the injustice.'

The destruction goes on for two whole days until there is nothing left to destroy. The fires continue to burn, the wooden houses smoulder and spring back into flame, a smoke pall hangs over the area, dogs howl, occasionally a wail of despair is heard in the night.

*****

The first snow of winter arrives on October 10 and the Generals issue orders for the immediate evacuation of Afghanistan.

We are going home but not before General Pollock has tried to shore up the rule of the new King of Kabul, Prince Shahpur. His brother Fatteh Jang knows it's useless and intends to accompany the army into exile but Shahpur is determined to brave it out. Pollock calls in the local chieftains, those who are still in the area, and makes them swear on the Koran to remain loyal to Shahpur but everyone except that deluded young man and Pollock himself knows these oaths will last as long as it takes Akbar Khan to re-emerge from the Hindu Kush and claim the throne in his own name or, at the very least, in the name of his father, Dost Mohammed Khan.

The next two months are hard going. The retreat is not trouble-free. The Ghilzais snipe, harass and raid whenever they think they can get away with it. Every day, men die at their hands. But we give as good as we get and this seems to deter at least some of them. The army does not meet any serious challenge as we withdraw through the Khoord Kabul and on through the other passes to Jalalabad, where we demolish the fortress, and back towards Hindustan through the Khyber Pass itself. Not before we reach Peshawar in early December can we be sure we have reached safety. Here we catch up with General Sale's advance guard and I am greeted when we ride into camp by Lady Sale and most of the others who spent so long as hostages in that fearful country.

'Major,' she says, 'I fear your wife has already left here for Bombay. I have a letter for you as well as other correspondence which has been piling up for months.' Then she calls on everyone to be quiet for a moment and goes on, 'Major Pottinger, it is my pleasure on behalf of your fellow former prisoners to express our warmest feelings of gratitude and admiration for your exertions in eliciting our release from prison in Afghanistan. The chief praise is due to you binding Saleh

Mahommed Khan firmly to our interests and of perfecting the whole plan successfully. The cheerfulness and determination with which you entered on the difficult task imposed on you must ever be gratefully remembered by us and in token of our esteem and regard we beg your acceptance of a piece of plate which will be forwarded to you as soon as it is completed.'

Her little speech is followed by a hearty round of applause and my friends break into song, 'For he's a jolly good fellow.'

*****

Letters from home. Handling them makes me tremble with delight, as if normal life really is returning at last.

Much has changed. My father and step-mother have moved from Belfast to Jersey. It seems my father's business interests have failed and he has been reduced to a state of bankruptcy. Yet at the same time he has been writing to the papers saying I should be awarded a knighthood for my services in Herat. Eliza, my step-mother, sends a cutting from The London Times in which my father argues that if Alexander Burnes deserves to become a baronet then so does Eldred Pottinger and – this is typical of my father – so does he for being the progenitor of such an heroic young man. Later letters, though, refer to the disaster in Kabul and some touch on my own role, suggesting I am somehow to blame for the whole thing. My brother John tells me he has heard these complaints and has written his own letter to The Times vehemently defending my character and person from such calumny. I must find time to write to everybody telling them all that has taken place but above all reassuring them I am safe and well. My uncle Sir Henry writes to say he has been dispatched to become Governor-General of a small Company outpost on the Chinese coast called Hong-Kong and invites me to visit him should I find the time.

First, though, there is the matter of money. I am owed much and need additional funds for poor Hoosein, who I think will never recover from the shock of seeing our army defile his own – our own – friends in Kabul for want of any other brown-skinned enemy to destroy. And I must report to Lord Ellenborough who is organising a great festival in Ferozepore for the triumphant army.

Yet all the strength which has seen me through the past year seems to have deserted me. I lie in my tent prostrate with exhaustion, going over and over in my mind all the events I have witnessed, the deaths I have seen, the brief flowering of love I have enjoyed among all this ruin and my heart is flagging. I am tired, tired to the bone. It is all I can do to rise from my bed, wash my face, eat the food Hoosein prepares for me and leaf through my correspondence. All around me is an army of young, vigorous men exultant at the success of their expedition and eager to participate in the festivities Ellenborough has prepared for them. By all accounts the Governor-General is so excited by his military parade he has prepared more than 200 elephants to take part in the procession and is busily painting the animals with his own hands.

We rest here only two days before marching down to Ferozepore for Ellenborough's ridiculous reception. On the way I am summoned to see General Pollock, who does not beat about the bush.

'The Governor-General will not see you, Pottinger,' he says. 'I am sorry to tell you this but Lord Ellenborough believes that, as the senor political officer in Kabul at the time of the surrender, you are personally responsible for the entire debacle. And I have orders that you are to be taken straight on to Calcutta where a Court Martial will be held into allegations against you of cowardice and misuse of public money. You will not be imprisoned or humiliated in any way but bound, on your honour, to remain with your escort all the way to Calcutta. I am told you will receive a modest sum of money for your expenses en route and any further payments due to you will be reimbursed at the conclusion of your Court Martial. In the meantime, you are relieved of any duties you may have…'

'I have no duties, sir,' I say bitterly. 'Since your arrival in Kabul I have been given nothing to do except write reports.'

'And very important your reports will prove to be, Major,' says Pollock. 'I must say, Pottinger, it grieves me to see a fellow member of the Bengal Artillery treated in this way and I do not for one moment believe these accusations against you will be proved true in court. Yet these are my orders from the Governor-General himself and I have no choice but to issue them. You must go down to Calcutta and defend yourself as best you may. Good luck, sir.'

Pollock holds out a hand, which I feel obliged to shake. I salute. He salutes in return. I turn with a click of my boot-heels and withdraw from his command tent to find Hoosein. At least he is pleased to be returning to Calcutta.

CHAPTER 60

Fort William, Calcutta, January 1843

The Generals and George Clerk file in after a long lunch at which much wine seems to have been taken. They all look tired and ready for an afternoon sleep. The day is still hot but the shadows have lengthened across the parade ground and there is a modest breeze which helps to keep the rest of us from somnolence.

I am wide awake. I have been pacing the grounds for the past three hours, sometimes accompanied by Broadhurst, sometimes by Lady Sale and Drina Sturt, occasionally by others including George Lawrence and Vincent Eyre as well. We talk of the future but every time I contemplate it I feel a shudder run through me, as if the floor has given way and I am tumbling hundreds of feet down a black hole, as I recollect that in a few minutes' time my life could be over. Cowards are executed, are they not? And they deserve to be. Perhaps this is the last afternoon of my life. I wonder if I care because I should not wish to go on living if I were to be found guilty of even the very least of the charges against me – my reputation, my good name, everything I hold dear, would have been destroyed for all time.

When we are summoned back into court, this sense of apprehension consumes me. I cannot think straight. I watch as my judges return to their seats, I hear as we are told to rise for their arrival, I sit when everyone else sits, I rise when Broadhurst tells me to and I wait as George Clerk speaks. But I do not take anything in, I do not hear what is said, I cannot tell what the verdict is even though I supposedly hear him speak it. The blood pumping in my head drowns out all sound, I cannot see properly, I cannot focus, I feel a noise sweep through the room but I do not know what it might be. I hear nothing, I see nothing, or perhaps I see and hear everything all at once. My legs start to shake uncontrollably. I must brace them though it pains my old wound. I try to clutch the side of a desk to steady myself. I feel a clap on the back, I see Broadhurst's smiling face in mine. I slump back onto the seat amid a cacophony of noise from my own body as it thumps and teems with apprehension.

And now the generals are gone. George Clerk is gone. Broadhurst is calling for water and air. A lady, Drina Sturt I think, is using her fan to blow air across my face. Somebody lifts my head and puts a glass of water to my lips, urging me to drink. I take a sip, then another, then I choke. I struggle to stand, with arms helping me, and sit again, looking out at the shadows on the parade ground and the Union Flag unfurling itself half-heartedly in the breeze. People are patting me on the back, saying they always knew it was nonsense and offering their congratulations. I look at George Broadhurst in confusion. Captain Whistler is also there, I see him in the corner of my eye. He looks on with an amused smile on his face.

'George, what has happened?' I finally ask.

'Not guilty, Eldred. Not guilty on all the charges, all of them. Completely exonerated. Better than that,' he says, 'Better even than that. Did you not hear?'

'Hear? Hear what?'

'The verdict of the court martial? What George Clerk said about you?'

'No,' I am ashamed to admit. 'I am afraid I missed everything.'

'Poor Eldred,' says Mrs Sturt, still fanning my face. 'It has all been so unfair. Poor boy.' She places a hand on my arm. 'I shall write to Eleanor this very day,' she adds.

'Eleanor, is she here?' I still feel groggy. I am not sure what is happening.

'No, silly boy, she's on her way back to England. And you will soon be joining her.'

Broadhurst kneels down so his face is looking into mine. 'Here,' he says, 'This is the judgment. Shall I read it to you, Eldred? Are you ready to take it all in?'

I wait before replying. The noise in my head, the sea-swell of anxiety, is abating, the tide is withdrawing, I gulp some water. I am calmer now. 'Yes, George. What did they say?'

He reads the proclamation made out in George Clerk's own hand, 'On all the charges against Major Eldred Pottinger, Companion of the Bath, this court finds the defendant not guilty – not guilty of cowardice, not guilty of conduct unbecoming an officer and not guilty of the misuse of funds. We wish to add that this court cannot conclude its proceedings without expressing a strong conviction that, throughout the whole period of the painful position in which Major Pottinger was so unexpectedly placed, his conduct was marked by a degree of energy and manly firmness that stamps his character as one worthy of high admiration. The court believes this verdict and its comments must be widely advertised to ensure Major Pottinger survives this ordeal without a stain on his character.'

CHAPTER 61

Fort William, Calcutta, April 1843

There is nothing to keep me here now.

My wife has abandoned me. I have been denied the money I am due for my additional responsibilities and my time as a prisoner of war. The world has moved on – we no longer hear mention of the name Afghanistan.

Nobody cares that Dost Mohammed Khan is back on the throne of Kabul with his son Akbar at his side. Nor are our triumphant generals concerned that the ruler we left in the Balar Hissar, Prince Shahpur, was betrayed by all the chiefs who had sworn allegiance to him as soon as our backs were turned. They are not interested that the Prince barely escaped with his life after fleeing Kabul, being captured by Akbar's men, escaping again and eventually sailing down river to Peshawar where, no doubt, he will be re-united with his exiled elder brother.

Nobody in power wishes to hear about the sufferings of the hostages. They are too concerned with making war on the Sikhs in the Punjab now that old goat Ranjeet Singh has died and in Sind, where our invasion has not been welcomed by the local chiefs.

Lord Ellenborough is especially indifferent to those of us who came back alive from Afghanistan. He's happy to arrange victory parades for the returning heroes – the contemptible little man even restored some ancient gates he claims were stolen from India centuries ago, though nobody has missed them and they are not the originals – but he has turned his back on any of us he calls 'politicals', claiming we are to blame for the whole disaster.

I write letters, I make visits, I apply in person, I meet officers and generals but never, not once, am I admitted into the presence of Lord Ellenborough. Ellenborough personally denies me the prisoners' pension paid to most of my comrades, he refuses my application for compensation for the loss of property I was forced to abandon, and he denies me the additional pay due as the senior political officer in Kabul after the murder of Sir William Macnaghten.

No doubt on Ellenborough's orders, I am summoned to meet Major General Lumley, one of the judges at my court martial. He is starting for the Punjab and is busily supervising preparations. He stands just outside the stable block as men rush to and fro preparing the horses with two of his adjutants. I march across to where they are waiting for me, salute and declare, 'Major Pottinger, sir,' as if he and I had never encountered one another before.

'Pottinger, yes,' says Lumley, stroking his thick moustache. 'You were fortunate, sir, in the verdict, you know?'

'I was, sir?' I ask. 'I was cleared of any wrong-doing.'

'Indeed you were, sir, but only after some debate. For my own part, I did not take such an indulgent attitude towards your handling of public money. Do you realise the financial difficulties your promises have caused the Company? Your unauthorised and impossible promises?'

'As I have said, sir, I am very happy to go through every item and identify those few we should pay and those many which are not payable under any circumstances.'

'Jolly decent of you,' says Lumley with a heavy irony. 'Now listen, Pottinger, the thing is, your promotion to Major was only ever temporary, for the duration of the campaign in Afghanistan and you must now return to your position as a Lieutenant in the Bombay Artillery. Is that clear, sir?'

This comes like a shot to the chest. I am stunned and close my eyes to withstand the impact of this blow. 'I am sorry, sir, I do not understand,' I mutter.

'How can I make it any clearer, sir? You are no longer a Major in the political service but you resume your duties as a Lieutenant in the artillery should you wish to do so.'

'And if I do not wish to do so?'

'In those circumstances, sir, I should think you would have little option but to resign from the service. Now if you will excuse me, I have to supervise the preparations. Please write to Captain Barrington here with your decision within the next fortnight. Thank you.'

Lumley offers the most contemptuous of salutes and turns away.

There is nothing to keep me here now. Seven years of service for nothing. No money, no fame, no advancement. I am where I started but older, less healthy and infinitely more disappointed, frustrated and angry. I spend time in church, praying to God for patience and fortitude but perhaps He feels He has done his duty by keeping me alive when so many others are dead.

There is nothing to keep me here now.

*****

Hoosein's wife and their two children gather on the quayside along with George Broadhurst, Vincent Eyre and Colin Mackenzie as we make our farewells. The sea is choppy in the sunlight, there is a brisk breeze and the brig 'The Prince Regent' is lying at anchor in the bay while sailors prepare to weigh anchor.

The ten-man rowing boat is waiting for us and it is difficult to say our goodbyes. Little Hoosein is in tears as he bids farewell once again to his wife and children. 'It is only for a few weeks,' he reassures them. 'I shall just see Major Pottinger safely to his uncle's and then I shall come home. We will be quite safe.'

I have secured Hoosein a writer's job with the Company, which will secure his income and give him a moderately prosperous future well away from any future wars. But the little man insists on accompanying me on this voyage even though he has still not forgiven Nott and Pollock for their destruction of Kabul.

'Major Pottinger, sahib,' he tells me, 'You are a prince among peasants, a star in a sky filled with clouds, a shining ray of sunlight in the monsoon season. We will travel well and arrive safely with your uncle.'

Broadhurst, Mackenzie and Eyre are, naturally, much more matter-of-fact about this farewell. I shake hands with each of them and say to my fellow former captives, 'I am sorry we have not managed to persuade Ellenborough to sort out our pay, gentlemen. It is unfinished business but now he has referred it to the Company in London perhaps we shall still receive what is due to us.'

Mackenzie is vehement. 'We'd bloody better.' He is returning home soon to get married and needs all the money he can get. Eyre, on the other hand, is publishing a book about our incarceration, together with his sketches of all the prisoners; it's sure to sell well and make him some money. 'Lady Sale is writing her own book,' he tells me, 'And Lady Macnaghten has landed on her feet.'

'Has she?'

'Yes, she is to marry the Marquess of Headfort. As she told my wife, "Every time I marry, I marry higher and higher." First a mere Lieutenant-Colonel, then Sir William and now a Peer and a friend of Lord Melbourne's.'

'I trust he likes cats,' I say as we shake hands.

The boat is waiting. Hoosein and I are helped aboard while our bags are thrown recklessly from the quay, the wind carries away our cries of farewell and the boat surges through the choppy waters towards 'The Prince Regent'.

*****

As we pass the low-lying Sagar Island heading for the open sea, I stand on the deck and look across at the long beaches and rocks where I see three tigers fighting each other for the corpse of a stag which one of them must have killed. The tigers are ferocious, teeth bared and their agonised yelps and furious growls come to me over the water. We sail on and as the island recedes I cannot tell which of the tigers emerges as the victor or whether the other two lie slain at his feet. Perhaps it does not matter anyway. There will be more dead stags, more furious tigers.

CHAPTER 62

Calcutta, December 1843

Monument to the late Major Eldred Pottinger, Bombay Cathedral

This monument, erected by public subscription, to the memory of

MAJOR ELDRED POTTINGER CB

of the Bombay Regiment of Artillery and placed in the cathedral church of Bombay, is in token of the admiration and respect to which his character as a soldier and conduct as a man are held by friends of this Presidency.

Major Pottinger's successful defence of Herat, his gallant bearing and judicious counsel throughout the eventful period of the British reverses in Afghanistan and recorded in the annals of his country need no eulogium here. The recollection of these services must add to the regret universally felt that one whose early career gave such promise of future eminence and distinction should have found a premature grave. Compelled by long exertion, anxiety and fatigue in the discharge of his public duties to seek a change of climate for the recovery of his health, Major Pottinger was returning to England via China when he was attacked by a malignant fever at Hong Kong where he died on the 13th November 1843 aged 32 years.

THE TRIALS OF ELDRED POTTINGER

From the **Calcutta Star**

He became a prisoner of Akbar Khan but was honourably acquitted of any responsibility for the overall fiasco. With a shattered limb, he returned to the British lines and was then abused in every respect until offered employment in Hong Kong. His life serves as a model for all young Englishmen. He was a credit to the uniform.

From the **Bombay Times**

He was requited for the valuable services he had conferred by being remanded to his corps, as a lieutenant of artillery, stripped of his employment and denied acknowledgement.

CHAPTER 63

Balmain, Sydney, Australia, November 1844

A beautiful Spring day. A brisk breeze chops up the water in the bay where perhaps a dozen schooners, clippers and brigs ride at anchor. This is the tenth day I have spent sitting outside the Dolphin Hotel watching the light in the bay slice through the scudding clouds and turn the sea a luminous aquamarine.

I can wait. It is not expensive to live here, though it can be dangerous. Robberies are commonplace though I do not think anyone will come after me.

I can wait. The days pass pleasantly enough, though whenever I am addressed as Mr Alexander it still takes me a moment to realise they're talking to me – George Alexander, a retired soldier from Dublin via Cape Town, that's me. I sit here, day by day, I do nothing except perhaps read a book or the Morning Herald, passing the time, waiting.

I go for walks round the bay and watch builders busily constructing a city out of the scrubland and dockers shouting to each other in an almost impenetrable language which purports to be English but not a version I have ever heard before.

Here I can look back. It is strange, being dead. But there was really no alternative.

After I left India for Hong Kong, to join my uncle Sir Henry, and long after Eleanor had departed from Bombay for England, I realised there was no future for me either with my uncle in that pestilential colony or at home in Britain. With or without my wife, what was I to do there other than write my memoirs setting the record straight and eke out a living as best I could? My feckless father has fled his creditors and settled in Jersey where my step-mother makes the best of things, ekeing out her own paltry income.

I sent her some money but not enough because I had still not received the money due to me when I died. Instead, the British East India Company finally agreed to pay an allowance to her, as reported by my brother John, who has managed all these affairs most satisfactorily.

I would love to see Eliza again but I would just be a burden to her. Perhaps one day I shall write.

It was as much for Eliza as it was for Eleanor that I decided to die. Typhus was rife in Hong Kong and, while Sir Henry was all for me remaining in the township he's building there, it was plain to me I would perish if I stayed for long. I was exhausted, my leg injury had flared up again and one sight of the long medical hall with its dying typhus cases was enough to convince me I would be a fool to remain longer in Victoria than was absolutely necessary.

Engineering my death was easy enough. I did not tell Sir Henry – it would have compromised his position too much – but Hoosein took care of it all for me. He procured the body of a European of about my size and had it carried into the infirmary where he persuaded one of the orderlies this was the corpse of the Governor-General's nephew, the infamous Eldred Pottinger. Neither Sir Henry nor his wife, Lady Anne, cared to view the body thanks to a natural fear of the typhus.

The funeral was held quickly, the body buried, the grave marked with a wooden cross, notice was sent to England and India of my death and I took the first boat out of Hong Kong bound for Sydney, armed with a little money, a few books and clothes and a new identity as George Alexander.

Australia is the place for new identities and new beginnings. Here in this new-found land I can breathe again.

And as I walk the beaches and rocks of this safe haven, watching out for the arrival of ships from home, I feel a new hope dawn, a new energy surge through me, a new desire for life and the future. I try to avoid thoughts of Afghanistan though occasionally news filters through – Dost Mohammed Khan is back on the throne in Kabul but one story I have read suggests his son, the vicious and charming Akbar is now dead – poisoned on his own father's orders, so they say. And Shelton is dead as well – he fell from his horse on the parade ground in Dublin and died three days later. When his men heard the news, they rushed from their barracks and gave three cheers at the news. I cannot say I am sorry for either man.

What we shall make of our life together here, I do not know yet. But I have been invited to join the New South Wales mounted police. They are eager to recruit English officers, though the force has a reputation for corruption, which might prove troubling. I suppose you can put a man in a policeman's uniform but once a criminal, always a criminal. Which is why they need good British officers to set an example. We shall see.

I do not yet know if Eleanor will be as good as her word. I wait and watch, from dawn to dusk, in the expectation of an arrival from England carrying my wife here to start a new life in this newest of new worlds. I have taken her into my confidence, explained where I am and why and she has written promising to take passage to Sydney. I have no real reason to doubt her but we haven't seen each other for well over a year and the voyage to Australia is long and dangerous. Even if she has embarked, there is no certainty she will arrive to disembark.

She said she told her brother and her sisters all her news. They were shocked and angry. They refused to see her new husband. They doubted the legality of our marriage. They accused her of ruining her life. She left home and stayed a few weeks with an aunt. She writes that the aunt is sympathetic, she has given Eleanor money and paid for her passage to Australia. In her letter, she said she would be leaving in a month or two's time. That was five months ago and the voyage usually lasts about 110 days. She must arrive soon, if she arrives at all.

Meanwhile I am sitting here outside the Dolphin, drinking my coffee and squinting out to sea in the bright sunlight. That life I led, those battles I fought, those people I knew – it was all for nothing. I could not stay in India, humiliated, demoted and abandoned. I could have gone home, I suppose, but the allowance I have secured for Eliza is enough to protect her from poverty and the depredations of my feckless father. Death – real death – was an option I seriously considered but why waste a life when so many have already been destroyed?

Here I will be free to re-make my life.

I pick up my telescope, a remnant from my time in Afghanistan. It is battered but it still works. I run it out and put it to my eye because somewhere on the horizon I think... I think I see... I think I see a sail.

A ship. A ship from London? Perhaps she is carrying my dear Eleanor.

Out towards the horizon, I think I see a ship.

Acknowledgements

This is a work of fiction but I didn't make it all up, I plagiarised, borrowed, copied and otherwise ripped-off a range of other people's books. I make no apologies for this, nor for the inaccuracies or omissions of which I am consciously guilty though, as to those I am unconsciously responsible for, I must, of course, seek the reader's forgiveness.

This book was inspired in the first instance by one given to me by my wife's late uncle, Mike Wescott, called 'The Afghan Connection' by George Pottinger (Scottish Academic Press, 1983), an account by one of Eldred's indirect descendants. It was only by reading this book that I became aware of the First Afghan War and wondered what it might have been like to live through.

Since then, I have discovered my extensive ignorance of the war was not for want of literature about it, dating back to the contemporary accounts available from journals of the time now to be found on the internet and books like Lady Sale's own 'Journal of the Disasters in Affghanistan', Alexander Burnes's 'Cabool', Emily Eden's 'Up the Country' and so on.

Other books I have devoured include 'Afghanistan' by Stephen Tanner (De capo, 2009), 'The Honourable Company' by John Keay (Harper Collins, 1993), 'The Great Game' by Peter Hopkirk (John Murray, 2006) and, of course, 'Return of the King' by William Dalrymple (Bloomsbury, 2013). I also read Craig Murray's 'Sikunder Burnes' (Birlinn, 2016).

As well as contemporary accounts and histories of the period, I have had recourse to the overheated, semi-fictional two-volume account by Maud Diver ('The Hero of Herat' 1912, and 'The Judgment of the

Sword' 1913), the latter of which appears once to have been owned by an E. Pottinger. I was also entertained by George Macdonald Fraser's account of the war in 'Flashman'.

I am very grateful to a number of people for reading this book in various states and suggesting improvements and corrections, in particular Bethany Jones and Chris Kelly, Tom Madden and Derek Williams. And, of course, to Fiona for her constant support and forbearance.

NIGEL HASTILOW

Nigel Hastilow is a journalist by trade. He was Editor of 'The Birmingham Post' in the 1990s and worked for the Wolverhampton 'Express & Star'. He has also worked for the Institute of Directors, the Institute of Chartered Accountants and his own publishing company.

He stood as a Conservative parliamentary candidate in 2001. He has written four other books, two of them novels: 'The Smoking Gun' and 'Murder on the Brussels Express'.

He was born in Birmingham and lives in Worcestershire.